Praise for Amy

The Californi...

"My favorite kind of book. Doan wea... ...ly relationships and a mystery that pulls you ... ...nd like a powerful riptide. Unforgettable!"

—**Jessica Anya Blau**, bestselling author of *Mary Jane*

"A thoroughly enjoyable, tender story about the heartbreak of long-kept family secrets. I now have a soft spot for every member of this lovable clan. You will cheer for the Merricks!"

—**Tracey Lange**, *New York Times* **bestselling author of *We Are the Brennans***

"Equal parts mystery and family drama, Amy Mason Doan's latest is a love story to an era of sun, salt air, and freedom. I promise, you will devour this novel."

—**Julie Clark**, *New York Times* **bestselling author of *The Last Flight***

"A masterpiece! Told with breathtaking empathy and a uniquely satisfying complexity of spirit and character, this sun-drenched saga will stay in your heart."

—**Allison Larkin**, bestselling author of *The People We Keep*

Lady Sunshine

"Amy Mason Doan creates a whole world and mood with her exquisitely crafted novel. A delicious daydream of a book."

—**Elin Hilderbrand**, *New York Times* **bestselling author of *Swan Song***

"An engrossing tale of secrets, memory, music, and the people and places you can never outrun. A fantastic summer read."

—**Laura Dave**, *New York Times* **bestselling author of *The Last Thing He Told Me***

"With lyrical writing and a page-turning plot, this sun-dappled book has it all: heart, smarts, and an irresistible musical beat."

—**Karen Dukess**, author of *The Last Book Party*

"This book is gorgeous. A gold-drenched, nostalgic dream with a fierce female friendship at its heart."

—**Marisa de los Santos**, *New York Times* **bestselling author of *I'll Be Your Blue Sky***

Also by Amy Mason Doan

The Summer List
Summer Hours
Lady Sunshine

THE

CALIFORNIA

DREAMERS

a novel

AMY MASON DOAN

GRAYDON
HOUSE

If you purchased this book without a cover you should be aware that this book is stolen property. It was reported as "unsold and destroyed" to the publisher, and neither the author nor the publisher has received any payment for this "stripped book."

GRAYDON
HOUSE®

Recycling programs
for this product may
not exist in your area.

ISBN-13: 978-1-525-80468-7

The California Dreamers

Copyright © 2025 by Amy Mason Doan

All rights reserved. No part of this book may be used or reproduced in any manner whatsoever without written permission.

Without limiting the author's and publisher's exclusive rights, any unauthorized use of this publication to train generative artificial intelligence (AI) technologies is expressly prohibited.

This is a work of fiction. Names, characters, places and incidents are either the product of the author's imagination or are used fictitiously. Any resemblance to actual persons, living or dead, businesses, companies, events or locales is entirely coincidental.

® is a trademark of Harlequin Enterprises ULC.

Graydon House
22 Adelaide St. West, 41st Floor
Toronto, Ontario M5H 4E3, Canada
www.GraydonHouseBooks.com

Printed in U.S.A.

For Kelsey and Wesley Mason

PROLOGUE

Ronan Merrick

1985
El Zafiro, California
Fifteen years old

I lie on my board, eyes closed, and let the gentle swell lift me skyward. Up up up, then over, down into the valley and up again. When I was younger, I didn't understand how surfing is as much about this—waiting—as it is about the thrill. Patience, solitude, surrender—they're all names for the same thing.

When I open my eyes, the sky is coral-swirled and I've drifted toward Cap. He floats on his white-and-blue longboard, his hands trailing in the water. A lazy-looking gesture, but under the surface his fingers work expertly, little fins keeping the perfect right angle of his body aimed at the horizon.

Cap. My father. Named for the Greek fishing captain's hat he wears on land, tilted far over his eyes. My brothers and Mama went in long ago to nap in the shade, but it's peaceful, this near-sunset hour, when good waves are rare and for long stretches of time you can sit and watch the light change and let your thoughts float.

A green helix of kelp twists past the nose of my board, and

I dip a hand in. The water's cold but my back is warm, catching the last of the sun.

I hear it before I see it, a distant whisper that breaks free from all the other noises out there, building to a friendly roar. Only seconds away, there's a fine little wave shaping up. It'll be two or three feet overhead, nice and wide. It's Cap's—he's closer.

But to my surprise he calls softly, "Yours, Ro."

I don't hesitate. I paddle hard, stretching my arms as long as they'll go, then turn toward the shore just as the swell heaves me up. I pop up fast and shove hard with both heels, skitter up to the nose just in time. A half step back, a little crouch, half a backbend…and I'm right where I want to be.

For a precious, pure moment, the world is a rush of sound, light, color. My board is a streak of ocean that happens to be a different shade of blue.

And then it's over. The wave breaks into white foam and I grab the nose of my board as I plunge beneath it, waiting for the surface to calm before kicking up to the light. My board's cool slickness under my chin is as familiar as my pillow.

Cap told me something once.

"Each wave is the ocean pushing us back to land, commanding us to go, be mortal again. But every time we paddle back out we're saying, 'Not yet, please. Not just yet.'"

I straddle my board, rake back my wet hair, and aim at the horizon. Cap nods at me, then continues squinting ahead, the sun now an orange hill melting into the water. I hold on to the last seconds of feeling immortal.

Until the next time.

PART ONE

1

Ava LeClair

2002
LeClair Family Lavender Farm, Oregon
Thirty-two years old

I saw it the morning before the boys left for camp.

A flash of light on the edge of the old copper birdbath. From the grassy clearing, it begged me to come closer—to see if it was only a drop of water kicked up by a bird, or a coin winking at me in the sun.

Standing on our farmhouse's white-pillared, slightly sagging front porch, I had to slow my breathing. For a second, I was no longer Ava LeClair, farmer, mother, PTA vice president. Expert at filling sachets and tying them with purple satin ribbon to sell in the gift shop.

But Ronan Merrick. The wild girl I'd been.

Barry burst out the door and joined me on the porch, tugging me back to the present. "Are you sad?" my son asked, clutching my leg, looking up at me with round blue eyes. He'd posed the same question for days in the run-up to his and his brother's departure for camp, meaning *Are you sad we're leaving you behind?* He had always been an empathetic child, attuned to everyone's emotions, and especially mine. But he could not possibly have guessed at the layers of my sadness now.

I turned my back to the birdbath and knelt, smiling and holding my son close. "Hey, little Bear. I was only thinking about your packing list."

"You can come with us," he whispered. "There's lots to do in Seaside besides swim."

Lou, his father, followed him out the screen door, a syrup bottle in his hand, our other son, Jack, at his heels. "Yes, come, Prairie Girl."

I smiled even brighter and rose. "ZBoy and I have big plans here this week," I said, and started tussling with our placid yellow Lab. "Boys, tell me again about the tricks you'll be learning..."

For the rest of the day, I resisted the birdbath's glint. As long as I didn't get closer, I didn't have to give up hope. I weeded in the fields behind the house. I helped my sons pack, chased them around upstairs. I tried to give them all of myself, but they sensed my heart's distance, as kids always do.

It wasn't fair to them.

So in a stolen moment before dinner, I sneaked out to the birdbath to prove to myself there was no coin, that it had only been wishful thinking.

But there it was, on the ledge, a bright penny with our Merrick-family mark. An *M* and a seagull and a wave, all at once.

Hand shaking, I covered it with the coin I always carried with me. A thousand-peso piece, my only bit of flotsam from a different life. I lined it up neatly, de la Cruz's profile over Lincoln's. The childish code returning as naturally as a first language:

I'm here.

When everyone was asleep, I grabbed a flannel shirt from the peg by the front door and pulled it over my T-shirt as I crossed the grass to the birdbath, where the water reflected the crescent moon.

Both coins were gone now. I touched the spot where they had been, as if the cold, green-patinaed copper was a doorbell. I knew who I was summoning, and my heart ached to see them. But I didn't know what door I was opening.

"Are you there?" I whispered into the misty night. The little cherub on the rim of the birdbath looked so carefree in the moonlight, pouring his urn into the bowl as if nothing momentous had happened on his watch.

A twig cracked low behind me and I whirled. A rush of wings, haughty chirrups—only a quail.

"They're asleep, it's okay," I tried again.

After a few moments, there was another crackle in the dry leaves. Higher, louder. Not a quail's. I held my breath.

My brother Griffin stepped into the clearing.

He stood silently for a long time. Tense, hesitant. And maybe this was for the best. I had to get used to him being here first. The fact of him, tangible proof of my old life, here in my new one.

Griff pulled the thousand-peso piece I'd left for him from his pocket and held it up, and I knew we were both thinking the same thing, that the old family code still worked. He clinked the coin on the birdbath rim—*tinnng*. "Copper on copper," he finally said. His smile was sad, rueful, here and gone fast. His voice was the same, and he was still thin as a whip, but there was an adult's caution, a weight to his movements now.

I wondered how different I seemed to my big brother. Ronan Avery Merrick, the sister he'd known, had curly blond hair as wind-tossed and sandy as the beachside hiding places our family had called home. Ava LeClair's hair was dyed brown and flattened, cut to a sensible shoulder length. Her life was as deeply rooted as a lavender stalk, as upright as the 150-year-old farm-house behind her.

He held out his hand, dropping the thousand-peso coin into mine, and I slipped it back into my pocket.

"Hey, Griff."

"Hey, Ronan." He surveyed the dark fields past the house. "Beautiful farm. It looks just like the postcard."

I cleared my throat. "We've bought the neighbor's acreage since." When I'd sent the postcard fifteen years ago, I'd only wanted them to know I was all right. I'd been certain I wouldn't be here for more than a month or two. I'd written only, "I'm fine. I'm happy, and I hope you will be, too." But this place had become my new world.

"I thought I should give you a little warning, in case you didn't feel like reliving old times in front of..." He gestured limply at the house. "How much do they know?"

"They know Ava LeClair."

"Nothing, then."

"No," I admitted. Ava, a twist on my middle name, was the only hint of my past. I was grateful that Griff had guessed about my secrecy, but ashamed.

Griff dipped his hand into the birdbath and we watched ripples break the moon's reflection into quivery slices.

I couldn't stand it anymore. My big brother wouldn't have come here after a decade and a half without a serious reason. "Griff. You have news, don't you?"

He nodded.

"Is it Mama?" Red-haired, gentle Mama. Warm and loving. She'd named me. Taught me. *Seen* me...though she hadn't seen everything.

I kept myself perfectly still, not knowing if I was ready for the answer.

Griff shook his head. "No. No, it's Cap, Ronan. He died. Three weeks ago."

I clutched the edge of the birdbath. *Cap.*

Our father. Everyone thought he was immortal.

I pictured him as I'd last seen him, riding a perfect dawn swell at San Onofre. Fearless, free from the modern world, at peace.

"I'm sorry." Griff touched my arm in comfort but it was quick as a button push, a strange, nervous tap. "Mitral heart valve irregularity, they said. Whatever that is. He'd slowed way down this year but wouldn't say why. He must've realized something was wrong, but he hid it until it was too late."

Cap hadn't believed in doctors. His formula for long life was salt water, fresh air, freedom, and his special date-and-coconut cereal for breakfast every morning.

"How is everyone?" I wandered over to a barbera bush, its flat maroon leaves black in the pale moonlight, and picked dead leaves from its spikes. *Cap is gone.* Impossible.

Griff hesitated. "It's been rough. Mama… She took it hard, that first week. But she seems better now."

"She's all right, really? And Dyl and Mag?" Now that the floodgates were open, the questions that had swum in my head for more than a decade rushed out. Had the boys struck out on their own? Was the Gull still their home, still running?

"You care, then," Griff said.

"Of course I care," I whispered, facing him.

We stood for a minute, spent by this little sputtering of honesty.

Then I turned and walked over to a maple, caressing its rough bark. "Have they had it yet?"

"Not yet. Soon."

"Where will it be, that break at SO?"

"No…not too far from there," Griff said.

This was a small comfort. I would know where it happened. The paddle-out—the ceremony in which the ash that was left of the dear one was poured into the ocean to say goodbye. Because this was how it was always done when a king of the old days, a god of the waves, died. Everyone in his family, biological and aquatic, paddled out to a calm expanse of sea at sunset or sunrise. They straddled their boards to form a ring and took turns speaking. And they tossed flowers and mementos into the center. I'd attended two such ceremonies, for Cap's friends, when I was a girl. Both times, Cap had led the proceedings.

Now it would be his ceremony.

"Will you come?" Griff asked.

I stiffened; I was afraid he'd ask that.

"I borrowed a truck," Griff said. "I'll take you."

I tried to envision this. Driving down to California, seeing the others. Their faces as I fumbled to explain what happened the day I left and never came back. The truth wasn't an option.

It had taken courage just to meet Griff here in the dark, in my own garden.

"You were good to come all the way up here to tell me in person, Griff," I said quietly to the tree trunk.

"That's your answer?"

I turned to him slowly, speaking to a point in the air midway between us. "You can sleep in the old drying shed behind the gift shop tonight. There's a bunk, it's comfortable. I'll sneak in the house and get fresh sheets for you, and—"

"Ronan."

"I'll bring you some food. And coffee? It's the least I—"

"Are you coming back with me to our father's funeral or not, Ronan?"

"I can't, Griff," I whispered. "But I can give you some beautiful lavender to bring back with you. And I'll write Mama a letter. And I can give her a little money, if she'll take it."

"Money." Even from ten feet away, I could see that Griff's expression reflected what I knew already: I was a coward.

"Griff grins," we'd always said. Now it should be "Griff is gruff."

But it was good to see him, however changed he was. I missed the Merricks, every one of them, even more than I missed the water. I had longed to know they were all right, but this… I couldn't risk more heartbreak. The possibility that once I went back to my old life it would be impossible to continue in this one, with every tear and fracture raw again. I'd worked hard the last fifteen years to patch a new one together.

"They've been okay without me for this long, haven't they?" I pleaded.

"Is that what you tell yourself, *Ava LeClair*?" He pronounced my alias with great effort, as if doing so pained him.

"Well. Then they can't hate me any more than they do. I'm sorry you drove all this way. I should go, my family might hear us." I headed toward the house, crossing the glade, through the prickly bushes, the trees.

"Wait." Griff ran after me and grabbed my sleeve. "I'm sorry."

I shook my head and pulled my arm from him, walking faster. At the crunch of gravel I pictured the three LeClairs, my loved ones, sleeping obliviously upstairs with open windows, and stepped off the walkway that led to our front porch steps. "They'll wake up," I whispered.

Griff lowered his voice to a murmur and avoided the gravel, but stayed on my heels. "Coming here, seeing you… I didn't want it to be like this. Let's start over? They need you. And *I* need you. To help me with them, just for the paddle-out, help get them through it. You and I were always the grown-ups, remember?"

I stopped, staring down at a baseball mitt one of the boys had left on the lawn.

"Ronan. Please. Mama's convinced *you* are what will help most right now. One good thing, 'a little brightness,' she said. 'Go get our girl, of course she'll want to come.' I told her it was a waste of time, but she said, 'She'll come,' so I promised

I'd try. At least think about it? You can do this last thing for your family, for her."

"Griff, *no*." I realized too late how harsh it sounded. "I…"

But when I turned to face him, Griff had already vanished into the darkness.

I made my way back to the house in a daze, closing my eyes as I sank onto the top porch step, gripping the cold wood under me on either side. Ours was the biggest, oldest place in the county. What would Cap have said about such a house? Once, the whole Pacific had been my home…

Go get our girl.

Of course she'll want to come.

She'll come.

2

Change in migration

1983
El Zafiro, California
Fourteen years old

Something is different this morning. It's fall, a few months after my fourteenth birthday, and I sleep past dawn—the first sign.

Instead of the scrapes and clangs of Cap's long metal spoon from the other side of my window, soft thunks on the roof wake me. Maybe we've parked under a coconut palm...

Outside, I squint against the morning sun. I'm used to rising in the dark, surfing so early there's rarely anyone else on the waves. But right now, it's bright, and there's no fire, no Cap's cereal or Mama's tea. No Cap or Mama. The twins stand on the roof of the Gull—those were the noises I heard—and the sight of their tall silhouettes against the sky, their concerned stillness as they shade their eyes to peer at something down the beach, jolts me fully awake.

We're parked not in one of our customary tree-shrouded spots, but on a weedy, narrow road. The surf is distant; we're stopped much farther from the beach than usual.

I clamber up to join my older brothers on the roof and stand on tiptoe, straining to see what they do.

Across the dunes and trees, there's a huge hotel, the kind we usually stay away from. Golf courses and tennis courts and a long chain of buildings with sapphire-colored tile roofs. A big, oval-shaped structure in the center, like someone flung a necklace of blue jewels onto the sand.

Overnight, we've flown south. I can tell from the heat, the palms and yucca bushes. The trees here are different from the central California pin oaks and poplars we parked under yesterday.

"Where are we?" I ask.

The twins don't answer right away. They turn right as if rejecting the existence of the hotel's deep blue roofs, gazing at the blue of the ocean and its smattering of surf breaks, already dotted with boards since we slept late.

Finally, Griff says, "A town called Almost-Mexico." He points. "There's a less crowded break that way. C'mon."

"Where's Cap?" I ask as we climb down. Mag, then Griff, then me.

Griff offers me a hand but I jump on my own.

"He's got a garage gig nearby."

That must be why Cap's brought us here. Cap's clever with his hands. He fashioned straps from old seat belts to hold our bunks against the walls of the van when we flip them up. He can make the Gull's transmission run for another year even when some mechanic shakes his head. He can comb and wax a board perfectly, quiet the crank on our food mill with a drop of nut oil in just the right place. He knows how to pop Mag's shoulder back in before he panics. And when we need money for food and gas, he spends a few days working at auto body shops.

Mama's good at other things. Tinctures, and lavender soap, and cooking, and her homemade orange-and-clove salve. The names of birds and flowers. She teaches me what she knows.

"Here." Griff hands me a tin cup of walnuts and raisins from the food bins inside the van.

Mag rolls his eyes, an expression that says *I see you, acting grandiose, trying to fill in for Cap*, and Griff playfully swats at him with his surf leash before they both hoist their boards and begin the long walk to the water.

I eat a few bites of what's in the cup, saving most of it for Dyl, then go in to wake him. He's still sleeping soundly in our shared bunk, his precious field journal, with its cover design of green kelp on a cream background, peeking out from under his pillow. It has the word *Mer* on the front, meaning *sea* in French, but I can only see the loopy seaweed-green *M*.

Mama found it in a thrift store long ago, and gave it to him as soon as he could hold a pencil. It's where Dyl records his observations. Mostly about animals and plants, but sometimes us, too. I'd once glimpsed over his shoulder: "Ronan" and "my sister..." But I'd forced myself to look away without reading more.

"Dylly," I say softly, tapping his arm. He'll notice we're in a strange town, and I can't let him worry. I pull my stuffed animal, Rontu-dog, from deep under our shared covers and dance him up Dyl's arm. "Come explore with me, Dyl. We're in the most beautiful place..."

Later that day Mama and Cap return.

Cap repeats what Griff said. "Mechanic nearby pays well. They're desperate for good help. How's the break?"

The twins rush to answer. They talk about their waves, how good it feels to surf in November without even a half suit.

The next morning, we fall back into our routine. I peer out the window into the lavender-gray light, and Cap's cooking his special coconut-and-date cereal over our little camp stove, the familiar scrapes and pings of his big metal spoon a comfort, though I heard him come home only a few hours ago from the garage.

I blow on Dyl's bare elbow next to me in our bunk. "Dyyyyyyylll-y," I whisper.

Cap says he doesn't need somebody stirring cereal or blowing on his elbow to wake him. He says the water does it, calling to him.

I help Dyl down and we pass Mag and Griff, still asleep in their bunks, one on each long side of the van. I hurry Dyl down the road to some bushes so we can pee.

As we're walking back he glances up and stops short. "Look," he whispers. "Twins."

He means two gulls. There's a real seabird hovering above our van, and it's somehow lined up with its wings at just the same angle as our gull's rusty wings, like it's showing off for us.

Cap and Mama nicknamed the van long before any of us were born, because the rusty metal shade awnings on her sides, from when she was a food truck, look like wings. Only her left wing moves now—her right is stuck a few inches up. The Gull's painted white and pale gray, every shade, with streaks of pink marine putty on her leaks. So she even looks feathery, like a real bird.

When we get back Griff is stretching near the van's door, and Mag is coming out, groggy and cloudy eyed. He says in a low voice so he won't wake Mama, "The break was packed with a jillion citizens on vacation yesterday. Poor suckers."

"Poor lost souls," Cap says, dishing out four big servings of cereal by the stove. He must have a little cash now from his overnight garage job.

Because milk is cow snot and makes you sluggish and clumsy, we eat our cereal with water, even when we have plenty of cash in the pipe. That's where Cap keeps our money—in the Gull's old stovepipe, neatly wrapped packages of cash in white plastic to keep it dry. We've been robbed a few times because Cap doesn't believe in guns, but no one has ever found our pipe hiding place.

Griff swallows his last bite and grins at me. His smile's as constant as the ocean, as bright as the puka-shell necklace he always wears, so we all say, "Griff grins."

"Griff grins," and "Mag is only civilized on water." And "Dyl is wise beyond his years."

I don't have a saying. It's not the kind of thing you can ask for. Mama calls me Little Seal—that's what Ronan means in Irish—but a nickname's not the same.

We clean our tin bowls and spoons, wipe them with the rag, and set them on a towel to dry.

"You lead calisthenics," Cap says to Griff, and heads back into the van to sleep.

Griff brings us to the sand and we line up before him in age order for sprints, squirrellies. It's early, so both the beach and the hotel are quiet. It's only our family and the seagulls up to appreciate the dawn.

With Cap absent, Mag modifies his own exercise form so drastically that he falls over, and we all laugh. Even Mag himself. But he's serious again when Griff finishes with our morning promises, the words Cap has us recite every day:

"I close my eyes 'til it all drops away. What's left is what I want."

Then it's time to grab our boards.

Our life has been the same for so many years I can't remember anything different. Up and down the coast in the Gull.

We drive at night and park by beaches under tree cover, never too close to anyone else. I shut my eyes in San Diego and open them in San Francisco. Read Dyl a bedtime story in Chinook, Washington, and help him brush his teeth the next morning in Eureka, California. When I wake after a driving night, I lift the curtain to guess where we are, though most beaches look the same before dawn.

We follow breaks and weather and wind, and sometimes

Mama tosses her arrow-shaped Marana seed pod in the air to decide north or south, laughing as it flutters down.

We never stay anywhere for more than four nights—Cap says it's not wise and Mama says it's not fun—and the Gull's usual resting spots are tucked away and safe, separate from the rest of the world. We trust Tina at the bait shop in Monterey, and few others.

And yet here we are, day ten, and Cap hasn't turned on the Gull's ignition once. We're still parked on the weedy road, too close to the blue hotel. The Sapphire, it's called. Named after this little town, which we've learned is El Zafiro—*the sapphire* in Spanish.

It's late morning and the twins and I are combing our boards together under a sweet-smelling bougainvillea. Dyl's reading Cap's old illustrated book on anemones. He's a beginning surfer and would be good if he spent more time at it, but he's more interested in other things. Wild creatures, and plants no one else notices, and the stories I invent to soothe him.

With a tooth of my balsa-wood comb, I scratch lines into the old wax on my board, one for each day we've been in this place, acting stuck.

Mag reads my mind. "When are we leaving? It's been ten days, we must have gas money by now."

"Well, when he gets back, ask him," Griff says.

Mag scowls and I laugh, and Dyl glances up from his book, head tilted, because he doesn't get the joke. Cap explains things on his own time, if at all.

"Seriously, why *are* we staying down here so long?" I ask. "That hotel's hideous."

"That's why you're always staring at it," Mag says.

I blow wax shreds at him, but that's all the comeback I have. The truth is, though I haven't ventured onto its grounds, once a day I climb atop the Gull and look out at the blue chain of roofs that is the Sapphire Resort, hoping something will explain what Cap won't—why we're still here. I gaze down at the kidney-shaped outlines of swimming pools and the olive-and-white rectangles of tennis courts, the shocking green of the golf course winding through it all. And the dots of people everywhere. The solitary dots, and pairs and groupings of them, their busyness and stillness.

The four of us went through a brief phase, a few years ago, when after surfing we'd gone on long walks from the Gull's hiding place to explore beach hotels. We'd even fished change from their elegant fountains, reasoning that it wasn't stealing, before Cap found out.

"They are empty places for empty people," Cap had said, when he realized what we'd been doing. "They spend hundreds of dollars to distract themselves from their emptiness."

We haven't done it since. And yet he's parked us here, adjacent to what he abhors. Maybe it's a test. He wants to know we will turn our backs on it. And maybe I'm failing.

"We've broken our rule about only staying places four nights," Dyl says now. He observes this as plainly as if he's reading statistics from one of his nature books. "And this is the third morning since we came here Cap didn't do cereal or morning exercises."

I exchange a look with Griff. I've done my best to distract Dyl, who's caught on to our confusion about how long this garage gig has lasted, how all-consuming it seems to be compared with Cap's others, and who misses Mama. She's been off on one of her long rambles nearly this whole time. That's what we call it when Mama's away—"she's on a ramble." She rarely tells us where she's going, although sometimes she returns with clues, from the items she's bartered, or flowers for Dyl and I to press.

Griff teases Dyl, "You want to do some squirrellies for me instead?"

Dyl shakes his head and returns to his book.

It goes quiet except for the sound of us running our balsa-

wood combs up and down. *Scccch, scccch, fffshhhh, fffshhhh.*
Every once in a while, someone brushes off old wax and rip-
ply ribbons fly toward the sun.

"He's saving cash for winter," Griff says. "I don't mind. I
had a perfect morning."

Though I wouldn't have called it perfect, because I was distracted, wondering why we're staying here so long, I'd managed to find a few moments of peace on the water.

"The swell at Zuma's been killer," Mag says. "I overheard
some men talking in the lineup. If we don't go soon maybe
I'll hitch up."

Griff and I smile.

Mag's all talk. He'd never go off alone.

The twins and I return to surf until the sun's high, unusual for
us, but it's better on the water than the crowded beach or the
weedy road by the hotel.

There's a boy in the lineup I've never noticed before. He's
good on his red-striped short board. So good that Mag and Griff
check him out, too, all three of us emitting invisible waves of
interest. He's tall, with slick black hair and sharp shoulders, an
unusual pop-up. It's fluid, and so late it's suspenseful.

I stay out long after my sore arms begin to protest, and my
brothers do, too; I can tell they're tired. But the new kid's presence is infectious. He swerves and dips with blasé precision,
taking what's his without ever dropping in on somebody and
stealing their ride.

I've never been a show-off, but for some reason I need this
new boy to know my cutbacks are as sweet as his. I take a little
hip-high wave that no one else wants and make the most of it,
bouncing my board up and down to prolong the ride, diving
off at the end, extending my body, imagining I am an arrow
from my fingertips to my toes. Cap once said I'm a good diver.

But if he knew I was trying to impress this stranger, he'd regret complimenting me.

Late in the session I luck out and a chest-high presents itself twenty feet behind like it formed just for me. It's big enough to wash every thought away. But when I resurface after, climbing back onto my board, I can't help but check stealthily; the kid's watching from far off.

An hour later, he floats near us, straddling his board, and nods at me. "Hey," he calls.

Griff, next to me, doesn't need to say it—that's a signal to head in. One syllable from the boy, but it might as well be a prolonged alarm bell. We don't interact with strangers unless absolutely necessary. A rule I've known since before I could speak.

I turn and paddle half-heartedly toward shore, but can't resist a glance over my shoulder. The boy tilts his head at me, puzzled by my snub.

"Ronan," Griff says.

After one last glance, I follow after my brothers.

"What was his deal?" Mag asks Griff as the three of us lug our boards across the hot sand toward the Gull. Despite all his big talk of hitching up to Zuma, Mag is quick to heed Cap's rule against interacting with citizens unless absolutely necessary.

Citizens. That's what Cap calls people who stay put, who have regular jobs. Who go to school. When he's feeling sorry for them, Cap calls them SSNs. Social Security Numbers. When I was little, I used to think he was saying "assassins."

"I think that citizen was flirting with Ro," Mag adds with a smirk.

Griff asks: "What did he say to you? Just 'Hi'?"

I nod, not correcting him. *It was "Hey," Griff.* How my big brothers would laugh if I made that distinction. They'd laugh at me, and at the new boy, and I couldn't bear that.

When we return to the Gull, Mama's back from her week-long ramble. She's preparing dinner on a new blanket, traded for her soap and tins of herbal balm. The cloth is purple with a beautiful gold paisley design, and she's spread it out over the gravel like an island, a bright oval atop the sad little utility road. The cloth is much bigger and brighter than the everyday Goodwill checked blanket we usually sit on for family meals.

She's baking potatoes on our camp stove—eight of them. Two apiece for the twins, who are growing tall and ravenous? There's a huge salad, and rice with her spicy cashew sauce, and a frying-pan strawberry-honey tart. It's a feast, for us.

"What's all this?" Mag asks.

"Oh, I just thought a treat would be nice." But there's a mischievous look in her green eyes. "Ro, would you wipe two more plates and take the extra chairs down from the rack?"

I untie the chairs from the roof and unfold them. Eight potatoes, not six. Two extra plates, two extra chairs… And then I hear a laugh. Three figures walk up the road toward us. Cap and two others.

Dyl tenses and Mama says, "It's only Bassett and his kid, Dylly. I shouldn't have teased like that, but we have so few surprises, don't you think?"

"Bassett!" Griff says.

Mama nods. "He wrote your father at the bait shop weeks ago to set our meeting place, but put *south* utility road and there isn't a south one so he's been driving around looking for us… Isn't that funny? What if we'd missed each other?"

"You could've just told us," Mag says. But even he can't sound too grouchy about it.

Bassett is Cap's oldest friend, I guess his only real friend, but he mostly stays in New Mexico because he doesn't surf anymore. He's one of the people who writes us letters via the bait shop in Monterey.

But I never knew Bassett had a child.

So this is why we've lingered here so long.

The figures are closer now and I can make out Bassett's round shape, Cap's lanky one, and the tall kid from before in between. Black hair. Angular shoulders. Walk as easy and confident as his surf style.

Mama strides down the road to greet them, her red hair and long white skirt fluttering.

I tell the twins, "I'm going to calm Dyl down." While our attention was on our visitors, Dyl has scurried inside the Gull. When I enter, I'm grateful for the refuge of our home, where every object, every rattle and cough and contour in the night is familiar.

I don't see Dyl at first. I look everywhere—up in Cap and Mama's bunk, behind the library. Then there's a thump and a shuffling-around noise behind me and I check our bunk. I swear it was the first place I looked, but there he is, burrowed under the covers, pretending to sleep.

I climb up and join him, curling around his body's lower-case *c* with my big *C*. I draw invisible waves on his back with my index finger, something I invented to comfort him. I even used Cap's old awl to carve waves in our wooden bunk base, so he can run his fingers along them if he gets anxious.

Over and over, I trace slopes and *W*'s and *V*'s, hills and valleys, over the thick blanket. I can't rush Dyl when he's like this.

"Who's Bassett Andiskid?" Dyl asks, his voice muffled.

"Bassett and his kid. He's all right, Dylly. You met Bassett when you were teeny, and we trust him."

"I don't remember him."

I pretend I remember more than I do, to calm Dyl. "He lives in New Mexico. He has a big beard, and long dark hair, and geodes on his dashboard, fool's gold and anthracite and amethyst. And his Winnebago van has beautiful wolves painted on the side. And he can tell you all about Hawai'i, the flowers and birds…"

Bassett's laugh booms through the windows, and Dyl, who

was just starting to relax, tenses again. There's a knock on the wall by Mag's bunk. Not a cop's *rap-rap-rap-rap-rap* but Bassett patting her right wing in a friendly way. "Old gal's looking good," he says.

"He's loud," Dyl whispers.

Bassett *is* loud, like he doesn't worry about anyone noticing him. He once knelt to say into my ear, winking and cupping his hand to his mouth though he hadn't lowered his voice a decibel, "Your dad is the best surfer I've ever known, but your mama's probably even better than him except she's a solo rider so I've never seen her."

"We'll get used to it, together. What'd you say we go out just for a few minutes to see how you feel? Dyl?"

No answer.

"Where'd you learn to surf like that?" Cap asks Bassett's kid. "Not from your dad."

So Cap had been watching us, from shore or another break. Watching me sneak a last glance at the boy. The possibility makes me flush.

"Can just us two have a picnic somewhere instead?" Dyl whispers.

I wish. And I wish Bassett the Second wasn't so good. I wish he was a replica of his father, goofy and clumsy on a wave.

"It'll be okay," I tell Dyl. "I'll trace secret waves on your back."

"And I'll do it for you. And I'll bring a book for each of us." He picks out *Island of the Blue Dolphins* for me, and I wait patiently while he climbs up to the big front bunk to pick out his book from our library wall, the stack of books that divides Cap and Mama's bunk from the rest of the Gull.

I know he's procrastinating up there, behind the vanilla wall, named because the spines of the books face the front of the van, and all that's visible to us are the creamy pages. From the kids' side of the van the wall is the exact color of vanilla ice cream sold on the piers.

Dyl descends the ladder without a book and instead pulls his field journal from under his pillow. Not technically a *book*, but I understand. He finds comfort in re-reading old entries and looking at his flower pressings and the botanical diagrams he's drawn.

My hands shake as I comb Dyl's hair and help him dress, but why should I care how this introduction goes? Mag and Griff will scoop up this new boy, now that we know he's safe, and claim him for their own, show him all our secret breaks.

When Dyl and I join everyone—Dyl hugging my *Island* and his field journal to his chest like armor and clinging to my side—no one notices us at first.

I look to Mama, who helped plan this linkup. That's what we call it when a meetup lasts more than a day or two. It means traveling in a convoy, parking near each other at night. We never do it, or at least haven't since that long-ago time with Bassett, though others who live like us do it all the time—I've seen them.

But Mama is preoccupied with our guests, and Mag and Griff are standing on the road a little apart from the others, still in their short-sleeved wet suits. I wish I still had on mine, too, that my hair was still wet. I feel like a waitress in my embroidered apron dress.

"That grown-up beauty can't be Ronan!" Bass booms.

"It is," Cap says in a hearty voice I don't remember ever hearing.

"Well, pleased to see you, Ronan. Even if your old dad can't follow simple instructions. We've been trying to find you for *days*. I never imagined you'd park so close to the hotel." Bass is the only person allowed to tease Cap like this.

"There is no *south* utility road, Bass. Would you care to see your letter?"

"The hotel's expanded since I've been here."

"Ah, yes," Cap says disapprovingly. "The chain of sapphires grows ever longer. Well, I'm glad we found you at last…"

As our fathers banter back and forth, the twins finally approach the boy. He's backlit by the dropping sun, so I can only make out his dripping wet suit, drenched dark hair. Griff collects himself enough to play the host, asking about his past surf haunts. And Mag waits attentively for his answers, guarded yet unable to contain his interest.

But the kid ignores my brothers, steps off the cheerful purple blanket, and comes right up to me and Dyl.

"Saw you out there this morning." His hand is still wet and cool from the ocean as I place mine in it. He offers a little nod. He means, "You're good." You never tell someone that outright. If you say "Nice four-footer you spotted" or "Looks like you had fun out there today," that means you're terrible.

The kid's hand goes from mine straight up, back to his neck zipper, and then it all seems to happen at once. Hand behind the long neck, oversize wet suit peeled down to the waist, long, wavy black hair shaken out, a strapless bathing suit top that's too small, almost like a bandage but far from flat, hips that curve out even more, all of these surprising lines silhouetted by the sun.

My brothers go quiet.

Bassett's kid is a girl.

"Easier out there this way sometimes," she says. She shrugs, then smiles. "I'm Charlie."

3

The back of beyond

2002
LeClair Family Lavender Farm

I got no sleep. I kept looking at the window, imagining Griff out there somewhere on the farm, sleeping on the ground and hating me. He probably thought he had me all figured out, the way he'd said "Ava LeClair" and "money," not hiding the judgment in his voice. He thought I was happily married, the past neatly tucked away. Rich, content… That my life was so easy I could slip away for Cap's memorial, then slip back in like it was nothing.

When just living this life, not letting the past swallow up Ava LeClair, sometimes felt impossible.

I tried to focus on Jack and Bear, in their room nearby. On their sweet, open-mouthed faces. But those pictures wouldn't stay. They fled, replaced by images of my siblings, my parents, Charlie. The pictures I've carried in my mind for a decade.

Lying in bed, the window open, I heard a whisper on the wind:
You owe them.
You owe them.
You owe them.

FIELD JOURNAL

Will she come?
I change my mind every hour.
I change it just as often about this question:

What will I say to her if she does?
She was only seventeen when she left. Then she had her children,
a whole new life.
And now that she's back in mine, I don't want to waste the precious
time we have together being angry.

Only a fool would do that. I want to remember only how good
she was to me.

But I am angry when I tell myself—she ran and hasn't thought
of me since.

How much simpler it was when I was younger,
and your pages held only flower pressings and sketches.

2002
Santa Barbara, California

"Ronan. You awake?"

My cheek stuck to the window and my neck hurt. Pacific Coast Highway had lulled me to sleep, the way it had for much of my childhood. But back then Cap drove, always. And now Cap was dust in an urn.

I got out, massaging the knot in my neck, and breathed in salt water and kelp. We were parked at a scenic lookout near the ocean. Below the rail, the cliff dropped straight down, revealing a stretch of water so vast and beautiful it felt wrong to look anywhere else.

I sat and dangled my feet over the bluff, the updraft of wind blowing my hair back. When I was younger, sights like this were as familiar as the nubby, wheat-colored curtains framing the window above the back bunk I'd shared with Dyl. Now it seemed miraculous.

So many surfers out. Paddling, scanning, riding waves. Mighty waves, and waves that promised mightiness but fizzled out before you could stand. Everything in between. For a moment, waves were all that mattered to me, too, as I watched them get born and live and die, all within seconds, never any two the same.

Uncanny, how the ocean could whip every useless worry

from your head, at least for a little while. I'd missed that. Missed the Pacific's smells and sounds, the peace and strength that came as if they were one thing. Some other language surely had a word for that.

Intoxicating, my first hit of ocean in fifteen years.

Griff joined me at the railing, leaning his elbows against it and looking out at the water. Then he glanced down at me and asked evenly, "Not once?"

I shook my head, avoiding his eyes. He only knew me as a creature who lived in the water. The natural next question was why. Why had I deprived myself of the water for so long?

Before he could ask it, I stood. "I'll drive the last leg so you can rest. Where are we meeting them for the paddle-out, anyway?"

"About that. The spot is…". Griff tensed, staring past my shoulder at something across the parking lot. "Not again," he sighed. "Come on." He hurried back into the truck.

As I climbed in after him I saw what he was reacting to—a woman a little older than me, with stylishly bobbed blond hair. She wore an orchid-colored pantsuit, a fuchsia purse bumping at her side, and she was trotting purposefully between the other cars, weaving and waving. Heading straight for us.

"Hello? Mr. Merrick? I don't want to bother you. I'd only like to ask a few questions. Do you have—"

Griff slammed his door.

"Who's that?" I asked as I yanked my own shut.

"Reporter." He gunned the engine. Wearily: "Buckle up."

Griff did a sharp U-turn, and as we passed the reporter I caught her crestfallen expression through my window, saw her lips moving as she called after us.

"What's going on?" I watched the woman shrink in the truck's high rear window, dreading his answer.

"The Merrick family is, apparently, what they call *a hot story*. That same reporter chased after Dyl and I on the beach last week. She's not the only one, but she's the most persistent. Damn it, she must've recognized the truck somehow. I borrowed it from the bait shop." He checked the rearview mirror and glared at his misfortune—and maybe how driving up to get me had caused it. He glanced at me with a rueful smile. "Anyway, that photo is still…shadowing us."

I had to turn away from him; the look in his eyes was too painful. I faced out my window, toward the sea. But all I saw was that photo. Always, the photo.

The California Dreamers. It was an uncredited shot of the six of us—Cap, Mama, Griff, Mag, Dyl, and me. The perfect surfer family. It had initially run in a student newspaper, just a fuzzy little black-and-white rectangle on the back page, in a collage of other beach shots. None of our names had appeared—there hadn't even been a caption. Cap had fumed when he saw it, but none of us had guessed how this was only the beginning, how it would multiply and grow. On beach blankets and tote bags and T-shirts. Even in rural Oregon, hours from the coast, I hadn't been able to escape it. Full color, me and my old family racing toward the Pacific, all of us washed in gold.

I hated that photo more than Cap did.

Had.

"So it's bad," I said softly.

"It was *bad* when the only ones who recognized us over the years were other surfers. Now it's relentless."

"Tell me, Griff."

"I'll show you instead."

He made a few turns, then we were on Santa Barbara's historic main street, boutiques with red-tiled roofs as far as the eye could see. He double-parked on a busy corner, craning his neck. "There. And that's a small one." He pointed at a bus shelter on my side.

"What do you—" But then I saw it.

CALIFORNIA DREAMERS
West Coast Beach Photography of the '70s and '80s
The Brand Museum

Under these words, a teenage girl stood with her back to the camera.

Me. But that picture had been taken so long ago, in another life, that the girl felt like a stranger. Her stance is wide, confident, her cobalt-colored surfboard held casually at her hip. She gazes off to her right so you can see her determined profile, and her sunlit hair, never cut, is a wild, bright mass dancing in the wind.

To her left are the fat roots of an old banyan tree, and the rear bumper of a van parked on the beach. Just enough of it visible to signal to the viewer that it belongs to the photo's subjects. Ahead of her, on both sides, five more surfers run toward the sunset-dappled water with their boards. Cap, Mama, the twins, and Dyl. Cap farthest away—about to dive onto his board and paddle. Mama ankle-deep in water, kicking up white foam. The twins follow her to the waterline, running so fast they look airborne. Small Dyl is just a step ahead of his big sister, at her right side. He looks up and to the left, as if talking to her. Although the others are spread out, ahead of her, something about their untamed hair, or their shared grace, or the parallel lines of their bodies and boards says they are a family.

Six beautiful and free creatures—golden amphibians returning to the sea.

≈

"Slick, isn't it?" Griff asked, driving on. "The exhibit's next month. We're on all the brochures, in national newspapers, advertisements, plastered over the museum's entrance. Bad enough when it was just cheap souvenirs, but now..." He shook his head.

"What?"

"A few months ago, when the exhibit was announced, the press suddenly became interested in us and tracked us down. They identified the van, pounded on the door, stuck letters under the windshield wiper. Worse than cops." He described the exact sequence of events, how the Gull's dented bumper had first given them away, how Cap, ill and wanting to be close to his beloved breaks, wouldn't move to where there'd be less interest.

Oh, God. Poor Cap. Poor all of them.

"I'm so sorry, Griff. I hoped. How sad for Cap, I mean for all of you that his last days were—"

"It doesn't matter now, does it?" He shook his head again as if to clear it and checked the rearview, but no one was tailing us. "Anyway, at least the paddle-out location Mama chose is secluded. They won't find us there."

"So we're paddling out from somewhere south of here, some quiet beach?" Because that's the direction we were headed.

No answer. I faced him again and his jaw was tight.

"Griff? What are you not telling me?"

He ignored me and drove downhill, winding through expensive homes until we were at the Santa Barbara marina.

"Hardly secluded..." I gazed across a field of white masts at a crowded oyster bar. Something was off.

"We take a boat from here to meet the others. The spot is rather far offshore. It's...not quite an approved location."

"We don't have the Neptune Society license to dispose of the ashes or whatever? I hardly expected that."

Griff breathed deep. "I wanted to tell you right away, but I was outvoted. I've been outvoted in a lot of things, lately." He pulled a map from his pocket, spreading it across the truck's dashboard.

He touched a spot in the vast swirl of water west of us. A sandy fragment of land so small I had to lean way down to read its name. The two words on the map were clear, printed in black against the pale blue ocean. I reread them several times before I could speak again.

"They're not on Manzanita Island."

Griff bit his lip, raised his eyebrows. "Except they are."

"But it's government property!"

"We have a friend who works for the government."

I stared at the map in shock. Manzanita Island—Cap had a book on the Channel Islands in the van library. Manzanita was the most rugged and least-touched mass in the archipelago that curved in a long chain off Santa Barbara. Eighty miles offshore and strictly off limits to the public. Maybe I'd been following the world's rules too long, but this seemed extreme, even for the Merricks.

"It's fine," Griff said, though he sounded as if he was convincing himself as much as me. "We've been there for over a week and it's deserted. The island's big enough, there's tree cover, we have a lookout post just in case, and we've got all the food and gear we need." He undid his ponytail holder and then tightened it again. "Mama thought if I told you on the farm, you might...balk."

She was right. "Griff, I'm a law-abiding citizen now." I remembered my fake IDs and amended in a slightly chastened tone, "Mostly. I have two kids. I can't get busted on federal land."

"We're careful. We could probably *move* there and nobody would notice." Griff tried to sound boastful but then continued in a more natural tone. "Mama claims Cap wanted it there." He folded up the map and stuffed it back in his shirt pocket. "Of course she won't give a direct answer on why."

I hesitated, then had to ask. "Is she...?"

"She's unpredictable and infuriating and hard to pin down. She vanishes when you most need to talk to her. She returns when you're convinced she's gone for good. But she's sound of mind."

"No change, then."

"No," Griff said. "So, anyway. It's not a terrible spot..." Griff went on, listing the many benefits of throwing Cap's ashes from the water off an uninhabited island instead of a crowded public beach.

I tried to listen, idly watching the bobbing boats, a man on the pier closest to us who'd pulled his gray hoodie over his head against the wind...

"...so it's the *back of beyond*, as Cap liked to say. Only a little fishing-charter traffic to worry about, and they can't see our camp so—"

"Is that a telephoto lens?" I asked, ducking. The man on the dock had retrieved something long and cylindrical from his backpack.

Griff lowered his head behind the wheel, spying through it, then relaxed. "It's a burrito."

I rose back up in time to catch the guy peeling foil and taking an enormous bite.

Griff said dismissively, "You have dark hair. Nobody would guess you were the girl in the picture."

I flushed, because in that panicked second I *had* been worried only about my own privacy. The very different life that would be jeopardized if someone outed Ava LeClair, farm wife, as the wild-haired teen girl in the iconic picture. How to explain my lies to my sons? To Lou, who I'd married with a fake birth certificate? To his strictly-by-the-book father and his best friend, the judge?

But also, Griff's words, his reassurance hurt—that nobody would think I was the girl in the picture. That golden girl.

He checked the clock on the dash. "There's a boat waiting for us, but we shouldn't linger in the truck since that woman's spotted me in it. And our boat driver can't wait forever. I promised Mama I'd bring you this far and let you decide." He raised his hands—*my duty is done.*

I looked out at the water as if I could see the island, the rest of my family on the sand waiting for me, beckoning me. The rest of my family, but not my father.

Manzanita—Cap had spoken of it once or twice, as a legendary surf spot in his younger days. He'd sneaked onto a fishing charter to get there. But he'd had so many beloved breaks.

"What other tidbits have you kept from me?" I asked.

Griff brushed sand from the dashboard, straightened the rubber mat under his feet. Tidying the truck he'd borrowed, or maybe just restless and ready to get on with things. "You know just about everything I do now."

The man on the dock had finished his burrito. His wife and son joined him, the little boy unfurling a Pokémon kite as they walked off.

"So what will it be, Ronan?" Griff asked. "Train or boat?" He flung the choice out impatiently.

A train home. I could feel it: a dark corner seat, my collar popped up high, a book hiding my face, speeding north. Back to the life I'd made on the farm.

And yet the little speck on the map tugged at me. They had waited, as if I was still one of them.

I swallowed. "Boat."

FIELD JOURNAL

The California Dreamers, *they call the photo.*

And, whether I asked to be or not, I guess I'm one of them.
Because I dream of what's captured in the picture.
Of freedom, youth. Of the six of us together, running toward sea
like we're untethered to earth. Or time.

The photograph, slapped on cheap souvenirs, has caused
so much trouble.
But I can't hate it. Souvenir means to remember.
It's helped me remember.

I was so young when my sister left.
The picture was my only way to see her, until now.

4

Rather pretty

2002
The island
Day 1, two and a half hours later

A few hundred feet from the island's shores, our driver cut the engine and Griff hurriedly prepared the tender, tossing it in the water.

"Better wear this until we're on the island, just in case," Griff said, and handed me a huge brown anorak with a DFW logo on the back, like the one our driver wore.

Wait, I felt like yelling as I shrugged on the jacket. *Wait, I'm not ready.* The ride had gone by in a blur, wind whipping my face as we passed a dolphin pod, a vintage wood schooner, beautiful sight after beautiful sight I'd barely taken in. Instead I'd been picturing my arrival at the island, seeing the others. Mama's red hair glinting in the sun as she waited for me on the beach with open arms. *Mama*—was her hair gray now, or henna red? Did she still smell like oranges and cloves? Would her voice still calm me? She'd summoned me, but she was changeable as the wind. What if she saw me, my brown hair and lined forehead, and was disappointed? She might let something behind her eyes drift away, the way her body often drifted away from me, from all of us, back then.

Dyl might cry, little-boyish, asking why I'd exited his life with only a scribbled note and a single postcard. Mag might not speak at all. He'd glower at me, or say something cutting, mocking. And though Mama would be waiting for me to fling myself into her arms, she would have questions, too, so many questions I wasn't prepared to answer.

Suddenly I wanted to stay aboard the *Popoki Kai*, the DFW craft connecting the world of the living and this world of ghosts, indefinitely. I fussed with the jacket, my "federal worker" disguise. It was so big there was more empty sleeve than sleeve, and I rolled them, stalling.

But when Griff jumped aboard the tender and offered me a hand, I had no choice but to take it.

"Thank you," I called to our driver before climbing down, but got only a small nod from the brown hood in return. They hadn't spoken a word or looked at us during the hours-long trip, and the message had been clear: their identity was on a need-to-know basis.

Our little rubber craft glided off, Griff behind me in the stern guiding the outboard motor. I glanced back at the *Popoki Kai*. She bobbed alone. No other boats, no news helicopters, no amphibious SWAT hydroplanes on our tail. The captain of the boat stood tall, head tilted back to gauge the clouds, DFW parka whipping in the wind, then started the motor and sped out of sight.

"The island is shaped like an eight," Griff was explaining. "One circle rocky, one green, with the highest spot in the center. See…there." He pointed over my shoulder at the highest trees. "It's a nice lookout if you're willing to put in the sweat— 2,400 feet. On a clear day, you can see the mainland. The rocky side gets the wind, so not as much grows there. Well, Mama and Dyl say—"

"'You have to look closer for life.'" It burst out, the sweet memory overcoming my nerves.

He paused. Maybe surprised that I remembered what Mama always used to say. Maybe just fiddling with the motor. He quickly retreated into the safe topic of the island. "And on the greener side…" Griff trailed off.

"What?" I turned to him.

"You'll see. It's rather pretty."

But what I saw, when I turned back to face the island and we rounded some rocky steppes so the green, east side of the hourglass-shaped mass came into view, wasn't just *rather pretty*. It was primeval, untouched, impossibly lush. And it wasn't just *green*. It was every green.

So many trees—Manzanitas, of course. Ground-hugging ones, little ones like babies of the apple trees they were named after, and big ones, twenty feet or taller. Bright red flame trees, stately pin oaks, eucalypti with shredded trunks and little silver-dollar leaves fluttering in the wind, gnarled olive trees bent horizontal.

It was the perfect place to say goodbye to Cap.

Griff killed the motor and rowed us as close as possible. "We wade from here. It's calm now, we timed this well. The break nearly tipped us when we came, but even if we upend, it's an easy swim on this side of the island. The other side gets most of the rips."

He was ready to plunge in but I hesitated. "I haven't been swimming in fifteen years, Griffin."

"Oh. Right. I…" He gave up his fumbling apology and silently passed me a life vest.

Embarrassed, I looped it around one shoulder.

The two of us paddled the boat in silence until we were past the break, riding a miniwave over water shallow enough to see through to the sandy ocean floor.

"I'll pull you to shore," Griff said. "You don't have to—"

But I'd already shucked off my shoes and stuffed them in my

duffel. Bad enough Griff knew I was anxious about a little two-foot swell; he wasn't going to tow me onto land while I sat here like some princess. I tossed the life vest into the tender, threw my duffel straps over my arms, making it into a backpack, and jumped into knee-deep water. Cold, but not icy.

Griff sloshed behind me and together we dragged the tender the rest of the way and up onto the sand, quickly stashing it under tree cover. "It's half an hour to where we're camping," he said, gesturing toward the path that led uphill.

I followed him through the flora. The birdsong was like nothing I'd heard. Masses calling from high and low, riots of them. They seemed to know this was their domain, that they'd lucked onto a piece of land where ugly-voiced humans like us rarely came.

Beautiful, unreal, miraculous. All better descriptions than what Griff had offered.

Halfway to the peak, a bright copper-colored flower with straw-shaped petals caught my eye and I stepped closer to examine it, then the water below. We'd climbed steadily, and from this height, I had a good view of a small, circular cove. The same flower was clustered thickly around it on the rocks.

"Ronan?" Griff looked back to see why I was dawdling. "Mama named that cove Golden Cup. Our fishing spot—those rocks hide it from ocean traffic. Not that there's much."

Golden Cup—what a perfect name, so Mama. The bronze-yellow flowers meeting in a near circle around water so clear I wished I could sip it like an elixir to give me strength for this reunion.

But that wasn't what had pinned me to the spot.

There was a man down there fishing. A man I'd last seen as a little boy. Even from up here he looked tall, his long, sturdy legs flanking the trap. Strong, as he jumped up, returned too-small fish to the water, coiled rope. He was impossibly grown-up.

Griff joined me. "Oh." He emitted a sharp whistle and Dyl looked up.

Sometimes I imagined him late at night, when the skylight over my bed shape-shifted into the pop-up bubble window above the bunk where Dyl and I had slept; or when I was deep asleep, especially when the boys were young, when I was unguarded, exhausted, my move from the old life to the new still incomplete, and the feeling of a gentle weight, a small, patient hand on my arm felt just like Dyl's...but when I opened my eyes it was one of my sons. Or no one at all.

Dyl had stilled. I held up my hand in an awkward wave. Would he whistle back, call up a greeting? Drop his haul of shimmering silver fish and race up to me?

He only nodded and returned to his work.

Griffin and I watched him, and then, when it was obvious that was all the acknowledgment I merited, Griffin tightened his ponytail holder awkwardly and we walked on.

Dyl had once trusted me more than anyone. You can see it in *Dreamers*. In the picture, he looks up and to his left, at me. But his small body veers away from mine. You can tell by the rightward turn of his shoulders. He drags his board, as if it's lost his attention because he's noticed something out of frame. If you knew him, you'd realize he might not surf at all; he might drop the board, leave the rest of us, and wander off to the trees.

In his hair—you have to look closely—there's a leaf.

The little boy in the photo is half-wild. He's torn between the safety I offer and the safety of nature.

Maybe he knows, even at eight, that nature is the only one who will not let him down.

"Not long now," Griff said. "That's one of the old DFW work shacks. See that tin roof?"

And then we were there, on a rise above a grassy clearing. I spotted a picnic table and benches built from downed giant eucalyptus trunks. The tree was non-native, crowding out everything else, Griff explained. So the felled wood was everywhere. We passed a firepit, but there were no fires allowed, so someone had piled rusty metal flotsam into the center to mimic flames.

"Well, that's the work shed." Griff gestured at the shack a minute's walk from us, a structure of about ten square feet. As we approached, I studied it and tried to steady my heart. Corrugated tin roof rusted to burnt umber with only a few streaks of the original silver showing, walls and a crude door made of—what else?—eucalyptus planks.

We were at the threshold. I steeled myself for the sight of Mama and Magnus, hoping I'd come up with something articulate to say to them.

Griff swung the door open for me and my heart skipped, but no one was inside. Only a simple metal desk, a bare wood floor, and shelves stacked neatly with supplies.

"I'm just getting your bag," Griff said, noticing my reaction. "We're keeping gear here, but we've set up camp in the trees."

They'd brought my old sleeping bag, the one with the mallard-on-red-pattern lining that I'd found at the thrift store when I turned thirteen and could no longer deny that my old one was too short. Mama, so positive I'd come.

Griff was half out the door, but I lagged inside the shed. I'd noticed something in the far corner and couldn't move.

"Are you coming, Ronan? Oh."

"Is it?"

Griff nodded. "We didn't know where else to put it."

It was an urn, a simple, ocean-blue enamel cylinder.

He fit in there. The king of the waves.

"I'm sorry," Griff said. "I didn't think."

"It's all right." I hurried outside. Confronting the living would be enough for one day. If I let myself think too long about Cap now, how the urn was the last I'd see of him, I'd never make it until his memorial.

Griff scanned the family's encampment, the tidy setup of cooking pot and dishes next to a camp stove, neatly folded blankets and towels, the trees encircling it all. "Tread softly on the land," Cap always said. And the Merricks were treading softly on the island. They'd brought very little.

"Ahoy, Merricks!" Griff called.

No answer.

"It's windy today," he said, which seemed a feeble explanation. But as if to prove his point, a length of fair hair that had escaped from his ponytail flew sideways in the breeze.

"It's fine!" I admired the clearing's silky, celery-colored grass, butterflies flitting from stalk to stalk. They were lovely creatures, their wings a milky orange.

"Those are Catalina Orangetip butterflies," Griff said. "They only survive on the Channel Islands."

"They're gorgeous. And what's that bird with the pretty call?" I was only asking out of nervousness, but waited until it sang again, a low, wistful sound amid the happy chatter: *Whishoooleeee. Whishoooleeee.*

"I don't know, but you can ask Mama or Dyl." Griff looked around, clearly uncomfortable now that we'd stopped moving for the first time in hours. He'd hosted me—managed me?— solo long enough. "I'll show you the hammocks."

Tranquil and beautiful as it was here, I fought a growing sting of disappointment. Had I expected welcome balloons? Everyone bearing a cake with my name on it, faux candles fashioned from rusty nails?

I wiped my water bottle with my T-shirt hem, tightened my shoelaces. I checked my duffel bag zipper.

I hadn't prepared anything to say to them. It had twisted my heart in knots all day, trying. I kept telling myself there'd be time on the drive, on the boat, on the hike…but here we were. And based on Dyl's cold greeting and the clear lack of interest in my arrival from Mag and Mama, I should brace for the worst.

"Griff?" I burst out.

"Yes?"

"When you first saw me, on the farm. What did you think?"

He considered the question for a long time. "The brown hair was a surprise. But then I heard you talking to one of your sons, and I thought—*that's her.* You sounded like you. I don't know. The way you used to talk to Dyl."

It helped, knowing. It was something to hold on to.

"Thank you."

We crossed the clearing to a stand of tall Torrey pines where they'd set up camp. It was cool in the shade, but I was sweating hard. I wiped at the moisture running down my cheeks, but immediately more droplets tickled my scalp, the back of my neck.

And then I knew. The same inner shiver I got on the farm when one of my sons was hiding nearby behind a lavender row—

My body felt it. Someone was near.

5

Hōkūlani Charlemagne Akamu Winslow Keahui

1983
El Zafiro, California
Fourteen years old

Charlie shakes out her wet hair, sending fine droplets my way, but her focus has turned to Dyl. She doesn't come too close or look him in the eye, somehow knowing instinctively that she must take it slow. She points to the book he's holding over his chest, protecting his field journal: my water-rippled copy of *Island of the Blue Dolphins*, which she naturally assumes is his. "Are you at the part where Karana fights the Aleut yet?"

He nods, but seems like he's about to bolt back into the Gull behind us.

As Charlie holds her hand out—gently, asking Dyl if she can take a closer look at his book—I glimpse a small tattoo high on her right arm, two crossed oars, a flower behind them, then worry I've been staring and focus on the book. She studies the cover appreciatively, handling the novel with care before returning it to Dyl, and I feel him soften a little.

Griff recovers first, stepping away from the circle of chairs on the new picnic blanket, where Mama and Cap and Bass are, and coming over to where we're standing by the Gull's rear bumper. "I guess this place is nothing after surfing Hawai'i," he says.

Charlie gazes over her shoulder toward the ocean. From here we can only hear it, and faintly. It will be all chop now, but I know she's seeing how it was earlier, wide, steady sets.

"It's not bad," she says. "I've had a postcard of the California coast on our fridge for years, so being here is kind of surreal."

"This girl begged to spend her Thanksgiving break with me in the Winnie," Bass says proudly, appearing at her side.

"Hardly." She leans against him, ruffling his thick black hair, which is nearly as long as hers. "You snore."

"Wait'll you hear the tapes she makes me play, Merricks. Prepare yourselves."

"Is *Charlie* short for anything, sweetheart?" Mama calls from the picnic blanket. "There's a Steinbeck book…"

"*Travels with Charley*! I love it, but that's not where they got the name. Listen to what they stuck me with. My real name is…" She pauses dramatically. "I don't expect you to remember this—Hōkūlani Charlemagne Akamu Winslow Keahui."

Bassett laughs. "A killer, beautiful Hawai'ian name like that and she makes us call her Charlie. Her mom and I never got over it."

"I liked *Charlie's Angels* when I was little," she says, shrugging. She turns to me. "He was like this mysterious god. You know, just a voice with power? I didn't want to be an angel, I wanted to be Charlie."

I have no idea what she's talking about, but I nod.

"What does *Hōkūlani* mean?" Griff asks politely.

"*Lani* is like, heavenly, or royal. *Hōkū* means star. So, heavenly star." She rolls her eyes.

"We put a lot of thought into that name, kiddo," Bass says.

But Charlie isn't looking at him. "Can I sit by you, Dylan?" she asks. "I'm starved. Can I look at your other books sometime? I'll be careful. So you're studying botany, huh. I loved botany in school. I have *Island* but my copy has a different cover, with Karana by her hut."

Bass, too, is open, easy. He works a spell on Mama and Cap. Mama feels rooted right here with us, laughing. Not like she seems sometimes, as if her mind's half on her past ramble, or her next one.

And Cap—all four of us kids are mesmerized by the effect Bass has on him. His hat is tipped far back and laughter crinkles his eyes all night. Bass even swirls Cap's sacred radio dial in the Gull from KOLD to KZSD—and for an hour after we eat he and Charlie give us lessons on her taste in music, bantering back and forth. "This one thinks Talking Heads are gods. I don't get it."

"Well, he won't admit it but he likes Madonna. And she sounds like Minnie Mouse on helium." Charlie gets blank stares and translates: "I mean her voice is beyond high."

After a while, conversation turns to old times.

"So how'd you swing the new wheels?" Cap asks Bass.

"Miguel's old rig flooded in St. Pete and molded to hell, so he gave me a deal. I paid him for as much as I could, but the shell's in the RV junkyard now. Bled and dead, poor thing. He's living in an apartment in Vancouver now, miserable summumma bitch. Excuse me, kids. Ella. I mean, poor sucker. So have you seen any of the crew from Taos?"

"Shelby and Mick," Mama says. "She had a little girl, last I heard. They bought a sweet cottage in Arizona somewhere."

It's strange hearing someone call Mama and Cap Ella and Merrick, but within his portly body, Bass seems to hold great stores of information about my parents. I understand only fragments here and there. Old friends, old towns, the Gull's longlost RV cousins, travels far east of where we go now. I wonder when Mama and Cap stopped venturing inland. Why we fly up and down, but not side to side.

When Bass tells a funny story about how after some surgery

he fell in his bathroom in New Mexico without his pants on and his seventy-four-year-old, eighty-pound neighbor had to crawl in his window to hoist him up, Charlie says, "Hey, Dad? I'm sure everyone will hate to miss your next no-pants story, but can I give them a tour?"

"Sure. I mean…" He glances at Cap, who hesitates before ever so slightly nodding his approval.

"Half an hour," Cap says. "I'm sure these two travelers need their sleep."

The four of us follow Charlie along the weedy road toward the water, then north along the sand, away from the hotel. It's a steep walk up to the regular parking lot where Bass has parked his Winnebago. The Winnie, he and Charlie call her.

"We can't get it down where you are because it's too long to turn around, and my dad can't back up," she explains over her shoulder.

She calls her RV "it." We climb up the railroad-tie steps behind a family of citizens who are headed home—huffing, sunburnt, gear-laden—after their precious beach day.

"One of us can back her up for you," Griff offers. Then, hastily: "I mean *it*."

"You two have licenses? I thought you were fifteen."

We don't volunteer that the twins have driven since they were ten, as soon as their feet could reach the pedal extenders Cap made. He'd wrapped our steering wheel in dried kelp so their small hands could grip it more easily. In a few years Dyl will learn, too.

Mag glares at Griff. He's right to, I guess. Griff has thrown caution to the wind, forgetting that the twins' driving is illegal. Charlie's not one of us, no matter how accepting she seems, and how friendly her father is with ours.

Griff recovers, "Oh. We only learned in case of emergencies…"

"Wow. I wish you'd teach me to drive."

We round one more switchback on the trail up to the parking lot, pass a truck, a van, and a convertible, and then Charlie says, "So here it is, ta-da!"

The first thing I notice is a parking pass hanging from the visor.

We circle the sleek vehicle, airbrushed on all sides with a design of a racing wolf pack. It's three times the length of the Gull, tall enough to stand in without bumping your head.

Our silent admiration feels like a betrayal of the Gull, cobbled together, made of rehabbed parts and Cap's creative additions.

But I trail my fingers along the painted fur of the wolves. "I remember these," I say half to myself, finally finding my voice.

"You do?" Charlie asks.

"Your father told us a pack of wolves followed him once, thinking these were real, and I believed him. I was six, maybe."

Charlie laughs and swings open the door like she has nothing to hide. "That's so him. He doesn't get the whole this-might-not-be-age-suitable thing. My mom said he took me to some horror movie when I was younger, before they split, and I got nightmares. I think that stuff was a bigger factor in busting them up than the cultural differences."

"But they're both Hawai'ian, right?" Mag asks.

"Oh yeah. I meant because she loves our house and Bass was a vanner at heart before he had to slow down. That culture difference." She shrugs, shakes her head. "Speaking of, welcome to our palace on wheels."

I've never been in someone's house before. I don't think any of us have, and Charlie doesn't seem to recognize how momentous this invitation is. As we enter the long, gleaming white Winnebago, I realize she probably doesn't even think of this as a house.

Griff and Charlie keep up a steady stream of conversation as we all roam the space. How long is her vacation? What's our favorite break? And on and on. I tend to Dyl, who clings to me, but I'm alert to every detail. The roomy front seat, the fixed wooden ladder leading to the sleeping berth above, which is at least three times the width of Cap and Mama's. In the middle of the rig, there's a two-burner cooktop and a refrigerator, an L-shaped eating nook with two orchid-patterned placemats. Across from this, a little bathroom with a sturdy wooden door. And in the back is Charlie's own soft bed that's as wide as the whole Winnie, wide enough for the four Merrick siblings to fit.

Only two people in all of this space—it's unreal. But it's also a pigsty. We wouldn't leave the Gull like this even for a morning.

"So is this the first time you've traveled with your father?" Griff asks.

I pretend to look out Charlie's bunk window so that I can concentrate on her answer. Dyl, too, is listening attentively; he's in his fact-finding mode. Charlie is a new species and demands analysis.

"Yeah," she says. "Usually I just visit Albuquerque for a few days. I want to get my GED next year so I can road-trip with my dad even more, but my mom's not into it."

I don't know what a GED is. Something to do with school, and I store the term away for later.

I study the stack of books in built-in shelves surrounding Charlie's bunk. Cap would not approve of some of the titles— cheap-looking mysteries and fantasies mixed in with classics. Her collection is not as big as our library, but almost, and all for her.

I wonder what she'd think of the books, held in place with a length of chicken wire, that form the vanilla wall between Cap and Mama's bunk and the rest of the Gull.

The walls and ceiling around Charlie's bed are a mosaic of taped-up mementos: postcards and maps and concert tickets and posters of music groups I don't know. What surprises me most are her photographs. Little doors into her world. Her mother, who looks like her, kissing Charlie's shoulder tenderly, the way you'd kiss someone's head, because she's shorter than her child. Her home on Oahu, a white clapboard place on stilts. Her cats, whose dishes have their names, Kealani and Kai. Sketches of tattoos she might get when she's older. Her hallway at school, lined with lockers. Her friends. Surfing friends, snacking friends, friends in their own enormous bedrooms. So many of them grinning and making funny faces back at me.

On the Hawai'ian-print comforter there's a brochure of a building I recognize—one with a blue roof. It's a list of spa services from the Sapphire Resort. Twenty dollars to get your toenails painted.

"Oh, I just gave that to my dad as a joke," she says over my shoulder, making me jolt. I'd been so immersed in studying her things, I hadn't realized she'd crossed to this end of the van. "That place is over-the-top, isn't it? I mean, how many fountains do you need? It's such a gross waste of water."

I smile vaguely and half turn from her, too embarrassed to admit that I haven't gone near the hotel, and pull a book from one of the cubbies under her bed—the copy of *Island* she'd described. I'm glad she wasn't lying about owning it just to woo Dyl.

"Want to trade copies before I take off?" Charlie asks as I flip the pages. "Temporarily, of course."

"Okay," I manage, startled by the offer. I have so few possessions, and the idea of trading, of owning something new, sends a spark through me. *Temporarily, of course.*

"So my dad said your mom homeschools you. That's so cool. Total freedom."

As if sensing I'm in deep water, the twins join us in the back, and we all huddle awkwardly next to Charlie's bed. I don't know what the rules are—are we supposed to lie to her? Cap and Mama teach us all the time, in their offhand ways, about surfing and nature, their classical and '60s music, philosophy. But it's not what Charlie's imagining.

We're silent a heartbeat too long before Mag answers, looking up at a poster on the ceiling. "Yeah, school's so lame. So who's this guy in the big suit?"

"Oh, that's only the genius David Byrne. Talking Heads? We heard 'Once in a Lifetime' after dinner, remember? Here, listen."

She drags out a boom box from under her bed and hits Play, and there's a bouncy driving beat, percussion, electronic and real music whipped together. Griff asks about her other posters and her surfing magazines and the many taped-up pictures.

"Now I want to hear about you four. Tell me every place you've hung out this year." Charlie shovels a pile of clothes from her bed to the floor so we can sit.

Mag and Griff trade glances, as if realizing we may have plunged into this visit recklessly.

"Thank you, but another time," Griff says.

"Really?" Charlie asks. "My dad said you might want to look under the engine. I can at least show you that before you go."

I know that Mag would love a look, but caution wins out. "We'd better take off," he says, resolved.

He's imitating Charlie's slang the way he sometimes copies kids on the beach, and I wince at how wrong it sounds. Charlie can say "hung out" and "lame" and "take off," but coming from Mag it's forced.

"Already?" Charlie asks. "Your dad said half an hour." She seems so comfortable. Unfazed by our nervousness in her fancy rig, or the way we evade her questions.

Charlie shoots me a look, but I need to leave for my own reasons, too. I need time in the dark, in my bunk, to sift through the events of this odd day.

"Dyl's tired," I tell her. Though Dyl seems content for the first time all night, and the only one of the four of us who's finally relaxed. He's settled on Charlie's soft bed with a fat reference book, and I have to place a hand on his shoulder to pull him back to us.

The four of us are out the door and walking down the hill when she calls down hopefully, as if we're just like all her friends in the pictures, "Same break at four thirty tomorrow? That's two thirty for me, but I'll rally!"

"You were quiet," Griff says as we follow the railroad-tie trail in the sand, back down to the beach. "Worried about saying the wrong thing and getting Mama and Cap in trouble?"

"Yes."

By instinct, we walk straight for the ocean, kicking off our sandals. There are some stragglers on the beach, but it's not yet dark enough for bonfires, and I'm grateful for this quiet, in-between time. I'm grateful for the caress of surf up to my shins, a familiar sensation after the foreignness of the Winnie.

"You talked enough for all of us," Mag says to Griff. "Why didn't you just go ahead and show her Cap's tin of fake IDs while you were at it?"

"He wouldn't have let us go off with someone he didn't trust," Griff says. "We should be careful what we tell her until we discuss it with Cap. But she seems safe."

I'm glad the twins have taken the focus off me. Griff may have picked up on how funny I acted, how withdrawn. But he is wrong about the reason.

I wasn't quiet because I was worried about saying the wrong thing.

I'd been quiet the way you're quiet when you don't want to break a spell. I hadn't known someone like her existed.

The way she'd yanked her hair out of her wet suit and shaken it out, the way she'd asked Griffin, straight-up, after Mag silently slipped off at one point during dinner, "What's up with Mr. Chatty?"

The way she figured Dyl out instantly. How she'd said to

me, like I was the only one who'd understand, "easier out there this way." Shrugging.

I can't get that shrug out of my head, that tiny motion, the few inches up and down of bare shoulders.

Hōkūlani Charlemagne Bassett Winslow Keahui.

I pronounce it in my head, picture Charlie's crossed-oar tattoo on her right arm. The photographs of beaming friends, arms flung around each other, the hallway in her big school, her cats lazing on that wide, sloping green lawn on Oahu.

"Ro?" Griff prods me now to back him up.

As the shallow water rushes back out to sea, foam tickles my ankles and feet, clinging to my skin. I bend to scoop up a handful of the fine white bubbles.

"She's okay, I guess."

6

The light was epic

Four days after Charlie and Bass's arrival

The twins, Charlie, and I sit on the sand combing our boards while Dyl reads a book on Oahu birds that Charlie loaned him.

Charlie's finishing a sno-cone and her tongue's blue. She offers to buy us some as a goodbye treat—she's flying back to her mom's tomorrow—but Griff explains kindly that we don't eat refined sugar or artificial dye. Cap's rules.

"Oh, that's smart." She quickly rubs her blue-stained fingers in the sand to try to clean them, but the sno-cone on her seems indelible. "When your parents split they drown you in spending money." She sometimes makes light of their divorce with sideways comments like this, but there is always something forced about her humor.

Charlie rolls up her white paper cone and throws it in the garbage, changing the subject: "One thing your beaches have on ours is prettier garbage cans." She examines this one—a rusted metal barrel with thin cutouts of waves near the base so rain, or beer, or god-knows-what can drain out. There are others with designs of dolphins, seagulls, California poppies.

"That's how Ro got the idea for our waves," Griff tells her.

"What waves?" Charlie turns to me.

I shrug. "Just these carvings I do."

"She engraves waves in all our woodwork in the van," Mag says.

Because even Mag has warmed to her. He held out for two days, feigning aloofness, but then couldn't resist her repeated invitations to inspect the Winnie's drivetrain and top off the oil.

Charlie stares at me quizzically, and Mag goes on, teasing, "We all carve, but Ro's a regular scrimshaw artist—no piece of wood inside the van is safe from her awl." It's practically a soliloquy for him.

"Cool. Maybe you'll show me sometime?" Charlie asks us.

She still hasn't been inside the Gull. Griff, ever courteous, offers to give her a tour now. After all, we've been inside the Winnie several times now, and when the twins asked Cap what we were allowed to say in front of Charlie, he'd nodded in approval of their caution and said simply, "We can trust her, but be sensible."

She hesitates, watching me, and when I don't respond to her interest says to Griff, "Show me next time we link up."

I shrug and focus on waxing my board. The harder I try to act normally around Charlie, the more I become Shrugging Ronan, a person I don't know.

"You use Mr. Zog's wax?" she asks me suddenly, horrified. Her mouth is slightly open and her tongue is still blue.

I shrug again. "Why?"

"One sec."

The twins jog to the ocean but Charlie runs up the bluffs, kicking back a wake of sand, and comes back with a *SWELL* magazine from her collection in the Winnie.

"Sex Wax: the Best for Your Stick," it says across a Mr. Zog's ad. And there's Mr. Zog himself in a trench coat, opening it to show his naked front to two girls my age: "Expose Yourself to Sex Wax."

"Disgusting!" I'm too shocked to be Shrugging Ronan.

"Right? Here." Charlie tosses me her tin of Mrs. Palmer's brand wax and I catch it in one hand.

"There's a board shop in Hilo that has every kind of Mrs.

Palmer's, but it's hard to get here on the mainland. You should make them stop using Mr. Zog's, too," she says of the twins.

Then she lifts her board. "C'mon, ready?"

I study the wax she's lent me. It's Plumeria scent. I read over and over: *Plumeria. Plumeria. Plumeria.* Even with the lid on, it smells like Charlie, like flowers under water. "I might come later. I'm making lunch for everyone. And Dyl needs me." Every night, I vow to stop being so intimidated by her. She's a citizen and she's slightly older and she's flown across the sea to drop in on our lives, but she's just a girl.

Except I've never known a girl my age. I've read about them in books, and observed them from afar, but nothing's prepared me for Charlie. For how desperately I want her to like me, and how desperate I am not to show her that.

Charlie glances over at Dyl, lying in a nearby dune and so lost pasting something in his field journal he wouldn't know if I'd hitched a steamer. She looks the other way, toward where the Gull's parked on the hotel's utility road. It's way too far to see, but Charlie's meaning is clear. She knows that Mama's on a day ramble and Cap and Bassett are off reliving old times somewhere, so *making lunch for who?*

When I stay silent, Charlie shrugs. "Suit yourself."

I stare down at my board and blow off a piece of wax. But then her shins come back into view. "Hey, did I do something?" she asks.

I look up, and the sun behind her is so bright I have to squint. "What? No."

"Because I get the feeling I offended you somehow and that's why you're not coming. Look at it out there." She peers over her shoulder at the ocean. "Perfect three-foot, offshore. Not too crowded." Swiveling her neck to face me again, with a little smile, she continues, "Don't miss it because of me. Hey. I promise not to talk once we hit the water. My mom says I can be a chatterbox, but I never talk when I'm surfing. You'd know that if you ever came near me out there. Even your brothers can attest to it. You'd be astonished! Amazed! Okay, I'm stopping now. Right now. Right. This. Second."

She pantomimes a zipping motion over her lips, and when I make no move to get up, she looks at me one last time and trots off to the water.

I sit next to Dyl in the warm dunes and shell sweet peas into our wooden bowl, watching the action on the water as often as I dare. Charlie's got her hair tucked down her suit and once in a while I catch sight of her wide smile. My brothers are still too wary to get close to the main lineup, but Charlie paddles easily between their break and that one, trading friendly words with the twins and the others. Like she's linking them. It's like a dance.

When she claims a wave, I clutch my wooden bowl. Her style is effortless, her body long and supple. I heard Bass tell Cap she first stood up on a board at three, but she has a newbie's joy on her face when she emerges from the froth, jumping off the nose of her red board at the last possible second.

I stand and take my blue board. I should be out there. Surfing is the one time I feel halfway at ease around Charlie.

"Goofy-foot?" she'd shouted to me yesterday during a lull. And I'd nodded.

"It took me a while to figure out," I'd called, too late. Because by then, thinking that was all the answer she'd get, she'd paddled off too far to hear.

I traipse in the warm sand toward the water, ready to lose myself in the waves.

And then I notice him. I'd been so busy watching/trying-not-to-watch Charlie I didn't realize I wasn't the only one mesmerized by her. Ten feet in front of me, there's a man on shore taking pictures.

His attention is on the twins, too, and when the three of

them together catch a glassy little two-footer, Charlie in the middle, he clicks furiously.

I wave to Griff, who senses my urgency from far off in the water, and gesture toward the camera guy. He and Mag duck-dive, pop up out of the photographer's view.

But Charlie straddles her board, paddles closer to shore to face the photographer head-on, throws a playful *shaka*, waggling her right hand, three middle fingers curled, thumb and pinkie extended, and sticks out her tongue. It's a glorious shot; I can see it in my mind, her tongue still sea-blue.

Charlie doesn't know our rule about pictures, that we're to avoid them. How Mama lets her red curtain of hair cover her face, or disappears into the van, if a camera comes too close and Cap's not around.

The photographer strolls off, training his camera on a sand-castle down the beach, and when he's a safe distance away the twins swim back in.

"Where's Dyl?" Griff asks when they reach me.

"There, way up the dunes," I say.

We all turn that way, checking on Dyl, then turn our attention back to the guy with the camera, who continues on toward the pier.

"He only got shapes," I tell them. I'm guessing, but I don't want them to panic. "You were pretty far out."

"Unlike the model," Mag says of Charlie, who is heading our way.

"What is it?" she asks us as she trudges up the sand. "Why do you look so worried?"

"We don't..." Griff says. "That photographer. We don't call attention to ourselves."

"It's okay," I say, to my own surprise. Charlie looks so stricken, her brown eyes wide as she senses our alarm.

"You didn't know," I continue. "Cap doesn't like photographers getting too close."

"What, is he a criminal on the run?" she asks, trying desperately to lighten the mood.

But Mag, unsmiling, shakes his head. "We should tell Cap."

"I told you, he only got shapes," I call after Mag as he stalks off, but Charlie has, in her innocence, undone her progress with him.

"Will someone explain?" Charlie pleads. She stakes her dripping board in the sand, and it casts a long shadow across the beach as she pulls her hair from her wet suit and rakes it back, squeezing it nervously.

So this is what it takes to make her nervous. Us. Mag, being unkind.

Griff hasn't staked his board. He's still clutching it to his hip, ready to take off toward the Gull if the photographer returns. "You didn't— Cap's not—" Griff wants to help, but he gets stuck when people fight.

"We have to be cautious," I start. "We…" I glance at Griff, who nods approval. "Our paperwork's not all current."

It's a beautifully vague statement, like "we're on holiday" or "we've moved often."

Charlie cocks her head. "You don't have birth certificates, you mean?"

I hesitate. "Mama and Cap might."

"But not you four kids."

Griff and I glance at each other again.

"Shit!" (Not the time to tell Charlie that swearing is against the rules, too.) But then she quickly lowers her voice to a conspiratorial whisper. "I'm sorry. Should I go after Mag?"

"You go, Griff," I say. "Talk to him." For so long, it's only been us, the four Merrick siblings, who swim away from cameras instead of throwing *shakas* at them. So who am I to know if Mag is overreacting?

When Charlie and I are alone the two of us settle on the sand, cross-legged.

"Your dad really didn't tell you anything about us?" I ask. I'd assumed Bassett had explained something to Charlie about our need to be cautious.

"He said your life is a permanent vacation. I didn't know he was being literal." She gazes out at the waves, the boogie-boarders and surfers floating among them. "Your folks told you they don't have birth certificates for you?"

I'm tempted to lie, to suggest that I know more than I do. Charlie and her dad have no secrets, they joke around about everything, present and past. And maybe I wish, just once in a while, that it was the same in our family. But I tell her the truth, and it feels good. "Griff figured it out. It's not something we talk about often." *Ever.*

"So Cap's allergic to photographs because he thinks they could lead to child protective services busting you for the van, or truancy officers because you don't go to regular school? I'm sorry. I just want to understand."

"I guess it's that. Partly. It's just a rule." Every nonexplanation sounds more ridiculous than the last, and a germ of frustration sprouts in me. "He's just careful about our privacy," I finish limply.

"I get it." She looks up the beach, where our photographer friend is now far in the distance, occupied with a flock of seagulls by the pier. "I feel like such a jerk. I was just horsing around." She gives her hair another squeeze, then turns to me with a big smile. "Hey! You're speaking to me! Actual whole sentences. What gives?"

I can't help but smile myself. I shrug. "I hate how Mag talks down to people sometimes."

"*Magnus is only civilized on water.* Griffin told me that yesterday."

"It's true."

"Well. Thank you, Magnus."

≈

The twins and I decide not to tell Cap about the photographer. He only got Charlie close up, really, and now he's gone. And we don't want anything to spoil Charlie and Bass's last night.

For the special occasion, we plan a late dinner at the beach, around a bonfire. Mama and I make abalone stew, and potatoes with wild rosemary we picked this morning, zucchini pancakes, towers of them, plums, spiced walnuts, and our big glass jug of sun tea, which we've been tending to all day, moving it around the utility road like a sundial so it never felt shade. With a sweet laugh at herself, Mama adds sprigs of mint to each cup. *She likes company as much as being alone,* I think. *At least this company. At least once in a while.*

The twins gather wood while Charlie, Dyl, Mama, and I tote the food from the utility road to the beach, scouting for the best spot, finally settling on the perfect stretch of sand. Not too close to other bonfires, not so close to the water that we'll have to run when the tide laps in. We rake the sand smooth with driftwood, then each of us takes a corner of the purple-and-gold paisley blanket, wafts it high, and even when it's clean of sand we keep waving it up and down just for the fun of it, watching it billow above us like a parachute. As we set it down, the boys start the bonfire, the sky darkening.

Charlie sits next to me on the corner of the blanket farthest from the fire and entertains us as always. Mag acts standoffish with her for a bit, but finally shakes off his irritation from earlier, succumbing to her infectious laughter—and her whispered apology about posing for the camera.

As a surprise, after our stew Charlie unveils a maple cake she baked in her little RV kitchen. It's lopsided and bitter, with clumps of undissolved baking soda that Bass teases her about. "We won't need to brush our teeth tonight—the toothpaste is baked right in!"

But I ask for a second slice. She's trying so hard to get our rules right—no store-bought cake, no refined sugar. Ever since the camera thing today, I feel oddly protective of her. I'd been so intimidated—by her confidence, her height, her two houses, and her snapshots—that I'd forgotten we outnumber her.

"You don't have to, Ronan," she says as I take a big bite of her terrible cake.

I eat every crumb while she watches, grimacing.

"The next one will be better," Charlie promises.

"I'll teach you how to cook skillet cake over a fire," I tell her. "I mean. If you'd like."

"Yes! Sign me up. I'll pay for my baking lessons in Mrs. Palmer's wax."

As she's pouring Bassett a final cup of her herbal tea, Mama urges him to link up with us again, anytime, and as we're clearing dishes, Cap claps him on the back. "You know our address."

Meaning 11641 Pacific Coast Highway, the location of Salt Bay Bait & Tackle in Monterey.

It's decided: Charlie will return. Maybe, if I'm feeling bold and Cap allows it, I'll write her a letter. I practice the casual request in my head: *Hey, can I write to you?*

After dinner, I fetch the dish tub from the rack on the Gull and fill it with seawater. Charlie helps Mama and me clean up, even when Mama protests, "But you're our guest!"

"I don't want to be a guest," Charlie says simply, settling next to me to wipe plates dry.

We work quietly, the job going fast with three of us. "So where do you keep the rest of your kitchen stuff?" she asks as we fold the blanket together.

Mama says, "This is all of it, sweetheart," with a little smile. She tells Charlie the zinc army tub we're washing up with will get lashed to the roof rack once we're back on the road, and it holds all we need—two big olive-wood spoons, one pot, one skillet, one rinse bowl, our camp dish sets and the scrubbers Mama makes out of clean straw.

On the other side of the dying bonfire, Bass and Cap and the twins lie back in a line with their heads on a fallen log, knees bent, Cap's chin so high his hat has fallen onto the sand. Dyl sits cross-legged behind them. Five heads tilted up to watch the stars. Our fathers spar about Jupiter's moons with the lazy ease of old friends, and Dyl informs them they're both wrong. Even Dyl has accepted these two new creatures into our life.

It feels right now to show Charlie my home, to invite her inside the Gull. Just like those friends in her pictures would, flinging open their doors.

But just then Mama sees something over Charlie's shoulder and murmurs, "There's someone shooting us. There up on the dunes, next to that palm."

We whirl around, and when my eyes adjust to the gloom up in the trees I spot him. Twenty feet from us, it's the man with the camera from earlier.

Mama glides south down the beach, toward the refuge of the Gull, Dyl a few steps behind. The stargazers stand, and Charlie turns to me, anxious.

"You there!" Cap calls, walking around the fire in our direction. He's picked up his hat, and he settles it on his head. "Come say hello."

"Merrick, behave," Bass says, jovial.

The man emerges from the trees. In the firelight I see he's only a boy, not much older than the twins. He passes us, approaching Cap, and Charlie and I are frozen in place as he looks at us, expecting a greeting since Charlie was horsing around for him earlier. But neither of us speaks.

"Now, would you like someone to skulk in the bushes and secretly take pictures of you and your family on vacation?" Cap asks. His voice sounds steady, almost good-natured, but his expression is hidden under the shadow of his captain's hat.

"I didn't mean to sneak. I thought it was okay, because of before." The boy looks helplessly at Charlie, the twins. Then me.

"They're called wild shots, outdoors, and you don't technically have to ask for permission, but—"

"He took pictures of me surfing today," Charlie jumps in. "Mama says I'm a ham. I was showing off."

The twins and I exchange worried glances across the firepit. We have made a mistake, not telling Cap about our near miss.

"We didn't want to worry you," Griff says hurriedly, and even from ten feet away, in the dim light of our dying fire, I can see how his face has gone taut. He and Mag walk up to Cap, flanking him, but Cap's focus is on the boy.

"He only got Charlie, close-up," Mag says. "We all left."

The boy looks baffled, and if I didn't know what was about to happen, it would be funny. "I'm doing local color for the *Daily Triton*. The UC San Diego paper? I'm new on staff this year."

"Charles *is* a ham," Bassett says. "Now, Merrick, there's no harm."

Cap looks across the firepit at Charlie, who still stands by my side clutching our picnic blanket, and offers her a small smile. "It's not your fault some people don't have manners, Charlie."

I feel sorry for the boy, with his swoopy bangs and polo shirt. He's no match for Cap.

"What kind of camera is that?" Cap asks. "It's a beauty."

"It's a Leica DRP Xl."

"Care if I check it out?"

I hug my arms around me and avoid Charlie's eyes, but I can still sense her confusion. Cap may not be mad at her, but soon she will be mad at him. Mad at all of us, for not stopping what's about to happen. Or instead she'll feel sorry for us.

I'm not sure which is worse.

The boy unclips the camera from the strap and hands it over, across the firepit. "Some alumni group donated a bunch of equipment—we have shelves of them."

Cap fingers a silver cylinder on the side of the camera. "What's this gadget here?"

"The timer. To take pictures of yourself with a tripod."

"And this?"

"Grip tape, for if your hands get sweaty. You're into photography?"

Cap ignores this, fiddling with the camera.

"So how long have you been on vacation?" the kid asks to fill the silence. He's still smiling awkwardly when Cap tosses the camera up and catches it with one hand. "Hey, what're you— Careful..."

A nervous laugh, another toss.

"Hey, hey, hey, that has ten frames left!" Still the kid doesn't seem to understand. Does he think my father, the engineer, doesn't know precisely what he's doing?

"Don't, Merrick," Bass says. "I'll talk to him, you can—"

Cap tosses the camera into the fire with our potato peels and abalone shells. There's an unsettling power in his gestures: the confidence with which he got his hands on the camera, rotated it as if to admire it, and destroyed it—and every image it held, including Charlie with her blue tongue. I hadn't expected that. Not the whole camera. In the past, Cap has only taken film.

The firelight is faint now, and his hat is too low over his eyes for me to read the expression in them, but I wonder if Cap isn't a little surprised by what he's done, too. The twins are silent, two tall sentries on either side of him, staring down at the ring of stones around our dinner fire.

"Was that entirely necessary, Merrick?" Bass asks.

The boy's too shocked to speak.

Cap's head is tilted down, and he could be looking at the dying fire, or his bare feet, or the boy's white sneakers. I wish I knew.

When he finally answers, there's a tinge of something I don't recognize in his voice. Regret? Embarrassment? But he says only, "He'll understand when he has a family of his own to protect."

Bass shakes his head and rises. "C'mon, Charles. We have a long drive tomorrow."

I feel her looking at me, can almost guess the hundred ways she'd try to make light of what just happened, the funny comment that might set things right again. But I don't want her pity. I stare down at the fire.

When she and Bass leave, Cap says quietly to the college boy, "Someone on the beach stole it and you didn't see their face, it was too dark."

The kid swallows. Nods.

"And you won't come back here."

The boy nods again.

"Thank you." Cap strides away, toward the Gull, and Mag and Griff follow. Griff trotting up so he's right at Cap's side, Mag a little behind, walking rakishly, as if nothing has happened, but I know it's a cover. I picture Cap chastising them for not keeping him informed.

I watch down the beach as they pass another bonfire, then a second before disappearing into the dark. They've left me alone with this stranger, this boy. Forgotten me, or assumed I was right behind them.

"I guess I should've asked permission," the boy sputters. "My editor at the *Triton* assigned me this beach, that's all. I wasn't trying to be rude. But I guess he felt..." He gazes up at the stars, grasping the camera strap around his neck. "The light was epic today, and I got some great shots on the pier. In the dunes..."

At the sight of him, his wistful expression, my tangle of emotions gives way to certainty. Because somehow I know. I know what he's seeing up there. Not Orion or Ursa Major or the Big Dipper, but the photos he took. He's going through his real pictures, one by one. He's remembering the light, the angles, what he left in and what he left out. But they'll never be pictures now. They're melting plastic, or whatever film is made of.

"He only did it because…" But I have nothing to offer him. No comfort, no explanation.

Why *are* photographs such a grievous sin? The chances of the wrong person seeing us in one are minuscule.

And yet No Cameras is one of our laws primeval, like in our Plutarch book in the vanilla library. A commandment.

The first time Cap defended us from a photograph—that I remember—I was six or seven. It was morning, the end of our predawn session, and a lady in Santa Cruz was taking pictures of me surfing, squealing to her husband, "Just look at the cute little thing go!" like I was a baby duck. Cap had calmly sloshed out to her, his board still leashed to his ankle, and asked for the film. It was too windy for me to catch his words. But she'd handed it over, then she and her husband had hurried to their umbrella, gathered their stuff, and left, the woman sending one last, confused look my way. Only once they were gone did Cap unleash his board and drop the film, with its sad little brown plastic tail, into one of the festive beach garbage cans with a wave cutout for drainage.

Three or four times since, Cap has thrown film away after tourists tried to take a photo of us. Twice he's asked to see a pocket-sized camera as if to admire it, removed the film, and dropped the cameras carelessly onto a beach towel rather than handing them back.

But this…

Before I can find anything to say to console the boy, he hurries off in the dark, the camera strap around his neck attached to nothing.

The next morning, as we're saying our farewells next to the humming Winnie, Bass pulls Cap into his bear hug and pretends last night was no big deal. "No more camera smashing, Merrick. We're getting too old for it."

I race for the Gull, but Charlie runs after me and puts a hand on my shoulder, stopping me from going inside without a goodbye.

"I'll come back," she says.

I nod but I can't look at her, and I don't believe her. Seeing what Cap did through her eyes, I'm certain now we'll never link up again.

Then the Winnie is a cloud of dust on the freeway.

7

Do right by Cap

2002
The island
Day 1, early afternoon

I looked up right as another trickle of water fell. This one hit my forehead and I blinked, swiped at my eyes. When I opened them I saw someone above, lying in a Jacob's ladder–style hammock high in the trees and holding a dripping handkerchief.

I called softly, "Hello, Magnus."

He jumped down from his hammock, kicking up tawny dust like a magician reappearing in a cloud of smoke after his act.

But there was no performer's smoothness. He took a few halting steps toward me, then stopped a body length away, clutching his wet bandana. Surely, he'd heard us earlier, wind or no.

"You're hurt," I said.

Griff shifted nervously beside me; he thought I was getting into the heavy stuff, that I meant hurt by me. By my absence.

"His knee," I explained, gesturing at Mag's leg. "He's bleeding."

Griff inspected the slash of garnet on Mag's shin. "How'd you do that?"

"It's nothing. I went to the lookout and bit it a little climbing down the shortcut."

"Bit it a little"—a classic Mag-ism. An oxymoron, like saying, "Wiped out...sort of."

I observed my big brothers, fraternal twins who could pass for identical if you weren't looking carefully enough. Both were tall, broad shouldered, their straight blond hair well past their collarbones. But Mag's locks were rougher, hanging loose, and Griff's baby fine, still ponytailed. Mag had always held his shoulders higher, his hands closed, had always looked at the world through eyes slightly narrowed.

How long had I been staring? "I have twins," I blurted. "Did you know?"

Mag shook his head.

I set my backpack on the ground and pulled a snapshot from my wallet. In the picture, Jack and Bear sit on the porch, oblivious to me and my camera. They'd found a rusted toy train in the south field, and I'd given them an old toothbrush and can of mineral oil to shine it up. They're hunched over the ancient toy, Jack scrubbing a wheel, Bear waiting for his turn. You can almost see his little hand twitching with impatience.

I handed Mag the photo. "That's Jack and that's Barry. Bear. They're six here. Eight now."

Mag examined the picture for a long time. Anyone else would smile, offer up the requisite *cute* or *sweet*. "Do they go to school?"

"Yes."

Mag looked again, searching for evidence of the classroom in his nephews. What would the stamp of formal education look like? Cap had spoken of school as something that "marked you" forever. He handed the snapshot to Griff, who dipped his face close to it politely but didn't say anything.

"We can't afford an infection," Griff said, clearing his throat and giving me back the photo. "I'll get the first aid kit from the shed."

Now we seemed to be out of small talk. I fought the urge to fill the silence, to ask if Mag would sit and elevate his scratched leg, to ask, *Did you hurt anything else? Do you want a fresh Kleenex from my pack?* Anything to drown out the lonely *drip, drip, drip* of the cloth in his hand.

"So you made it," he said at last.

"Looks that way."

He bent to dab at his cut. "Griff and I made a bet."

"He bet he could get me to come here?"

"The other way around. I knew you'd do right by Cap." He straightened again and shrugged, but it was a monumental gift, more shocking than a hug.

We gazed over toward the work shed, where Griff was taking his sweet time, and I thought of the blue urn inside. "I'm so sorry he had reporters hounding him his last few months, because of that museum thing. Cap."

After showing me the museum poster on the bus shelter, Griff had recounted the miserable chain of events. Cap had collapsed on the beach, and someone called a medic who happened to surf—so he recognized the bumper of the Gull as the one displayed on a banner outside the Brand Museum advertising the exhibit, the distinctive, dented chrome blown up to massive proportions. Days later, the first reporter showed up outside his crummy hospital room.

"You know about that, then. Yeah. It wasn't fun." Mag sighed, regarding me for a heartbeat or two with understanding, then quickly collecting himself and turning his attention to his cut, swabbing it roughly with his bandana. "We tried to distract him from that whole…mess. Played his records to drown out visitors. Moved the Gull as much as he let us, once he came home. We offered to drive inland, but he didn't want to leave the coast for his last…near the end." He paused. "We stayed east for three months when the picture was on the cover of *Time*, and it made everyone miserable. Oh, did you know we were on *Time*?"

I nodded. I'd wondered how they had dealt with *Time*. *Dreamers* appeared on the cover in 1992, six years after I'd left, along with a roundup of other shots depicting "families in America." I'd seen it on the farm and my dinner had nearly come up—but it was only a wire service image, and no article or identifying details had accompanied it.

Dreamers had caused trouble back when I'd lived in the van, too, forcing us to change our lifestyle, to think of the outside world far more than Cap wanted in order to stay one step ahead of those few people who recognized us in the picture.

But our problems had been nothing like what Mag described now. It seemed the family's luck had run out.

I imagined a scene like in a movie, reporters hurling questions when anyone opened the Gull's door:

Is it true you live in your van?

Is it true you kept your kids out of school? Did you ever ask them if they wanted to go?

Mr. and Mrs. Merrick, how did you elude social services?

On and on...

"Was Cap aware of what was going on?" I asked.

"Sure. Livid at first."

"Only at first?"

"Later he seemed...resigned." Mag balled up his bandana. "He said if anyone's foolish enough to waste six dollars on surf pictures in a museum, or scribble articles about us and our van, instead of just going in the water themselves, we should pity them. Not hate them."

It occurred to me there was another family member I'd never see again. The Gull.

"How's the Gull running?" I asked, my voice so pained I felt silly.

"She's at the yard in San Jacinto."

The yard, otherwise known as the RV graveyard. I didn't want to picture her on concrete blocks among thousands of motorhome carcasses. *Bled and dead.* A rush of wind blew through camp, shaking the tree branches encircling us and lifting the leaves at my feet in a mini whirlwind. Absently, I knelt to catch one, thinking of the Gull in flight, on the road. I split the leaf in two, like wings.

Mag added, "She's not beyond repair. We were just getting the cash together for a new engine and paint job."

I rose eagerly. "How much do you need?"

"Why, you going to make a donation?"

"I could give you some. Sure. What does a new engine cost, a thousand?"

Mag waved me off. "You don't need to worry about it, seriously."

"But I want to—"

"Look at the parade marshal."

I turned; Dyl was here, just stepping out of a tree's shadow. And his arrival *was* a parade.

He dragged a makeshift litter, two long branches webbed crosswise with reeds, holding a basket trap brimming with silver-white fish. Behind this, two sand-colored kittens followed. High above him, also drawn by the day's catch, three gulls wheeled.

Closer up, Dyl's hair was as thick and lush as ever, still as wildly curly as mine would be if I didn't iron it straight. But unlike when he was a boy, and I'd struggled to comb it, even after working Mama's orange oil into the tangles, it was now unsnarled. And leaf-less. My little brother had grown into a handsome man.

Mag took a canteen from the picnic table and tipped water onto his cut. "You going to say hello to Ronan?"

"It's all right. We saw each other when he was fishing."

"Hello, Ronan," Dyl said dutifully, and his voice was a man's. Of course it was. He was twenty-six now, though I'd locked him in my memory as a boy. He'd once been almost like my son, but this baritone-voiced adult wouldn't look at me, hadn't even glanced in my direction.

"Now who's uncivilized?" Mag mocked Dyl for his greeting.

I focused on the kittens, who were keeping a safe distance but hadn't taken their round eyes off the fish, which Dyl now laid out and salted in a wide metal pan. Our dinner, I assumed. I held my hand out, palm up, but the cats wouldn't come near.

After Dyl finished prepping the fish, Mag shot him a dirty look: *Talk to her.*

Reluctantly, Dyl came and sat near me. He pulled his green-and-white field journal from his pack and busied himself scribbling intensely.

I waited to speak until he closed the journal; I would never win a quiet contest with Dyl.

"It's beautiful here." I stared straight ahead at a beam of sunlight sifting through the dark trees. "Like Karana's island."

"Who's Karana?" Dyl asked.

A dagger. He knew who she was.

But after the hurt subsided, a wave of tenderness washed over me. Dyl's knit brows and sullen expression were exactly like Jack's in the rearview mirror the time Lou and I'd missed his *Oregon Trail: The Musical!* performance as Meriwether Lewis because the truck blew a tire.

"Karana is a character in this book I love," I told him, daring a glance his way.

"Oh."

"*Island of the Blue Dolphins*," Mag said, walking past toward the shed. "He still has it."

So at least my cherished old copy wasn't at the bottom of the ocean, tossed by Dyl in anguish, or anger, after I left. It was something. I hopped up and wandered over to a tin of fish bones Dyl had saved, gesturing at the cats. "May I?"

He nodded. I sat back on my heels and held out two scraps of fish, palms up, the treats nearly on my fingertips. I looked sideways, not at their four alert eyes. Give the vulnerable in this world time to know you, to assess their risks, before going closer.

We'd calculated risks constantly in the old life. Unconsciously, like breathing. Talk to that stranger or walk away? Park the van by those dunes or under that tree? Use the campground showers at 1:00 a.m., when the site hosts are asleep, or when they're busy selling cords of firewood?

Trust me, cats. It felt important. An example for the human I really wanted to win over. Inch by inch, they crept closer, then they lapped from my hands, bolting back the fish as they shot back into the trees. Four eyes, bright in the dusk, watched me suspiciously, waiting to see if they'd made a mistake. But Dyl refused to face my way.

FIELD JOURNAL

My sister is on the island.

Can it be true?

*I've wanted this reunion for so long. Wondered how she was,
in her new life.*

I practiced a million conversations.
Do you remember the stories you used to read to me?
I do. I still hear every word in your soft voice.
My private and precious bridge to our past.

Do you read them to your children?
I hope so.

But now that we're here together, so close,
I'm afraid I'll say everything wrong.
That such questions will come out like blame, or jealousy.

Or I'll stay tongue-tied until she sails away again,
and it's too late...

After dinner, my brothers and I cleaned up with few words. Then Mag went to work whittling something out of balsa wood, Griff tallied supplies, and Dyl wrote in his journal. I pulled a seed catalog from my duffel and pretended to read it, as though my attention was on the price of *Augustifolia* instead of completely tuned to my brothers spread around me at camp.

I could do this. Was doing it. Things were awkward, and Mama's continued absence stung, but my arrival had not led to accusations, or shouting, or whatever ugliness I'd feared. We were fumbling through things all right, considering. Perhaps, given the alternative, I should be grateful for silence.

And then: *Din-din-dtooonnng. Din-din-dtooonnng.*

A bell, far-off but insistent. An urgent ring that brought to mind ancient mariners, farm villages where you warned neighbors from acres away when there was trouble.

"What's that?" I looked in all directions.

All three of my brothers had snapped into action, moving gear in the shed. Startled, I tried to help, stowing my unused hammock and sleeping bag.

"You know the plan, we'll hide up in the Web," Griff said

to all of us, as if he wore an invisible captain's hat. "We'll stay there and wait for news."

"Will someone please explain what's going on?" Panic seized me as I exited the shed on Griff's heels, bending to hurriedly tie a shoelace.

Mag, looping his fishing net up in a tall eucalyptus, said over his shoulder to me, "Two rings from the bell on the west dock is a message from—"

"From our DFW friend," Griff interrupted, glaring at Mag. "Let's go."

The three of them dashed into the trees, beckoning me to follow.

We ran in a line, along switchbacks with no trail markers, uphill, then a little down, then up, up, up again until I felt like my lungs couldn't take another step. Then thick foliage forced us to slow down. The island seemed to be narrowing, so I gathered we were headed toward the center, that lookout way up high. The middle of the 8.

We were crossing a flat ridge when Mag, dropping to his knees so as not to be spotted, inched to the edge, pulled binoculars from his pack, and scanned the water below, "There's a boat, all right."

Griff joined him and took the binoculars: "And it's anchored. No fishing gear, either."

"Pirates," Mag said glumly.

I peeked out, holding a root for safety. Below was a white Kris craft, narrow and sleek. Someone was on board but they were only a fuzzy oblong from up here.

Griff, sweeping the binoculars around, locked on to something and whispered to himself. "It can't be. We shook her off. How did she—" He handed me the binoculars. "Is it?" he asked, his voice disbelieving.

My view through the binocular rounds was horribly clear. *Oh, God.* Blond bob, fuchsia bag. "Yes. It's her."

"She's a reporter who tried to wave us down in Santa Barbara," I explained to the others, handing the binoculars to Mag.

"Well, you obviously *didn't* shake her off, Griff," Mag said. "Thank God for Ch—" He looked at me and caught himself. "For the bell."

But it was too late—I knew. My heart had sensed it. The brown-jacketed driver of the *Popoki Kai*, my family's mystery helper, had a distinctive carriage. The set of the stranger's shoulders, their height, the confident drape of their forearm on the wheel…and the way they'd stood, after Griff and I disembarked, lifting their chin to the sky to check the clouds.

I don't trust forecasts, Ro. I trust the clouds overhead and the wind on my cheeks.

She'd kept her hood cinched tight, her back to me. But the name of the boat that had ferried me here should have given it away. Kai was one of her childhood cats.

I faced my brothers. "You can say it. Thank God for *Charlie*. I know she's your DFW helper. You can explain why she's involved later. Now let's go."

We took off running.

The Web was a network of rope ladders strung horizontally twelve feet up, about six feet square, in a dark grove of trees near the center peak of the island. Like a panic room, but in the air.

"Impressive," I said once I was seated, my back against a broad trunk, but the word came out shaky.

Mag said, "We can't surf. We had to stay busy somehow. But we never thought we'd actually need to use it…"

Up here we'd be nearly impossible to spot. We had food, water, blankets. But our safety was an illusion; the reporter could be making land this moment, and there was no hiding from the fact that we'd been found. One phone call and we'd be jailed for trespassing.

We were not safe so much as trapped.

Had I lingered too long at the dock? We'd been so careful, on the boat and out of the marina in seconds, well camouflaged in our DFW getups. And Charlie (Charlie!) had driven around in loops, making sure no one was tailing us.

"What if that…woman spots Mama?" I didn't want to say the word *reporter*.

"She'll hide—you can hear that old bell anywhere on the island," Griff said. "We worked it out with Charlie in case any of her DFW colleagues paid a surprise visit."

"Better a coworker of Charlie's than a reporter," Mag said.

"Charlie will handle her. Flash her badge, or… It's fine." Griff checked in his pack. "Let's inventory our food and water."

"We have plenty," Mag said. But he complied, showing Griff all he had brought. An extra-large canteen, pounds of nuts, a huge tin of chokecherry leather Dyl and Mama had dried on the island.

I unzipped my own duffel as if I didn't remember precisely how much food I had: four granola bars and a Ziploc of chocolate-covered raisins melted into a clump.

To feel more useful, I rummaged around, tidying my things. A packing cube of clothes, fleece top, knit cap. And a tiny object I'd forgotten I'd brought—a little glassine pouch with snips of blond hair in it.

My twins wouldn't expect a call for a few days. They'd be done with their early dinner now, worn out from skate camp, settled on the sofa bed at their uncle's. They still believed they had only one uncle.

I missed my boys. I'd never felt so far away from them. Never been in a different state before, even.

Dyl seemed to notice the clear bag and its silky contents, and I let a beam of sun play with it, wishing he'd ask what it was.

This is my boys' hair, Dyl. They secretly cut it and gave it to me to make our dog smell it so he wouldn't miss them. They're so sweet and clever, Dylly, just like you. Their names are Jack and Bear, short for

Barry, and our dog's name is ZBoy after famous skateboarders, and I wish they could meet you and you could meet them and please please look at me my heart is splitting.

He looked as if he was about to say something, but stopped himself, instead directing his attention at a squirrel in a nearby tree.

We'd been waiting, wafting up in the trees, for more than an hour.

"Charlie'll ring the all-clear bell soon," Griff said. But his voice was less convincing now. He scratched his calves distractedly. "Sand flies." He took a small green dry-bag from his pocket and opened it, removing a tin of Mama's salve, and rubbed the mixture onto his bites, a little more aggressively than he needed to. He was worried, no matter what he said.

"They didn't get you?" he asked me, because I was observing him so closely. "They're bad on that beach where we landed today."

I'd been dying to scratch, and now pulled off my shoe and sock, showing off the pink welts on my ankle. Griff handed me Mama's tin. Oranges and cloves. Rubbing my ankles and feet, half lost in scent memory and half anxious about whatever was happening with Charlie and the reporter far below us, and why it was taking so long, I got careless.

Dyl noticed my right instep.

I clapped a hand over it. I'd forgotten the tattoo. "Oh. I did that a long time ago. Ugly, isn't it?" I said.

"No," Dyl said, facing me directly for the first time since I'd arrived.

"Look," he said to the twins. They stared, waiting, until, reluctantly, I removed my hand.

On the farm, it was second nature to hide it. Even back when Lou and I had been trying to make a go of our marriage and had made love, slept in the same bedroom, it was surprisingly easy to hide the arch of your foot from your partner.

I'd drawn it myself late on the night of my eighteenth birthday, a year after I'd arrived on the farm, when I still bunked in the seasonal picking cottage and had only just begun to notice Lou's warm smile and the muscles in his bare back. With India ink, an antique pen nib, and rum filched from a bunkmate, I'd carved our family wave pattern from memory—the same one Mama had on her instep, the same one Cap and the twins had, and the one I'd tattooed into the Gull's wood over and over. A longer version of the symbol on Cap's coins. The same Merrick pattern of *V*'s and *W*'s and pen swells that Dyl, presumably, had hidden inside his boot right now, marked onto his body on his own eighteenth.

It had hurt. But still I'd dug deeper into my flesh, deeper than necessary. The pain was nothing compared with my ache for the Merricks, and my growing fear, after no one responded to my postcard, that they had soared on without me.

"Mama will like that," Dyl said to me now. And I was grateful for every sand fly that had feasted on me.

From there, my brothers only seemed to soften further. Griff reached back to his ponytail and tugged on two lengths of hair to tighten it. "I was thinking, you could sleep in the work shed tonight. If you like." And it didn't sound like a jibe at my civilized life, but simple courtesy.

With an insistent headshake: "No. I'll make camp with you three. A blanket on the ground is fine for one night."

Mag said, "I braided a hammock for you. But unless Charlie tells us the coast is clear soon, we may be sleeping right here."

"She's here," Dyl said, looking down.

We all followed his gaze, peering down through diamonds of rope. Glossy leaves, stretches of rich dark soil, branches so heavy with buds they arced like grade-school rainbows...and, half-hidden behind a pale bamboo trunk, the top of a brown anorak hood.

"It's okay, Charlie," Griff called, flinging the ladder down for her. "You can show yourself. She knows."

Charlie tipped her head up, scanning the rope web, finding me. My sock still in my hand, I waved down at her wanly from my strange perch. She shook her head—a wry, understanding gesture just for me. *Fancy meeting you here. Some reunion. What next?* It said all of that and more, and I shook my head back at her: *I know.*

She climbed up expertly, her long legs taking the swaying white rungs three at a time, and sat next to Griff. She looked across the platform at me without hiding it. Clad in her khaki uniform, her long hair braided neatly, the tip covering her official-looking badge, she was perfectly composed, and smiling. I tried to act just as unfazed, but it was surreal, her being here. I busied myself, trying to put my shoe and sock back on, but in my distraction I was clumsy, and they plummeted through the rope, rustling through the leaves and smack into the center of a pale green, cabbage-like plant the diameter of an inner tube. They perched there, as if determined to extend the moment and make me feel even more ridiculous.

"Bull's-eye," Charlie said with a kind laugh.

"I should get those," I said without looking at anyone. "They could give us away."

"You don't have to worry about that," Charlie said. "Your visitor won't come up here—I talked to her."

"Thank God you saw her boat and got to the bell in time," Griff said. "Any idea how she found us?"

"Damn that photo," Mag said. "Did she follow the *Kai* today or last week?"

"Neither." Charlie pulled an envelope from her pocket, and her voice sounded so curiously altered, so business-like compared to a moment ago, we all went silent, our rope platform going utterly still. Birders on an expedition had nothing on us.

"Griff, she wanted me to tell you she was only trying to chase you down on the mainland to talk to you about—" Charlie smoothed the envelope on her knee and tapped it. "About *this*." She looked at each of us in turn, worry in her warm brown eyes.

Charlie went on, her expression grim. "She didn't need to follow any boat here. She already knew exactly where you were hiding out."

"What?" Griff asked, panicked.

Mag, furious: "How?"

Charlie sighed. "Cap invited her."

8

Quiver

1984
Santa Cruz, California
Fourteen years old

Cap studies his mug of lemon tea. "Infestation week is here."

We've finished dinner, and the six of us sit on our every-day plaid blanket in the shade of the Gull. We're parked in an abandoned lettuce orchard miles inland from the Santa Cruz shore, behind a collapsing farmhouse. The trees are neglected and scraggly, but the house's decaying white clapboard screens us from the road, and though it's a half hour walk to the water, no one's hassled us.

We don't park close to the sand during spring break.

Or *infestation week*, as Cap calls it.

I'd spotted the first sign this afternoon. I'd been floating on my board under the little dock. Not the big Santa Cruz pier, which is always heavy with tourists, but the battered, skinny one the crabbers use.

In the cool shade under the dock, I looped my arm in a frayed rope around a pylon gone soft with age and lay face-up, lulled by baby waves, watching clouds change through the wooden slats. It was sweet relief to get away from the van, which feels smaller these days. I've grown an inch, and my feet dangle over the end of my and Dyl's bunk. But that's not why the van feels small. Maybe it's Jarvis Germaine—Cap's surf idol, whose gentle, elderly voice lectures us from Cap's oldest, most-played record. Jarvis talks about freedom, about "rejecting the machine," about "sermons in stones" and "wisdom in waves." He's the source of our morning promises: "I close my eyes 'til it all drops away. What's left is what I want."

Jarvis Germaine is one of our few clues to before. Before the Gull. So his voice never bothered me when I was younger; I always listened to him reverently, trying to imagine I was a younger Cap, becoming inspired to live like we do. Jarvis Germaine talks about quiet, about thinking for yourself.

But now his voice crowds our home.

I thought I'd found the perfect escape under the crabbers' dock. They keep to themselves, like we do, lassoing their traps, plunking them in, waiting. Whir, splash, silence, again and again. There's a peaceful rhythm to it, like surfing.

I hadn't been floating long before the cracks between the boards above went dark. "Hey, cutie! Thirsty?" Two boys stared down at me.

They wore Sun Devils T-shirts, the loud one also sporting a baseball cap with a plastic harness for his beer can, a clear tube running to his mouth.

So much for my hiding place—I flipped onto my stomach and paddled fast, out into the sun.

"Wait, share my IV drip!" the hatted boy said. "Have a suck!" He yanked the straw from his mouth and rained beer on my legs.

His friend grabbed his shorts so he wouldn't fall in. "Leave her alone. Sorry!"

"Come back! C'mon, don't be like that, Gidgey!"

"Gidget," the friend corrected.

"Whatever. Don't go!"

I didn't turn again until I was far out where the twins were surfing. When I glanced back, both boys were gone.

"Were those college kids hassling you, Ro?" Griff asked, his brow heavy with concern.

I shook my head.

Griff gazed off to Mag, who'd drifted close to two girls on a raft shaped like a flamingo. *Mag is civilized on water.* Lately, extra civilized when pretty girls were involved. Mag didn't seem to know what to say to them, but he ventured closer and closer.

"God, I hate spring break," Griff said.

Now, as dusk falls on the lettuce field after our dinner, we wait for Cap to go on as usual about the wasted money, the littering and vomiting. How we should pity college kids who try to squeeze a lifetime of freedom into one drunken trip.

But this year something astonishing happens.

"What do you kids know about the Quiver?" Cap asks, looking at us each in turn. "Griffin? Magnus?"

They shake their heads no.

I'd just plunged my hands into the dishwashing tub, about to wash our dinner plates for Mama to wipe dry.

*Quiver...*did I overhear the word in the lineup? *Meet me at the Quiver...*

"Is it a restaurant near here?" I ask, and Cap and Mama chuckle.

"No, Little Seal."

"I know." The five of us turn to Dyl, flat on his back atop his worn green beach towel, a few feet from our picnic blanket. He's observing cumulus clouds, fuchsia-streaked because the sun's setting, and has a book about sea lions tented on his narrow chest, his field journal at his elbow ready for important transcriptions.

Dyl continues evenly, quietly, as if reading from one of his encyclopedias, "A Quiver is an annual spring gathering of surfers. They dig and pile sand next to a creek or river stream to widen and redirect it, until it's a chute down to the ocean, forming a perfect, constant wave on shore. They pick a remote beach without day-trippers. And no cameras are allowed because it's secret."

A spring break for surfers.

"Why's it called a quiver, genius?" Mag doesn't look up from his whittling.

"Your collection of boards is your quiver, like an archer's quiver of arrows. The gathering, the Quiver by the River, is a collection of surfers."

Griff, who was eating an apple, pauses midbite in appreciation, and asks with a face as pensive as Mag's was mocking, "How do you know all that, Dyl?"

I wipe my hands dry, waiting. But Dyl's lost in his sea lion book again. He's so quiet and small he can become invisible, free to observe people outside the van. But he's more interested in the speckled, slug-shaped animals than the rituals of strangers.

I watch Cap; his hat is tilted over his eyes, but I can imagine the disapproval in them. He believes the paddling, the patience, are as important as the thrill, the flight of surfing—he probably thinks a man-made wave is cheap. A shortcut.

I envision a crowd of people throwing *shaka*s at each other, all the "showoff Beach Boys garbage" Cap detests. An impure substitute for real surfing.

But it only makes me more curious. I want to know what it feels like to ride an endless wave carved into the shore.

"That sounds awful. A fake wave?" Mag says to please Cap, though I can tell he's equally intrigued.

Griff nods in agreement. "It does sound synthetic. A wave on land?"

"Awful and synthetic," Cap repeats.

His ironic tone confuses all three of us. Griff tightens his po-

nytail nervously, and Mag looks down at his wood and whittling knife.

I try to help them. "They probably leave beer bottles and
trash."

"That would be terrible, wouldn't it?" Mama's voice holds
mystery…mischief? "But it isn't like that. It's not a gathering
many citizens know about."

"You've seen it, Mama?" I dare. "Before us?"

For a second, the air stills. Then Mama and Cap share a soft
laugh.

"A million lifetimes ago," Mama says to Cap, only to Cap.
And he smiles at her. "Shall I tell them?"

Cap nods and rises, hoisting his board, striding off on the
long walk toward the beach.

"Tell us what?" I ask with a throb of excitement.

"Well, simply that it's too bad you three think the Quiver
sounds synthetic and messy, because there's one nearby. Blue
Beach. And we thought you might visit as a birthday present
for the twins. Was that foolish of us?"

"No!" Griff and I nearly shout.

Mag shrugs. "I guess it could be interesting."

Mama reassures Dyl, who's grown tense, sitting up abruptly
on his green beach towel and watching her with wide eyes, his
books forgotten, clutching his journal in both hands. "You and
I won't get close to the Quiver, Dylly. Would it be all right if
we watch sea lions instead?"

Dyl loosens his grip on his journal, nodding in relief.

Griff and Mag and I sit in silence for a moment, regarding
each other with expressions of surprise. My dish tub, Mag's
whittling block, and Griff's half-eaten apple forgotten at our
knees.

We're seen-through, we're shocked, we're confused.

But underneath, I know they feel the same frisson of ex-
hilaration I do.

≈

"Is this really happening?" Griff asks as the twins and I hurry along a narrow dirt road toward the ocean.

I take two steps for every one of theirs. Quiver, Quiver... who named it? How does such a ritual get started?

Cap, who will join us in two days, has still not explained his decision to send us here. Not that he ever explains his decisions. Not to us.

When I questioned Mama this morning, she seemed to have forgotten claiming this adventure was the twins' birthday present. She only said, "He must have his reasons." Like always. When I asked why she and Cap hadn't joined a Quiver since that one "a million lifetimes ago," she'd said, "We don't need it now. We have our Quiver of six. Now let's braid your hair..."

But after preaching to us our whole lives about staying separate from the crowd, about the evils of music festivals and surf contests and "mainland luau clambake hokum," he's granted this exception, and it feels foolish to waste more time on why.

"We must be close," Griff says when we've been walking on the windy road toward the beach for an hour.

We know only that we're to turn right at the red mailbox. But we've passed many mailboxes and none have been red. White, tin, tin, black, brown...but not a speck of red on the long dusty road ahead, and my board is heavy at my side.

"Look!" Mag points ahead.

Not the red mailbox, but a parked yellow Chevy with a balsa wood rack. A minute later there's an old Woodie wagon, peeling green paint streaked with white—the telltale sign of a life in ocean fog. Ahead is the most impressive vehicle of all, a VW van with a jagged surfboard nailed on the roof sideways, like a dorsal fin.

Mag sounds thrilled: "That board was bitten!" The VW's

plastered in *Jaws* movie stickers, and the message is clear—the owner survived a shark encounter.

Finally, in the distance—a beautiful dot of red. A crimson mailbox in front of a ramshackle house, and past its dirt driveway, a narrow opening in the trees, a sandy trail.

"I smell ocean," I say, and suddenly my board feels lighter.

Griff sucks in air, grinning, and even Mag breathes deep and half smiles.

A wiry old man appears on the path, walking toward us with his ancient white longboard at his hip. As he passes he throws a *shaka*, barely raising his thin, sun-speckled arm—just an automatic curl-in of his middle three fingers, a friendly wag of his wrist.

The three of us throw our own *shaka*s back to him.

Cap wouldn't like it. He said "Don't forget you're not one of them, even if they're vanners."

But Cap and his disapproval are miles away.

We string our hammocks in dune palms, a quarter mile of beach between us and the roaring river wave, the beach fires where everyone else is surfing and hanging out.

Cap commanded that we stay together, but the twins *cling* to each other, and I feel a surprising rush of tenderness. Tough Mag, protective Griff, a world of two since minutes after they were born, a world within our already-small one. Both now trying to hide their discomfort in these uncharted waters.

When it's dark, the wave lit by torches, I'm the one who insists we march over there at last and step up for our turns. It's not a choice: the wave's unceasing rush sounds too inviting to resist any longer.

"I guess. Now or never." Griff forces a smile.

We approach the lineup in the sand, and the man ahead of us turns, sizes us up. He's about forty, with long brown hair and a tattoo of a shark on his shoulder. "Your turn, Duchess," he says with oily politeness.

"I'm not next." Nervousness has crept in. Not of the wave, but of these strangers, even if they're fellow vanners. I don't know the etiquette here.

"Fiat of this place—first-timers cut in line."

"They're first-timers, too," I say tentatively of the twins, who are stiff and silent in front of us.

"But ladies first." Slowly, in an exaggerated gesture of courtliness, the dark-haired man rotates his wrist until his palm faces up. His eyes flash mockery.

"Listen to Jaws," some other man says, respect in his voice. So, clearly this Jaws character owns the VW with the shark-bitten board on its roof.

"Indecision is a decision, Ronan," Cap said when he taught me to surf.

I'm holding everyone up, waiting too long. My last thought before I push Cap's voice away is that a man nicknamed Jaws just called me Duchess. I shove in, onto the wave, right here, now, now, NOW!

It's a new feeling—everything has to happen in one swift, decisive motion. Commit, grip your board like you're a skateboarder, shift onto the current and you're soaring. For a second I fear I'll wipe out in front of everyone, but I find my feet quickly, closing my eyes after I get the rhythm. Long minutes of just feeling it. No wondering why Cap brought us here, what nostalgia or birthday generosity or other mysterious impulse stirred him, or how Dyl's doing on his ramble with Mama; or anything else in the world. A never-ending wave—what a sweet, strange thing.

"Goofy-foot!" someone yells approvingly from the sand.

"Go, Ro!" Griff's voice, far away.

"Nice, Ronan." Even Mag has words of praise.

I open my eyes, trail my hand in the man-made curl, taking everything in.

Fires dotted around, encouraging faces. A perfect wave made by a bunch of people just because, and the pink-orange-red layers of the sunset light hitting the hills.

The wave is like a campfire—it requires stoking, tending. The three of us help eagerly, and as I'm reinforcing a wall of sand, shoving great cold mounds to the edge of the rushing water with both hands, a woman on the other side of the water chute stands to observe something behind me. Soon all of us have paused to watch.

An incongruous sight: A family of four follow a photographer carrying important-looking equipment. Father, mother, a baby in her arms, and a citizen girl about my age. They're in matching white shirts and jeans, even the baby, whose fat legs kick in denim pants. They walk gingerly across the sand, clearly embarrassed, and avoid making eye contact with our ragged group.

"No cameras are allowed," Dyl had said. It feels like ages since Cap dropped the college student's Leica in our fire, but I'm still on high alert whenever I see a camera.

The family and their hired photographer show us little interest. To them, we're just surf bums messing around.

"Got to get those Christmas cards done in March now, gotta keep up with the neighbors!" the red-bikinied woman next to me says, and I oblige her with a laugh.

The photographer leads the white-and-denim family out onto picturesque rocks and everyone gets back to work shoving sand. But I can't help glancing over my shoulder a few times. The photographer kneels, checks the light, repositions the four on the rocks. For the final pictures, he drags a trash can down the beach, upturns it, and stands on it.

After, they retreat across the beach and I eavesdrop as they pass behind me.

"I meant to tell you, the Morrison house sold," the mother says. "Two-fifty. A lot, but it's got the biggest yard on the kulldasack. Here, Kelly, you dropped your sweater."

I steal one more glimpse as they approach the road. The father carries the baby, and as the daughter pulls on the sweater she'd dropped, she stops and gazes right at me for a minute. Then her mother calls back to her and she hurries after them. The sweater's white and fluffy, ESPRIT on the back, the *E* three horizontal lines like Morse code. The brand rich citizen girls wear.

I wonder what Kelly would say if she saw where I live. Six people in one small van? No toilet, no shower? Outsiders never see our Gull clearly.

A roach coach—that's what some of them call her, because she used to be a lunch truck. When I was little, and someone was laughing at us, our van and our clothes, I'd asked Mama, "Why don't those people like us?"

"Because they trudge and we glide," she'd whispered.

I must have seemed confused because she knelt and looked me right in the eyes, cupping my face in her soft hands. "We glide, Little Seal. We get to live how we want. Those others, they're stuck. We glide."

The Gull is battered and she used to be a roach coach, but she glides. If a town doesn't make us happy, if the people are nosy or the break is bad or cops knock on the window too much, we glide away. Like a gull sailing on the wind.

Late that night, settled into our hammocks, the twins compare stories. Everyone seems to admire the vanner called Jaws, the one who called me Duchess, but Mag knows a secret about him.

"That board on Jaws's VW? With half the nose gone? Jaws was telling this kid in line today how it's from one dawn when he surfed Trestles alone. And he looks down and sees a gray shadow. Great white…twenty feet. But he keeps his cool." Mag growls, imitating Jaws. "'Every muscle in my body knew if I wiped out, I was dead. Two hundred pounds of red chum.'"

I envision the long, pearly gray shadow and shiver.

Mag lowers his voice. "'And then…'"

I lean half out of my hammock, intent on Mag's face.

"'Crunch!'" Mag claps his arms together and Griff and I nearly tumble from our hammocks. When we're done laughing Mag goes on. "Except it's a lie. He cut the board *himself*, with an old bear trap."

"No!" Griff and I shout, as disgusted as we are amused. Vanners are supposed to be above that. Trying to impress people with props—that chomped-out board is no different from a citizen's ESPRIT sweater or BMW hood ornament.

"It's true. Apparently, he stole some antique bear trap from Big Bear Lodge. Years ago."

"Why would you ruin a perfectly good board for a story?" Griff is genuinely mystified.

"I have no idea," Mag says. "But Big Bear sounds cool. We should try snowboarding someday. I heard you can get work in those mountain towns, easy. Two years…"

Two years until they turn eighteen and Cap might let them work.

I let their talk wash over me as I pull my sleeping bag up to my neck. It's cozy, here with my brothers, listening to their funny stories, the wind off the water rocking us back and forth in our hammocks.

What a day it's been. I picture the ridiculous vanner Jaws, cutting his board and concocting his boast. I think of citizen Kelly and her family in their denim and white, and the photographer who'd stood on a trash can to get the perfect record of their lives.

I wonder what their pictures will look like, what wall they will hang on, at their house on the kulldasack.

"What's a kulldasack, Griff?" I ask.

"Cul-de-sac," he explains, spelling it. "It means expensive houses on a dead-end street."

Mag adds, echoing Cap, "Dead-end lives."

As I'm drifting off, I picture Kelly from today. I raise my hands like her family's photographer, steadying his camera.

Click, I think, crooking my index finger in the dark as I sway in the hammock. I try to recapture the look on her face when she stared at me.

Had it been scorn, or longing?

9

Guests

The four of us, spread before Charlie on the rope web as her midair audience, froze. The island world continued on, oblivious—petals fluttering, birds calling, palm fronds rattling.

At last, Griff spoke. "Cap *invited* that woman here."

Shaking his head in disbelief, Mag said, "A reporter."

Dyl crept to the very edge of the platform—next to me—so he was as close to the cliff, as far from the letter Charlie held, as he could get. His face taut with anxiety, he gazed down through the leaves as if he could see the boat holding our invader.

Griff reached for the letter in Charlie's hand. He read it several times, nodding, then smoothed it, folded it exactly as it had been, and passed it to Mag.

Mag read quickly, huffed out a strange little laugh, then balled the letter up and threw it toward me in frustration. I barely saved it from dropping through the rope.

I straightened the paper and recognized Cap's handwriting, though it was wavier than usual, illness visible in strained

pen-strokes. He'd offered no preamble or apology. No explanation. Only:

> I have asked Pauline Cowley of *SWELL* magazine to
> show you this when she arrives at 33.2489 N, 119.2881 W.
> *SWELL* requested an interview because of the Brand Mu-
> seum exhibit, but her coming to you is my idea alone, and
> I believe it will be "a worthwhile endeavor."
>
>   Please allow her to ask her questions; how you answer
> is up to you.
> C.M.

An interview. After we'd been commanded all those years
to avoid people, to hide who we were and how we lived. Suddenly now he wanted us to talk?

Charlie broke the silence. "Those numbers are—"

"Coordinates," the twins and I said at once. How like Cap
to work in latitude and longitude and a Cook reference, edu-
cating us until the end, instead of simply naming the island.
But not one word about why he would agree to an interview.
Or any concern for us, dealing with what he'd set in motion.

Because my brothers were struggling. I could feel it, their
distress pulsing across the grid of white rope that held us all.

Dyl looked like any second he might leap to the ground and
disappear into foliage.

Griff was trying to appear cool and in command but couldn't
stop moving, jostling the ropes, causing swells that rolled the
rest of us up and down. He kept tightening his ponytail, checking the ties around the gear we'd hoisted up.

Mag slowly wound a rope end around and around in his
hand. "A man. Rages against photographers. His whole life.
And then. Invites a reporter to his funeral," he muttered.

"Could she have taken advantage of Cap when he was weak,
near the end?" I asked.

"That's unlikely." Griff was striving for his reasonable-adult tone, but couldn't keep the shock from his voice. "Cap was compos mentis until his last breath. He says right in the letter this is what he wanted."

"Remember when…" Mag shook his head, trying to close off the memory.

"Remember what, Mag?" I asked.

He hesitated. "The Quiver. Remember how he had Mama tell us we were going? After…*toying* with us about whether it was a good thing or not?"

I remembered it vividly. How our father had given us a rare treat—an adventure among strangers—and how the twins had tried so hard to come up with the right opinion on the Quiver to please him. "And he just strolled off to surf after," I said. "No explanation. All of a sudden, the rule about approaching strangers unnecessarily went out the window, but we weren't told why."

Exactly like now.

But while the interview seemed to go against Cap's every fiber, we couldn't deny that the note in my hand was utterly him. Perfectly, exasperatingly Cap. There was no "*if* you choose to answer her questions." Only *how*.

"You two loved the Quiver," Griff said, as if this was an argument for doing the interview, but his voice lacked force. He sounded so defeated I didn't argue with him.

For a moment I was back there. Confusion pushed aside, laughing with my brothers in our hammocks. The river wave rolling under my body, its spray steadier and warmer than the ocean's. The thrill of being on our own, the amber glow of torches and bonfires…

Of course we had loved the Quiver—all three of us had. That wasn't Mag's point. But Cap sending us there had been so jarring. Couldn't he have explained, just a little, why he'd wanted us to go? And couldn't Griff admit that Cap's opacity hurt?

"Are you suggesting we'll love sitting with that woman for an interview?" Mag asked. "Because it sounds as appealing as getting dragged naked over a reef. We're grown, Griff. We don't have to blindly accept Cap's commands like—"

"We don't have to decide yet," I interrupted. I knew exactly what Mag had been about to say: blindly accept Cap's decision *like always*. Things were getting too heated, and we needed a break before the twins' fight got too ugly. As much as I wished Mama had run to me the second I'd set foot on the island, I was glad she wasn't here to witness this mess.

"Maybe Mama doesn't need to know about the reporter yet," I said. *Or at all.* I assumed we'd vote against this absurd interview idea and send Pauline Cowley quickly on her way back to the mainland. "She's in mourning and—"

"She knows," Charlie said from her corner of the rope platform. And even Dyl, at the opposite corner, turned around to face her. "Your mother knows, sorry. After I dinghied back from talking to Pauline on her charter boat, I found her at camp grabbing supplies because she'd heard the warning bell, and I showed her the letter, and she…"

"What?" Mag pressed. "She freaked, right?"

Charlie shook her head. "The opposite. For a second she seemed surprised, but then she smiled. She got that serene look…you know. And she said, 'I'm sure he had his reasons. Does our journalist guest have a camera?' I said yes, and she said, 'Well, there. Maybe he wanted to make up for the cameras.'"

I pictured them now, the cameras Cap had gotten his hands on.

One thrown into flames.

Two hurled onto beach towels.

Many more disemboweled—their translucent amber entrails dangling to the ground after Cap had popped the windows open and yanked their film out, ruining shot after shot.

We hadn't been famous, not then, not yet. But he'd already

treated anyone who took pictures near our campsite as paparazzi.

"That makes zero sense," Mag said. "'Make up for the cameras?' What, she wants us to pose for a photoshoot for the article?"

My palms were sweaty and raw from gripping the rope so tight. *Just breathe. No one's agreed to any interview, let alone a picture...*

"Well, anyway," Charlie went on. "Your mother said we should invite her to stay for now, to keep her comfortable. So we sent the charter boat back with a story about her writing an article on my work here, and I set Pauline up in the big stat shack—the main DFW shed, you know, where we log our data—on the west side of the island. Just while you all decide what to do."

Mag sighed, not protesting any longer, but his voice was still prickly. "Nice of our mother to join us in a timely fashion."

"She's off finishing her secret project for the paddle-out, she told me to tell you," Charlie said hurriedly. With a concerned look at me, she added, "All of you."

"Oh," Mag said wryly. "That's fine, then. If it's for the secret project."

She's grieving and she's not here to defend herself, I wanted to jump in, but held back. Because Mag was right. As the note was utterly Cap, this was perfectly, exasperatingly Mama. She appeared and disappeared when she fancied. Went along with Cap's decisions no matter how strange or sudden. *He must have his reasons.*

Nothing had changed since we were younger.

You owe them, I'd told myself back on the farm. But the idea of a journalist getting cozy down the rocky hill, not two miles from where I sat, made my heart skip.

I had never told anyone besides Charlie how we lived. The occasional comments—"roach coach"—the flashes of confusion or disgust in strangers' eyes, had told me others didn't and would never understand.

Six of us in ninety-eight square feet. I knew how it sounded. Knew how other people's faces would change if they learned how I'd grown up. How we'd never gone to school. How we'd fished for coins in phone booths and fountains until Cap stopped us. Used rest stop toilets and public beach showers. "Interesting," they'd say.

They'd say "interesting," but mean "wrong." *Dreamers* hadn't captured that; it didn't fit with the fantasy.

I waited for Griff to weigh in, but he only reached for the letter again. I handed it to him, and it was painful to watch him reread it, as if there was something he might have missed. A message from Cap, just for him, that would explain everything. Maybe he hoped the white space between the body of the letter and Cap's "C.M." would miraculously sprout a "Love."

Or anything but emptiness.

10

Pour one out

After a long time, Griff folded the letter and slipped it into his pocket. He said wearily, "Yes. Give her some food, Charlie. Keep her from injuring herself on the rocks."

Maybe we could at least delay this interview, keep Pauline on the other side of the 8 until we all agreed it would be a mistake to even talk to her, no matter what Cap wanted—or thought he wanted. "What if we ask her to write her list of questions for us first so we can consider them?" I asked. "It'll stall her while we figure out what to do."

"Fine," Mag said after a pause. "It's not like we can boat her back to the mainland before dark, anyway."

"She'll stay on the other side of the island." I hoped to calm Dyl and maybe reassure myself. I needed to "paint a story" like I'd done when he was little. The stranger confined to the other circle in the 8, while we stayed, safe and hidden, in our lush, leafy circle. Dyl nodded, but his distraction told me I hadn't entirely succeeded.

"She's a tenderfoot," Griff said, trying to regain his confidence. "She couldn't find her way over here, in any case."

"You really saved the day, Charlemagne," Mag said. "Without your bell, that woman could've snuck up and taken pictures of us."

I swallowed. Charlie kept looking my way, her expression searching, like she expected something from me. But what? She was the one who had kept that brown hood cinched tight back on the boat.

"And...thank you, Charlie," I managed, not meeting her eyes, speaking to a spot a little higher than the DFW patch on her left sleeve. "We owe you. This is a risk for you."

Charlie shrugged. "Pay me back with a wave sometime."

Back at camp, I busied myself packing food for Charlie to share with the reporter. The "kitchen," as my brothers called it, sat atop a rectangle of pebbles near the picnic table. A tidy line: butane stove, cooler, pots, the deep zinc washing-up basin Mama'd plunged her hands into forever.

Charlie watched from the other side of the gear while I knelt and scooped and sealed way too much fish and rice into metal navy supply containers.

"That's plenty!" she cried. "Sure I can't help?"

But I shook her off, packing more and more.

"Thank you," she said stiffly when I finally stood, handing her the last tin. "It's enough for an army."

"Well, you can feed the army, too, when our visitor phones them and they bust us on their property." My voice was strained, my attempt at lightness a failure.

"We won't let that happen." Then Charlie cocked her head. "Hey, I wanted to tell you the reason I hid from you on the boat—I know you're wondering why."

Why, given the chance to see me after fifteen years, you hid in an oversize anorak? Hadn't crossed my mind at all, Charlie.

"It's fine," I said.

"I just thought you'd want to focus on Cap's memorial. That you were dealing with enough. And I was only supposed to ferry everyone here and keep watch. I didn't think we'd have time to talk, to really talk, until after the paddle-out, anyway. I thought maybe we'd catch up after."

"I get it," I said. "I mean, let's do that."

We had it now, though—a chance to catch up. Yet we were both stuck in awkward silence. I knelt, wiped at a nonexistent smudge on the basin. Stood with the rag in my hand, willing myself not to twist it. *Charlie. Two feet away, after all this time.*

Then something occurred to her. "So why *did* your brothers tell you it was me driving the boat? I don't mind. I'm just surprised, since it wasn't the plan."

How could you imagine that would work? I felt you there. Remembered the way you tilted your chin at the sky to check clouds. You did it the first day I saw you, when you wore your too-big wet suit with your hair tucked down…

"The twins let your name slip," I said. "You know, in the confusion of your bell, running up the hill to hide. Well, speaking of, better not keep our honored guest waiting."

"But we'll catch up later. Right?" she asked.

"Yes! Definitely!" I smiled, a bright shield of a smile to match her own, until she was out of sight.

Dyl signaled that dinner was ready and I followed him to what the boys called "the clearing," though the weeds were so tall it hardly felt clear. They'd set aluminum camp chairs around their faux flames, the stack of pointy red rocks and rusted metal I'd admired earlier.

"Dyl and I gathered the metal scraps from a little cove on the west side, the rough side," Mag explained. "It collects every piece of flotsam in the Pacific, we'll show you. If there's time."

After that, the four of us dined in eerie silence—still no Mama.

I watched Dyl out of the corner of my eye, grateful he hadn't bolted, spooked as he obviously was. Griff was fidgety, barely eating. And Mag ate, but kept disappearing abruptly into the trees with his knapsack. His movements were loose, his hair damp and messy.

After Mag's third trip, when he sat and placed the bag at his feet, there was an unmistakable clink. I'd written his behavior off as a natural result of the day's surprises, but now I spotted the reflection of sunset on glass in his bag.

"I *knew* the weight of our cargo felt off," Griff said wearily. "Exactly how many beers did you sneak onto the boat, Mag?"

Mag squinted and held his thumb and forefinger together, indicating *a teeny bit*. Then, slowly, he widened them into an *L*. "Who remembers our book on Roman numerals?"

I had to laugh. "Fifty beers, Magnus. You've got *fifty* beers stashed on this island?"

Griff rubbed his hair. "Magnus Pertinax Merrick. You could've capsized us. You'd better account for every one of those fifty bottles when you clean up."

"I will *leave no trace*." Mag finished the bottle he'd been concealing, reached into his pack for another, pulled out an opener and popped the cap. Then he took a long swig.

Griff echoed Cap's old phrasing: "Alcohol is for the weak. For pathetic spring breakers. For citizens who have nothing else to come home to after a workday. Cap's rolling in his—"

"Urn?" Mag asked, holding his bottle aloft.

Dyl and I traded glances, worried that this would set Griff off, but he seemed to have little fight in him.

"He's not even drunk," Griff said to me. "He's acting like a clown to get to me."

"Says the prig."

"We're all upset because of the letter," I said, to prevent this moment from spiraling due to the twins' age-old grievances. "We're angry at—" *At him. Because he never explained himself, not back then, and not now.* "We're angry at the situation. Let's not take it out on each other."

"I'm not angry," Griff insisted. "Cap had his reasons." Yet he seemed lost in memory.

Mag pulled another beer out of his bag and cracked it open. "Anyone else want to partake?"

I could taste it—icy Pacifico. I was here for another twelve hours at least, there was a reporter eager to dredge up god knew what questions about our history, Mama was MIA, and the conversation between Charlie and I had been hopelessly awkward. I held my hand out.

Mag passed me the bottle, singing to the tune of "Row Your Boat": "Ro, Ro, for your throat…"

Griff abstained, ever loyal to Cap's rules. "You're an ass, Magnus." But he smiled tiredly, and didn't say a word about my drinking.

It was getting dark, our metal plates, at our feet, long since emptied. When there was a crack in the trees behind us, we all flinched and Dyl rose to his feet. Not worried about an animal, but our human visitor, I guessed. Pauline Cowley.

"She's far away, Dyl," I said.

He nodded and sat back down. Then he asked thoughtfully, "Why do people care so much about that photograph?" It was the first time he'd spoken since she'd arrived.

There was a long silence. I'd wondered the same, often, but had always stuffed the question down. My feelings about the photo's popularity were painfully complex. When I'd first seen it, there had been a surge of pride…before everything the photo wrought took that away.

But now, for the first time, I was compelled to answer honestly.

"I guess it makes them happy," I said at last. "It's California like it is in dreams. It's…freedom. Sun."

"People think surfers have mastered the most elusive trick

in life—how to empty your brain," Mag said. "Like we have no worries. People are stupid."

Griff added, "They tape that poster of us to their office walls, Cap told me once. He called it 'an imaginary portal out of self-imposed drudgery.' He called them 'poor souls.' Remember?"

I nodded, smiled. Cap *had* pitied citizens, in his best moments, when his other feelings toward them didn't crowd that one out. It was easy to forget that.

Dyl spoke quietly. "Charlie showed me a poster of a fox family that her work friend taped inside the big shed." He tilted his head in thought, a mature gesture, but when he spoke, he seemed to channel the piercing simplicity of younger Dyl's worldview: "Pictures of happy families make people happy."

The other three of us were silent again for a moment. Surprised, humbled that we'd missed this simple point—*Dreamers* portrayed a family. I smiled at him, "You're right, Dyl."

Mag cleared his throat. "So, Ronan, speaking of families. What was it like, seeing yourself on T-shirts and assorted bric-a-brac up in Oregon?"

"Surreal." I sipped my beer. "I was at a gift shop with my boys the first time. A hundred miles inland—we're not talking tourist hotspot." The boys had been four: I hadn't left the farm much until then, but had begun venturing out, realizing I couldn't hide the world completely from my sons. "They wanted something special for Lou, for Father's Day."

"You and your husband seem happy," Dyl said.

I hesitated, then admitted it: "We're separated. That is, if you count our marriage as legitimate, since I used phony papers. He still doesn't know about that."

Mag raised his eyebrows. "Complicated."

"Yes. Anyway…that day in the gift shop. I'm looking at dog mugs, cat coasters, and there the six of us are, on some cheap plastic tumblers. Over the words West Coast, Best Coast."

"Cute," Griff said dismissively.

I had held one of the tumblers in my hand a long time, over-come that I was so many miles from the Merricks, by how I'd left, worried about how they were doing. It was bizarre, how the photo comforted and thrilled people—it had to be, or they wouldn't pay for it. It *gave* them something.

But with me, it only seemed to take.

"And is that what your twins bought for Father's Day?" Dyl asked, pulling me from the memory. His eyes were bright with anticipation; I knew he was trying to visualize my life now.

"Oh, thank God, no. They chose a barbecuing apron with a yellow Lab who looks like ours on it."

The daughter on the next farm was caring for ZBoy; I'd told her I was going to Portland for a few days to buy a sur-prise birthday gift, and she shouldn't mention my leaving. The farm, my life there seemed so far away.

Mag blew a low, dramatic note with the mouth of his beer bottle. "I have an idea. I could hit a gift shop on Catalina be-fore the paddle-out. Get a cup with us on it for Pauline Cow-ard, as a souvenir of her visit."

"Brother." Griff's tone was kind.

"Pauline Cowley," Dyl corrected.

I wondered how many beers Mag had drunk. He went on, "It's perfect. I'll get T-shirts, too. Let's all paddle out wearing them, and Pauline Coward can photograph us for her article."

Mag wouldn't let up. "It's brilliant, it'll be like those por-traits within portraits. Remember that painting in the art his-tory book in the vanilla library?"

Dyl and I said in unison, "David Teniers."

I pictured our younger doppelgängers, printed on cotton, tag-ging along for the paddle-out. Thirty-five Merricks, total, like that old Teniers painting crowded with portraits and real people.

The image was disrespectful, grotesque, bizarre. But it made all four of us laugh.

At first, Griff's laugh was just a sputter behind his hand that he tried to pass off as a cough, but it was undeniable. "We shouldn't," he said. "We're awful."

That only set us off more. An exquisite relief, to laugh about that damn photograph.

"So, Ro," Mag said. "Since we're talking about our education. How're those geometry lessons serving you?"

I held out my Pacifico bottle as if to shake beer on his foot. "Fabulously. Mag, you fiend."

He yanked his leg away, smiling mischievously. "When did you realize?"

"When I was trying to help my sons with their extremely basic math homework." Because Mag's geometry "lessons," I'd learned as an adult, were impressively intricate tall tales. I filled in the others: "Do you know he taught me Pythagoras was an early surfer with a triangular surfboard?"

When our laughter ebbed again, I asked, "Did Cap know about that?"

Mag shook his head. "I told him his antique math primers were all anyone needed."

I wished I'd clued into Mag's tiny rebellion back then. Maybe he and I would have been better friends. Or maybe I'd have seen only my own vulnerability as the butt of Mag's joke, not appreciating that he was just a kid, too.

"Let's pour one out for the old man." Mag tipped his beer onto the edge of the synthetic fire. "Oh, Dylly, want one?"

Dyl stood, not saying a word, and for a minute I feared he was upset. He crossed the clearing, over to the shed, and went inside.

He emerged a moment later with a wood crate labeled Saline Filter-Tabz 144-ct and set it between Griff and Mag, then made a second trip to the shed as we all exchanged confused looks.

This time, he came out holding the blue urn. He positioned it gently atop the crate, returning to his seat in our circle.

For a moment, we all regarded the urn in silence.

Then Griff fumbled in the backpack at his feet, pulling

something from it, and rose, approaching the urn so quickly I couldn't see what he'd carried over. He knelt in front of the urn, his back still blocking my view of whatever he was doing. For a sick second I thought he was kneeling in worship.

He straightened, evaluating, then stepped closer to the crate, made an adjustment. Satisfied, he took his seat again.

Griff had set Cap's Greek captain's hat on the urn. Tipped forward and slightly tilted, the way Cap always wore it, aslant over his left brow.

Griff wiped his cheek, a punishing swipe. He did it so fast I couldn't tell if his face had glistened, or if it was only my imagination, and then he cleared his throat. "He looked too small before."

We listened to the night sounds of the islands. That wistful bird call: *Whishoooolleeee… Whishoooolleeee…* The Pacific's breath, calm now, whispering through a million leaves.

"Any minute he's going to start calisthenics," Dyl said.

Mag, his face lit dimly from the lamp in the firepit, smiled wide. "Squirrellies. God, those made your ass hurt."

I remembered the calisthenic routine perfectly, had even taught a modified version to my boys. But it was only something we did for fun, out in the fields. And there was no wind-sprint race, no fiercely coveted hat-tip at the morning's winner. The companionable silence, the joy of rising early and running outdoors, though—they were the same. Sometimes consciously, sometimes not, I'd tried to hold on to the best of what Cap had given me.

"I tried to make his coconut-date cereal a few times, but it wasn't the same," I said. "That metal scoop. Do you still have it?"

"Of course! That thing could jolt me from a coma." Griff tapped his tin fork on his plate, a soft echo of Cap's meal bell. Two raps, no more, because if you didn't get to breakfast by the second clang, you weren't hungry enough. "Mama always slept through it."

"If she was there at all," Mag said.

We went quiet. I'd always thought Dyl and I were the only ones who'd minded Mama's absences, how she blithely came and went as if we didn't need her.

We sat in our campfire circle like we had so many times before, when Mama was off on a ramble. Me, Griff, Mag, Dyl. Despite Cap's near-constant and at times maddening silence, he had been more physically present than she had. If he knew he'd be on a garage gig, he appointed one of the twins to lead exercises. Made sure we at least had cereal or nuts for breakfast.

I swallowed at the memories, raising my beer to my father.

Mag copied me, lifting his bottle to the blue urn, and Griff and Dyl raised their canteens.

"To Cap," Griff said solemnly.

And the three of us echoed him. "To Cap."

In our hammocks later that night, we avoided mentioning the reporter, who was probably at this very moment scribbling her questions for us.

Mag, swinging himself back and forth by holding a branch, said, "Tell us about the lavender business, Ronan."

"She goes by Ava now," Griff reminded him.

"You can call me Ronan." I had gotten used to it, after the initial shock of hearing my real name on the farm. It felt strange, but good. I began to rock myself as Mag was doing, gazing up at the first smattering of stars. "Well. We have four hundred acres. We produce for a local organic toiletry company. Soap, lotion, room spray. It's great for the bee population."

Soon I'd put everyone to sleep.

"And her family owns the farm," Griff said, filling the others in.

I winced at *her family*. "The LeClairs are...good people. They..."

I pictured Lou's father, who couldn't be more different from Cap. Whenever people camped on a patch of his great-great-grandfather's four hundred acres, he had his assistant dispatch them swiftly, commanding, "Handle it." Not *them*, but *it*.

I told my brothers none of this. "They've been on that land for more than a century."

"Griff tells me you haven't dipped a toe in the water since you split," Mag said. "Why the hell not?"

Griff sounded imperious: "Have some tact, Magnus."

"It's okay. I don't mind talking about it."

And maybe it was the dark, or the soothing *whishooolleeee* in the distance, but I *didn't* mind.

"It wasn't something I planned. At first it was because I'd told them I couldn't swim. There was a beach outing on our day off, some of the younger farm pickers. That was... I was young. I'd only just arrived."

"This is when you were seventeen?" Mag asked.

"Yes. Right after I'd hitched up."

"Why didn't you go on the beach outing?" Dyl asked.

I was afraid my heart would break if I saw the water and thought of you all.

"Oh. I was still keeping to myself as much as I could, those first months. I wanted that day off to be alone." That was true, too. It had been so jarring, so overwhelming at first. Living and working with dozens of strangers after my tiny Merrick world.

I hurried on. "So I told that lie about not knowing how to swim—it just felt easier. They got this idea that I had an ocean phobia and I didn't correct them. But I always thought I'd go to the coast. I missed it." God, I had. I could hear the surf now, familiar and forbidden, sweeter than any drug. How to explain? "Maybe I didn't feel like I deserved the ocean anymore."

After I left you.

The only sounds now were the sea and the soft night wind in the leaves.

"You know what's funny, though?" I asked, surprising myself. "I realized something on the boat today. Our lavender, it's a blue varietal. Waves and waves of it, when it's in bloom. And it's beautiful. So I guess I was subconsciously finding a different ocean. The closest I could get to one, anyway." I laughed nervously.

But this gathering wasn't about me; it was about Cap. I stopped talking, waiting for someone else to speak.

"Hard to believe we're doing it tomorrow," Griff said softly. "Pouring him in the ocean."

"It's not really him," Mag said. "He'd be the first to say that. No sogginess, no sentiment or superstitious talk."

"He paddled out for other surfers two times," Dyl observed, wise as always.

"Only out of respect," Mag said. "He didn't believe it meant anything."

Mag acted like it was nothing, the paddle-out. Would he be able to maintain that fiction when we were floating in a circle, when whatever Cap had crumbled into was tipped into the Pacific? I tried to picture the scene. Us on our boards tomorrow, forming a ring. But I couldn't.

"Will we hike down to the beach before first light?" I asked.

"Depends when our ever-punctual mother decides to return," Mag said. He turned to Dyl. "What's this secret project? You must know."

"I promised I wouldn't tell."

Mama and her secret projects…taking her sweet time before saying hello to the daughter she hadn't glimpsed in over a decade. She couldn't help how she was, and maybe wanted to greet me when we could do it in private. Maybe she was shaken by Pauline Cowley's appearance, no matter what she'd told Charlie, and needed to be alone to deal with it. But I yearned to see her.

A little rustling and shifting, then stillness. We were all lost in our private bedtime thoughts, recalling today or imagining tomorrow's ritual, and soon we'd all be asleep feet from each other like we used to.

Swaying on the rope, lulled by birdsong and surf and the pull of the past, I did something impulsive.

I whistled.

I was still an excellent whistler. Jack and Bear, and Lou, at one time, enjoyed listening to me. I could do "Buffalo Gals" and "Goodnight, Irene." And nothing could get ZBoy to turn from trouble faster than my sharp wolf whistle.

There was a terrible pause, and I wished I could pull the sound back from the night. Maybe it was folly to think I could so easily recreate something that had been lost.

But then Dyl responded.

Mag followed, his whistle slightly higher, a perfect middle C.

Then a longer wait. An owl hooted, a gull screeched, something skittered on the ground below. Maybe that was all I'd get.

When so much time had passed that I'd given up, Griff gave an abbreviated whistle.

In the dark, I reached up as if to catch it.

The next morning I woke first; it had been a long time since I'd slept in the trees. Though I kept my bedroom window open all year, and sneaked out of the farmhouse some nights to bed down on the porch.

Was this real? The surf, the smells, the diffuse light all told me it was. I was on an island with my family, and hadn't dreamed it.

I peeked over at the three nylon cocoons which were my sleeping brothers in their mummy sacks. Griff still snored, Mag still thrashed—a wonder he hadn't plummeted in the night, his leg was dangling over the side of his sleeping bag—and Dyl still slept as curled and quiet as a possum.

I stretched, rolled onto my stomach, looked down, and below me was a cloud of hair, unmistakable—wild and blond. Curly, as mine was when I didn't tame it.

Mama.

FIELD JOURNAL

This is a blue hyacinth I found today.

Although fuchsias were her favorites, Mama always loved these, too.

*They grow in nooks and crannies, and they're
particular about humidity,
but when they find a spot they like,
safe from nibbling animals and blight, they flourish.
I saved this one from a vole.*

*I wish I had Mama's flower-pressing book, the one she brought
on her rambles, here with me.*

*Blue hyacinths, she said once, are symbols of tranquility
in the face of trouble.*

*I think I should collect one for each of us here.
We may need them.*

11

And God looked upon it

1984
Blue Beach, California
Fourteen years old

Early in the morning, Mama and Dyl and Cap join us at our campsite.

"Happy birthday, my loves." Mama is radiant, smothering the twins in hugs, kissing me tenderly, trailing her hand down my wild hair. The two of us waft out the fancy paisley blanket and spread it, and we all sit.

Then she tells a story we've heard many times, one of her few. How her labor began weeks early and she had to deliver all alone in the Gull. There was no time to drive to Carlsbad, where Cap had heard a midwife would help her for nothing. There was barely time to wave Cap in from the water.

She finishes the story as she always does: "I told him, 'Isn't it better, no strangers, just the three of us?'"

"And then, just as we'd swaddled Griffin, another pain hit. And you came, Magnus." She turns to Mag and he holds still, no longer dodging her kisses. "And I said, 'Isn't it better, no strangers, just the *four* of us?' And then I fell asleep."

Cap tips his hat back, the lines around his eyes crinkling deep from pride in Mama, I think. Or maybe it's a private joke they share because she's left out some part of the story. His reaction is the same every time she tells it.

Mama pulls our battered kettle from her pack but I tell her, "You relax, Mama. I'll make breakfast."

"You act as if I delivered those boys today instead of seventeen years ago," she muses in her soft voice. But she lets me take over.

She missed us, I realize. The twins and I were the ones on a ramble this time.

I build a fire and serve apples and hard-boiled eggs with our tea—a feast. Dyl unveils his birthday presents, drawings of birds that look like the twins. I bought the half-used charcoal pencil for him years ago, with fountain coins, and he's gotten good. Mag is a myna, with hunched shoulders and suspicious eyes, scrunching his forehead, and Griff is a fluffy, smiley yellow budgie.

Cap tips his hat back for a second, studying the sketches. "Uncanny."

Mama has traded her homemade soap for thick hand-knit sweaters and the boys pull them on even though it's warm. "And on your eighteenth, you'll get these. Look."

She hops up, lifting her right foot above us with a little laugh to show us how, while we've been separated, she has tattooed her arch. A wave, the pattern I carve inside the van—our pattern. It was our family's private joke that the design had come from a garbage can. Like turning "roach coach" into something regal. The joke was on them.

Then Cap, who's sitting cross-legged on the blanket, his back impossibly straight, brushes sand from the bottom of his right foot and, in a gesture as slow and deliberate as Mama's was sudden, flexes it. He keeps his foot taut only for a moment, enough for us to see that she's etched the mark into his flesh, too, then relaxes it so the tattoo's hidden again.

"Will Ro and I get them?" Dyl asks.

Mama's radiant. "Of course, when you turn eighteen. All six of us will have them. We're all Merricks."

I give the twins new pucks of board wax bought with the two dollars Cap allotted me for presents (Mrs. Palmer's brand, NOT Mr. Zog's). Black Licorice for Mag, Blazing Cinnamon for Griff.

Griff sniffs his and pretends to pass out from cinnamon fumes. When he sits up again he says, "This is terrific, Ro. Thanks."

Mag says, "I'll strip my board right now."

"Not just yet, Magnus." Cap stands. Unhurried, leaving us all in suspense, he walks the few hundred feet to a stand of palm trees, strolling between two and disappearing into the oleander bushes.

We all stand, our backs to the surf, trying to catch a glimpse of him. A minute later, he reappears, his body tall and straight, his hat level, despite the heavy burden he's toting. Under each arm, he carries a gleaming, custom-made board, the resin coating like glass.

At the handful of board shops we trust, it's thirty dollars just to fix a ding. New short boards of this size, wooden, shaped to perfection...they had to cost Cap at least seven hundred dollars each. There are cheaper boards out there, but Cap detests polyurethane because it's made from oil. So was this why he suggested we come to the Quiver? So he could get the boards and surprise the twins?

He sets them down near the blanket and the twins listen reverently, running their hands along their new babies as Cap describes them:

"Yours has a more squared-off tail than Mag's, Griff. It'll help you turn when the waves are small. Mag, yours is an inch thinner, a pintail, but the float should be right even though you've gained muscle this year..." And on and on. Our father doesn't speak much, but right now he's positively chatty, boyish in his excitement. I take a mental picture of his animated face, his expressive eyes that for once aren't shadowed under his hat. I want to remember them.

Mag is so happy he teases Cap. "New boards at sixteen. Is that a rule we didn't know about?"

Cap's expression goes far away, and his flow of words stops. I want so desperately to know what he's thinking. Maybe he's recalling a favorite board, or a first one. A birthday of his own from when he was a boy. But all he says is "Thought it was time."

Mama and Dyl depart for the Gull, but the rest of us want one last run, and Cap decides he'll ride the river wave just once.

As the four of us trek over to the Quiver, boards balanced on our heads, Cap says, "Haven't tried one in decades."

Decades…was this the same as "a million lifetimes ago"?

"A million lifetimes ago" is also how Mama answered when I asked where she and Cap met, when I was four or five, and we passed a wedding on the beach. It's how she answered many of my questions when I was younger, and even then I'd known that "a million lifetimes ago" isn't truly a place.

I hesitate, but curiosity forces the question: "You rode one at a Quiver like this?"

Cap tips his hat up with his right index finger and looks straight ahead, at the wave. Still so distant it's just a bunch of people who could be admiring anything on the beach.

He takes so long to answer that I regret asking. *We don't ask him about before*: the unspoken rule.

But at last Cap faces me and smiles. "Just kids. Miles from any ocean."

Cap, a kid, miles from any ocean—I can't picture it. But the six words are almost as good as a new custom board.

It's an amazing thing, how the crowd parts for Cap when

he approaches. It's not new for people to admire Cap's surfing, to recognize his carriage and his unusual hat. Most older vanners know him, and regulars at our favorite breaks certainly do. But we rarely get to see their admiration up close. Someone gestures for Cap to go but he insists on waiting in line. And when he takes his turn, he's casual and grand at once. He surfs the man-made wave like he's alone with it, his old black, gold-trimmed captain's hat like a crown. I'm proud and grateful, and wouldn't change one thing about him.

And then a single shadow appears on our trip.

"And God looked upon it and saw it was good." A deep male voice behind me.

I whirl, trying to discern who said it, if he meant it as unkindly as it sounded. If he was mocking Cap's demeanor. The man named Jaws smiles.

The twins share my confusion; I sense it. They're thinking it, too:

Is he making fun of our father?

As expertly as he hopped on the wave, Cap hops off. But as he nods at us, about to give a word or two of advice to the twins as they test their new boards, his expression changes. It had been far away again. A million lifetimes ago, maybe.

And now it's surprised, fully here in this moment on Blue Beach. He's spied Jaws. It happens quickly: Jaws practically bows, and Cap responds with a nod so short I wonder if it was voluntary. Then Cap walks away.

I look at the twins, whose faces reflect my own wonderment at the exchange, our father's abrupt departure.

"Your turn next, Duchess?" Jaws asks, all feigned innocence. "Or would you like a private tour of my van, instead?"

Griff, with a rictus of a smile, seems unsure what to do. The veins in Mag's forearms show themselves. At the insult to Cap or to me? *Were* these insults, or is it simply that we don't know how to be among people?

"Do you mean the van with the shark-bite board?" Mag asks Jaws. "Because I heard how you really broke it."

"What do you mean, *really*?" Jaws asks with a too-merry laugh. "Who told you how I broke my board, your *captain*?" He scrutinizes Cap's small shape in the distance. Then he lifts his right hand to his temple in a sarcastic salute.

As if Cap's hat is anything like the absurd adornment, the *lie*, on this charlatan's VW van. He's had his hat since before we were born, Mama told us once in a rare moment of reminiscence.

Griff places a hand on Mag's shoulder, and I shake my head at Mag. *Remember Cap's rules. Don't spoil everything when these people mean nothing to us. He's just jealous because people admire Cap here—they know a pure surfer when they see one...*

Mag steps back, unclenching his fists. Quietly, his voice strained from the effort of backing down, he says, "What I mean is...we heard about the shark. Must've been terrifying."

Griff leads Mag away, calling back, "It's his birthday, he's had too much beer."

Jaws monitors the twins' retreat, then relaxes—some kind of exemption granted. "Your brothers?" he asks.

I nod without looking at anyone.

The river wave rushes on, wasted.

We help fill in the wave and rake sand until there's no trace left.

Walking back to the rest of our family, we try to laugh about Mag's near fight. It was one tense minute, and nothing happened, not really.

"Your teddy bear friend didn't stay to clean up," I say. "That's what I'm calling him. Teddy Bear." The flimsiest of jokes, to take the teeth out of a shark, a bear trap...a small, nothing man who laughed at our father.

"No wonder Cap didn't want to stay. Can you imagine resorting to a trick like that to make people respect you?" Griff smiles to himself. I know what he's thinking—Cap doesn't need such tricks.

"Pathetic," I agree.

"Psychotic is what it is," Mag says.

We don't mention the man's disrespect toward Cap. Or muse aloud about how they knew each other, what may have passed between them, or when.

Or how Cap's warnings failed us this time. Citizens aren't worth the trouble, he's always said. We don't mention how that pathetic jagged board is attached to a van, not a citizen's commuter car.

Cap doesn't ask what happened when he left. We leave Blue Beach and the Quiver miles behind.

But late that night, Mag sky surfs. It's this thing only he does. When Cap's driving at night, sometimes—not very often—Mag climbs out his bunk window onto the Gull's roof. There, at our top speed of fifty-one miles an hour, he stands behind the board rack without holding on and balances, legs bent like he's riding an epic wave.

I've never gone up there to watch him. I made Griff tell me about it, the third or fourth time I saw Mag twist out the window in the dark and heard his thumps.

Griff had said, "It's his way of dealing with stuff."

What stuff? I'd thought. Mag had always seemed so sure of himself, always seemed to bask in Cap's admiration for his toughness. He seemed unbothered by Cap's edicts and inconsistencies, Mama's disappearing. Maybe not as blindly loyal as Griff, but like nothing could get to him, pierce that thick Mag shell.

Now I know better.

I'd love to see him sky surf. I bet it's beautiful.

PART TWO

12

We manage to stand

1984
Pismo Beach, California
Fourteen years old

On the surface, life after the Quiver is no different from before. Long, golden days on the water, just us and our boards. We have our world of six, and don't need anything more.

Cooking lunch in Pismo three days after we reunite, I dare a question of Mama: "Did you and Cap meet at the Quiver in Blue Beach?"

"Did someone say that?"

"Not exactly."

"We met far from there, but not far from the beach. Now, let's wash these apples…"

I comply, tamp my questions down. But I am frustrated by her riddles, the blankness that is Cap and Mama's past, more than when I was younger.

And whenever I steal time alone, I take mental pictures.

Once I start, I can't stop imagining all the photographs a person could shoot, mentally framing them, then saying *click* in my head. I realize it's something I've done all the time, less consciously—trying to preserve bits of my life. Trying to grab hold of them to understand later. Painting stories for Dyl, Mama has always called it.

Now it becomes a tic, a physical ritual. I hold my hands up like two Ls facing each other, adjust them, closer together, farther apart, up, down until I like what's inside my imaginary rectangle.

Then…*click.* I pretend to snap with an invisible camera. I do it just for me, to lock things in my memory.

Soon I'm taking pretend pictures everywhere. On my board, shooting the sky, the swell, an otter, a sandcastle behind foam. So much of surfing is waiting, watching, observing changes in water and light, and when I'm between waves I imagine what I look like from above. From land. I watch color spread on the water as the sun inches over my head to the horizon.

Click, I say in my head. *Click.* It's just for fun—not against the rules.

My pictures make me feel powerful. Like someone who can erase every part of the world she doesn't want to see, who can conjure frames around what matters most.

Someone who can stop time.

For a year, it is just us.

Then one warm midday in Santa Oro we come in after surfing and the light over the bluffs is a soft salmon color I've never seen. I frame the picture in my head. Clouds, sky…and then a glorious sight.

Wolves. Beautiful, bounding, acrylic-painted wolves.

"Ahoy, Merricks!" Charlie shouts from the Winnie's roof. She's in boxers and a cutoff top, her black hair whipping straight up. Bassett, broad and smiling next to the bumper, wears his favorite shirt and matching baggies with the green magnolia pattern.

I call over my shoulder, "Mama! Cap!"

They follow my gaze. Cap tips his salt-stained hat up and his eyes flash surprise, confusion. Then the crinkles around them deepen as he smiles his biggest smile.

"Coming in already?" Bass descends the steep dirt path, slow and clumsy, toting a green webbed beach chair. "You must be getting old!"

"I'll know I'm old when I'm carting one of those around!" Playful Cap is a rare thrill.

In seconds Charlie scrambles down the hood of the RV and pulls on her black wet suit, grabs the battered, red-striped board she keeps in the Winnie. She helps her father the last few feet down the path, then runs to me, her board at her hip. "C'mon, this offshore's not gonna last."

The seven of us head back out together, Bass plopped contentedly on his beach chair to watch and sip Pacificos. Charlie's laugh is so exhilarating, her hop-off so gleeful, they warm me inside. So does Mama on her board, a rare sight because she usually surfs alone. She and Dyl study kelp beds as much as the swell, but it feels right to have them near. We all watch as Cap ventures out farther than anyone. He's fearless, all inimitable style and strength and focus. He's thirty-seven but faster than a twenty-seven-year-old.

"Your father," Charlie says, shaking her head to show her awe. Moments later she spots a woman on shore with a Polaroid camera and immediately swims far out of her view—though it's nothing even Cap would mind. Just a mom taking pictures of her toddler daughter.

When there's a lull between waves, I say, fiddling with my leash, "Thank you."

I'm not sure she's heard but she shrugs in response—*it's nothing.* That's our full acknowledgment of the Cap camera incident.

A minute later she spots a waist-high wave that could rightly belong to her or Griff or Cap because it's an A-frame. All three compete for it, paddling in. But it's a clean race, and Charlie, whose arms are nearly as fast as Cap's, gets it. She carves a couple of times, bails as it turns to mush. Cap says a few words to her that make her smile, and I wish I could hear him.

I thought we'd never see her again, but now Charlie feels almost like one of us.

Not as if she'd never left. But because, in her reappearance, we can fully appreciate her.

Late in the day, Griff's got his eyes closed, trusting his ears to tell him when he needs to open them, trusting his distracted parent, the ocean, not to topple him from his water-cradle. Yawning, he asks Charlie what I'm dying to: "How long are you with us?"

"A whole month!" She sits up to a straddle and splashes, windmilling her arms next to her board. Then another wave catches her attention. "That's yours, Ronan!"

We travel with Bassett and Charlie for three weeks, the pack of wolves airbrushed on the Winnebago wheezing, Bass jokes, as it tries to keep up with our swift little Gull. Bassett says if he pushes the Winnie more than forty, the wolves'll go belly-up—meaning its engine is twenty years old but he can't afford to replace it.

"Sorry you're here?" Bass asks Charlie one day by the side of the road in Mendocino as he pours water in the Winnie so she won't die crawling over a steep pass.

"You know I'm not, goof. You're fishing for compliments." Charlie punches his enormous shoulder.

"Wait'll we break down in the desert in Barstow in 110-degree heat."

These things still amaze me. The way they're planning their upcoming Mexico travels, the pin-studded map taped over Charlie's bed in the Winnie. She's the one poking pins in—every stop her choice.

A convoy of two, we drive from San Francisco up to the Oregon coast, then Washington, which Charlie says is beautiful but freezing. She has to wear Bassett's ancient, way-too-big full wet suit and hood and booties, and Bassett calls her Bassett's Hound because of all the rolls in the neoprene, like the dog's.

One sunless afternoon in Hummingbird Beach, Washington, when the waves are steady and inviting, she foregoes surfing and stays on the sand with me and Dyl, who rarely surfs more than once a day. I've neglected him for Charlie and I'm trying to make it up to him.

"You don't want to get back in?" I ask.

She shrugs. "You two are more interesting." She gestures at the lineup. Meaning the boys or the waves? I'm not sure.

Dyl leads us to a tide pool, and the quivering creatures' jewel colors feel miraculous in such a gray place. He's in his element, and Charlie's genuinely interested in all he shows her. Spiny sea urchins, kelp wheels, lichen. He explains how he'll sketch them, explaining even our family joke—how his kelp-patterned field journal says Mer on the cover so we call it his *Mer*rick journal.

He wanders off, and Charlie, kneeling close to the tide pool, asks, "Ever been to Canada? We're so close." The signs for BC ferries are everywhere.

I say it to the rippled image of her face in the water: "We don't leave the US."

"Of course, your parents don't have real driver's licenses. Otherwise you'd come to Mexico with us. I'm an idiot."

She puts it all so matter-of-factly. Not hiding the truth in euphemisms, not acting like it's disloyal to wonder about Cap's choices for us. As if she understands exactly how Cap and Mama's silence, the way I have to be satisfied with Griff's sifted-down, incomplete explanations make me feel. I offer something in return: "If you were an idiot, I wouldn't tell you one real thing."

She gazes at my reflection, serious for a second. Her lips part, head cocks. "Is that a compliment, Ronan Merrick?"

I plunge my hand in the tide pool and flick a little water at her. "Don't get vain."

This becomes our routine. Charlie and I surf with the others in the morning and explore with Dyl in the afternoon. That day I assumed she would peel off with the twins seems so long ago now.

One afternoon I show Charlie the Port Angeles hotel, with its octagonal courtyard peopled by crumbling statues of sailors. Before I can stop him, Dyl explains how we once fished for change in the fountain of the enclosed courtyard. "And a hundred others."

She runs her fingertips down a bas-relief design of fishing nets on the peach-colored stone wall. "Why'd you stop?"

"Cap didn't like it. Even though Ro invented a family signal to keep us safe." He explains about the code I invented when I was eight—how a Merrick-stamped penny on the southernmost point of a fountain meant one of us was hiding, waiting until the security guard left so it would be cleared for fishing. How a peso on top meant *all clear*. Other coin placements had other meanings—*hide*. *Extra treasure*. I'd dreamed up all of it, stretching our afternoons in those elegant courtyards when Mama was on a ramble and Dyl needed distraction.

Even the twins had become intrigued by our coin adventures and joined us, until Griff told Cap what we were doing and he made us stop.

"Ro was clever." Charlie's voice has a playful lilt. "She still is."

Dyl wanders off to inspect a mossy wall and Charlie and I sit on the fountain's edge. It's warm, sun reflecting off all the stone, and she cups her hand and trickles water down the back of her neck.

As we watch Dyl, I murmur, "We didn't need our code. I just liked the idea. And it kept Dyl entertained for hours. I'd even make up dangers. An undercover hotel inspector we had to outsmart. Fairies and birds to help us."

"I was an atrocious babysitter." Charlie laughs. "Not creative like you."

"It wasn't babysitting," I say a little too quickly, defensive about how Cap and Mama delegated Dyl to me.

"Oh, I know. I only meant Dyl's lucky, that's all."

Outside the hotel, Charlie presents Dyl with a dripping bicentennial quarter. "Nobody told me I couldn't fish."

Dyl pays her back in Ruby Beach. Cutting through an alley, he shows her one of our regular bins, lifting the bag of leftover crushed peanuts they toss out from the ice cream shop at closing. When he offers it to Charlie, I'm so embarrassed I can't look at her. Coins are one thing. Dumpster diving—Mag told me long ago that's what it's called—that's another.

"You don't have to eat that," I say.

"It's evil to waste food." She unknots the plastic and tips gold peanut flecks into her mouth. "Yummm."

Secret by secret, Charlie has entered our lives.

Charlie's gotten into tricks since we last saw each other, and we're trying to surf two on a board. Not to be outdone, the twins race to master it before us. For days, it's all we work on, using a pair of Cap's old longboards.

Because I'm smaller, I have to be in front, so I can't see Charlie. I have to imagine her hair, her smile, the beads of water on her smooth neck. But it frees your tongue, not having to show your face.

As we're scouting waves, I turn to the right so she can hear me. "Charlie?"

"Hmmmm?"

"Do you miss your mother?"

"I do. But she's not like yours. She's always watching me. And she wishes I was different."

"How?"

"She tried to schedule me into being a proper lady. Comportment lessons and ikebana lessons and wholesome outings with eligible boys."

"And none of that interested you?"

"Flower arranging was okay." She laughs. "Let's take that one."

We paddle too late and miss the pocket, as I'd known we would. Charlie, usually so direct, has tried to change the subject, but this is a new and intriguing peek into her heart.

"Was your mother always like that? I can't picture Bass with someone *proper*."

"My aunties and everyone live practically on the same street. And they're traditional—they never liked Bass. I don't know. I guess after they split, she was afraid I'd become like him."

"She lets you visit him for, what, fourteen weeks a year?"

"Now that I'm practically an adult. And only because I threatened to move here full-time if she didn't."

I didn't think I could admire Charlie more, but after this glimpse into her home life—her *other* home life—I want to hug her. Doing so would topple us, and make her think I pity her, when really, I'm overwhelmed with gratitude that she's opened up.

Resting in a calm stretch of sea, we watch the twins. They're twenty yards north, straddling their shared board, backs to shore. Mag in front, Griff behind. Horsing around, Griff falls in. Mag paddles off as if he's going to leave him, but paddles back fast and offers him a hand up.

Behind me, Charlie laughs. "They don't even seem stable when they're sitting. We'll beat them to a stand for sure."

"We just need something rideable."

"You're so lucky to have your pack," Charlie says wistfully. "I mean, most of the time. Don't you ever— Never mind."

"Don't I ever what?"

"Want privacy in the Gull?"

"Sometimes I'd like a bathroom of my own, like yours in the Winnie," I admit. "But just once in a while, I'm not asking you to feel sorry for—"

"I don't!"

"I know!"

We talk over each other, then go quiet, the only sound waves lapping over our board.

Charlie breaks the silence. "Use mine anytime. And anything in it. Shampoo or whatever."

For a horrifying second I wonder if my hair smells bad to her. I wash it as much as I can. I stiffen and she quickly adds, "I didn't mean you're dirty. You're cleaner than me, Ro. You smell like your mom's potions. I want the orange-clove soap."

"Okay."

"I just meant what's mine is yours. Ugh." She drops forward, leaning against my back, and I shiver at the contact. "Maybe no more talking. Here's a decent one, let's show your brothers what's what."

We race for the wave, paddling in sync. We manage to stand for a few seconds only, but the feeling is sweet.

One week before her Mexico trip, I finally find the right moment, when no one else is around, to invite Charlie inside the Gull. She kicks off her huaraches, brushes sand from her feet, and climbs the broad metal steps below her right wing, entering my home.

"Mama and Cap sleep behind those books. Griff here, Mag here. Dyl and I in back, here. That window looks tiny but it lets in a lot of cross draft." I tap the bubble window in the ceiling over our bunk. "Our beds are really comfortable, they don't bounce too much when we're driving because of those special hinges. Cap made these straps from old seat belts. And—"

A gentle hand on my wrist.

"What?"

"I love it, Ro. It's wonderful."

I look down at the rust-colored shag that covers up all of the ridges and bolts from the Gull's former life, before she was our home.

"I've never had anyone in here before."

She says quietly, "I know."

I hesitate. "Okay, then. When Mag was twelve and I was ten and a half, and he wanted to make me mad, he'd say this was the Gull's *guts*." I give the carpet a little brush with my bare foot. "Because of the color."

"That boy." Charlie waits patiently for me to go on.

"I was born on this rug. We all were."

"And this is Rontu-dog." I hand her my cherished stuffed animal, who in my nervousness I'd ignored a moment ago. "I found her in a parking lot behind a Crocker Bank in Bodega Bay when I was nine. They had a giveaway for opening five-hundred-dollar accounts, *Crocker* Spaniels from Crocker Bank, but someone didn't want theirs, I guess. Rontu is a little miracle. I'd seen those stuffed animals in the window, and I wanted one so bad."

Charlie smiles, scratching Rontu-dog's ears. "Rontu, from the dog in *Island*?"

I nod, so grateful I almost tell her more. That Rontu's stomach has a Velcro opening, and inside, behind a cheap little stuffed heart that says Highest CD Rates in Town!, I dug hiding places. That her plush paws and ears once held fountain coins, before Cap forbade taking them.

Now Rontu holds only her heart. I promised a tiny Dyl that I'd never open her again; he thought it hurt her.

The Gull has another, bigger hiding place, in one of the twin rear doors that we never use because Cap attached our bunk to them, bisecting the vertical line where they join. That sturdy right rear wall is double, and there's an opening in the inner layer of metal, where a handle once was. Anything secreted inside must be affixed to an old shoelace, the other end knotted on a bolt, because it's a steep drop down to the bottom.

Rontu is empty, but the door holds something now, a secret no one else knows about.

Something stops me from telling Charlie about it, even as she traces waves under our bunk with a soft smile.

"And this is our school." I lead her to the vanilla library, explaining how Cap approves our books. How he taught the twins and they taught me—Griff in charge of humanities and Mag math and science. "And I taught Dyl, until he outgrew me."

She bites her lip for a moment. "The lessons you pass down to each other. Cap to the twins to you to Dyl. Does that go for everything?"

"What do you mean?"

"I mean, what do you tell Dyl when he asks why you live how you do?"

She wants to understand why we live how we do.

I've ached to know. Not why this life is better than citizen life—that I understand. But what Mama and Cap's past homes were like. What first sent them away, onto the road.

Except just asking the question has always felt disloyal.

When I was little and first read *Oliver Twist*, I'd asked Griff if our parents were beaten as children. He'd said, "Of course not. They wanted something better than the SSNs, that's all."

But I knew that. What I didn't have—still don't have—is a picture of their other life, before.

So I asked sideways questions, hoping to get at the truth from other angles. Once, when there was a half inch of white-gold hair in Mama's part, between the red, I asked her why she hid it. It's naturally blond like mine, under her SunDrops Henna.

"Don't you want to match the rest of us?" I'd asked.

Mama had whispered, "I like secretly matching, don't you?"

Another time, a little older: "Do you ever miss your family, Mama?"

She'd squeezed me and said, "This is my family."

Or Mama would say silly things. Like "Before? I was a mermaid." Or "We were grunion and I wanted five baby grunions so Cap and I made you."

Mama was good at that—changing the subject, redirecting. I'm good at it, too, I realize now—I do it with Dyl all the time. I learned from the best.

"Ro?" Charlie asks now, sitting on the rust-colored rug, resting her back on the cupboard Cap built below Mag's bunk. "I'm prying. I'm sorry. I *love* your home."

I sit under Griff's bunk, facing her, twisting fronds of shag rug in both hands.

As we got older, I became aware of the flicker of hurt in Mama's eyes when I probed her, and the message was clear. It pained her to talk about *before*. Eventually I asked only rarely, when I couldn't resist.

"Dyl's never asked that question. I guess he stored away what he's overheard, the answers Mama gave me when I asked. But…"

Charlie leans close.

"But if he did, I'd tell him the only part that matters. Mama and Cap ran away together because they were unhappy living like everyone else."

13

Four pups

2002
The island
Day 2, early morning

I peered down through the white rope diamond to where Mama sat in the glow of the solar lantern. She wore a green sleeveless dress and had a brown sack slung across her chest diagonally, like a contest winner, Ms. Nature.

She looked like she belonged here. She smiled up at me and mouthed, *My girl.*

I climbed down and fell into her arms. Oranges and cloves, ocean. "I knew you'd come," she whispered. She cupped my face, stroked my hair. Not asking why I dyed it, why it stopped at my collarbone instead of my tailbone.

Mag and Griff and Dyl slept on above, high in the air, like fairies from one of Dyl's old stories.

For a long time, we didn't say anything. She squeezed my hand, and it all came back to me, how when Mama squeezes your hand, the memory of it has weight and edges, like it's something you can carry.

"Cap," I whispered at last. "I'm so sorry."

Her voice was surprisingly steady. "He was ready. He didn't want to fade out in some dreary bed, stuck to machines."

Of the reporter we'd stashed in the other work shed, she seemed as accepting and untroubled as Charlie'd said she was when she first told her the news: "Cap must have had his reasons for inviting her."

About the Gull's thousand dollars in repairs, which I offered to help pay: "We'll scrape it together like always, maybe the Gull deserves a little rest, don't you think?"

And on this setting for the paddle-out: "Don't you know why it had to be here?"

How could I know? I hadn't even known that Cap was sick, or that the six of us would soon be on a museum wall in LA.

"I thought it was maybe so we could hide from reporters, because of that museum exhibit. But if Cap invited one, then that doesn't make sense."

"Oh, is that what you and your brothers think?" She gave me a look. Not as in *you're right*, but as in *you could not be more wrong*. "I'm glad you're getting along, you four."

"It's a little strange, because of that reporter—"

"And you have a family in Oregon?" She was radiant with expectation for more details. She looked at me as if I was still a teen, that windblown girl in the picture, and her eyes showed none of the accusation or disappointment I'd feared for fifteen years.

"I have two sons, Mama. Jack and Bear. Fraternal twins."

"Well. It runs in the family." She ran her index finger down the part in my hair. A glimmer of blond would be visible now, between the brown. I hadn't colored it in two weeks.

"And you're raising them alone?" she asked.

I shook my head. "Their father, Lou. He's wonderful."

She tilted her chin a degree at my answer. Mama always knew when there was truth between words, in the interstices. It was the way she communicated herself. But she didn't ask about my long-dead marriage.

I had so many questions for her, though. I needed to know

what happened after I left, after I mailed my postcard of the lavender farm in full bloom, why I never got even an acknowl-edgment they'd received it. "I've missed you so much, Mama," I said, my voice breaking. "I have so much I want to talk about with you."

"I missed you too, Little Seal. But we have time." She beamed again.

But we didn't. Couldn't she understand that? It was impen-etrable, her beaming, the light she gave off. It was blinding. Maybe I did want her to accuse me, to bring up my leaving. It would show that my absence had mattered, at least. It would allow me to respond—*But you didn't come for me.*

Why didn't you come for me?

Instead she blithely ignored that I'd fled. I had never, in a decade and a half of daydreamed conversations with her, imag-ined that.

"Mama. When I left, I mailed a postcard and—"

"Look at those bites!"

"They're fine. Mama—"

"You need more salve." In the dim predawn light, she ex-amined the pink welts on my ankle with a frown that turned to a wide smile as she gazed up: "Boys! Isn't this nice? All of us, together?"

Because Griff was climbing down, Dyl had sat up, and Mag was stretching.

Griff was in take-charge mode again, ensuring Mama that "our" plan was to confine the reporter to the other side of the island while we decided about the interview. "She'll be far away from the paddle-out," he said, joining us.

Mama was unconcerned. "I thought we'd have our little ceremony tomorrow. It's so beautiful here. There's no rush, is there?" she asked, with that dazzling smile.

The boys looked at me, waiting for me to jump in and say, *Yeah, there kind of is.* I couldn't get the words out.

"Mother," Mag said. "Ronan goes back today."

"You do?" She turned to me, startled.

"I... That was the plan."

"Your sons are waiting for you on the farm, I suppose?"

I couldn't lie to her. Her eyes were still so trusting. And though I'd told myself this would be the briefest of visits, now the idea of an extra day with my family was tempting. "Well. Actually, they're away at camp."

Mama said tenderly, "Did Ronan tell you about Jack and Bear?" She seemed to relish using these names, and I stored this away as a little gem, two gems—how I'd only mentioned them once and she'd locked them into her memory so quickly.

"She did, Mother," Mag said. "So have you finished your secret project for the paddle-out?"

"Nearly," Mama said. "Ronan. Could Lou spare you from the farm one more night, do you think?"

Uncanny, her sorcery. It was stronger than ever; she seemed to sense that Lou could perfectly well spare me.

Lou and the boys could not only spare me, they didn't even know I was here. It was one thing to tell myself on the farm that this would be a two-day trip. Like saying "Just one quick wave, and then I'll get out of the water."

But I was immersed in my family, enchanted by them again. The way they'd adapted to the island without harming it, their ease here, beyond civilization. And the pull of Mama's sweet, expectant face was irresistible, no matter my frustration with her. "Well," I admitted. "He's not on the farm, either. He's staying near the boys for the week. Seaside."

"Mother, Ronan planned on only two days here..." Mag leaped in.

Griff and Dyl hadn't spoken in a while, but they watched

me closely, waiting for my answer. It was no longer dark, and the faint dawn light felt like a sign.

"It's okay," I said. "Mama's right. The sun's almost up so we should wait 'til tomorrow. I'd hate everyone to rush through the ceremony on my account, it's too important. I can stay one more day."

"Perfect," Mama said. "Thank you, Ronan."

"We should talk about the reporter, though," Griff said tentatively, looking over his shoulder for a moment, as if he could see the west side of the island and the shed where we'd installed Pauline Cowley. He turned back, looking at each of us significantly, ending with Mama. "We need to decide what to do."

Mama didn't answer, and her expression didn't change. She merely took one last sip of her tea and set the tin mug down on the ground.

"We asked Charlie to get her list of questions, to stall her," I added, hoping for something, *anything* solid from Mama. The tiniest acknowledgment that Cap inviting a reporter had jolted her, too. That stalling the interview was wise or foolish.

A hint, a *flicker* of distress at the existence of that list, which Pauline was creating as we spoke. Of a citizen-stranger who couldn't possibly understand the choices Cap and Mama had made, poring over them. Judging them.

"Well, you four talk it over when you see the list," Mama said. "You decide what to say to her, that's fine with me. In the meantime, does anyone feel like a hike?" She clapped her hands together with excitement.

"Mama?" I tried again, panting, when we were nearly at the summit.

"I want to show you something. There. Do you see it?" she whispered, pointing at a dull arc of twigs far above. A seagull nest. She smiled distantly. "Now, gulls never let their young leave until they're completely ready to fend for themselves."

I nodded. I didn't know if I wanted this to be a coded message for me or not. I only wanted her to stop moving, to look me in the eyes, to let me speak above a whisper. And to acknowledge that, even if she didn't have answers, she shared some of my questions.

"... And I saw an eagle's nest the other day on the west side of the island. I'll show you tomorrow or the next day..."

I told her I couldn't stay long after the paddle-out, but she didn't react. My departure plans had begun to seem arbitrary—my sons wouldn't be home for a week—even foolish, when there were such wonders as eagles still to see.

So I gave in to her nature tour. Let her describe the moss and lichen that bald eagles used to line their nests, how they were protected here.

She'd made it clear. She didn't want to talk about the past.

When we rejoined the others she asked, "Now, does anyone feel like a swim?"

I tensed, gazing down at the whitecaps. Paddling out for Cap's short memorial on a board before sunrise, then hopping on the boat to leave, was one thing. But swimming in the ocean, in daylight, just for kicks? I didn't relish the prospect of fighting that surf, or pretending I wasn't scared. And what if we attracted attention, and someone radioed in that a pack of people were treating Manzanita Island as their personal resort? It seemed absurdly risky.

Dyl spoke then, directly to me. "It won't be the ocean. I found a warm swimming hole—the rocks hide it from boats." His reassuring tone was exactly the one I'd used on him when he was a little boy and he was nervous.

Comforted slightly, I said, "That sounds wonderful, Dyl."

≈

I stared out at where Dyl had led us. "It's... How is this...?"

"Right?" Mag laughed.

"Our first backyard pool," I said, in awe. "Amazing what

sixty or seventy million years of volcanic activity can create." The fact, straight from the vanilla library's fat *Geology of the Pacific* reference book, came automatically.

The others stared at me, pleased by my pleasure, surprised by my sharp memory.

We stood on a rocky ledge curled around a deep, oval-shaped cove. Across the water, on the ocean side, the wall of rocks wasn't as high, but it provided enough vertical cover to hide anyone swimming inside the nature-dug pool.

"Dyl found it the third day," Mama said.

"It's warm enough for no wet suits this time of year, but don't expect *backyard* warm," Mag said. "There's a little churn from the tides, but enough of the water stays in here all the time that it warms up."

"Do we jump, or sort of scooch in?" I looked dubiously at the rough sides of our "backyard pool." Five feet of scooching would mean a lot of scrapes. Climbing out would be worse.

"Neither," Griff said.

Mama nudged her youngest. "Dyl, why don't you tell her?"

Instead of explaining, he darted back into the trees. He returned with a snare he'd fashioned, made out of a loop of braided reeds lashed to a stick, and, demonstrating slowly for my benefit, used it to catch the end of a manzanita branch and pull it down.

He rappelled down the side of the rocky ledge in front of us a few feet, then let go and plunged gracefully into the water. Instead of snapping back up, his grabbing device now dangled within easy reach.

"See, he weighted the handle with stones, so it makes climbing out a snap, too," Mag explained.

A snap, huh? I swallowed. They were all watching me—I was next. Shaky, trying to hide my nerves, I unbuckled my sandals and unzipped my shirt until I was only in my shorts and sports bra.

It seemed to hit the others that in their excitement they'd forgotten I was no longer an ocean child. Mag shot me a worried, apologetic look, and Griff opened his mouth as if about to speak, maybe recalling my nerves when we'd disembarked from the *Kai*.

But I had to be a good sport. My little brother was floating on his back, waiting for me.

It wasn't pretty. Dyl had been so quick, so agile, some rare, island-bred hybrid of chimp and porpoise. I was nothing but quaking, landlocked farm mom as I took the makeshift safety bar and worked my way down the rough edge of the "pool." But I made it. And when I dropped in, the water felt like chilled silk.

I back floated toward the center, where Dyl was. With a little whoop, Mag splashed in, and then Griff made his more dignified entry. Then Mama joined us, and for a long time, there was no need to do anything but float. I started with a dog paddle. Then a sidestroke. Then it came back, my old, rolling crawl. How I'd missed this.

I paddled to Mama and said breathlessly, "I'm glad I came."

"I'm glad you're glad."

"It's just like that time we snuck into the San Andrea cove, remember? Cap was working and we were boiling in that heat wave. And Dyl was so young. He brought a cup of water back for the Gull, to trickle on her hood."

"He should do it with this water. Anoint the Gull."

"Bring a container back to the RV graveyard, you mean?"

"The Gull's here." Mama looked dreamy.

"You mean…in spirit, like Cap?"

"No, truly here." She laughed and swam off.

Always unpredictable, always floaty, had Mama lost her grip on reality? Floated off to sea?

I signaled to Mag and he surged over in two strokes. "Mama

didn't— This sounds nuts. You didn't hire a ferry or barge to bring the Gull here to the island, did you?"

"What are you talking about?" he asked.

"Mama said the Gull's here."

"Oh, you know how she is. Always talking in riddles." Mag dipped a finger into the water from above and swirled it as if to demonstrate the conundrum that was our mother.

At least Dyl seemed less anxious today. He'd swum the other way, to the far rocks. Nimbly, he scrambled up and sat on the thick ledge there, peering through a craggy, window-like oval onto what I'd assumed was open ocean.

He looked over his shoulder at me, beckoned happily once, and turned again.

Shivering, I swam to him. He offered me a hand up—such a grown-up hand, with such strength behind it.

I was still processing it, this man's strength in my tiny little brother—would it ever be anything but shocking?—when I saw what he wanted to show me.

Down below, the rocks descended sharply to a narrow strip of beach. And there was another family there. Elephant seal sows and their new young. The long, portly animals were silvery gray as they sunned themselves, conversing in clicks and foghorn-deep calls.

"Four pups," Dyl said.

Overcome by the sight, how sweetly *Dyl* it was to share this coincidence with me, I tried to keep my voice steady, but it came out ragged. "Like us. The Merrick kids."

Dyl smiled at me under half-closed lids, then descended gracefully back to the water and duck-dived expertly, showing me his right instep. That was my answer—his eighteenth-birthday tattoo.

From my perch a few feet above on the rocky ledge, I laughed with joy. Dyl surfaced and water streamed down his eyes, his

smile. He had Mama's serene smile. I'd missed it so much I had
to jump into the water with him again.

Water was always the cure. *We float, we glide, we need no one else…*

We splashed and floated like the old days, our worries forgotten on dry land.

Then, everything changed.

Dyl spotted her first, over my shoulder, and it was like watching an animal, one second lost in pure pleasure, sense a predator,
and remember that earth holds danger, too. His smile faded.

I paddled around. On the rocks, gazing down at us, Charlie
stood with an envelope in her hand: our interview questions.

We slowly climbed out of the water, dripping and shivering,
and surrounded her, all of us staring at the thick white envelope. I'd expected a page; this was a novella.

Dyl's voice came out thin, young sounding. "What does she
want to ask us?"

Charlie said, "I didn't read them. It's…family business.
But she was up all night writing by lamplight. Scribbling and
scratching things out. Crumpling up paper. There's a whole
recycling bag full." Clearly, Charlie hadn't slept, either; she
was red-eyed and looked exhausted. Now she was circled by
drenched, anxious Merricks; we hadn't even let her sit and rest
after yet another cross-island hike.

I wondered if she was weary of being our liaison to the outside world, just like when we were teens. But she was gentle
and respectful as she offered the envelope of Pauline's questions to Mama.

Who wouldn't take it. "Oh, I don't know anything about
magazines. You four decide what to say to her."

"If we say anything," Mag said. "We really need to figure
that out, Mother."

Charlie turned to Mama. "Oh, she really hopes you might
come visit her soon, Ella. And she mentioned some kind of

small honorarium for the interview. She hasn't told me how much, but—"

"Isn't that sweet? First Dyl and I have something to show everyone. Dyl, let me check that it's all ready, and then you follow in a little bit, all right?" A smile, a gentle squeeze of her wet hair, and Mama was downhill, out of sight. Happy to pretend Pauline Cowley and her questions didn't exist.

"What's an honorarium?" Mag asked.

I explained reluctantly; Pauline dangling this surprise carrot, when the Gull sat in the graveyard needing a new engine, might make it harder to say no. "Money." I sighed.

"Did Cap know about that part?" Griff asked.

"I don't know," Charlie said. "She wouldn't say."

"There must be a lot of questions in there, for her to *pay* us for the answers," Mag said.

"Well, let's see what they are." Since no one else seemed to want it, I took the fat envelope from Charlie, unsealed it, and pulled out what Pauline had sent us. She'd wrapped her questions in a sheaf of blank paper, I saw to my relief, and her note for us was only on a single four-by-six card. Maybe the interview wouldn't be so grueling after all.

I read, flipped the card over.

And laughed.

"What?" everyone asked.

I held up what Pauline had written.

Griff narrowed his eyes, reading. "She's unhinged. Or she thinks she's Sartre."

Dyl tilted his head, looking thoughtful. Analyzing Pauline Cowley as one of his creatures. He respected unpredictable animals.

"*One* question?" Mag said. "She was up all night to write *one* question?"

Pauline had written only four words: "Is this the truth?"

"Is *what* the truth?" Mag laughed. "Life? The island? Well,

now I'm curious about all the questions that went in the recycling bin. Hey, it's good—it means we can tell her anything."
My heart sank; Mag seemed to have warmed to the interview
because of the money. And Griff seemed to be a yes out of loy-
alty to Cap. "She's just some rich eccentric. We can control the
interview and send her on her way."

But Pauline Cowley wasn't unhinged, or pretentious. That
was the most unnerving part. It was a perfect, brilliant question. The only question.

"She means is *this* the truth." I turned the message around
so they could see what Pauline had used as paper: a four-by-
six color glossy of *Dreamers*.

FIELD JOURNAL

Is Dreamers *the truth?*

I've stared at it more than anyone, I guess. Stared into it.
I've tried to see it as others do.
I've studied it by the ocean, like now, and when I was far inland,
but could taste salt and smell kelp because of one
tastefully framed photograph.

It captures something truthful—no one can deny it.
The joy of racing from what doesn't matter toward what does,
surrounded by the tiny group of people on the planet
who understand you.

My childhood was lonely, though I had everything.
And few people understood me, after she left. So that joy is real.
I'm reaching for it now.

But capturing something truthful isn't the same as telling the truth.
It's a moment in six lives.
There are so many moments, unphotographed, outside its margins.
Can we talk about them without blotting out the joy?
I don't know.
I don't know if we're brave enough.

14

Underground

Charlie's time with us flies, and too soon, it's her last day.

We're lying side by side in her bunk, and as she walks her feet up the wall under her Billy Idol poster I take a mental picture: her chipped fluorescent-white-painted toenails exactly match the white teeth in Billy's sneer.

Life will be gray and dull without Charlie in it. It'll be LaPush Beach in winter, without anemones. I ache to cross the border with her. But I look up at her map, studded with its thirty-seven pins, and ask enthusiastically: "Tell me about Guanajuato, again?"

A silence, then Charlie says, "You don't really want to hear about Guanajuato."

"Of course I do!"

An even longer silence. Does it hold pity because my world is confined to California, Oregon, and Washington? I have more freedom than any citizen girl. Freedom is our motto. Cap's logo, even. I show Charlie now, pulling a penny from my pocket, tracing the design stamped out of the center, telling her how Cap punches coins after each garage job.

"He uses a tiny die he made. Coins minted before 1982 work best because they're all copper, without zinc." Cap had said that long ago. What he hadn't explained, what I'd been too young to wonder about then, was when he'd started making them, or why.

"Take this as a going-away present."

Charlie traces the shape cut into it as I did, the *M* that's also a seagull and a wave, but says, "I don't need a present. C'mere."

"Why?"

"Just c'mere."

So I do, holding my breath. She whispers in my ear. "We're not going."

"What?" I laugh, shocked.

She grins. "You're better than my thirty-seven pins."

The next morning

Cap tips his hat back at Charlie, who's joined exercises.

The hat-tip is high praise. Charlie deserves it for her perfect form, when even showing up impressed him. It can't be past four, a misty predawn, but she's foregone half an hour of sleep in the warm Winnie to wind-sprint and squirrelly with us in the dark, by flashlight, on wet sand.

She beams at us as we head to the water, but seeing how Mag keeps his distance, Charlie murmurs to Griff and me, "Mag's pissed."

"Don't mind him, he'll be civilized after a few waves," Griff says, walking ahead.

I fill Charlie in. "Cap hasn't tipped his hat at Mag after calisthenics in months. It's this age-old battle between the twins. Mag slept through exercises once last fall, and Cap acted…"

"Pissed?" Charlie finishes.

"That would've been better. Cap pretended Mag hadn't been missed. *Griff* took Mag aside later and lectured him."

"And how many times have you won a hat-tip?"

"Oh, it's a competition for the twins. You know."

"The male Merricks," Charlie says.

"The taller Merricks. Dyl's not included, either." It's not the first time she's prodded me like this. The larger half and the smaller half, the male inhabitants of the van and the female/baby, and how we fit. Once, spotting a Student Driver car, she asked why Cap taught the boys to drive at ten, but still won't let me helm the Gull.

"There's no point in talking about it," I'd said, and her silence argued that there was.

But it's too beautiful a morning for self-pity, and I head her off: "Charlie, I'm five-two. These aren't wind-sprint legs. But speaking of wind, it's perfect right now." I slosh in and paddle off.

Cap finishes surfing early—he's driving Bass to the RV graveyard to hunt for an air-conditioning compressor for the Winnie, although he doesn't believe in AC himself, and won't return until late. Mama and Dyl are going along to explore a lake nearby.

Mag was supposed to go on the graveyard trip, but he's still prickly over this morning and says he'll stay behind with the rest of us instead. Mag's hurt, I know, when instead of protesting, Cap says breezily, "It's your day."

But the offshore wind's perfect, and the four of us stay out a long time. Eventually the twins bail to nap in the Winnie, since the Gull's gone until late tonight.

It's just me and Charlie now. When I catch a twenty-second ride that carries me way in, she gestures with her index finger next to her temple, pushing up through her wet hair.

I tilt my head in confusion.

She does it again, more slowly, and I laugh. She's tipping an invisible hat at me.

≈

When we paddle in for the day, a boy wades over to us in the shallows. "Where'd you two learn to surf like that?" he calls, which always feels like an insult.

He's tall, with a brand-new board, brand-new orange baggies. Rich. His Talking Heads concert T-shirt is the secret password for Charlie's attention.

"Did you go to that concert?" She coils her leash, ignoring his question.

I resist the urge to tug her away. She's forsaken her thirty-seven pins for me, and I can't bear for her to decide it was a bad trade.

The boy's been to Hawai'i, and they discuss KPu'ena Point, her tattoo, how big-wave surfing's cool but not their thing. How he applied to University of Hilo but attends UC San Diego. They talk easily, the boy reaching for a strand of kelp stuck to Charlie's board and brushing it off.

It's so intimate, like removing an eyelash from someone's cheek without asking.

I want to join the conversation, but how? *Hey, do you know a classmate who works at your school newspaper? My father threw his camera in our fire… Hey, I know every kelp section by heart because there's a diagram on my little brother's journal! Canopy, stipe, blade, float, sporophyll…*

I can only watch, a child, with nothing to contribute.

"Hey—there's a party today," the boy says. "An underground party—467 Monte Rialto, in the hills."

"Nice!" Charlie says.

Does *underground* mean a secret party? One in a basement?

The boy asks where we go to college, and Charlie says casually, "I'm applying to a bunch, but I'm not sure college is my thing."

My skin prickles like she's thrown sand at me. She's never

mentioned college, not once. I'd been so focused on her return to Oahu that it never occurred to me: soon she'll leave me behind in another way.

I tell her brightly, "You should go to that party," and wander down the sand to the public restroom's outdoor shower.

"What's up with you?" she asks when she joins me under the water, peeling down her wet suit. "That's freezing! I didn't tell him. You know. Anything I shouldn't've."

"I know you wouldn't." I shut my eyes, letting icy water pound my face. "You should go to that party. Your flight's not 'til midnight, right? He likes you."

"He asked if *you* had a boyfriend, Ro."

I'm supposed to be flattered and fluttery in my stomach, I know. But all I can imagine is Charlie at college, forgetting me. Worse—learning to pity me.

In the Winnie, Griff snores, sprawled on the kitchen banquette. Mag's spread-eagled on the floor. We step over them, Charlie making faces like it's a game, and I pretend I'm still in a good mood. We grab bread and orange juice and climb onto the roof where it's shaded and breezy, wind rattling through silver eucalyptus above us and all the way down the bluffs. Charlie's penthouse—that's what she and Bass call it.

"I went to an underground party in Kailua." Charlie lays her wet suit out to dry. "It was a good time. Here, I'll do yours."

She spreads my suit carefully, and it looks so small next to her long one, the elbows and shoulders grayed and worn, while her suit is as deep black and shiny as a seal's coat. She's ten months older, but it feels like ten years.

Charlie has thrown herself so headfirst into our lives it hasn't occurred to me until now that I haven't returned the favor. She probably spends every weekend at home partying. Our big plan for this afternoon is sketching tide pool diagrams for Dyl.

I blurt it out: "Let's go."

"Cap would let you?"

I don't answer.

"Oh no. I'm not sneaking you to a party while they're away. I'd never get a hat-tip again. He'd never let me near you guys again. He'd *kill* me."

"He doesn't believe in violence."

"Hilarious. Why are you interested in parties all of a sudden?"

"Who's getting killed?" Griff's bleary-eyed face appears above the ladder, and he climbs up to the roof, sprawling on his back next to us. "Too hot in there."

"It's nothing," Charlie says.

"Charlie and I are going to an underground party," I announce. Childish, because I know Charlie will say no. And obvious, too. But I can't undo it now.

"No, we're not," Charlie says.

"Well, I'm going," I say. "467 Rialto."

Charlie lies flat on her back, like Griff, and bats at a eucalyptus branch. "*Monte* Rialto. Great, Ro. Wander into some stranger's mansion and get shot to prove a point."

Mag joins us just as Griff says, "Of course you're not going." Like he's Cap. Like it's a rule of the universe.

"Thanks for waking me up." Mag scowls, his face red and creased from his nap.

"There's an underground party nearby and Charlie and I are going," I say. "Mag, you should come, too."

Mag's too proud to admit he doesn't know what an underground party is, either. "A citizen party?" He hesitates.

He talks about rebelling sometimes, hitching or earning money. But Cap's rule about mixing with citizens unnecessarily is sacrosanct. Charlie and I will end up sketching tide pool diagrams for Dyl to paste in his field journal, which is what I'd vastly prefer anyway. And at least she'll know I tried.

"It doesn't matter what kind of party because it's not happening," Griff says.

And that does it. Mag gets steely eyed. "You don't decide what I do, Professor. I'll go with Ro and Charlie. I'm not afraid."

Griff replies, "I didn't say you were! I'm just trying to point out that... Charlie, reason with them."

"Oh, no. I'm not getting tangled up in your Merrick mess."

Griff rubs his hair, weighing options. Then he sighs. He's outvoted. "All four of us will go. For *one hour.* We'll take a walk nearby and just..."

"Just scope it." Mag seems as surprised as I am by how this plan came together. "If it's lame we bail."

Charlie laughs. "Mag, I'm sorry, but you cannot pull off 'scope it' and 'lame' and 'bail.' Okay, guess we're going. But do not blame me if Cap finds out."

The four of us are high in the San Diego hills, minutes from a party packed with college citizens. We've come for the flimsiest of reasons—because Mag didn't get a hat-tip this morning, because a stranger on the sand stole Charlie's attention for two whole minutes, and because she sent away for college brochures.

Now it all feels foolish.

But we keep walking, passing estates, gated neighborhoods. Green lawns fade to gold as we climb higher into the drought-stricken hills. There are homes in every stage of construction— some just foundations, some complete except for gaps where there should be windows and doors, some still boasting For Sale signs. But even these look given-up-on. The geraniums in their pots are as crispy and faded as their front lawns.

Cap told us people can't afford houses, that developers overbuilt into the hills from greed and now it costs too much to borrow. *Poor, deluded souls,* he says.

"This is pretty high up for an underground party." Griff tries to sound light but his voice is strained with nervousness.

His ponytail is too tidy, too dry, and he doesn't smell like himself. None of the three of us do: we showered in the Winnie, so instead of Mama's orange-and-clove soap, we used Charlie's. Plumeria and coconut.

We pass three empty lots before Charlie says, "We're here."

Young voices and music in the distance, but where? The sun's dropping behind us, casting our shadows east. But beyond these four elongated shapes, there are only weeds, rolling up, inland, as far as I can see.

At last Charlie offers a hint. "These are parties made possible by drought. Can you water-babies even imagine it?"

In the distance, a boy on a skateboard shoots above the golden weeds and arcs back down, invisible again.

Underground means it's a party in an abandoned swimming pool.

I spend my first party in an empty hot tub.

There are at least a hundred people, presumably college students. We weave through them, a blur of neon tops and sunglasses and bangs arcing as high as the waves off Mavericks.

The four of us cross the weedy back lawn, passing a hip-high black speaker throbbing the song people belt along to on the beach: "Red, red wiiiiiyiiiine…" Charlie glances back at me often, checking on me, but it's useless to try to talk with the speaker so close.

No one challenges our presence. We keep moving, getting a feel, finding our spot. So this is a college-citizen *rager*. The heart of it is the pool, where skaters roll and swoop in and out. A long, curved bench rims the shallow end—the blue tiles are half-finished, and now it's a bar: beers and cans of Hawai'ian Punch and bottles of liquor cover it.

There! Charlie mouths, points, leading us to the empty hot tub on the other side of the pool, where it's quieter.

When we reach it I turn to talk to the twins, but they've gone off on their own.

"Will they be all right?" she asks as we settle at the bottom of the tub.

They'd been so unsure at the beginning of the Quiver. But that adventure, nearly a year ago, seems to have emboldened them. "They can study the concretins," I tell Charlie, using Cap's name for skateboarders, whose preference for asphalt over water he says he'll never understand, though he has a grudging respect for them.

"Are *you* all right?" She taps my foot with hers.

I admit it. "Now I am."

"You stubborn girl, Ro. It's our last day together! I would've been happy sketching urchins for Dyl to glue in his journal."

"Let's analyze these creatures for him instead."

I like this spot, apart and hidden. From down here, we occasionally catch a glimpse of a skateboarder midair, the fiery sunset behind him. But it feels cozy and safe, just big enough for the two of us to lie on our backs, knees bent, while scraps of conversation waft overhead:

"A babe. Total babe."

"Hello, beer goggles."

"Forget your board?" I have to remind myself the voice means skateboard.

"Coach'll kill me if I thrash my pitching hand…"

"You skank, you snaked my woo woo!"

Charlie and I knock knees, make faces, cover our mouths to stop from laughing too loud and drawing attention to ourselves.

"'You skank, you snaked my woo woo,'" I mimic, and when she comes up for air, Charlie explains that a woo-woo is some strong drink with cranberry and peach liquor. "You sound so utterly *wrong* talking like that, Ro. Don't be like Mag. I love the way you talk."

"Don't snake my woo woo, skank," I say gravely, for the pure joy of watching her collapse in laughter again. It feels like it did six hours ago, when we surfed together.

A girl above complains about Botany class: "I got a B, I'm so pissed. Like I know which soil chaparral grows in…"

I boast, softly, for only Charlie to hear: "North and east-facing."

"A-plus." Charlie lifts her arm, her right index finger up high, and moves it in deep concentration. "Hey, I've invented something relaxing. Tracing the clouds. Let's show Dyl."

I copy her, tracing clouds. "You always seem relaxed, whether you have something to trace or not."

"You see me here, with Bass, and you, and the rest of the lovely Merricks. You relax me."

I keep tracing. Her voice has an edge I've rarely heard. "Because your mom schedules you and all that?" I remember every word of our conversation on our shared board.

"That, and… I hate the men she dates. They dump her and break her heart. I envy how much your folks worship each other. And I feel guilty about splitting my time between my mom and dad. Sometimes I'm on the plane halfway there or halfway here, and I want to turn it around, right over the Pacific."

Charlie projects such ease and confidence, I've never realized how torn she must feel between her parents.

She traces wordlessly for a long time before adding, so fake-casually I know she's only bringing it up because of what I heard her say earlier, "My mom wants me to go to college. She's always on me about it, because she went, and her sisters and aunties and all the way up the line. You know, got to keep up the glory of the Akamus going. That's her family name. But my dad says it's up to me. They fight about it."

My heart seizes up again. "You should go."

"It's so much money. Maybe I should just surf, be like you guys."

I hesitate. As much as I don't want things to change, college is an opportunity for her. "You're smart. You should go."

"Your parents are smart. They didn't go."

"Cap went."

Charlie, shocked, rolls onto her side to face me. "Really?"

"He studied engineering for a while, Griff told me. Cap doesn't believe in it, though. Not anymore."

"Not for you."

"Mama doesn't believe in school, either," I point out.

"Sure, but...you know. He makes the rules."

The truth is I have thought, once or twice, about Dyl going to college. I don't know how he'd fare among citizens at a real campus, but he seems like a natural scientist.

And me? The botany that Mama has taught me is interesting. I'm curious about psychology, how to make kids comfortable. I'm good at it, if Dyl's any test. Maybe I'd enjoy studying in a library far from the vanilla one.

A wisp of cloud moves across the sky, a flossy curl dipped in pink. I take a mental photograph: *Click.*

That's what I would study. Photography. Really learning, instead of watching photographers on the beach when no one's looking.

≈

The sky darkens and someone wants to start a hot tub bonfire so we climb out and help. They've got a stack of old newspapers and they're separating pages, twisting them for kindling. Charlie and I do the same, then after making a dozen or so I notice a familiar three-pronged Poseidon staff logo on one of the sheets.

"What?" Charlie asks.

I show her the cover page in my hand: it's the UCSD *Triton*.

It takes her a moment, but then, remembering the *Triton* photographer from her first visit, she says, "We could've been in this. Famous!" Her tone's ironic, because it's just a dinky student newspaper. Soon to be kindling. "Was that only a year ago? Hey, listen…"

She reads an article about a sand dune–preservation project, how a professor takes her class to seed native grasses, and I half listen, my focus on the back page's collage of black-and-white photos. "SunDays," it's headlined. Students and townies lazing on a lawn, playing Frisbee. Shots taken in town, on the pier. The subjects aren't named, and neither are the photographers; it's just for fun.

There's a cheerful line underneath:

Got a news item or photo to share with the *Triton*? (818) 555-1234, Eustice Hall, 44 Jacaranda…

"Ro! Charlie!" It's the twins, calling us to join them on the grass.

A bunch of people build a fire in the pool, too, twisting more *Tritons* for tinder, piling branches. There's no shortage of them, and the fire doesn't stop the skaters rolling in and out; they merely adjust their ellipses by a foot or two to avoid the flames.

On the sloping lawn at the rear edge of the lot, someone's set a row of skateboards upside down, their wheels up. And a boy's "surfing" down the wheels on his shortboard.

"What a circus," Mag says. But I know he wishes he'd brought his surfboard.

"Someone's going to get hurt," Griff murmurs. "Or thrash their board."

Mag doesn't answer. He's too mesmerized by the surfers gliding down the line of upside-down skateboards. Twitching to try it himself.

Eventually he turns his back on them and, like the rest of us, focuses on the skateboarders in the pool, how they "drop in."

Charlie explains. In surfing a drop-in's bad—it means you stole someone else's wave. In skateboarding it's riding your board on nothingness, over an edge and down, onto a ramp or into a pool, like these kids. We watch the concretins roll, wipe out, laugh.

I like the rhythm of it. The sound. Thunderous rolling, a breathless pause while they're aboveground, turning, then their wheels hit concrete again and the thunder returns.

While we're watching, a girl offers us paper cups of red gel.

"A Jell-O shot," Charlie tells us. "It has alcohol." She hesitates, then slides it down her throat, winces, beams. She's always said she doesn't drink much, even when she's not around us. I wonder if her interest in it now has something to do with what she revealed in the hot tub—how when she's on a plane headed home or here, she sometimes wants to turn it around. She'll be on that plane in seven hours.

Griff tosses his drink in the garbage, and when Mag and I don't immediately do the same, he shakes his head at us.

I think of what Charlie said regarding Cap: *You know. He makes the rules.*

Impulsively, I tip a bite of red goo into my mouth and grimace: underneath the sickly sweetness of the Jell-O there's a burn. Mag follows my lead, swallowing his.

"We should go," Griff says. "It's after nine and it's getting too crowded."

It's true—there have to be three hundred people here now, and by the looks of them, they're not just college kids. There are older people, some sloppily drunk. And if we don't beat the Gull home, we'll have a lot of explaining to do. But I know Griff really wants us to leave because he's lost control.

We were only coming for an hour, to "scope it out." And now we're taking shots. Charlie and I stop at one, but Mag asks for another, forcing it down with zero evidence of pleasure.

"Mag," Griff says. "Let's go."

But Mag marches around to the other side of the pool.

"He's not getting more alcohol, he'd better not…" Griff trails off as it becomes clear what Mag's doing.

He talks to a skinny boy with a bleeding elbow, borrows his sticker-covered board. Not hesitating, not looking at us, Mag sets the skateboard on the ground and stands on it. He mimics the skaters, the blasé expression, the mysterious heel-press-lean-swerve that they make seem so effortless when they drop into the pool.

"Come on, Mag," I whisper. But his board flies away from him immediately and he skids to the bottom of the pool on his left hip.

"Shit," Charlie says.

Griff flinches, feeling his twin's pain.

"At least he's in the shallow end," Charlie says, as Mag jumps up, heaves himself out with his left arm, the other hugging his borrowed skateboard, and tries again. This time he anticipates the fall and separates from his board even earlier, sliding down the side of the pool, scrambling back up.

"He's going to try a hundred times 'til he gets it." I stand next to Charlie with my arms crossed. "Give him some coaching or you'll miss your flight."

"Should I, after the hat-tip thing this morning?" Charlie asks me.

"Yes."

"Help him so we can leave," Griff says grudgingly.

Because Charlie knows how to skateboard. Maybe Mag's just too focused on nailing this move to worry about his pride, but he accepts her advice willingly. "Lean forward *way* more than you think you have to. Commit. See?" She drops in, rolling back and forth easily, letting her momentum subside and climbing out.

With Charlie's pointers Mag fares slightly better, but he hasn't got it, still finishing in a heap at the bottom of the pool each time.

Now Griff can't resist a go, even though moments ago he was trying to shepherd us out of here. "Let me try."

The twins take turns, scraping their legs and arms. Seven times apiece, eight, but their feet and the board never seem united. At one point they both gaze longingly at the other hub of activity—the line of upside-down skateboards and the drunk college kids "surfing" down them. I know they wish they could try that instead.

"The *solidity* under you feels so different from surfing, right?" Charlie says as they're catching their breath by the rim nearest us. "You'd think it'd be more natural, and once you nail the drop-in it will be. But the start, getting used to concrete instead of water, is brutal."

I like the certainty in her voice: *It will be.*

I hold my hand out to Griff, indicating that I want a turn, but he shakes his head. "And how will I explain you breaking your arm to Cap?"

Also, I'm in a sundress from the thrift store. So much skin to get scraped, way more than the twins in their shorts and T-shirts; they've got road rash everywhere. Well, pool rash. But I'm in a funny mood. Charlie's leaving, and the twins' competition is tedious, and I need to prove to myself I don't need any of them.

I go up to another kid and ask to borrow his board.

"Sure!" he says. "I just had the truck tightened."

Whatever that means.

As I approach the pool and step on the board Griff says nervously, "Don't, Ro."

"Oh, let her," Mag says.

Charlie says nothing.

I don't look at any of them. *Commit, commit, indecision is a decision.*

The last thing I see, before I go over the edge, is the fire. A bright blur of amber in the corner of my left eye.

Griff carries me from the party on his shoulders.

Not because I'm hurt. Because I did it.

"The only one to drop in," Charlie says, gleeful. "On your first try!"

My ride was jerky and I'll have a beauty of a bruise on my left elbow tomorrow from hitting the pool wall to stop myself, but I did it. Hurled myself into a pit of concrete for a two-second, lopsided-U-shape of a ride.

"I think I prefer surfing," I say.

"She's so modest." Even Mag seems to share in my triumph. "We should buy you a skateboard and—" He gazes across the street, stops walking.

Griff freezes, too, catching sight of what's startled Mag, and from my perch on Griff's shoulders I see it.

"What?" Charlie asks.

"That VW van," I say. "It belongs to this weird guy we met once."

Griff sets me down. "C'mon."

We walk off, filling Charlie in on the ridiculous citizen we met nicknamed Jaws, on his tall tales of a shark attack and the bear trap he used to make it look like a great white had chomped his surfboard, and how he affixed the "bitten" trophy to the top of his VW bus, like a fin, to impress people.

We leave out his disrespect to Cap, or how he and Mag almost came to blows.

"I'm so sorry you didn't get to meet him, Charlie. He's such a pleasant person," Griff says. "Mag? Time to go." He has to tug Mag's elbow to get him moving faster.

"You Merricks lead such interesting lives," Charlie says in awe. "I'm going to miss you."

In bed, I comfort myself with the idea of our letters.

I drift off, but it's a jerky sleep, interrupted by someone leaving to use the bathroom. Mag. Sick from that gross jelly drink... I drift off again, feeling a skateboard under me, seeing Charlie's hat-tip on the water, in the window... At least I know when I'll see her again—her fall break. Three months from now...

And then, far away, glass breaks. Not a new sound—distant glass shattering is our home's familiar nighttime chime, dependable as the grandfather clocks I've read about in old books. Beer bottles get kicked, thrown. In anger, celebration, frustration. We ignore it all. But this sound is closer than usual. And when I scan the darkness over Mag's bunk and his familiar mountain-range shape's not there, I know the broken glass has something to do with him. I extricate myself from Dyl, slip down and over to Griff's bunk, tiptoeing, pausing to check that Cap's steady snoring continues.

I touch Griff's shoulder and he grunts.

"Mag's gone," I whisper.

Griff has the same gut fear—he scrambles down from his bunk and is out the door before I am. "I knew he was going back to that party. I just *knew* it..."

We spot Mag slumped on the parking lot curb two hundred feet away, his head in his hands.

I run to him. "Mag, are you—"

His board. His absurdly expensive, custom-made, Cap-designed board is at his feet, broken in two.

I touch the splintered edge, too astonished to speak. Griff lays a hand on Magnus's shoulder.

Mag doesn't look up. "He'll kill me."

"Tell us what happened." I lean close—Mag smells like gas station. I pick up a bottle from the pavement with a pissed-off-looking bird on it: Thunderbird: The American Classic.

"Where'd you get this?" Griff asks.

"I lifted it from the party."

We don't drink. It rots the heart.

We don't steal. They expect us to steal.

"Get to this, Magnus." I touch the wrecked board, anise scented from the licorice wax I gave him.

Mag gestures with his right hand on his left: a chomping motion.

"Jaws," I say.

"He did this?" Griff says, furious.

"He and…"

"They ganged up on you at the party?" Griff balls his right fist, like he and his twin have swapped body language.

"Snapped it over a keg, had his friends hold me down. Funny, huh?" Mag looks up and Griff and I gasp. His cheek's raw meat, his right eye only a slit.

Griff clenches both fists this time. We don't ask why Mag returned to the party with his surfboard. We'd both felt him itching to "surf" down that line of upside-down skateboards.

"But *why*?" I daub a corner of my T-shirt on Mag's eye. What to say? *I'm so sorry*? *We'll make them pay*? We can't. We're supposed to leave no trace—on land and with people.

"I don't know," Mag says. "He was drunk. I didn't go back to make trouble, I swear. I only wanted to try surfing the wheels. He said, 'Here's a message for your captain.'"

"We should tell Cap," I say. "Right now. This is ridiculous."

"No, Ro," Mag pleads. "Griff? I'll tell him something else. I'll tell him I wiped out and the board broke."

"It was my idea to go to the party," I say, more bravely than I feel.

Griff says thoughtfully, "He'll want to see the pieces. And it won't explain your face."

I take in the pitiful sight of Mag...and the smell. If we tell Cap we went to a citizen party, that there was alcohol, that two-thirds of us drank it, any parts of the truth, he'll be livid. He could blame Charlie, and I couldn't bear that.

But there's more to it for Mag. He's ashamed he lost a fight.

And Griff... I see on his face that he could never deliver such an insulting message to Cap, whatever his connection to Jaws. I ache to know, but even I don't want to give that *joke* of a man the satisfaction.

"Wait here." Griff takes off, then hurries past again with his own board.

Mag's twin telepathy alerts him instantly. "Griff, don't!" he calls.

But there's bashing noise, a sickening crack as Griff breaks his board over a bike rack. He's sweating when we get to him— Griff's grown strong, but a beautiful board like that doesn't give up its life easily. He hurls the two parts in the parking lot dumpster without a second glance.

Then he throws Mag's pieces out, too.

Griff's calm, as if he's just tossed four ordinary pieces of garbage. "Tomorrow we'll disappear early, and pretend we're surfing, and when we come back we'll say they were stolen. That we both got careless."

"You colossal idiot." For the first time since we found him here, there's a little normal Mag attitude in his voice, and it's a relief to hear.

Griff grins. "It will be better if he's mad at both of us. It might...spread out the rage."

I jump in, "I'll say I saw your boards get stolen, but we have to explain your face, too."

"You're the storyteller, Ro."

"You two are..." Mag shakes his head, but can't hold back his lopsided, grudging smile. "Griff, man. You just wasted a perfectly good seven-hundred-dollar board."

"Hey. I never gave you a birthday gift."

Cap believes us. He's furious at the twins, but more furious at the fancy convertible of punk college kids I invent, the fictitious board-thieves.

I use my best storytelling magic. I take pictures in my head until I can see what I describe, how the three of us ran after the car together, how one of the rich citizens threw a bottle and it hit Mag's face because he was the fastest, and closest. By the time I'm done, Cap nods in something close to approval.

For Mag, it seems to mean more than all the hat-tips Cap has withheld over the years.

15

My beautiful home

2002
The island
Day 2, afternoon

As we walked down the steep, thickly wooded terrain toward the ocean, which got louder by the second, I tried not to think of Pauline's envelope in my backpack. Neither twin wanted to carry it, so Charlie ended up handing it back to me as we followed Mama to her "surprise."

"A hot potato," she'd said wryly as I took it. "I understand, though. Hard enough dealing with Cap being gone, without a reporter raking over your lives with him."

With each step, my pack felt pounds heavier, somehow weighed down by a single envelope. I'd heard how crafty reporters could be. They put you at ease and you found yourself disclosing things you'd never planned to. Lou's father had spoken to a newspaper reporter after a county meeting, about a farm-tax bill, then bitterly regretted it—and he was tough.

We'd hoped we could content Pauline with a sunny story to match the photograph. But her four-word question seemed to promise hundreds more.

"Tell me about the photo of you six," she'd say. "Tell me how you felt when it spread…"

As I came around a bend, I glimpsed something on the sand below, and for a moment, it swept all thoughts of Pauline Cowley and her questions away.

The Gull *was* here. Just like Mama had said.

Out of boughs and branches, flowers and kelp, she and Dyl had made a replica van. They had built her secret project in a little cove, a cozy notch of the island protected from wind by steep, U-shaped cliffs. From a boat, you'd never know it was man-made. It would blend in with the trees and flowers behind it.

Mama beamed while we surrounded her, and Dyl ducked his head modestly as the twins clapped him on the shoulder.

Mag said, "So this is where we'll do the paddle-out tomorrow morning. Out there, with the Gull II watching over us."

A sweet idea.

"He would've liked it, Mama," I said.

She nodded, gazing at us with shining eyes, then turned and walked toward the water's edge, knee-deep in the lapping waves.

"It's to scale," Mag announced from the other side of the structure.

I paced the flower Gull out, the front and the side, to double-check—it *was* the same size as our real van, or close to it. Fourteen by seven feet. I fingered the rounds of dried willow mimicking wheels, the intricate braiding of a kelp strand over the bower's "front window." There were even wings made of reeds woven between branches.

Mama said the Gull was here, and it was. And this wretched interview? Maybe she was right not to worry about that, too. Cap had wanted us to talk to Pauline, here on a private island, even if he didn't share the reason why.

I stepped inside the structure, which smelled like sea salt and ozone and orange blossom. In the doorway, I turned to Charlie, who was hesitating behind me. "She used to be a food truck, did you know that?"

She nodded, hanging back on the sand while the rest of us explored the interior. "I'll leave you guys," she said. "This is for family."

"No, step in, Charlie," I said. If it weren't for her, we wouldn't be here on this magical island. And she had helped my family when I'd left. Though I hated to think I was replaceable, I was grateful.

Mag sat on a stack of palm fronds—the driver's seat. "Where to?" he asked her, looking up earnestly.

"Hmm… Can you take me to Haleakalā garden in Hawai'i?"

"No problem."

"Shotgun." Griff took the stack to Mag's right.

Sitting on the sand in the center of the creation, Dyl observed me contentedly as I explored the inside. Our bunk was a ledge of dried willow, placed at the same height I remembered. Pale weeds dangling from the roof near the front hinted at our vanilla library, and the steering wheel was a daisy chain. "This must've taken you days, Dyl. It's beautiful."

We'd thought the Gull was beautiful, too, that rusty old white-and-gray Grumman Olson…no one else had.

"Fourteen by seven," I said. "And all six of us lived here." I shook my head.

"Remember how Cap only let us have one cookie tin each for our possessions?" I asked. To this day, I could name every item I had stored in my Deluxe Belgian Chocolate Biscuit Round. The things I treasured most were free, plucked from garbage, or, when I was small and it hadn't been forbidden yet, bought in secret with stolen coins.

"'Material goods weigh us down,'" Mag recited. "'They are both bait and trap of a sick society.'"

"You were shocked when you saw my bunk in the Winnie, all my posters and clothes," Charlie said.

"It was a pigsty," Mag said.

"Hey, I'm neater now." Charlie punched him.

Nobody spoke again for a long time. After a while, Charlie wandered out and over to the shoreline behind Mama, pretending to look out for boats. Giving us time alone in our Gull. In the eerie sunset light, we could pretend she was real.

"I wish…" Griff said. And that was all.

Dyl curled up in the back of the flower rectangle, and I settled next to him. Griff stretched out on the right side—facing forward—where his old bunk had been hinged. And Mag stood in the center, doing something I didn't understand at first. Then I recognized his wide stance. He was sky surfing.

I swallowed back tears. When Griff had first come for me, back on the farm, I'd feared the truth about my past getting out. That while Lou would at least try to understand, most of the people in that life, people like my sons' living grandfather, wouldn't approve.

But maybe I also feared their reaction might change how I remembered it. If I had to talk about it, defend it out in the open. My secrecy had kept it sacred.

Yes, maybe outsiders would think my childhood was ugly. But they would see only the facts. When I let myself look for the beauty twined around them, when I could bear it, there was so much.

Like how it had felt to close my eyes in San Francisco and open them in San Diego. To know with one glance at a scallop of foam if the wind was offshore or onshore.

Our home had been an entire coast. The next wave. Home had been wherever the arrow-shaped seed pod fluttering from Mama's delicate hand said we'd go next, and it was boundless.

Griff cleared his throat. "We'll get her back," he said confidently.

There was a long silence, broken at last by Dyl.

"Ronan?" he asked from next to me, his voice so serious I feared what was coming. "Why did you leave?"

This was my chance to tell them the truth. I knew I wouldn't get a better one.

I looked at him, but his eyes were so wide, so trusting, I couldn't bear it for long and stared straight ahead. "Oh, pride, I guess. I was a foolish seventeen-year-old who thought this…" I looked around, mentally replacing vines with metal, the circle of daisies with our sweat-stained and much-taped white vinyl steering wheel, sand with our old rust-colored shag rug. "I thought this would wait for me."

But if I told them my secret, the weight of my betrayal would sink this island.

Because I'm the reason reporters want to talk to us.

I'm the reason that photo became a sensation.

The reason the life Cap wanted for us—private, peaceful, wholly unconnected from the world—disintegrated.

I took *Dreamers*.

16

Leica DRP

1983
El Zafiro, California
Fourteen years old
The night of the Triton camera

"I got some great shots on the pier," the boy said mournfully. "The light was epic today." This last part was soft, and wasn't said so much to me as to the sky.

The boy hurried off in the dark, the camera strap around his neck attached to nothing.

It was only me and the dying fire.

I'd watched the camera fall. Cap had been busy monitoring the kid's face, savoring his dismay, and then, perhaps, feeling a pang of regret for causing it.

Not me. My eyes had been on the camera. I'd seen it bounce off Dyl's serving of abalone, a translucent pink-white trampoline, into the safety of a large, mottled shell.

The flames had died in the misty air, and the spent logs on the camera's side of the pit looked like little gray-white crocodile backs, crosshatched and still. It was an impulse, as impossible to resist as whatever made Cap toss the camera.

I grabbed our log separator and poked. Surely it was ruined, a melted glob of plastic. But I wanted to see it, this thing that Cap had destroyed so ceremoniously.

Then—a bit of orange, near the edge of the pit, that wasn't flame. The film in the camera's window. I prodded the camera over the stone ring, onto the sand.

I'd imagined the camera popping open, film and camera a black-and-orange puddle from the heat, but it was intact. I tapped it fast with my index finger, and it was barely warm, so I picked it up.

Maybe the pictures the boy took are even okay, I thought. *I could get his film back to him, somehow. Take a bus to his college...* The silver timer gadget screwed into the side, to take pictures of yourself, the boy said, was cool and smooth. I examined the dial, which let you set the timer for ten seconds, twenty, thirty, a minute. There wasn't even a speck of ash obscuring the numbers.

Even the camera name, Leica DRP, and a little blue-and-yellow label on the bottom—University of California San Diego Communications Dept.—were unwarped.

It's like the camera was hiding in a little A-frame hut made out of the two abalone shells.

Waiting for me to claim it.

I knotted a shoelace around the camera and hid it deep in the Gull's double rear door, below my bunk, securing the top end of the shoelace to a long bolt. It was enough, at first, to know the camera was mine.

17

Bitter and bright

2002
The island
Day 2, afternoon

All of us sat at the sunny picnic table back at camp, staring at Pauline's envelope.

Secured between a solar lantern and our dry-bag of almonds, it fluttered cheerfully in the breeze.

Taunting me.

Pauline could soon sit us down and bombard us with all kinds of questions about *Dreamers*. It was the only reason people were interested in us. If the others found out I'd taken it, they'd never forgive me.

"Fifty thousand dollars," Mag said. He'd repeated it three times. Because that was the absurd amount Pauline had offered as her "honorarium."

Charlie had delivered this news a moment ago, after paying a visit to Pauline, and making an excuse for Mama's declining to visit her as Pauline had requested. Mama had waved off the invitation:

"I don't think it's necessary, do you?" She'd taken my hand

as we'd climbed back up the hill after our visit to her flower Gull. "This visitor is all that interests me at the moment."

The compliment lifted my spirits in the moment, but didn't exactly help us with the Pauline situation.

Charlie had told us that the cash was nothing to Pauline—she had family money. Then Charlie'd slipped off again, shooting an apologetic look my way, murmuring something about gathering island fox data.

"A bribe doesn't sound very professional," I said now as calmly as I could.

"That's Pauline Cowley's problem, not ours." Mag still couldn't take his eyes off of the white envelope.

Griff said, "Let's settle this fast so we can focus on the paddle-out."

Mama stood. "It feels like a storm, I'd better go check the water barrels. Why don't you pull the chokecherry off the racks before it's spoiled by rain? Goodness, if it's not calm enough for our little ceremony tomorrow morning we might have to do it the next…"

We all glanced up—perfectly clear. But when we looked down, Mama was yards away, her mass of gold hair shining in the sun, disappearing into the woods.

"She hopes it storms because she doesn't want to do the paddle-out," Griff said quietly.

I already had a lump in my throat from Mama calling it *a little ceremony.* "She can't even say the word."

I understood her not wanting to say goodbye. But Mama had left us to handle this huge decision alone, as if we were simply choosing which break to surf.

"She'll use any excuse to delay," Griff said. "Weather. That." He pointed at the white envelope encircled by our tin plates. Inside was the photo with Pauline's question written on the back. "Maybe we should just rip it up and send her back to the mainland."

The twins' switch on the interview had me spinning. After a lifetime of blind fealty to Cap, Griff would ignore his final wish?

"I can't rip up fifty thousand dollars." Mag pocketed the envelope. "And that's what the interview is now. You suddenly want to disobey him? Griff, you have no idea how that money could help. While you were pacing around outside Cap's deathbed, some of us were handling the living."

"What are you talking about?" Griff asked, looking up in surprise.

Mag glanced at Dyl, sitting on my right. Dyl had his field journal open in front of him, but since Charlie's reappearance and her bombshell about the money, he'd only mindlessly traced yesterday's sketch of an elephant seal, digging into the paper, piercing it. Dyl's eyes, as he met Mag's, seemed so sad, and now he gripped his worn charcoal pencil as if it was the only thing holding him here on the bench next to me.

What were he and Mag hiding?

"Nothing," Mag said. "I just think fifty thousand dollars is pretty good for an hour's work, that's all. I don't want to reject the idea outright. Come on."

An hour's work. As we trekked through the trees to the chokecherry-drying area, I thought of Cap's stamped pennies and pesos. How he'd drilled that seagull shape in them, and then we decided it was an *M* and a wave, too. Cap's symbols of defiance. They meant even on the job, he could make time his. Because even when our stovepipe had been hollow, we were rich enough to turn the world's currency into a Merrick code, something entirely ours. Circles with pretty markings but no value.

Long after I left and became a parent, when I had to earn money, and budget on the farm, and it went so quickly—for roof repairs, my boys' shoes, water bills—I'd realized that Cap's defiance was actually denial that money was part of our lives, a fiction that deserved pity more than admiration. Perhaps he thought his garage gigs would humble him in our eyes if he didn't come home with his special coin.

Money did matter. Even on this primitive island, it had found us.

After a twenty-minute walk we made it to Mama's fruit-drying area, a sunny field banked by low Hosta plants with plate-sized leaves and, stretching from above and below, long sprays of white-and-purple flowers. The mashed chokecherry was spread out to dry on rounds of eucalyptus, the kind from the felled trees that were scattered all over the island. Non-native, invasive, I remembered Griff telling me as we'd passed piles of the wood discs. And Mama had put them to clever use.

We all got to work, peeling strips of dried chokecherry paste from the wood, setting them inside Mama's old critter-proof tins, between layers of brown paper.

Mag perched the dreaded envelope on a stump lengthwise, bookended by two eucalyptus rounds, so it looked like a little sail, but the rest of us tried to ignore it. For a while the only sound was the *rip, rip, rip* of us working.

Sun shot through the coral-colored strips—one side was grainy, the other glossy as stained glass. The tart-sweet ribbons used to be a delicacy, the only thing close to candy that Cap allowed. Dyl offered me a morsel and I ate it. A strange flavor, bitter, then addictively bright, then, only after you'd swallowed, tinged with sweetness. Our childhood treat was an acquired taste.

Rip, rip, rip. Little shreds of my heart. I was just beginning to feel close to my family again, and Pauline Cowley could ruin everything if she asked too many questions about *Dreamers*. Or—the realization was sickening—what if she somehow knew already that I'd taken it?

Mag had given up all pretense of working and leaned against a tree in the shade. Then Griff stopped, too. He paced, undoing his ponytail, running his hands through his hair, securing it in the leather band again. Only Dyl and I continued to work steadily. *Rip, rip, rip.*

And then another sound: the *flap-flap-flap* of Pauline's envelope in the wind.

I crossed to the other side of the field, hoping that there I wouldn't hear the envelope's rattle. On the ground, in the shade, was a knee-high container, one of Mama's old ones. I uncapped it and found at least two gallons of the jam-like liquid, ready for drying. Mama had boiled enough fruit to last months. Did she hope to *stay* here? Yet another worry. What a mess things had become. And I couldn't leave her now, add to her heartbreak. I felt trapped. *Flap-flap. Flap-flap-flap.* No use—the envelope was still taunting me, even from over here.

I returned to the others and got to work again, but tore at the dried fruit recklessly, until my hands hurt and the sticky bands folded in on themselves, balling into clumps.

"Are you all right, Ro?" Dyl asked.

I smiled at him quickly and turned away. I had to calm myself, to focus. "I'm a great lavender picker, but I guess I'm out of practice at this."

"You're doing fine."

"Dyl." I hesitated. "This island, it's beautiful. I wish it could be all yours. You and Mama seem happy here. But. She understands you can't stay, right?"

"Did you know we're only twenty miles from the real island, San Nicolas, where the real Karana lived alone for eighteen years?"

"So you do remember." In spite of everything, his admission warmed my heart.

Dyl nodded shyly. "Her name was Juana Maria. I was camping in Santa Barbara a couple of years ago and I found her burial place in this big mission when I went to fill up my water jug. The Lone Woman of San Nicolas Island, they called her. The mission was a beautiful place, I guess. But not…" He looked up at the dome of blue sky, empty except for a solitary gull.

"Not like this," I said.

He shook his head.

"So she ended up on the mainland," I said softly. "I wonder how that felt, after living alone on a place like this for so long."

"The plaque at the mission where they brought her was awful. They said she was *rescued*."

"Dragged off it by missionaries, more like."

I knew from Dyl's pained expression that he was picturing this, same as I was. He switched to a happier topic: "What're your sons' favorite parts of the book?"

I smiled. "Jack's is where Karana makes a skirt of yucca reeds, in the spring. And Bear's is where she sees the devilfish in the sea cave. And they both love the part where the birds swoop down and take Rontu's fur to build their nests.

"I wonder what happened to my stuffed-animal Rontu. Remember how we named her after Karana's wild dog?"

"Rontu-bank-dog," Dyl said with a secret smile. Remembering Rontu, I guessed. "You missed her, Ro?"

"I—I missed everything." I looked down at his tousled hair, his charcoal-stained fingertips. Over at the twins sitting on either side of the same tree trunk, their long legs bent at identical angles even as they fumed at each other silently. I thought of Mama, down on some beach, overcome with her love for Cap. The real Gull, and the one she'd painstakingly constructed of branches and reeds and flowers. Charlie's bright eyes, the wisdom and concern in her voice then and now.

My next words came out raspy. "When I read *Island* to my sons, Dyl, their imaginations are so beautiful." I stopped myself before saying *Just like yours was*.

It was wrong to confide in him like this when so much hurt lurked around the corner…or on the other side of our island. It would shatter Dyl to learn that I'd taken the picture that caused so much trouble for him.

We were finished; the drying racks were empty, and Dyl and I crossed over toward the water tub to wash our hands.

"I'd like to meet them sometime," Dyl said. "And ZBoy."

"I'd like that, too. Maybe when… We'll figure it out." I was ashamed of my feeble answer. I had no clue how I could knit my old and new families together. If Pauline outed me as the *Dreamers* photographer, Dyl and the rest of the Merricks might never want to see me again.

"Close your eyes," Dyl said, reaching into his pack.

I obeyed, and soon felt something silky and soft in my hands.

Rontu, my old stuffed-animal dog; Dyl had retrieved her from the Gull. I nuzzled the ratty old dog, whose paws had elongated from stuffing that had migrated to the tips. I felt the Velcro seam in her midsection to check what she held in her belly.

The film I'd secreted away when I left the Gull was still there.

Rontu had been pregnant with my secrets for a long time.

Did Dyl know that? He'd vowed as a little boy that he'd never open her up again. But we all make silly promises when we're young.

Anxious, I cradled Rontu to my chest, but Dyl's warm smile told me he had no idea what she concealed.

"I didn't want her to stay in the junkyard all alone," he said.

"Oh, Dyl. Thank you." I settled the dog on my lap. "Remember what Rontu means?"

"Fox eyes. She names Rontu when she decides she can trust her."

I touched the toy dog's silky fur. I was so glad Dyl hadn't hardened over the years. But maybe he was only opening himself to more pain. Surely his heart had scars, rows and rows of wave-shaped scars, from how I'd abandoned him. But he'd let me back in, here.

If he found out I'd taken the picture, hidden the truth for so long, would he ever trust anyone again?

FIELD JOURNAL

Why should they trust me?

They'll think I'm a silly landlubber (oh, and even the word landlubber is so quaint they'd laugh at it. I feel both hopelessly younger than them, because of all they've experienced, and so very much older).

They assume I couldn't possibly understand the dualities and contradictions in their unconventional life.

But I do understand.

How's this for a contradiction—within the same moment, sitting in the library at home with the photograph on my lap, caressing its sterling silver frame, I could both cheer that life and question making it possible.

2002
The island
Day 2, afternoon

We joined the twins in the shade over by the fruit tubs, where Griff was still trying to make Pauline's fifty-thousand-dollar "honorarium" fit the Cap he'd known. "He can't have realized she'd try to pay us."

Mag mused half to himself, "You know, Charlie told me about these eccentric philanthropist types who donate to Channel Island causes. They boat over here one day, hear a spiel about island foxes or elephant seal pods needing help, and they write checks."

"So you think Pauline Cowley *pities* us?" Griff stood and paced. He was back in full patriarch mode. Lordly, protective. Cap's family was not to be pitied.

Mag pulled a coin from his pocket and began throwing it up and down.

"What, you want to decide this by coin toss?" Griff asked him.

Mag stopped and held it up: one of Cap's marked pennies, the ones he'd stamped to tell himself, and all of us, that money didn't matter. Since I'd left, the single coin I'd brought had taken on a different meaning for me, despite its more painful associations. I always kept the answering coin in my pocket, to place on the *M* penny the way we'd done in hotel courtyards as children, telling others *I'm here*. It was an act of hope. Hope that someone would come for me, and they finally had. But this was not the reunion I'd imagined.

Mag said, "Here's my answer to her damn question. *No*. The picture's not the truth. It's a lie, because it pretends money doesn't matter. And it does."

"If you're greedy and brainwashed," Griff said.

"I am not. Being greedy." Mag threw the coin, hard, at the rattling envelope.

Griff stood. "But fifty thousand and we're to sell our souls?"

Mag got up, too, and grabbed the fruit-paste canister at the end of our little assembly line, hurling it at a manzanita. Fuchsia compote dripped down the trunk. Splatter art, like what my sons had done in preschool.

Griff and I stared in shock.

Pauline's mere presence here had rendered us children again. Confused, frustrated children, aching to understand what our parents didn't deem us worthy to know, ashamed because of that ache.

Cap and Mama had fought to give us a dream life, and that life was supposed to be enough.

Dyl rose and, calmly, stood beside Mag. He placed one pink-stained hand on Mag's chest. "We need to tell them."

"Tell us what?" Griff and I asked at once.

"Mag's not being greedy," Dyl said. "We need money."

I nodded. "A thousand or so to repair the Gull? I can help. It'll take a few months, but I want to and it's better than doing the interview, so—"

"You have seventy thousand more handy?" Mag asked. "Because that's how much coin we really need."

Griff said, "We could buy a used van for three thousand. What are you talking—"

"I did something," Dyl said, jiggling his knee. "I'm the reason we owe so much."

"Owe who?" I asked with dread.

Dyl looked at me and Griff, his eyes glassy. "I'm sorry," he began. "I didn't—" And then he hurried off, the only trace of him a shiver in the trees.

18

Empty ocean, secret ocean

1985
El Zafiro, California
Fifteen years old

After the underground party and Charlie's departure, we drive
south. But the Gull crawls instead of soaring. Gas money is
scarce since Cap insisted on replacing the twins' boards immediately. One dawn I wake and we're on that weedy utility
road again, the one next to the Sapphire Resort.

Outside Mama, not Cap, stirs our cereal. "Cap is earning
a little money at that garage in town," she says. "May I braid
your hair, Little Seal?"

This means she's leaving soon for a ramble, and it will be
a long one since we're nested on the bare road we both hate.
And Cap will be inexplicably tense, like he always is here by
the hotel, with no Bass to cheer him up.

I nod at Mama, gulping back disappointment. And my questions: *If we do have to stay here, can't we park in the trees, at least?*
Why is this the only town where we park on a road? Why can't I
come with you?

I sit on a stump while she smooths my wild white hair, working out knots. She talks to every wayward curl. "Aren't you the

sweetest little troublemaker?" Her closeness, her hands fluttering by my neck and ears, aren't enough to block the thunks of hotel tennis balls beyond the trees.

Mama kisses us goodbye, and I turn my back so I don't have to watch her go. "'My sweetheart is fleet in the trees,'" Cap says of her, a quote from a poem, and I picture her now, graceful as she flees us. The twins, resigned, head off to surf, but I don't have the heart to join them.

First Charlie, then Mama. A few days ago I was soaring on that borrowed skateboard, confident and brave and in control, but now I'm a powerless child again.

I want to crawl under the covers of the empty Gull.

But when Dyl asks, "Mama will be gone a long time, won't she?" I know I have to distract us both.

"We're going on a secret ramble of our own today," I say impulsively.

I remove the ever-present leaf bits from Dyl's hair, comb and part it, and dress us in our only shirts with collars, pulling them up high like the rich citizens I've seen.

We're going to the hotel at last.

Ahead of us, the resort's buildings and pools and gardens are divided by walls, miles of white-painted adobe with a flower shape cut into each block.

I say with gentle certainty, as if I'm Mama, "That's called a breeze block and the design is a chocolate cosmos flower, and it brings good luck. Isn't it pretty?"

Dyl shakes his head; I'm trying too hard. He's not keen on this ramble, and I don't blame him.

Poor Dyl; I've tugged him along without explaining my motives. But even I don't understand why I feel compelled to come here. After surviving the underground party, I'm no longer intimidated by the hotel, and maybe I needed to prove to myself I'm not completely at the mercy of Cap and Mama's whims? But

I'm doing to Dyl exactly what Cap does to us. Leaving him in the dark. He's dying to ask *Why are we here?* but he's too loyal.

"Well, okay," I admit to Dyl. "It's not as nice as a real flower. But you can still diagram it in your field journal. You can write about all of this." And this seems to calm him.

We pass a pool. Slick, still bodies surround it, but no one swimming—it's an empty ocean. A gross waste of water, like Charlie said. *Over-the-top.* Waiters in blue shirts trot around, delivering slushy drinks and tacos that must cost ten times what they do at food trucks. The bodies draped on the long chairs sign room numbers on their bills without looking, some too lazy to sit up so the waiters have to kneel. A girl and her mother lie side by side in lemon-yellow swimsuits that seem like they've never touched water, a tall stack of magazines between them.

I square my shoulders and try to look like I have a room number to sign. What would the girl in the sundress think if she observed me?

The way we slept, the six of us, "a six-pack in a cooler," as a kid in Santa Cruz called us once. The sighs coming from Cap and Mama's bunk, the grunts from my big brothers'.

But she wouldn't see everything. A mother who tilts her head at the sun and says it is too fine a day to pin down, and I should go *make my own classroom.* She's just another Kelly Cul-de-Sac, another squealing girl at an underground party, nothing to envy.

Dyl looks up at me, ready to move on. "Ro?"

"That pool might as well be dry for all they're using it. Don't you feel sorry for them?"

I hurry on, along the path, toward the hotel's front entrance. "A sapphire is bluer than the water in that cove where we saw the sea turtle when you were six. Remember, Dylly?"

What I mean is *never mind these flat rich citizens.*

Our path slopes uphill, and then we're under a white roof

like an open tunnel, breathing mist. *Click.* I take a mental picture of it. A chute of clouds between manicured greenery.

Dyl whispers, "Miracle fog."

To the right of the hotel's lobby door there's an aviary with glass walls, birds of every color trapped inside. Next to it a doorman in a uniform says, "Good morning."

I make my voice bored; I'm a rich girl. "Good morning."

Dyl looks up at me in awe, at the aviary birds in pity.

"I know," I say, of the poor stuck birds. I lead him across the cool marble lobby, taking in its high cream ceilings, its murals and palms in pots, and the people. Everywhere—too many, too close for Dyl's liking.

"Cap doesn't like us going to hotel lobbies," Dyl whispers.

"It's not against the rules," I whisper back. "Just taking coins from the fountains." I comfort him, explaining the hotel's wonders like I have known them all my life. I tell him a mixture of true things I'm reading on plaques, and words in our library, and things I just like the sound of.

"That fountain is called Fleet Sweethearts," I say of a trickling blue-tiled bowl with stone statues of two girls in the center. There are no coins on the bottom. Has someone taken them, or do these people have everything they wish for?

Dyl pulls an *M* penny from his pocket and places it on the fountain's southernmost edge, recalling the games we used to play, the signal that meant one of us was near. He smiles up at me.

"We won't get it back," I say of the coin. "Are you sure?"

"They need it more than I do. Someone can make a wish with it."

≈

On the way back we take a different path, between tennis courts. Two men smoke cigars on one, watching a boy my age hit ball after ball from a red machine called a Lob-ster.

Mesmerized, we observe them through the white adobe walls with the flower cutouts.

"That's your prescription!" one of the men yells at the boy. "A thousand balls from the Lob-ster dispenser, so you won't collapse again next weekend!" He crosses the court to a bench near us, coming so close I can smell his sickly sweet cigar smoke.

"Enjoying that Partagas?" he calls to his friend. "Make Cohibas taste like garbage..." He trails off. Stares straight at me and Dyl; he's seen us through the breeze-block wall.

Dyl's confusion and fear pulse through our clasped hands.

"Get," the man says coldly, like he's shooing an animal.

"We won't hurry for him," I say quietly, and keep my shoulders back proudly, like Charlie's, as we walk away. Only when we're safely on the dunes north of the hotel's beachfront, and the thunks and pings of the tennis courts have quieted, does Dyl let go of my hand.

"Skunk," I say, of the cigar man, laughing to show Dyl it was nothing to worry about.

It *is* nothing to worry about. But it was an ugly, unsettling moment, and I won't ever go back to that grotesque hotel.

Taking my lead, Dyl says, "Birds and skunks and a lobster. A zoo." He says it bravely, but without conviction. And his voice sounds young again when he continues, "I wish we could tell Mama..." He trails off, his attention diverted by something up the dunes from us, in the weeds. "What's over there?"

I see what's caught his eye—a bit of chain-link behind the weeds.

"I don't know."

I'm drained, but can't disappoint Dyl after what I just put him through. There's a little split in the bottom of the chain-link fence, just enough for one person to bend it up and belly-crawl through the triangular opening. We crawl in to explore, and the stillness is a balm after the hotel, and I'm glad I indulged him. Just a weedy patch of land, but it hasn't been touched by people for a long time, and Dyl finds insects, birds, flowers that have taken over. He's safe here.

When the sun dips low, we find a tile-lined pond and climb into it. We lie back and stare up at the clouds. From down here, we can't hear any hotel sounds. It reminds me of lying back in the empty hot tub with Charlie.

"Do you think this was a pool?" Dyl asks.

"Maybe a fish pond."

"I like it better than that hotel pool."

"Me, too."

"Will you name this place, Ro?"

Mama told me long ago that giving places new names makes them ours. I learned to swim near Santa Barbara, in her Floating Forest. I collected poppies for pressing in San Francisco, in her Goldest Glade. The old well by the abandoned farmhouse in Fort Bragg is called the Sunken Mirror, and the trail through the aster bushes in Santa Ynez is Constellation Walk. She named the Gull.

And she named me. Even my middle name, Avery. *Ruler of elves.* The twins used to tease me about this due to my height— or lack of it compared with them. But then Mama said, "My mother had a storybook about it."

It was the only thing she'd ever said to us about her parents, about her life before us, and Mama's explanation hushed everyone.

Now I think hard, because this place needs the perfect name. A strong, enchanted name that *alliterates*, like lines in our Hopkins poetry book.

"The Secret Sea."

Dyl smiles up at the sky. "And it's ours. Only ours, left here just for us, for when we have to nest by the hotel? And it will always be here for us?"

I hesitate. It may only be a grown-over vacant lot, but the fence means it's an owned place.

Though what harm is there in making Dyl happy?

"Yes, Dyl. It will always be here for us."

The fenced lot between us and the hotel becomes our refuge for the next week. Dyl wanders around happily in it for hours, distracted from Mama's absence.

And I discover a new hobby here. It starts late one afternoon, unexpectedly, when I notice a heron taking flight. Its peach-colored legs are elegant and alien both, and it just happens. I ache to photograph it. Not in my head—for real. It's like my craving for water—all-consuming.

Late that night, when all three boys are asleep and Cap's working yet another late shift at the all-night mechanic in town, I fish the camera out of its hiding place in the Gull's rear door, and I creep out, sneak into Dyl's Secret Sea.

Moonlight welling in the pond—*click*.

A baby rabbit up on its haunches, throwing a long, elegant shadow across the crumbled stone path—*click*. The rabbit spots me, freezes. Twitches its nose, vanishes.

I experiment with the camera's timer, to take pictures of myself in moonlight. I set the camera high and low, using what's on hand. Crumbled tiles, a log.

I don't know if or how I will ever develop the photographs, and I have only the film remaining inside it, so I must conserve it. I capture a hundred mental pictures for every one that's on film.

I begin taking pictures outside the Secret Sea, too.

One morning, one mild, beautiful morning just north of the Secret Sea, all of us family surf together for once, even Mama. When no one's looking, I prop the camera inside an overturned garbage can on the beach. I set the timer to take pictures of us through the drainage opening shaped like a wave.

After everyone else goes in, Cap and I surf close to each

other for a while, something that rarely happens. A precious, rare ending to a perfect day.

That week I spot a one-hour photo-developing booth in a Carlsbad parking lot as we drive past it looking for our next nest, but I don't have enough money for even their smallest roll of film or cheapest developing.

Anyway, maybe it would destroy the magic of keeping my memory undeveloped, hidden in the dark. Who could I show my prints to, anyway?

Maybe they're better kept in my imagination.

Late one night, I creep home after taking pictures in the Secret Sea, and the twins are waiting for me outside the Gull. They look so stern I reach back for the now-familiar weight of the Leica camera in my backpack, assuring myself that I remembered to hide it, wrapping it in socks and a knit hat and zipping my pack completely.

"Where've you been?" Griff whispers.

"Just walking."

"She's been to the hotel again," Mag whispers. "We have to tell her."

"I haven't, not tonight. But what if I had? Why are you—"

"Shhh." Griff tugs me away from the van, down the gravel utility road, up to the dunes.

Only there, under the rattle of an old date palm, does anyone speak.

Mag says, "Let's tell her. It's no big deal."

Griff gazes south down the sand, off toward the Sapphire's blue roofs. In the moonlight, they're still black rectangles among the waving palms. "Cap's working at the hotel tonight. He works there sometimes. But you can't tell anyone."

"He works in the garage?" I ask, confused. "He fixes golf carts?"

Mag snorts, laughs.

Griff says, "Just don't go near that hotel again. Cap wouldn't like it. Even the two of us don't go there."

This infuriates me. The "even the two of us," as if he and Mag are superior beings.

But now everything bubbles over. How they hadn't told me about Cap working at the Sapphire. How we're stuck here while Cap earns money, most of it to pay for the twins' new boards, when I know somehow I will get no new board at sixteen. How Mama rambles while only I must watch Dyl and keep him content.

How I'll always be separate. And lesser. Part of the smaller half.

I stalk off back toward the hotel, Griff hurrying after me, Mag following more leisurely. When we hit the breeze-block wall that separates the path from the hotel garage where the golf carts are parked, Griff whispers in resignation, "Just be quiet, at least."

Then, I smell it—cigar smoke. Sickly sweet.

"Spectacular night," a man says. It's the hotel man, the skunk that Dyl and I laughed about. The man who made his son hit a thousand tennis balls from the Lob-ster machine. "You know I only do this for you, come here personally."

"And you know I appreciate that," Cap replies.

"How's the family manse? Add a hot tub yet?" Another slow intake of breath as the hotel man must be dragging on his cigar. Then puffs it out, *huuuuuuhhhhh.*

"Stop being cute, Julian."

"You really do like things the way they are, don't you? I'll never understand it, but *chacun son goût*, as the frogs say."

What a strange conversation, what a foreign language. Not *chacun son goût*, which I know from our French primer means *to each his own*. But everything else they're saying.

Centimeter by centimeter, I edge toward the wall to peek through a petal. Through a chocolate cosmos flower cutout, I watch Cap kneel near a golf cart. He holds a long stick with a mirror, to view its undercarriage. He finds what he's searching for, reaches in. Pulls out a flat white package, exactly like the ones I've seen holding money in the Gull's drainpipe.

Pieces come together. So this is his garage gig.

Suck, puff. "How many thank-yous can you deliver on this run?"

"These three. No more. And this is the last time."

"You say that every time."

A soft weight on my shoulder—Griff's warm hand, comforting me, or holding me back from doing something stupid. Both.

Cap retrieves two more flat white plastic packages from under carts.

"Bollinger'll get you the badge names tomorrow, usual place."

"Business is good, then."

"We're blessed, friend."

"Are we?"

This is their goodbye.

Cap tucks the white packages into the back waistband of his baggies and walks away toward the dunes.

The cigar man stays, looking up at the moon. A little business taken care of, a nothing man under his thumb for money, and he's earned every last drag of his cigar. Inhale, sigh. A cloud in a ring, drifting up.

Inhale, sigh. The cigar man blocks more stars with each exhale. Finally, he leaves.

I close my eyes and rest my cheek against the cold stone wall until Griff tugs me away.

≈

I lead the twins to the Secret Sea; I can't bear to go back to the Gull, to pretend, to smell cigar smoke on Cap. Not yet.

I show Mag and Griff the little opening in the fence, and the dry fish pond, but there's no comfort or beauty here right now. The three of us sit on the edge of the pond, dangling our legs in the emptiness.

"Cool place," Mag says. "We thought you were going to the hotel whenever you snuck out, sorry." Nonchalant as ever. As if we'd spied on Cap fixing a carburetor or flushing an oil line.

"I've seen packets like that before," I say. "In the van stove-pipe, with cash in them. I'm so stupid."

I'd thought Cap just had a way with cops. He's so charming with cops. Everyone says so. Cap has always claimed it's because they wish for our lives but don't know it; their despair is just a grain of sand inside their uniform, but if you can find it they treat you okay.

But, Mag explains, most of those encounters are just ways to hand off thank-yous up and down the coast from the hotel's owner to dirty cops...thank-yous in the form of white packets filled with money.

"He delivers cash from the hotel man so police officers will look the other way...from what?"

No answer—it's bad.

"Drugs," I say. "It's drugs, isn't it? The hotel is a...a..." A conduit? A waystation? The word eludes me.

"You don't need to worry about it," Griff says. "Cap knows what he's doing."

"He told you that?" I ask.

"Not exactly," Griff admits.

"The two of us followed him one night when we first came here," Mag says. "We've never talked about it."

"Does Mama know?"

No answer for a long time. Then Griff says, "I think she understands."

"But she doesn't like when we come here. She always leaves on a ramble." I cling to this. Mama doesn't know, or doesn't approve. "What kind of drugs?" I ask. "Coke?"

Griff looks up at the sky, Mag scowls. That's a yes.

"And they tape the money under the carts to move it around or hide it until they need it…"

Mag nods.

A *front*, that was the word. I'd read it in some story long ago. The owner of the resort, for all his property's splendor, needed or wanted even more money than he could make from rooms and golf games and manicures. Who'd suspect Cap? Just a surf bum, van trash. I think of everything he says about staying separate. The times we have extra food—fish and abalone stew and glistening honey tarts, not like the lean days when it's only rice or windfall oranges. The money for the twins' boards.

Cap acts like it's just chance. Like the world will right itself and fill your belly if you're patient. His speeches about pathetic citizens grubbing for money. How they choose to be trapped, and if only they knew there was a better way…

"It's just something he does," Griff says. "For us. He only does it when we really need money."

"Don't let on that you know." Mag points at me.

The next day, we soar north, but I wish I didn't know that our gas money comes not just from Cap's late nights working on cars, but from helping to move poison around. Because that's what he's always called drugs. *Poison*, worse than alcohol.

I wish Charlie was here, so I could say to just one person, *We hurt people so we can live apart from them.*

I write this to her, in a letter I may or may not send. *Charlie…* Every morning I rub a shard of her Plumeria surf wax on my wrist. I smell it now, as I toss and turn in my bunk. I close my eyes and picture her agile turn, the last morning we surfed together. With my index finger on the inside of my arm, I trace the arc of her back, the exact line of it over the water.

The next day, all afternoon, miles north, I attack waves, throwing myself on anything with possibility. It's a perfect day, a beautiful chest-high swell, not too crowded. Cap joins us and

I feel him watching me with approval, but I can't look at him. I need the water to work its magic. It always helps.

But in a spent moment when I'm on my stomach, idly paddling while I catch my breath, memories come on me suddenly. A girl we once saw OD under the pier in Monterey. She lived, but I can still see her twitching, a skin-and-bones rag doll.

Or I see Cap kneeling on that greasy garage floor while the hotel owner looms over him. That rich man, who could surely hand Cap the white packets instead of making him scrabble on the ground.

I look at Cap—godlike, meant to live like this—and place the image of him surfing over the other ones. *That is what I will do*, I tell myself, *until it's the only picture I remember.*

But it's not enough.

The next day, on the same afternoon that Cap looks out the front window at a bunch of skateboarders crossing the street and tells the twins "You two would be good at that" and no one even glances at me, not Griff or Mag, who saw me *drop in* on a borrowed skateboard, we happen to park in La Jolla. We're well concealed in the shade of eucalypti, but walking distance from the UC San Diego campus.

I remember what I saw on the bottom of that newspaper page used for kindling at that skateboarding party. *Got a photo to share with the* Triton?

By now I've been taking pictures, but not developing them or sharing my habit with a soul, for months.

And what comes next all happens very quickly. While the others nap, I venture to a one-hour photo kiosk with four dollars in scrimped coins and a single roll of film hidden in my pocket. The roll holds eight of that *Triton* reporter's shots—

And fourteen of mine, taken months ago. Some of them from inside an upturned garbage can, using the longest setting on the timer. And to my surprise, the photographs look pretty good, at least to my untrained eyes.

There's one taken in El Zafiro where all six of us are clear, spread out in a pleasing symmetry, the light dancing on the water as we rush straight toward it. I remember the day well, because Mama surfed with us after returning from a long ramble. And Cap and I stayed out longest, just the two of us. Both rare events, especially in that place. But the water and our closeness brought peace.

I name the picture privately—*Perfect Day*. Not knowing that my perfect day will continue forever, on T-shirts and towels, and, long since titled *The California Dreamers* by someone I'll never meet, that it will be blown up larger than life-size to loom high over museum visitors.

Late at night at a rest-stop picnic table, I clip out that negative with Mama's sewing shears. Two days after, I take a bus to the UC San Diego campus, find the newspaper office address on my camera's label, and push my photo submission through the mail slot.

It's shocking, how little time it takes. How quickly the pent-up anger and resentment of a lifetime can boil over.

It's like that narrow mail slot cut into the newspaper office door was waiting for me. Pushing the picture through it is like mailing a protest letter to myself.

I don't know that the whole world will see it.

And I feel better. Like I've balanced things out, somehow. Declared that Cap doesn't have all the answers.

Later, after the picture runs, and spreads, and gets bigger, and is put on objects for sale, bigger, in full color, bigger, and bigger still, and when it pursues all of us in a way I'd never intended or craved, I won't remember what made me do it.

Three days after I submitted the photograph

Dyl and Mag and I are sitting on the roof of the Gull reading when Griff pounds up the ladder in back. His movements are so loud and hurried, so unlike his usual steady demeanor, I know something has upset him before I turn and see his grimace. He skirts our board rack and in seconds he's looming above us, holding a newspaper. He hands it to Mag without a word, stabs the back page with his finger.

I look over Mag's shoulder: It's the UC San Diego *Triton*. There's a picture of the six of us running toward the water with our boards. It's barely three inches wide, on the fifth page, and it's in a collage-thing with a bunch of other beach photos. It's not the biggest one in the collage. There's a man eating a chocolate-dipped frozen banana who's four times our size.

Above the group of photos it says, "SunDays."

Dyl asks, "Is that really me?"

I shake my head, the only reassurance I can muster. I'm too shocked at the sight. I swallow. I'd forgotten how I looked in the picture. My hair's flying out in a cloud, taking up so much space. I'm gazing off to the side with this look on my face, like…like *I* have all the answers.

When right now, I can't even make sense of one simple fact: *I did this.*

The twins debate whether we should show the newspaper to Cap, their words barely audible, there's such a roar in my head. A roar like a thirty-foot-wave at Mavericks in November.

"…kid must've come back. As revenge…" Mag says.

"…should tell him…know how he is about pictures, and now…"

"It's just our backs, Griff. You can only make out Ro's hair, that's all. No one but us'd recognize it…a tiny college paper, forgotten tomorrow. We should just throw it away."

"…might see it himself, though."

"Lighten up," Mag says. "You only saw it because you were at the board shop, near campus, you said? Well, Cap'd never venture near UCSD. *Or* read a newspaper."

There is no name on the picture, not even the silly pseudonym I'd used on the note I'd pushed through the *Triton* office with the negative and print. As I'd observed in the hot tub at the party, when *Triton* pages had been used as kindling, there's no detailed credit for any of the shots on the collage page. Just "Triton Contributors."

No one will ever know I took it.

I'd been so angry the day I'd submitted it. At Cap for his hypocrisy. At the twins for ignoring me, after I'd felt so close to them, conspiring to cover for Mag's fight with Jaws.

At least that's what I'd told myself. My anger at Cap, at least, had seemed...noble. But the second I'd pushed the envelope holding my photograph through the office mail slot at nine at night, I'd regretted it. If the *Triton*'s door hadn't been locked, I'd have opened it and retrieved my little envelope holding the print and negative from the rubber mat inside. I could still spot it through the slim, rectangular opening, atop the other mail strewed around. I'd written on the outside with my left hand, "Local candids for the *Triton*, Kelly Culsac. Sophomore." While writing the cheerful note and the pseudonym, I'd thought, *This is either the most or least mature thing I've ever done. But they won't run it, not when they look up their student rolls and find there is no such student attending their fancy college...*

At last, with the twins and Dyl still huddled around me, I speak. I say it to the newspaper page with us on it, not raising my eyes to meet theirs: "I agree with Mag. Cap doesn't need to know."

"I vote with Ro," Dyl says.

"Looks like you're outvoted again, Professor," Mag says. "C'mon, the swell's picking up."

Griff hesitates, then sighs and hands me the newspaper. "Throw this trash out, will you, Ro?"

He and Mag take off to surf away the problem.

A college paper, forgotten tomorrow.

What is that expression I've read? "Lining birdcages tomorrow." The silly photograph of us will line birdcages tomorrow.

But I can't bring myself to throw it out. The negative I submitted to the *Triton* was the only one—and it means something to me. Like the coins Cap makes in garages. It's a tiny piece of defiance.

In the public restroom I tear out the picture, roll it into a black-and-white curl the size of my pinkie finger, and hide it behind a beam so I can return for it later.

19

Sapphires and coins

2002
The island
Day 2, late afternoon

"What have you and Dyl not told us, Mag?" I asked after Dyl ran off, as Griff sank next to me on the grass.

Mag took a deep breath. "Dyl got into some trouble. Last month."

Pacing in front of us, occasionally pounding a tin of fruit leather in a frustrated drum solo, he explained. He began with a quote of Cap's: "'The chain of sapphires grows ever-longer.'"

The chain of sapphires was the Sapphire Resort in El Zafiro.

"Dyl got into trouble at the hotel?" I asked.

"That plot of undeveloped land abutting it, near where the picture was taken," Mag said. "Remember? You and Dyl were pretty fond of it."

An understatement. We'd treated it like sacred land.

"I remember," I said.

Mag hesitated, then went on. "They're finally developing it, expanding the hotel. New time-share and spa and conference wings. Five-star all the way, no van trash allowed within a mile."

"They're destroying the Secret Sea," I said softly. "How sad."

"Yeah," Mag went on. "Greedy prick, that hotel owner."

I wanted to stop my ears from the rest, but I needed to understand where this was all leading.

"So Dyl and I were surfing nearby," Mag continued. "This was five or six weeks before Cap died, right before we realized the press had identified us and the van bumper in the museum-exhibit picture, the whole other nightmare waiting. I didn't know the hotel expansion was coming, I was trying to cheer Dyl up. Cap couldn't hide being sick anymore, Mama was a mess…

"So anyway," Mag went on. "I was at the showers and Dyl was alone on the beach. And this reporter from the *Sun-Register*…" Mag shook his head, envisioning it. "He approaches Dyl and tells him about the land development just south. All the gory, money-making details. Asks if he wants to comment, given his family's 'unique ties to the area.'"

"No," Griff said, anger flaring in his eyes.

"Yep," Mag said. "Dyl wants to bail but he's desperate to see the development, of course. So the reporter walks him over there where it's fenced off. Hoping to get quotes, his reaction, whatever. And the design renderings have just gone up, showing the finished development in all its glory. Slick placards staked in the ground, with diagrams, and photos of people getting seaweed facials, and taking meetings with a view of the golf course, sitting under umbrellas, swimming… And…" Mag paused dramatically. "Guess what other picture they're using to lure potential time-share buyers?"

No.

"Ours," Griff said. "Since it's uncredited, they consider it fair use."

"Yep. Taken near that very sand—you can tell from the banyan tree roots when it's blown way up," Mag said. "A historical touch."

He continued, his voice a murmur in the background. I was right there with Dyl, hearing the birds in our secret sea, feeling the cool shade of its overgrown boughs. Feeling his pain, his powerlessness in that moment.

"… In fairness, the reporter was trying to get the environmentalist angle on the development. And it's not like we have a telephone, or like he knew Dyl's…personality…"

I pictured the Sapphire Resort owner with his cigar, lording it over his ever-growing empire. Over Cap. How dare that vacuum inside a Tommy Bahama shirt destroy our refuge.

But a steady beat of shame also pulsed through me. Because the Secret Sea was never ours, and I shouldn't have made Dyl believe it was. He'd trusted in the magic of the place, the stories I'd concocted there. Our own little reality. I'd promised, *It'll always be here when we need it…*

"… Dyl walked off without a word. That's what the guy put in his article. 'One long-time area surfer too shocked to comment…' But Dyl was…" Mag shook his head.

I stood and paced, trying to collect myself. "So when Dyl learned they were ruining that land he took it hard."

"That's one way to put it," Mag said. "Another is he booked down to the resort in the middle of the night, yanked the sign with our picture on it out of the ground, ran over to the hotel, and used it to smash the glass walls of the aviary all to hell."

I closed my eyes, leaning my forehead against a fir branch. *Oh, Dyl.*

Mag said, "He cut up his arms and feet, left a trail of blood that led the cops to the van." He went on with the grim facts. "Trespassing, destruction of property, B and E. He did five thousand dollars' worth of property damage, apparently. A felony is anything over a thou. It's thirty thou, if you include the birds that got out. But that part of the charge sheet is bogus because I know for a fact nearly all the stupid birds came back.

They only lost one hyacinth macaw and, I don't know, some green-toed warbly-face chacalacha."

None of us laughed.

"Dyl got arrested," I said.

Mag nodded. "Arrested, but not charged. I dealt with it. His record is clean...for now."

"You bought someone off in the PD?" I asked.

"No. But we settled it, shall we say, paralegally."

"Is that like paranormally?" Griff asked with dry resignation.

"It was the only way," Mag said. "Could you picture Dyl in county, even for a night?"

No. God, no. The idea was heartbreaking.

I said, "So you borrowed money to make the problem go away, and I take it you don't mean from a bank."

Mag shook his head.

I sank against the tree trunk and buried my face in my hands. I wondered what kind of lowlifes had loaned Mag the money to help Dyl; maybe I didn't want to know.

My family wasn't just struggling; they were every flavor of screwed up. They didn't even have proper shelter, with the Gull in the RV graveyard. Mag claimed they'd been crashing with friends, but I wondered if this was true. I imagined them camping on cold beaches, sleeping in the park, cops shoving them at 3:00 a.m. If they didn't get money from Pauline, that would be their lives forever.

And I would be to blame.

"Mama doesn't know," Mag said. "She was dealing with enough. And we never told Cap, but I wonder if he found out."

"Quite the coincidence," Griff said, then didn't speak for a while, considering.

When Griffin had first mentioned "media attention" due to the museum show, I'd pictured reporters tramping over our sweet-smelling lavender fields, hounding my sons. I'd feared the truth coming out about who took *Dreamers*, and the Merricks turning their backs on me for good.

But now, only two days later, I found *I* couldn't turn my backs on *them*, come what may. That would be a permanent obliteration of all they meant to me. And not just of the five Merricks on the island, alive and dead. Of me. My history. The years of my life that made me who I was.

"We should do the interview," I said softly.

"What about your life in Oregon?" Mag asked, brow furrowed over my reversal.

My life...meaning my *lies*.

"I don't know what I'd tell people there if my past got out," I admitted. That was a risk I would have to take. "But I want to help."

My brothers went silent. Dyl crept back then, visibly weighed down by shame, and I guessed he'd been eavesdropping. He sank to the ground next to me and I hugged him hard. I whispered, "Mag told us how they were provoking you, about the development. None of this...*none of this*. Is your fault."

He nodded at his feet, but I knew I hadn't convinced him.

"It'll be all right, little brother." Griff squatted next to us, clapping Dyl's knee. "Cap would have understood."

Mag sat, too, tapping Dyl's foot with his. "We'll handle it together, the four of us."

Dyl was still so quiet, so stricken with guilt, that even though he was twenty-five I pulled Rontu-dog out of my pack and set him on his knees, in the center of our circle of four, to try to cheer him up. "The five of us."

After a few minutes, Mag said, "It's moronic to be afraid of a...snapshot." There was a strange relief in his voice, as if disclosing this mess with Dyl and the Secret Sea had lifted a weight off him. "Is *Dreamers* the truth? Sure. Life was and is still perfect. We only need sun and waves, nothing more."

Griff: "And Cap had all the answers and explained them to

us in minute detail, just like he did inviting *SWELL* magazine to his wake."

Mag and Dyl's sudden, wide-eyed silence said they were just as shocked as I was. Griff had never, to my knowledge, admitted frustration with our father.

But the twins were right; we could tell this stranger anything. That our upbringing in the van had been one blissful day after another, that Cap and Mama had been perfect parents, perfect people, and none of us had a single reason to long for anything different. Perhaps that's all she wanted—a pretty article to match the pretty photograph.

"Right," I said. "We'll sit for the interview. We'll plan it all out and control every word, and Pauline Cowley will never know we're lying to her."

"Excuse me."

It was Pauline, resplendent in a silk fuchsia pantsuit.

20

Kulldasack

2002
The island
Day 2, late afternoon

Pauline stood on a small knoll above us. She was sunburnt, wobbly, panting. Sweat stains bloomed on her short-sleeved fuchsia shirt, and she waved a crumpled white paper at us, seemingly too tired to talk.

Griff collected himself first, walking up to her and beckoning all of us to follow. "Ms. Cowley, welcome!"

Mag asked bluntly, "How did you get over here?" At a sharp look from me he covered quickly, "I mean, wow, you're a good hiker!"

"Rest," I urged her, spreading a clean towel in the shade and helping her sit. I offered her my water canteen and she glugged gratefully.

At last she spoke. "I feel so foolish. I found this map in the shed. And it didn't seem far. I wanted to see you. Explain." A cough—she'd gulped too fast. "It's…harder than it looks on the map. Excuse me." She was still pale, faintly green, in fact.

Charlie burst through the trees behind me, panicked. "You

won't believe it, but that fucking reporter's disappeared! I left her alone for five minutes and—"

"Charlie, look who's here!" Griff said, and Charlie strode over, coming to a stop between Mag and me. Now we formed a tight circle around our visitor. A nervous, embarrassed foursome.

"I'm sorry," Charlie started. "I was worried about you, so—"

"So foolish," Pauline repeated, cutting Charlie off as if she hadn't heard her cussing her out. "Those rocks were something. And then the elevation."

"The terrain's difficult, especially those rocks on the west side of the island," Griff said kindly. Now that we needed the money, we had to put on the right face for Pauline.

"So you write for *SWELL*?" Mag asked. He towered over her, and maybe that's why it sounded more aggressive than he'd intended.

We were all thinking it…but with a disbelieving emphasis on *you* that Mag had, luckily, resisted.

You write for *SWELL*? With her prim, short-sleeved pantsuit, her salon-highlighted blond coif, and her general air of "indoor infection," as Cap used to put it, Pauline hardly looked like a surfer. Or even someone who dabbled in surf writing.

"I." Pauline swallowed. She was definitely green. "I freelance. This will be my first—first piece for *SWELL*. I usually write for…"

I took the map from her—it still had tape on the edges from where she'd peeled it from the workshed wall—and waved it at her neck to cool her, while Charlie pulled an energy bar from her pack and unwrapped it. Pauline pursed her lips and shook her head with a polite "No thank you, Charlie."

It was hard not to feel for her. Summoned here by Cap, and from the looks of her outfit and gear he hadn't told her how rugged the setting for her interview would be. We'd stuffed her in an old tin-roofed shed on the other side of the island, assuming she'd wait for us. You had to admire her pluck. But even as I wafted the map up and down at her and she nodded at me gratefully, I reminded myself, *She is not our friend.*

"I'm Magnus," Mag said. "And that's Griffin, and this is…" He cast a confused glance at me, wondering, I guessed, if he should say Ava, or Ronan, or some alias. Mag settled on no name at all, hurrying on, "And Dylan."

Except there was no Dylan, we realized, looking around at the bushes and trees surrounding us. He must have bolted again when Pauline appeared.

Already this was not the controlled, carefully planned interview we'd discussed five minutes ago.

Pauline said, with great effort, "I'm so glad to meet you all. I—I recognize you from." A nervous swallow. "From the photo."

Then she threw up.

"Finally, someone outside the family gives their honest reaction to that photo," I whispered to Mag.

He snorted, covered his mouth just in time. "Not funny, Ro."

Griff and Charlie had taken charge of Pauline, who insisted she was fine now. Charlie had declared her overheated and maybe a little altitude sick from her too-quick climb uphill. She rested in the shade with them with a damp cloth on her forehead, all apologies for her "impulsive" decision to hike over to our side of the island alone.

Mag and I, out of her view, scribbled notes on the back of a LeClair Lavender Farm brochure I'd found in my duffel. Safe things to talk about during our interview, topics to avoid. We figured we could eat up half an hour just detailing the surf conditions where *Dreamers* was shot.

Now that Pauline was here, a fuchsia presence on our side

of the island, I couldn't stop thinking about how we had underestimated her.

"I hope I didn't insult her too much with that *SWELL* comment." Mag checked over his shoulder to be sure Pauline was still out of earshot. "It just came out."

"She's hard to read. She's so genteel on the surface, but there's something tenacious about her." Tenacious and hard to trust. It seemed unlikely that she only wanted a sweet story to match the photograph, so the more time we could eat up with preplanned answers, the better. "Oh! We could tell her how Cap taught us to respect locals before we could even swim. Surf etiquette."

"That's good, write that down."

"And we throw technical surf terms at her. That's another half hour, at least."

"Hey, what if we do the interview on the boat? Pretend it's so we won't be spotted. She doesn't know anything about the marine traffic here, or where the government workers visit…"

"Then whenever we want, we say, *time's up* and the Merricks disembark!" I said. "Mag, you're brilliant."

"And Charlie ferries her back to Santa Barbara on the *Kai* before dark. Easy."

Griff came over. "I'm going to grab one of our boards so we can carry her to camp. It'll work as a stretcher. She says she doesn't need it, but I'm not taking any chances. And—"

"Let's take her down to the west-side dock instead," Mag interrupted. We filled Griff in on the plan to conduct the interview on the boat so we'd have an easy getaway.

"Good thinking," Griff whispered. "If we carry her, it won't take long. Let's get this charade over with."

FIELD JOURNAL

There's a poem in the library. Robert Frost.
I like this line →
"… Has given my heart. A change of mood.
And saved some part. Of a day I had rued."

That was today.
I felt weak and alone and frightened. And so very foolish.
I was ready to steal the boat and leave.
Seeing their kind, familiar faces swept all that away for a moment.
Seeing how they fit together so perfectly made it worthwhile.
Flying here, fumbling my way into their memorial.
Vomiting.
(Note for future magazine assignments—silk shantung pantsuits
are best reserved for interviews in hotel lobbies)

A family, together again after years of separation, is more beautiful
than any dust of snow…

2002

The island

Day 2, late afternoon

We took off, heading southwest. In front, Griff and Mag carried an embarrassed but compliant Pauline, who lay on her back on Griff's tan-and-white-striped board, secured by a pair of someone's pants knotted around her and the board at her hips. Griff at the nose, both hands behind him gripping Pauline's "stretcher," Mag holding the tail.

Charlie and I followed, weaving around trees, as the grade turned to a slight, steady downhill.

Another parade, like Dyl's arrival at camp with his wild menagerie yesterday. But this one was even more surreal. The board holding Pauline curved, rose, dipped. When the boys climbed over a downed fir trunk and Pauline rode her board, strapped in, it looked exactly like she was coasting over a steeply pitched little wave.

"At least she's getting a taste of surfing," I murmured to Charlie.

She laughed. "That's a two-footer, at least. Five if you measure mainland-style."

For a while after that Charlie and I said nothing, eyes on the odd trio in front of us. Then the trees thinned, and we began the steeper descent down rocky, dry terrain I hadn't seen yet.

"I really can walk now." Pauline's gentle voice wafted back. "This is so silly."

But the twins wouldn't hear of it, telling her she could turn an ankle in her exhausted state. Just as important—we were making good time.

"Life is so boring with the Merricks around," Charlie said archly. "Nothing ever changes."

"We *are* a dull family." I smiled, remembering what Charlie had said after the party in 1985, when I'd dropped into the empty pool on a borrowed skateboard and we'd explained our run-in with the man nicknamed Jaws.

That night we'd been walking downhill through a ritzy neighborhood. Now we were picking our way to sea level on island rocks.

Again came the low bird call, the pretty one I'd asked Griff about when I'd first arrived. Only yesterday? It felt like much longer: *Whishooolleeee… Whishooolleee.*

"That's a burrowing owl. They nest near the low vegetation on this side," Charlie explained, reading my mind.

"I like your office," I said. "It's special here, Charlie." I looked at my sandals, not wanting her to see how good it felt to say her name. I'd whispered it, alone in the fields, over the years. "You could lose your job, though, couldn't you? For bringing us here?"

"I wanted to help," Charlie said at last. She shrugged. "Your family…they're important to me."

She had a white gleam of sunscreen above her right eyebrow, a fingernail's-width smear that she hadn't quite blended in. A precious bit of evidence that she wasn't perfectly efficient and organized, that she had retained some of her teenage chaos despite her crisp light brown Department of Fish and Wildlife uniform. I hoped her bedroom was messy, cluttered with books and posters, even if the writers and musicians had changed. I hoped she still raced to get outside every morning.

"I'm glad they could see this place," Charlie said. "I wish I'd brought them here before. It shouldn't have taken, well, a funeral. I wish… Anyway, you know who sparked my love of natural science, don't you?"

I smiled. "Dyl." I wondered where he was. It wouldn't surprise me if he was tracking us just out of view. He would want to keep tabs on Pauline's location, and knew we needed him for the interview.

"So I wouldn't have any job without the Merricks," Charlie added. "I owe you."

Drizzle hit my shoulders and I glanced up; I'd been so focused on our strange convoy and Charlie's equally surreal presence at my side, I hadn't noticed the sky turning pewter.

Charlie tipped her head up, too, checking the clouds and wind. "Storms come fast here. We should hurry." Looking ahead of us at the twins, she asked, "What are your brothers doing now?"

We watched the twins, twenty feet ahead of us and downhill. They'd stopped to make a little roof over Pauline using their two windbreakers zipped together. They tied the sleeves of one windbreaker onto the back of Griff's backpack straps, pulled the fabric taut above her and the board, and knotted the other two sleeves to the front of Mag's pack.

"We can tell Pauline about Cap's cleverness with his hands," I said. "We inherited that, I guess." I mentally scribbled another note on the back of the lavender brochure in my pocket, adding to the list of anodyne topics for Pauline: *Resourceful, frugal etc. Environmentally friendly*.

"Will you help us in the interview, Charlie?" I asked. "Jump in and change the subject if she digs into anything we don't like? And make sure I…you know, act controlled and calm and mature, like the civilized citizen I've become?"

"Of course I'll help. But." She shook her head. "Never mind."

"What?"

Charlie didn't speak right away. And when she did, she sounded worried. "You're preparing for this interview like Pauline's hell-bent on ripping Cap apart. I'm not going to call it *obsessive*, but it's…interesting."

"Cap died and we want to protect him. That's natural, isn't it?"

"Of course! I just wonder if… Look, I get it. You don't know her, you never asked for this attention, you all deserve privacy. But would it be the worst thing in the world to admit to an outsider that the life he chose for you wasn't perfect? Could it maybe be healing?"

I didn't answer.

She touched my wrist. "I'm sorry."

"It's all right. It's a fair question."

We walked on for quite a while, and then Charlie said in a lighter tone, "I hope you're not too 'controlled and mature' in real life, though. The Ronan I remember could be impulsive."

I looked askance at her. I'd thought of myself as obedient, with some notable exceptions. Which did she mean? "Impulsive, how?"

"Oh. Throwing herself into swimming pools her first time on a skateboard." A pointed pause. "And other things."

Like the impulsive thing I'd done a certain night when I was sixteen. I couldn't tell if that's what was on her mind or if it was only me remembering, but reliving that moment, my cheeks warmed and I rushed to fill the silence:

"Mentally I'll be throwing things at Pauline for coming here. So share some happy anecdotes about Cap and your dad if things get tense, please— Hey, how is he, by the way?!"

"He's good. Heartbroken he couldn't come, but he just had knee surgery… So anyway, I'll quote Pauline a poem he gave me to recite in Cap's honor at the paddle-out. 'O Captain! My Captain!'"

"That doesn't sound like Bass."

"It's not. He made up one of his atrocious limericks for me to recite. But I memorized that 'O Captain!' poem in school and Pauline'll never know. We'll deal with her, and then I'll run her to Santa Barbara before nightfall."

I hesitated, but couldn't stop from blurting it out. "But you *will* come back, right? I mean. In time for the paddle-out tomorrow morning?"

Charlie stared at me without smiling. "Would you want me here?"

I nodded, my heart picking up its pace.

"Okay," she said. "Just checking."

The wind increased, rattling palm fronds and leaves, and the clouds over the ocean, down the craggy hill to our left, looked ominous, coming closer every time we glanced that way. The drizzle had fattened to rain. "If the twins slip on these rocks and drop our honored guest, we're not doing any interview today," I said. "How far are we?"

"Another thirty minutes."

Ten minutes later, rain was sheeting down my back.

Just twenty minutes more and we'll be safely at the boat, I told myself. Then a tree limb snapped in front of me, thwacking my shoulder.

"You okay?" Charlie called.

I nodded, but my shoulder felt far from okay. Nothing was broken but pain sliced down my right arm when I tried to lift it more than a few inches.

"Let's hurry," I managed. But my voice was lost under a roll of thunder. And then a giant Z of electric white crackled in the sky down to the churning gray water.

"The boat's too far!" Charlie shouted. "We have to make a lean-to!" She ran ahead to tell the boys.

Our carefully laid plan to get the interview over with and Pauline back on the boat before nightfall had been washed away with the rain.

I had no idea what Charlie's plan was—build whalebone huts on the sand like Juana Maria had? Hardly time for that.

But we all followed her south, toward the water, a blur of brown coat with a black mirror of hair down her back, obscuring the top of her DFW logo. We ended up under a stand of palm trees overlooking the sandy beach Griff had described, which collected "every piece of flotsam in the Pacific."

Charlie pointed—three DFW rafts like the one I'd seen yesterday morning when I made land on the other side of the island. Orange rubber ovals, each the size of two surfboards side by side.

"We use these for gathering water samples!" Charlie shouted, dragging one by its rope. She gestured at the boys, who set Pauline's rig down and ran over to help.

The four of us flipped the rafts and set them under palms, hurriedly propping them on ocean debris to raise them, fortifying the sides with even more flotsam to hold them in place. We used whatever we could grab: an igloo cooler, an aluminum chair, a gray Rubbermaid trash can, driftwood. In the end we had three decent if homely and slightly drippy shelters.

As I was leaning Griff's surfboard against the side of one to make it more watertight, a pair of familiar, long-fingered hands appeared next to me. A faint scent of oranges and cloves, diluted by rain but unmistakable: Had she been following us the whole time, or waiting for us here?

"Did you hurt yourself?" Mama asked over the wind.

I was favoring my left arm, but thought I'd hidden my banged-up right shoulder well.

I shook my head, but she insisted on patting me to check

my injury as rain drenched us. "It's not broken or dislocated. But rest it, promise?"

I nodded, then watched in disbelief as Mama dashed to Pauline, leading her under the shelter with the surfboard.

Thunder clapped, the twins dived under the second pontoon.

After a second's hesitation and a slight laugh, Charlie pulled me into the third.

So here we were. Two of us in each shelter. A little triangular neighborhood of three houses.

I pictured it from above—how our orange shelters would look if I took a stick and scraped a circle along the inside, in the wet sand. Double lines leading to each entrance.

A cul-de-sac.

FIELD JOURNAL

"The best-laid plans of mice and men…"

*I don't have the energy to transcribe every line of that poem right
now, though I know it by heart. When I was younger
its Scottish words fascinated me. Well, they still do.
We are Scottish by ancestry, Mama once said, and she gave Burns a
prominent place in our library, above the wide fuchsia volume
of Botanica Americana she loved so much, and from which
she taught us nearly every day.
Unhurried, meandering lessons, taught as often in the library as
out in our vast garden, on a "ramble."
While Father paced in his office…or seethed through the window,
tapping his watch to remind Mama that we had places to go.
They were so different.*

*Curling up next to a library shelf sounds like heaven right now,
but it's so far away.
And no longer ours.*

*It's cold, and raining hard, and everyone has taken shelter.
The interview will not happen today.*

*I don't expect to sleep tonight.
My impulsive actions got us here, and I can't back out now.*

*Would I undo what I've set in motion?
I'll tell you tomorrow.*

PART THREE

PART THREE

21

Bruce Balboa & Kenny's Surf Outfitters

1985
Morro Bay, California
Sixteen years old

I turn sixteen, and as I expected, there's no new board or mention of one in a year. Not even a fresh puck of wax.

But I understand. Money is tight. Cap sprained his right wrist badly, hitting reef at Trestles, and can't do garage work. He looks worried all the time. His face drawn, his shoulders taut. He checks his bandaged hand constantly, probably slowing its healing when all he wants is to have it back.

And Mama…lately she exists only as a whispered discussion behind the library wall, a touch of Dyl's cheek, the tip of one of my braids in parting. She's off trading her soap, gathering windfall fruit, maybe just trying to get her mind off our money troubles.

I guess Cap was telling the truth when he told the man at the hotel "This is the last time." We have no more white packets in the stovepipe; I peek often now. And we haven't gone near the hotel.

With wave after wave, I have tried to drown the memory of Cap in that hotel garage, and I have failed. But over time, I have washed it clean. He did it for us. He only did it when we really needed money. And he's stopped.

He's stopped, but I still take pictures. Since the one in the *Triton* was published, I have taken a thousand mental pictures and eleven real ones.

But they're only for me now—I'll never share them.

Mag, Dyl, and I are reading on the sand, in the Gull's shade. Charlie mailed me a puck of Mrs. Palmer's wax, gardenia flavor, and I put as much on my wrists as my board, and as I read *Island*, I breathe in the scent, like it's part of the story.

Charlie. When I saw her handwriting on the package, I felt a curious flutter, deep in my stomach. I didn't just miss her company, her conversation. I missed the *feeling* of her, in the simplest sense of the word. Her breath on my neck, as we sat two on a board, scouting waves. Her hand on my wrist. Her knee knocking mine...

Cap says *Island* is "too young for me," so I'm careful to open it less than I want to. Since my birthday I've read *David Copperfield* and *Call of the Wild* and *Dharma Bums* and *Travels with Charley.* But I always come back to *Island.*

I'm just at my favorite part, where Karana fights the wolves, when Griff collapses onto the sand by us. "Does she *hate* the island this time?" he jokes. At one time his good mood wouldn't have been notable, but now it catches me off guard. He's been acting off for months. Frustrated by our lean rations, counting down the months until he turns eighteen and Cap will let him earn money.

I've missed Griff's cheer. I didn't realize how much until this moment, witnessing its return—his smile in the middle of his new chin-hair dots that are trying to be a beard.

"Where've you been all morning, bro?" Mag asks him.

"I walked down to Morro Bay." Griff glances at Dyl, who's copying coral diagrams from a book into his Mer field journal, and lowers his voice. "There's a surf contest next week. Amateur stuff, but they're giving out cash prizes."

Mag knows where this is headed. "You're kidding yourself."

"What if I registered under a fake name? Stuffed my hair down my suit like Charlie does? We need cash."

"It's risky," I say.

"You already registered, didn't you?" Mag asks. "You're delusional, bro."

"Have you seen our meals lately?" Griff's good mood has vanished, and he hurls his towel in the bushes. "There's no rule about surf contests."

"You can't. Griff?" I shake my head. "You're outvoted. You know he hates contests even if it's not a rule."

Bad enough that I have betrayed Cap. I can't watch Griff do it.

Mag proposes something to cheer his twin up; Griff won't participate, but we'll go watch the 18-and-Under contest together.

So the next day, the four of us rise early for the long walk to Morro. From the safety of the dune grass, we spy on the competition, and it's clear Griff would've won easily. The scene is chaotic, though. Loudspeakers, blaring music, judges recording points, countdown clocks, sponsors, T-shirts. So much money to be made off what we do every day just for the joy of it.

"All four of us could've swept our divisions." Griff's shoulders tilt, sway. Even sitting down, he's imagining what he would do on the current swell, where the competitors have a few more minutes to impress the judges. When the female contestants battle it out, Griff says of the leader, "Look at her. Ro, you'd crush her."

I can't argue. And a fifty-dollar prize would be a dream right now. Yesterday, in secret, I fished twenty-three cents from the fountain in the Hilton lobby to buy Dyl a pack of cheese crackers.

Griff rises and zig-zags down the bluffs toward the contest before we know what's happening.

"What's he doing?" I ask Mag, worried.

"You think I can read his mind?"

"You usually can." Because Mag had whispered something to me as we walked over: Griff secretly dreamed of competing. My heart broke for him, but it was also frightening. Griff was our steady one.

I watch Griff as he approaches one of the long white tables on the beach, talking to a woman, taking something from her… Relief surges through me. "It's okay. He's only taking free things."

Griff returns, raining energy bars with a surfer logo down on us. Only pride stops me from devouring mine on the spot. Then something else flutters into my lap—a brochure from the event.

"Happy?" Griff asks.

"What am I looking for?" I ask.

"Page two. Guess who I was going to be?"

There, I see it. "Bruce Balboa, Covina, Calif.—withdrawn." Or, as we know to be the real case, a no-show.

"Bruce Balboa?" Mag laughs.

Of course Griff'd pick that pseudonym. Bruce after Bruce Brown. Balboa for his favorite break near Newport.

As the four of us trudge back to the van, I poke Griff. "I'm sorry, Bruce."

"It was a ridiculous impulse. Cap's right about contests. I'll find another way to make money."

We stretch those energy bars out for a week.

Three nights later

Over a beach campfire, I'm idly reading between stirring our pinto beans, the boys lazing nearby, when Cap's voice pulls me from Karana's world to this one.

"Entertaining literature, Ronan?"

I hand him my book. When Cap's upset about something in the citizen world, he paces and gestures, his voice rising like a preacher I heard once through an open chapel door. But this quiet voice like ice—we don't hear it often.

He's thumbing through the contest brochure I'd used as a bookmark.

I shoot Griff a worried look. Does he somehow know Griff entered that contest? That he's the flaky "Bruce Balboa"?

But Cap's not searching for the list of entrants. He unfolds the contest brochure to a page we all flipped right past earlier, spreads it out. And what he holds up for us is surreal.

It's us. Our picture.

My picture, the same one that ran in black-and-white in the UC San Diego newspaper months ago.

Except now it's bigger. Placed in a circle with a yellow border and rays. We're inside a cartoon sun. A full-color ad for Kenny's Beach Outfitters.

It feels impossible. And yet there we are, the six of us running across the sand toward the ocean.

22

Grins

"You knew that college student with the camera came back after that night, that he took more pictures of us. And ran this one in his newspaper, but you. Didn't. Want to. Worry me."

Cap's voice is even, quiet, but I know he's full of rage. We've confessed about seeing the *Triton* nine months ago, and how we kept it from him.

"It was my decision." Griff holds himself high. "I made a mistake."

"We voted," Mag says.

Drowning in cowardice or shame, I let the twins do all the talking. I wish Mama was here to soothe Cap with her tincture pots. Lemon-honey balm on his temples to clear his thinking. Lavender under his nostrils to calm him.

Cap pulls more contest brochures from his trunk pockets. Stacks of them.

They're all folded open to our picture. Cap's breathing is heavy as he sets them down on the sand between us, one by one—we're everywhere. And in this printing, I'm not just a black-and-white silhouette with a cloud of hair. It's clearly me in the photo. And you can see part of the Gull's bumper.

"You're the oldest, Griffin. I'm so disappointed, you—"

"It's not his fault." I have to scrape it out.

"Ro's right. It's that weasel college kid who's responsible. Maybe he even made money off this." Mag's picked up one of the brochures and he's studying the picture, disbelieving.

Cap ignores us both.

Griff tries to change the subject from blame to the *how* of it— by what dark magic did our photo jump from a little college-paper collage to a color advertisement a hundred miles away? "Did that boy sell it to the store to use in their advertisement, do you think? Or did the college maybe—"

"They don't care who they hurt," Cap says. "Whose lives they taint." His voice breaks, hidden rage turning to hidden despair, and even in my confusion I ride a small swell of pity for him.

Cap scoops up the brochures and marches off toward the water, Griff trailing after him. "I'll come. I'll help, we'll get to the bottom of it."

But Cap only raises his hand in dismissal. Ankle-deep in the shallows, he hurls the bright sheaf of papers into the Pacific.

I don't want to look at Griff. If he's crying, I'll cry, too.

I gather up the brochures Cap missed, staring at my own profile, replicated on each one. How strong I look. How care-free. What's happened is so unexpected, it simply doesn't seem possible that I took the photo now.

"He's worried," I say softly. "About money, his hand."

"It's fine," Griff says, his voice a little steadier. "It's my fault he's upset. I should've told him the second we saw the picture in the newspaper."

Mag says, "It wasn't our fault that guy came back, or ran it in the *Triton*."

"So you think Cap went to that Kenny's store to confront

them about their ad or…" Clutching the stack of Kenny's Surf Outfitters brochures, I realize what's missing.

"Karana," I say senselessly. What I mean is she's gone—my *Island* book's gone. Cap swept her up with the brochures.

Griff races to the water, duck-diving. Though I'm wishing desperately for a glimpse of the bright yellow cover with Karana standing proud on the rock, her hair streaming to the side, I know it's pointless. Cap has a strong arm and the book's nowhere.

Cap returns hours later, eerily calm. Mama's with him. He always seems to know how to find her. His expression is indecipherable under the shadow of his hat.

Maybe Cap did confront the Kenny's Surf Outfitters owner, and now he'll let it go. He'll never learn how our photo really got in the paper. *It's over*, I think. I deserved to lose my book, and maybe that's punishment enough.

"We'll be on the move tonight," Cap announces. "Pack up."

Late that night after I've brushed my teeth at the public restroom and I'm walking listlessly over cold sand, Griff catches up to me from behind and hands me something clumsily wrapped in a brown bag.

It's *Island*. A hardback edition, with the same picture on the cover as the one I loved—Karana with her hair flying out, dolphins leaping behind her. In vain moments, I've thought she looked a little like I would, if I darkened my own wild hair.

I hug the novel to me like it's Karana in the flesh, come back from the dead. "How?" Then I see that his neck is bare. "You sold your puka necklace."

"Only fair, since it was all my fault. I should've warned him when we first saw that picture in San Diego." He's talking himself into worshipping Cap again.

"Griff," I whisper. "It wasn't your fault, you have to listen—"

"He worries about our privacy, for our safety. Don't waste time being angry, Ro. I'm not."

I don't answer.

Griff says, "I'm going back out there before we leave, interested?"

"What'd you think is going to happen? Cap's acting like…" I check over Griff's shoulder, but Cap's far off, entering the shallows with his longboard. "Like we're running away from that picture."

"Cap said it's just a precaution. It's just one silly advertisement. So, coming with me?"

I shake my head.

So quickly, back to waves and smiles and everyone getting along. He'll join Cap in the water like Cap never scolded him. Griff—generous, grinning, good—he sees the best in everyone.

But I can't ignore the feeling of the world closing in.

23

Shelter

2002
The island
Day 3, 12:30 a.m.

"It's not letting up, Ronan," Charlie said.

It was after midnight. Officially my third day on this island.

I'd been alert to any change in the weather, hoping the drops would subside, but if anything, the rain pounded harder on our overturned-raft roof, making sleep impossible.

Not that my nerves would have let me.

Mama, sweet-natured and trusting, could be telling Pauline anything in their shelter. At least she didn't know about Dyl's troubles, or our debt.

I filled Charlie in on that now, and her face showed that she was heartbroken, imagining Dyl in jail, the Gull in the junkyard.

"Mag knows I have student loans," she said. "But I wish he'd told me. I have a spare room in my apartment."

"They wouldn't take it. You know that." I peered out, soaking my cheek, and yes, there was still a lamp on in Mama and Pauline's shelter. There was a glow from the twins', too. "I'm going to check on everyone."

Charlie raised her eyebrows—she could tell I was more rest-less than interested in everyone's comfort—but she didn't argue, silently passing me her brown anorak. I pulled it on and crept out, dashing across wet sand to the boys' lean-to.

I crawled under the opening and found them in the center of it, sitting back-to-back like they had as kids. The crowns of their heads touched the orange rubber ceiling, as if they were a double pillar keeping their makeshift roof aloft. They each had a flashlight on the ground; Mag was whittling something with a small block of balsa wood and Griff was reading a slim yellow Yeats book. Cap's favorite volume.

Griff directed his flashlight at me. "Are you all right? You're holding your right arm funny."

"Oh, it just looks that way because Charlie's work jacket is so huge. Can you get that out of my eyes? Do you think Dyl's okay?"

Mag turned and leaned forward to peek out the drippy en-trance, which faced inland, as if he could see Dyl in the rainy blackness. "He's probably built a whalebone hut worthy of your Karana by now."

I scooched in close to them. "So what did you and Pauline talk about while you were carrying her?"

"She's a strange one," Griff said. "She asked where our favor-ite places to surf in Southern California were, so I asked her if she knew the area, and she said, 'Sure. I kind of feel like I do.'"

"What's that supposed to mean?" I asked.

"I don't know. So then I asked where she'd surfed, and she said, 'This is the closest I've ever come to a surfboard until now. The picture of your family is the second-closest.' And then I asked her what she meant and she said, 'Oh, I'm just tired and punchy. I don't know what I'm saying.'"

The three of us sat listening to the drumming rain, watch-ing the water stream down in a glassy oval around us, puzzling over Pauline's words.

Then Mag slapped the rubber raft edge above his head. "I wonder. When she said she 'kind of' lived in San Diego. Do you think she went to college there?"

Griff jumped in. "You mean maybe it wasn't that boy who took *Dreamers*. I always thought it was odd he'd come back after Cap spooked him. Pauline's a little old to have been a student back when it first appeared in the *Triton*. But she could have been a graduate student, or—"

"It would explain a lot," Mag said. "She feels guilty about the photo, she came clean to Cap, and she wants to pay us to make up for it!"

I swallowed at the coincidence. "I'm going to check on her and Mama, wish me luck."

I darted out, leaving my brothers to their wild theories. But instead of hurrying over to the third lean-to, I stood on the wet sand, heedless of the rain pouring on me.

I'd felt so *together* with my siblings, strategizing about the interview. But that would change the second they found out the truth. *No, boys, nice try, but I'm positive Pauline didn't take Dreamers...*

How can you be so certain, Ro?

Ro. They were calling me Ro again. Accepting me as a Merrick.

Because I happen to know the photographer very well. You're looking at her!

Talk about punchy. I hadn't slept more than seven or eight hours since I'd left the farm. The wisest thing to do would be to skulk back under my shelter and rest for the interview.

Instead I tiptoed outside Mama and Pauline's lean-to to eavesdrop, to collect whatever information might prepare me for what was to come.

They were utterly silent. But when I inched closer, I saw that Pauline was showing Mama something by flashlight. What?

I crept as close as I dared, holding my breath, rain dripping down the inside of Charlie's jacket collar. Was it *Dreamers* they were examining?

Mama, still with her back to me, said, "Hello, Little Seal." A voice so serene and low I could barely hear it over the rain.

I crawled in, feeling foolish. "I was just checking to make sure you were warm enough."

"We're fine." Mama touched my arm. "Is your arm better?"

"It's nothing."

A little pause. Disbelieving? I guessed so.

"Pauline was just showing me some snapshots from her wallet to pass the time." She held up the one I'd glimpsed. Not *Dreamers*. Just a picture of a big, pale house with black shutters. It was hard to make out in the darkness, but it suited Pauline.

"Oh. That's nice. Is that your house, Pauline?"

I glanced at Pauline, whose expression was shadowed in darkness. She gave me a slight nod.

I looked back at Mama: sweet smile, beautiful, distracted eyes.

Mama and Pauline seemed so focused on each other; I felt like an intruder. Reluctantly, I said, "Well, sleep well, you two."

"You, too, Little Seal."

"Mama and Pauline looked quite chummy, which is just lovely," I told Charlie, crawling under our upturned raft next to her. "And in other news, I'm officially losing it. I've begun to see *Dreamers* everywhere." I told her about Pauline sharing her wallet snapshots with Mama.

"So you still hate that picture."

"What's to like?" I stopped up a leak in our shelter with a wedge of Styrofoam. "I don't think I could've survived eighteen years here alone like Juana Maria. She's the one who should be on T-shirts. Not me. She was heroic."

"Confession. I own a drawer full of those shirts."

"No!" I turned in surprise.

Charlie nodded. "And two posters. Hey, my first love is an icon. Who else can say that?"

Love. She'd never used the word back then, and it almost hurt to hear it now. I'd dated other girls, other boys. Then men and women. Not many, but enough to measure everything I felt against the intensity of my love for Charlie. Even when I'd dated Violet, a singer/potter on the picking circuit, for five months, and even when Lou and I got pregnant and impulsively married, I'd loved Charlie.

But I'd been convinced she'd never felt real love for me, after how we'd parted.

"Anyway," Charlie hurried on. "You didn't exactly leave me with a photo of yourself. It's a beautiful picture. And you're the most beautiful of all in it."

"Charlie."

She wouldn't let me stop her. "You look serene but full of life and…" Charlie seemed to fumble, embarrassed. "And it's mainly how you're looking to the side. I know you. Knew you. And *I'm* mesmerized by this girl. *What is she thinking? Is she happy? Is she thinking how lucky she is to be one of those unearthly creatures?*"

"You, of all people, know I wasn't thinking that."

She didn't answer, but I felt her yearning to.

"What? Say it."

"It's like you've rewritten over everything, Ronan. The good parts. You're frantically trying to list safe things to talk about with Pauline, like if you don't, you won't remember the good parts at all. But that picture. It isn't all a lie, is it?"

"An hour ago you said acknowledging the bad parts would be healing."

"That's no different. It's allowing yourself to really look. Without a cheat sheet, without being afraid of what you might see. Or remember."

I squeezed rain from my shorts hem, letting this sink in, seeing *Dreamers* as clearly as if it was plastered to the bottom of the boat above me. For a second I imagined I was back in the Gull on a rainy night, as we sped to the next beach. Rain drumming on the snug roof.

"Oh, Ronan. I don't have a clue what it was like to be the only girl growing up in that van. And I haven't forgotten the bad parts, the little bits you shared, anyway, what I could piece together. So whatever you had to forget to run away, and stay away, it wasn't wrong.

"If you had to make it all bad, or forget, in order to break away… I understand that, because maybe I'd've had to, too. Back then, I always envied your big family. And how much your parents loved each other."

I pictured Mama and Cap, images from my life with them. Secret glances, soft smiles, the comforting glow of their reading lamp from behind the vanilla wall. "They did love each other. Too much, maybe? Too much to see what they were doing to us. I don't know."

We were quiet for a minute, listening to the raindrops patter above us.

"Ro."

It was the first time Charlie had called me that since before.

That was how I thought of my life. Before I left, and after I left. Before Ava LeClair and after.

I shifted onto my back, staring up, and murmured, "Every time I've come across that photo, there's a second before I realize who it is. I see the boards and the water and there's a…a breath of feeling good, basking in something I lost. There were days when I didn't want to leave the van, ever, and felt sorry for anyone who didn't live how we did. There were so many of those."

Charlie lay back next to me. Water was sheeting all around our little shelter, and everyone else felt far away.

"I *do* remember the good things, Charlie. You. You were one of the best things." My heart was beating hard.

Charlie swept her thumb across my cheek gently, completely, then looked down at her hand glistening like my tear was a precious thing she had to hold for safekeeping.

"Tell me about one perfect day," she said.

The rain had slowed a little, the drumming on our roof steady but no longer angry. I could hear the ocean again, and its friendly roar brought image after image of good days. Perfect days. It wasn't hard to find one to appease Charlie. I had hundreds. But I told her about one I still cherished, in spite of everything. The ordinary surfing day when I was fifteen, and secretly took *Dreamers* as we all ran in the water.

I don't mention that part. But I described the rest. Every color, every sound.

Pink sky, five dark silhouettes on boards, a deep feeling of peace.

≈

After I described my perfect day to Charlie, the one I secretly captured in the picture, we were both quiet for a long time.

"You see," I said. "I didn't obliterate everything good about the van. So don't feel sorry for me."

"No. Never."

"Charlie?"

"Hmmmm?"

"Will you tell me about one perfect day when you were younger? One you want back so bad it hurts?"

That's how it always was with her. We'd never poured our hearts out to each other for hours and hours, even as teenagers. We'd tipped them out, a bit at a time. A little pain sloshing over the edges here and there, when we got careless.

We lay side by side, on our backs, under the overturned boat. The right side of my body touching her left—there wasn't room for safe distances here.

Charlie took a deep breath and I could feel her chest expand.

When she exhaled, sort of sadly, I felt the warmth as the sigh left her body, floated up to our makeshift roof and back down to us.

"Here's one." Charlie turned onto her side and faced me, propping herself up on her elbow, head in her hand, and I did the same. It was dark in our shelter, but I could still see the wistful smile that passed over her face.

"I'm seventeen and I'm in Santa Barbara," she said. "And I wake up super early, but you and Cap and all three boys are out surfing somewhere. So I go to the fancy hotel and put a coin on the fountain for you so you'll know I'm there and I haven't seen the security guard."

My breath caught. But there was no room in here for that. She'd feel it—the slightest change in the atmosphere. I tried to breathe normally as she went on. We were killing time until the storm passed. That was all.

"You and Dyl come an hour after I put the coin out," Charlie went on. "But that hour. It feels like a week. I get enough change for us to take the bus somewhere, then I spend the time pacing back and forth, and going into the restroom to check my tattoo. See, I've drawn a little turtle inside the real tattoo. Remember the game I played with Dyl? How I'd put things in there and see how long it took him to notice?"

Dyl had loved that sweet, simple game. Charlie had drawn animals, words, symbols. "Just keeping you sharp, Dylly," she'd said.

"So, this day. You're wearing your sundress. Do you remember it?"

A spaghetti strap Gunne Sax, three dollars from a thrift store. Stained at the waist, but I'd cut off the lace tier on the hem and used it as a sash, covering the stain. I felt beautiful in it.

"And your hair's pulled back, except for this one wild curl that always escapes by your right cheek. You have your yellow swimsuit on under, because we're going to the beach.

"And you ask, 'Have you been stealing coins, ma'am?' in this serious voice.

"And the whole time, I'm thinking, *Notice my tattoo, Dyl. Notice my tattoo.* Because sometimes, after he checks it, you touch it, too.

"And then we're on the pier. You, me, and Dyl. And right before we go down the stairs to the sand, Dyl says, 'Hey. You put a turtle on it!' And I kneel for him to touch the fake part of my tattoo, the turtle. Because it's our ritual, right?

"But you don't touch it. Not today. You laugh, but you don't touch it.

"And then we go down the beach."

One word from me, one shake of my head so small it wouldn't be visible, but would change the air just enough to feel it—*No, Charlie. It's too late for us*—and she'd stop.

"I measure that day in all the times you don't touch me. When you take off your sandals and I offer to carry them up to our hiding place in the shade—it doesn't happen.

"When you're showing me new footwork, and I'm standing on your board pretending I'm listening even though I can't pay attention to what you're saying for the life of me. I think you're going to touch my instep, showing me what to do. But it doesn't happen.

"We go for ice cream and I have chocolate on my lip, but you only point to your own to let me know. You don't touch me. You have to leave any minute, and it's not going to happen.

"And then."

Charlie looked at me for a long time, and my breathing must have been the loudest thing on earth for me to hear it over the rain.

"And then, when we're walking down the dunes right after sunset, and I've completely given up on you touching me today, and we're making our plans for tomorrow…

"You just… You hook your pinkie in mine. Your left, my right."

Charlie demonstrated, raising her hand to the hull of the raft and hooking her right pinkie over the edge of the wooden bench seat above us.

"And you don't say a word," she said. "You just stop walking, and hook our pinkies. And give me this look, like, *Is that all right?* And it's a perfect day. Because I knew we weren't just friends anymore. I knew it was just a matter of time."

24

Shells, seagulls, flowers, sandcastles

1986
Half Moon Bay, California
Sixteen years old

After we appear in the Kenny's ad, the six of us cavorting in a cartoon image of the sun, the twins and I vow that we will never again hide anything from Cap, that we will follow his rules and stay close to the van.

"We'll be a good example for him," Griff announces, meaning Dyl.

I tuck the camera away, deep inside the Gull's back door, and any time I get the urge to take a picture, mental or film, I plunge into the water to swim or surf instead. My stomach is a hollowed-out cave from the constant exercise, and my limbs have never been so strong.

Three weeks after the advertisement appears, I finally get a quiet moment alone with Mama. We are in Half Moon Bay, washing clothes in our plastic tub with water I've retrieved from the rest-stop pump. Dyl and Cap and the twins are napping, and this is my chance to ask Mama about the photograph, to ensure there's no chance of my being discovered. I'm wringing out Griff's favorite T-shirt and ask, casually, between squeezes,

"Did Cap ever get any answers about how our photo appeared in that ad?"

She rests back on her heels, examining her water-pruned hands. "Are you still worried about that silly flyer, Little Seal? It's nothing to worry about."

"Cap worries. He made us leave that town."

"Ohhhh. Well, that's just habit from when he was younger. I'm sorry, have you been thinking about it all this time? It's nothing you need to bother about."

"I know. But what did they say to Cap at that shop, about how they got the picture for their advertising? Did he ever tell you?"

"The man who does their advertising got the picture from what they call a photo pool, so it wasn't their fault."

"What's a photo pool?"

"It's… Well, I don't know, exactly. Now help me hang these up while it's nice and sunny."

For a while, it's just as Griff predicted. If anyone besides our friends at the bait shop asked Cap about that advertisement from Kenny's Surf Outfitters in the contest brochure, he hasn't mentioned it. New ads without our photograph come out. The old ones get tossed. Nothing awful happens.

It's a strange, uncomfortable feeling to know we still can't return to Santa Oro or any other town that has a Kenny's—four favorite stops wiped from our migration. Four beloved breaks we cannot surf until Cap decides the advertisement has been forgotten.

He hasn't told us when that will be, or how we will know.

But otherwise our life has gone on like before, at least on the surface. Though Cap's hand will never be the same, it has healed enough for him to pick up a little garage work, and we have enough money to get by.

We wake to cereal and exercises, we surf, Griff grins, Mag

scowls, Dyl writes in his field journal and reads from the ocean-ography books Charlie has shipped him care of the bait shop.

And when I find a precious few minutes to myself, I swirl the radio from KOLD to one of Charlie's stations, searching for clues of what she might be doing, if she's thinking about me, in the lyrics.

≈

Mama, Dyl, and I collect salmonberries and late-spring mush-rooms in a field adjacent to a public park. We're excitedly dry-ing and preserving for our feast with Bass and Charlie, who will link up with us in three days.

"Are these all right?" I ask Mama, though I know the differ-ence between edible and poisonous mushrooms as well as she does. I like how she cups her hand next to mine so that I can tip what I've gathered into it for her inspection.

"Ohhh, aren't those beauties?"

We're walking home when I stop short on the sidewalk.

By the public sprinklers, a girl flaps her beach towel out, and the design on it… No. No. Impossible.

Her friend blocks my view before I can make it out, but for a second, I'm sure it's us. The same image that was in the *Daily Triton* and then the Kenny's advertisement in Morro Bay—somehow blown up and printed on terrycloth. Someone's sick idea of a souvenir.

I swallow, glance over. The girl has wrapped herself in the towel. I can't make out the image at all. It was a blurry shape next to a surfboard, that's all. It's guilt playing tricks with my imagination. There are so many things to print on a towel. Shells, seagulls, flowers, sandcastles…

"Hurry up, Little Seal!" Mama and Dyl are in high spirits, their faces brimming with happiness. Our precious friends are coming, Cap is working again, our baskets are full. What is there to worry about?

25

Curl of glitter

"Miss me?" Charlie asks.

A question so laughable I don't bother to answer.

It's not just Bass who's good for Cap; Charlie is good for all of us. She stares, rapt, as Mama flings up her Marana seed pod one morning to decide our next direction. It lands in a perfect V on the asphalt, and Charlie whispers reverently, "South."

Cap and Bass go off for long talks, and Cap always steps lighter when he returns. Charlie teases the twins about being *adults* now, and asks if they're going to settle down. She says it like it's the most absurd thing ever, and even Cap laughs.

Ten days after Charlie's arrival, I see a flyer from the Parks Service in the restroom when I'm brushing my teeth. I get an idea, and ask Mama to help me. We tell everyone we're going on a midnight ramble.

"It's a surprise," I say. "Not far."

"What do I wear?" Charlie asks.

"Your Police sweatshirt with the hood, over your full suit and booties. And bring your board."

"One more hint," Griff says.

I take a mental picture in advance and describe it. "It will be like surfing a curl of glitter."

Cap hasn't spoken, but he smiles at this, tipping his hat back for a second to peer at me. He knows where I want to take them.

Mag balks. He and Griff got into a fight earlier because Griff teased him about paddling close to some girl. Some naiad, as Griff calls them. But Charlie persuades Mag to come.

"Magnificent, you don't want to miss whatever the surprise is, do you?" she asks him. Only she could get away with calling Mag *Magnificent.*

He relents, bringing up the rear.

"Where're we going? C'mon, I won't tell," Charlie begs me as we set off.

"Let's run to get warm."

"You're in a funny mood, slow down!" She laughs as I race ahead.

It's misty out, the moon watery, but it gives us just enough light as we carry our boards along the beach, and the weather clears just in time.

And then, up ahead, the sand flashes silver.

The grunion are running. Masses of them, thousands of silvery, wiggly fish flopping on the sand as far as we can see. We feel them on our ankles, tickly little creatures with their prehistoric minds on laying eggs.

The eight of us wade in, Bass only up to his ankles. Mama and I act nonchalant, paddling, careful not to look at the sky, as if the evening's only sight is on land. The rest think we only wanted them to view the grunion from afar, and it is something to see—from here, in the water, the beach is iridescent.

Mama and I glance up... Not yet, not yet, then she nods to me, letting me do the honors.

"Now look up," I say.

And there it is—a meteor shower.

Glitter above, glitter on the beach, great swaths of shine above and below. It's a long time before anyone bothers surfing.

Cap sees a little wave he likes. He's abandon and control together. The graceful, unmistakable arc from his shoulder to his bandaged fingertip, trailing in foam as he glides out of a perfect four-foot curl. As he backflips off, I know he's seeing the Lyrids.

The tension between the twins vanishes as they surf close to each other, almost too close, like they did as little boys, their laughter loud enough to carry over the pounding waves, the calls and shouts and delighted squeals from the silver-clad beach.

Charlie paddles near me. "This is glorious."

The voices of grunion-watchers on shore are only a soft murmur out here, everything unimportant except the sparkle of stars and fish.

"You're soaked, c'mon!" Charlie says. It began drizzling an hour ago, at least, but all of us stayed out long after the Lyrid show ended. The rain only seemed to make the grunion on the beach more happily frantic.

We sloshed to the sand, unleashed in a hurry, and dashed under the pier, toweling ourselves off.

"Why do you love them so much, you nut?" she asks, knocking my knee with hers.

"The grunion? Because they don't care about us, and they're ridiculous but sort of…beautiful. You know?"

Charlie smiles, nods, and I go on: "Our silly problems don't affect them in the slightest. And they're optimistic. Mama always says she can't respect pessimists, and how nothing could be more optimistic than a thousand fish mating, hoping for just a handful of eggs to survive into adulthood."

"You're an optimist, too."

"Am I?"

"You worry. You worry about your family. But yes, I'd say

you're an optimist. Only an optimist would plan an outing involving fish and rain and Cap and citizens and Magnus. But he loved it. Every last one of us did, Ro. Look at them."

We watch the others, who are heading back to the vans. Bass, in a yellow slicker and nor'easter hat, looks big and clumsy, walking backward to talk to Cap, but he's picking his way around grunion masses so he doesn't harm a single one. The twins joke around, boards balanced on their heads as roofs. Cap has Dyl on his shoulders; it's been years since he's done that. Dyl's hands gently rest on Cap's hat so as not to move it. His hands are cautious but his face beams. And Mama holds Cap's hand.

"Coming, you two?" she calls to us softly.

"Soon!" Charlie answers.

So everyone else goes back to the vans. It's dark under the pier, and we're alone and the flutter's back, the flutter that might only be wishful thinking or the otherworldly spell of tonight.

"You're drenched," she says.

"Am I?"

"Yes. You've collected rainwater. It drips down your hood to here..." She touches the side of my neck, runs a finger down and around to my left collarbone. "Then here. It's a little fairy pond, right here..."

I wait for her to laugh, to remove her hand, to change the subject. Instead her voice thickens. "Is this all right?"

I swallow, and surely she can feel it. Her fingers are right there at the base of my neck. It feels so obvious, like any fool could tell, with that one swallow, what her fingers grazing my neck have done.

"Ro?" she asks.

I nod, tilt my face. Hers is glazed with rain, and she's smiling at me, taking in my answer.

"I remember how nervous you were when you first met me. You didn't know why, did you?" She says it with a smile that clenches my heart. She knows. She knows she knows she knows. And she's thought about it, too.

Is it only the silver field of grunion working their magic, and tomorrow, when they're hidden in the sea, we'll be embarrassed and pretend it never happened?

The crowd's clearing out, so it's just me and Charlie in our shelter under the pier. And I am full of optimism, just like she said. So I do it—the thing I've been thinking about since we darted under here.

Or maybe I've been thinking about it longer.

Maybe I've wanted to do it since she first hugged me, saying goodbye before her flight to Hawai'i a week after we'd met. Or maybe, yes surely, since the first afternoon I saw her, and she shrugged her bare shoulders.

I lean in and kiss her.

26

Swell

2002
The island
Day 3, 1:00 a.m.

As Charlie and I lay side by side on our backs in the little shelter, I raised my left hand to hers. Hooked our pinkies.

She twined her fingers in mine, and I turned to face her, breaking our hands apart, stroking her cheek. She leaned into my touch, kissing my wrist, her lips so soft I had to kiss her mouth.

Everything else dropped away but the two of us, fast and desperate and inevitable. It was like the night of the grunion run, when the beach turned silver for a few hours.

I woke to the awareness of Charlie asleep next to me, holding me close. It was still dark.

She had wrapped her coat around us, and the rain drumming on the boat had softened, a steady, gentler beat. *Don't stop raining.* If it stopped, we'd have to face the day. The interview, and the paddle-out. The clouds would pass over the island, and the light would begin to change with sunrise. Each new color an ending.

I thought she was sleeping until she whispered, "Hey, Ro? You still give me hummingbirds in my stomach."

I laughed, burrowing my face deeper into her side. "God. What a *young* thing to say."

"Don't be embarrassed. It's still the finest compliment I've ever received. That, and the other thing you said to me. That last night?"

"I remember. I wanted so much for you to say it back."

"But I only said, 'You're lovely.'" She pulled me tighter. "I wanted to say it back. I was afraid you weren't saying it for the right reasons. You were adrift, then."

I was here with her, snug in our shelter, my forehead against her warm shoulder. But I was back there, too. Feeling the outside world, unrelenting, vast, and cruel. "Everything had started to fall apart."

When I emerged in the morning, the sun was out, birds chirping and singing in relief after the storm. I was the first up.

I was stiff from sleeping on the ground, my arm achier than before, and it was cold. But the island seemed to demand that I turn in a circle, take in every degree of beauty. Far to my right, the fog over San Nicolas Island, then a long stretch of impossibly blue ocean, and then the wavy column of sand to the east, strewn with palm leaves and other detritus after the storm, but wind-smoothed, glinting. Only when I'd turned fully around did I glance up and see a figure on the rocks high above. So I was not the first to wake; Pauline was perched up there, alone. Staring out to sea, bundled against the cold under Mama's red sleeping bag.

I started back toward my shelter but she spied me and called, "Good morning! Ronan, up here!"

I couldn't snub her, not when the interview was today. I climbed up, determined to act friendly, or at least civil.

"Did you sleep well?" she asked.

I flashed back to Charlie's face close to mine, shivered as I recalled our night. "Surprisingly, yes, and you?"

"Oh, terrific." Though she looked wretched. Her eyes red, mouth chapped. And her voice was unconvincing. Pauline seemed to work something over in her mind. "Actually, it was a rotten night. I don't think I slept more than a few minutes, here and there."

"I'm sorry."

"It's not your fault, Ronan." She held my gaze for a long time.

Too long. I stepped away from her, staring down at the three bright orange ovals under which the others slept.

"Is anyone else awake yet?" I asked.

"No. You're the only *Dreamer* not dreaming."

At her reference to the photo, all my joy from my night with Charlie vanished. I remembered why my first instinct, a moment ago, had been to scurry back under my orange lean-to.

"Our father isn't dreaming," I said sharply, on alert again.

"I was speaking figuratively."

Her tone was questioning—I'd anticipated that. But it was also knowing, and pained. This, I had not expected from her. Everything had a double meaning.

With great effort, I kept my voice neutral. "Explain, if you don't mind. What were you trying to say?"

"You left the life they chose for you."

Oh, she was sharp. "My mother told you that? No wonder you—" I stopped myself just in time. *No wonder you wanted to be her roommate the night before your interview. So you could do your research.*

Pauline sighed sadly. "Ronan. Here, sit. Please?"

At last I complied, and she continued. "Yes. Your mother told me you left the van…the life, at seventeen. *I* wondered why. You're speaking to me, not to *SWELL* magazine right now."

"Well, if you say so." My laugh sounded as forced as it was.

How swell of you. So then I trust you completely. "Flay me, display me." A line from a poem Cap liked...by cummings or Pound? Oh, what did it matter. She had succeeded in needling me.

Everything was strategy, and I had to remind myself of that, no matter how unsettling her gaze, how surprising her line of questioning.

"Let's start again. You left the van at seventeen."

And now she'd ask the natural follow-up: *Why?* I braced myself.

But she asked instead, "Did you ever wish someone had made you leave before that?"

I fumbled through my surprise. "Of course not. It was a great life. It was a...a dream life." *Careful, Ronan.* I gripped the hem of my shorts and felt, through the fabric, the list of interview topics in my pocket. "You know what's funny. You should write about this. The song, 'California Dreamin'.' It's about people who *don't* live in California, but want to."

She hesitated, but then nodded. "It's about people who have a cold life and want a warm one. Which your picture offers to the world. Right? And it's such a beautiful picture. The person who took it has an eye."

Hers were steady on me, her words probing. "It's a beautiful record of a life. A most unusual life.

"I know you think I don't understand it, but I do. I understand secrets. And seventeen-year-old girls running away. You know, I wish you could be proud of that *California Dreamers* exhibit in the Brand. Even visit it. We all have a right to bear witness to our own lives."

Could she know? My breathing caught and I looked longingly at the bright orange raft, wishing I'd ignored her summons. I blurted, "What's your favorite version of that song? It's been covered a million times. There's a Bobby Womack version, do you know that one?"

"Oh, Ronan. I didn't come here to trap you, or hurt you."

She let out a pained sigh, telling me my clumsy attempt to steer the conversation to safe waters was obvious, it was noted, and it was pitied.

A long whistle from below. Mag's perfect middle C.

"Up here!" I called gratefully. Mag emerged from under his raft shelter, and then Charlie. Then another camper joined them, someone with a bulging tan backpack. Dyl hadn't been far, then. I'd guessed that, and wondered where he'd bivouacked last night. He'd probably made himself more comfortable than any of us.

"Your little brother," Pauline said, watching him as I was.

"Look, Dyl brought a bunch of food, you must be starving," I said in relief. "And you must be impatient to get the interview done and go back, so you can sleep in a proper bed on the mainland—"

But Pauline grabbed my hand. "Ronan. I—I'm sorry I've bungled this visit. I have a lot of respect for your family."

"You're just doing your job," I said brightly, shrugging.

But she wouldn't let go of my hand. "To answer your question. I like the original version of that song the best. But it always makes me cry. It's so beautiful. So full of longing for a better life." Her hand held me, and the understanding in her voice held me. At last I looked at her, directly in her eyes for the first time. Dark blue eyes, shining with compassion, with intelligence and kindness.

I met them for no more than a second or two. But this seemed enough for her—the price she exacted from me so I could get away from her pitying gaze.

She released my hand.

27

Fame

1986
California
Sixteen years old

After the grunion run, Charlie and I steal off together whenever we can. Dunes, parks. We kiss and talk and laugh, giddy
with our new discovery.

"You give me butterflies in my stomach," she whispers.

"You give me hummingbirds."

One day when all of us are eating dinner, Dyl spies a ruby-
throated hummingbird and sketches it in his field journal. Charlie and I share a secret glance.

We've hidden the change in our friendship without discuss-
ing a plan to do so. We get so little time alone. It would be
wasteful to spend it talking about what everyone might think.

That's what I tell myself. But after a few weeks, I begin to
detect worry in the corner of Charlie's eyes. And once, after
we've been kissing for a long time in a warm, deep dune, she
finally whispers the question I've been dreading: "What would
everyone think about this?"

I don't know what my family will think about it—two girls.

My attraction to Charlie feels so natural I can't pinpoint when I started. Probably when I saw her surfing that first day.

Gay is used mostly as an insult. Citizens toss it around. *That's so gay*. It means lame. Stupid. Silly. And I've found boys cute, too. Thought about kissing them. So what does that mean?

Last week, Mag used *gay* to describe someone's bright, banded wet suit in Newport. And Cap looked at him sharply while I held my breath. "I mean immature," Mag had corrected. Just as he would when letting other citizen slang slip in Cap's presence.

Now I wished I'd been braver—that I'd asked Cap if the silent rebuke was only for using slang, or if that particular word offended him for a second reason. How he felt about couples different from him and Mama.

I feared the answer.

Charlie wants to talk about it, to be open. But I'm afraid we're something dirty.

"I don't know," I admitted. "What about Bass and your mom?"

"My dad wouldn't mind. My mom... We'll never know unless we tell them all."

"When you come back," I say. Stalling her. Charlie is going to visit in four months, at the start of her summer vacation. A long separation, but at least we know its end date.

She agrees, but our remaining time is heavy with need and confusion.

Then one night in the dunes, after she's slipped her hand under my suit, I cry out, "I love you."

Charlie sweeps my cheek with her thumb and says only, "You're lovely."

I stiffen with embarrassment and she quickly continues, "Ro. I'm falling for you, too. But I'm not sure you can be sure of that yet. You know so few people. I mean that came out condescending, but—"

"It's not important, forget I—"

"It *is* important. We should talk about it."

There's a long, awkward silence. We cover it with laughter, with a final late-night swim and promises to write daily. And then she's gone.

≈

My ache for Charlie is so all-consuming, her first letter so slow to arrive at the bait shop, I would have been unhappy even if life was otherwise perfect.

But two things happen within the month after she boards her 747 back to Oahu that add to my heartache.

The first is a knock in the night: *Rap-rap-rap-rap-RAP!*

I'm jolted from a sweet dream. I know cop knocks. They always use the side of their fist, not their knuckles, and there's almost no time between flesh hitting metal, and the number of knocks is always five, with a loud one at the end.

Rap-rap-rap-rap-RAP!

In our bed, I hold my hand on Dyl's shoulder—he's stiff and scared under our blanket, and I trace waves on his back, calming him.

Then: "Open up, City PD."

"It's just a police officer," I tell Dyl, and we both relax.

Cap hits the floor, slides the door open. He goes out to talk to the officer, shutting the door behind him, and Mama's quiet behind the library wall.

The officer laughs, says a lot that I don't hear, though I catch a sarcastic "celebrities." This is new.

The discussion takes a long time. There's a tangle of voices, rising, calming, rising again. Silence.

And then Cap says, "Fine. Yes, sir." I don't like the *sir*.

A flashlight beam shoots through Mag's window into the van, bounces around. This is new, too.

In the moonlight, Mag sits on his bunk with his back straight as a board, fists balled. He doesn't like the sound of *sir*, either. Griff, up in his bunk, smiles at me. Not his real grin but a nervous, pretending-it's-okay smile.

"Why is it taking so long?" Dyl asks me.

"Don't worry, Dylly," I whisper. I dig around and find his sweaty hand and we trace the waves on our bunk together. One time around, two times.

"I'll bet by the fifth time, it'll be over," I say, guiding his index finger slowly over the grooves.

"Is it a robber or a cop?" Dyl asks.

"You heard him say. Cop. So it will be over soon." Cap told the man at the Sapphire he would no longer transport money for him. But if that's not true, if a white packet is changing hands outside the Gull's metal wall, Dyl does not need to know about it, ever.

"But maybe he was lying."

"It's nothing to worry about, follow my hand."

At four times around the waves, Cap comes in and says, "All taken care of, go back to sleep." He climbs up and he and Mama talk, low, in their bunk.

"See?" I whisper to Dyl, who snuggles down to sleep.

But instead of sleeping, Cap jumps back down, hops into the driver's seat, and the Gull rumbles.

The magic did not work this time.

My heart's racing, and the twins exchange a shocked look in the shadows, but I make my voice as soft as I can and whisper to Dyl, "It's all right," drawing waves on his back with my finger while he traces them on our bunk. I know our pattern by heart, all the little points and slides and valleys. The same waves are tattooed on the arches of Mama and Cap's feet, and soon they will mark the twins'. Then mine, then Dyl's.

As I sketch along Dyl's back, I try to let the Gull's familiar engine humming rock me. But as I drift off, I think—she is not humming. She is shuddering. She is shaking.

≈

We drive south to the next beach, ten or twelve miles by my calculations, as I count by the yellow highway strip unfurling from the back window. We must be coasting on fumes; lately I have begun checking the gas gauge along with the stovepipe. Cap parks us under a tree and climbs up to bed. But I can't sleep.

"Are they all asleep?" Cap asks Mama.

I hold my breath.

"I think so," she whispers. "We were parked so far off the road, what happened?"

"It's like he knew where we were."

"But how?"

"I don't know. But he gave me this. Called me a *celebrity*."

What?

I wait a long time for clues, but they don't come. And neither does their deep breathing which means they're asleep. I imagine my parents, tense with worry on the other side of the library wall, and sleep very little myself.

We've stopped in a town that was no one's choice. There's no surf break, and we have to content ourselves with swimming. The twins and I try to amuse Dyl by creating a little river wave next to a creek, but it feels forced.

Cap finds work at a garage. He comes home drained, and doesn't make any coins there—it's not a place he has worked before.

I walk there to spy on him, sensing his despair. And he's not under a car, but he has a stick in his hand, and for a second I remember that mirror under the golf cart. But he's pushing a broom around. I hurry off, wishing I hadn't come.

But it's all temporary. When we have enough cash, he'll drive us another two hundred miles south, to a board shaper called Daniel's where he's respected and can make his own hours.

In the meantime, we all feel uneasy about the cop making us leave. Cap seems distracted. Mama doesn't ramble far, and I heard Cap tell her that just to be safe, she shouldn't.

The first night in the new nesting place, jerked from a deep sleep, there are thuds that at first I think must mean another cop outside. And then rocking.

Or had we started south already? Impossible. Cap has accepted garage work in town and we have no gas money. The rocking and thuds end—probably just one of the twins deciding to night surf, or sleep on the roof…it was so warm. Really, it might have been a good hammock night.

"Ro," Dyl whispers.

"Hmmm?"

"Look." I join Dyl, who's looking through the back window. Outside, Griff and Mag stare at something I can't see behind them.

We tiptoe out, not wanting to wake Mama.

Blurry from sleep, it at first only seems like a word floating in the dark. Sideways, in fuchsia glow-in-the-dark paint: "HYPOCRITE."

Then I realize it is written on a board. Cap's board. The letters smeared on in Stick Glo surf wax.

The four of us circle the garish monolith.

At last, Griff speaks. "They knew it was Cap's board."

Someone must have unstrapped it from the roof. They left the others, didn't steal anything. Only a childish, chilling message.

"I heard Cap tell Mama yesterday when that cop knocked, 'He gave me this.' What? Did he tell you, Griff?"

"A notepad with that same picture of us on it," Griff confides. "Fifty pages, us at the top next to 'Hang Ten!'"

Celebrity. Hypocrite.

"How can someone just use our picture on souvenirs without permission?" Mag asked, balling his fists.

Then we hear Cap, whistling along the road. He comes into view, tossing a coin up and down. He seems happy. So he'd managed to make his coin. My heart swells for him. For a second, spotting the four of us there, he seems touched to see us, as if we'd sensed his return from his long evening's work and come out to greet him.

My first impulse is to block his board with my body.

Cap stops tossing the coin, and all the joy drains from his face.

"Is everyone all right?" he asks. "Where is your mother?"

"Still asleep," Griff assures him. "I should have woken. I'm sorry. I should have stood guard after the cop yesterday."

Why would any cop, let alone two of them, care about a cheap souvenir notepad?

Cap shakes his head slightly, indicating that Griff's not to blame.

The four of us help our father scrape his board, then we wash it in the moonlit waves.

"I'll wax it for you now," I offer.

"Thank you, Ronan," Cap says. "But I won't need my board for a little while."

Mag says, "Does someone think we *posed* for that souvenir trash. Made money from it? And who would even care if we did?"

Cap looks out to sea. He has rakes of fluorescent fuchsia on his rib cage where he wiped his hands.

"I don't know if they truly believe it," Cap says. "People often pretend to believe, when it's helpful."

"Helpful for what?" Mag asked.

"For hurting. Helpful for hurting, Magnus. Well. Let's strap this back on the roof."

"So we're just going to leave?" Mag sputters. "We're not going to fight back?"

Griff glares at him.

But Cap's expression is soft. "There is no fight, Magnus. This is only someone to pity."

"I'll drive so you can sleep," Griff says, his chin lifted defiantly.

But Cap, weary as he is, insists on taking the wheel wrapped in dried kelp. He sits in the captain's chair, his hat on, and we roll onto the road.

None of us asks where we're going.

Four more towns south. Nowhere we like. The glow-in-the-dark board paint doesn't appear again, but Cap can't work because he doesn't want to leave us alone, even with the twins on guard.

After two weeks of this, I confer with them in the dunes. Mag says, "Maybe it's one of the old-school board shapers stirring trouble with the cops, telling them when we're parked illegally. Or another vanner, mad because they think Cap made money off our picture. *Hypocrite.*"

And I remember what the police officer said after pounding on the Gull and making us leave in the night—that mocking *celebrity.*

"It doesn't explain why the police would care," Griff says. "A vanner would never willingly approach a cop, or have any sway with them, if they did. It could be someone from the Sapphire hotel, angry because Cap quit working for them..."

Mag: "Or the opposite! A cop who's gone straight could be behind it?"

"Then why did that officer mention us on souvenirs? He said 'celebrities...'"

"I don't know. Just to be a jerk, maybe..."

They go on like this, theorizing. Who might have a grudge against Cap, or if it's only a coincidence, us having to move twice in one week.

How easy it is for outsiders to control our lives, after all. Knocks in the night, a little paint, and the Gull's favorite nests are smashed.

The boys can debate for hours about the details, the exact chain of events and who our mysterious nemeses might be, but the picture links everything. None of this happened until the flyers, the souvenir Hang Ten! notepads, the towels…

Celebrity. Hypocrite.

I know who's to blame for whatever's happening to us. Me.

Cap decides the six of us will hide the Gull behind the bait shop and split up for a few weeks.

He'll go off alone to see how far the merchandise with our picture on it has spread, try to make amends with whoever is mad at us—however unjust their grievance. He is sure that he will get work again, shaping boards, if he can just explain.

"And the twins will hitch to Big Bear. You've been curious about snowboarding, right, boys? And you three will camp, somewhere inland. Ronan and Dyl, you'll remember what you see and tell us all about it when you return. Interest in that… picture will subside by then."

"I have a beautiful ramble in mind," Mama tells me and Dyl.

Everyone's being so kind to me, but they wouldn't be if they knew this was my fault.

28

All blown out

2002
The island
Day 3, morning

"Are we ready?" Griff asked.

No one answered.

The four of us sat on a wide steppe of gray rock overlooking the wooden west-side dock, in the shade of an ancient manzanita. It was the biggest I'd seen in my life, and one of the few trees on this side of the island. Rocky and wind battered, the west oval felt like another world from the lush east oval where I'd arrived only a couple days ago.

Mama and Pauline and Charlie waited on the boat below, under a blue awning Charlie had set up on the *Kai*'s deck so we'd be comfortable for the interview. We'd told them we were gathering wild mint for Mama's sun tea, and though they surely guessed it was a pretext for a final sibling conference, no one questioned our story.

"How old is this tree, Dyl?" I asked.

"At least a hundred years." He reached up to caress the trunk.

Drawing my index finger across warm stone, I traced the outline of the thick manzanita branch shading me. The wind's constant pressure had made every tree limb point east, as if they grasped for the mainland. As if the tree was saying, *That's where you'll end up, in the end.* Back in civilization.

But I wasn't ready. Not to return, not for the interview. And I could tell from my brothers' tense expressions that none of them were, either.

Mag gazed down at the blue awning, then, smiling wryly to himself, pulled a length of balsa wood from his pack. "Look what I made last night." It was a model surfboard. A foot long, beautifully sanded. "I thought it would be helpful to demonstrate turns, since she's a noob. I had nothing else to do." But he also sounded a little embarrassed, seeing the thing in broad daylight.

"It's terrific, Mag. May I?" I asked, and he passed it to me. It was perfectly shaped, even had a fin and a miniature leash of braided reed strands. We had a prop. Our list of safe topics. We couldn't stall any longer. "Charlie thinks it means something, our elaborate preparations for the interview. She says it could be healthy to talk openly. Even about the less-perfect parts of the life Cap made."

Griff asked, "Is that what you three think?"

I waited for Dyl or Mag to jump in. To say, *No way. It doesn't mean anything. We give her our scripted answers and nothing more.* But they remained silent.

"I don't know," I eventually said. "I just wish Cap had told us what the rules were, for the interview."

"Well, he didn't, so we stick to the plan." Griff reached for the little board and examined it. "We could have a signal. If anyone says something they shouldn't, put your hand over the board like this." He clamped the nose of the board between his thumb and forefingers like a jaw snapping down.

"Shark chomp," Mag said.

"Bear trap," I murmured, remembering the night I'd learned that anyone could submit a photo to the *Triton*. That had started it all. Our troubles, my flight from the Gull. "Remember that party where Jaws showed up? Remember how the UC San Diego kids used their school newspapers as tinder for the fire in the empty pool?"

Guess. Please, just guess. Right now, while I have a scrap of courage left.

Instead Dyl said, "Maybe you would have stayed and taught me to skateboard, if the photo hadn't made things so hard on us that year. I heard how good you were."

"And what really happened to our boards," Mag said.

"You stuck together, but you could've trusted me, too," Dyl said playfully.

"We did," Griff told him with a smile. "You were just so young."

They would never guess. Their trust in me, their acceptance that I was still one of them, was pure. And overwhelming.

Dyl stood and came over to Griff, reaching for the little board. He handed it to him, and all of us watched Dyl walk a few steps away, toward the open ocean, and stretch his right arm out, holding the surfboard against the expanse of blue sea from a distance so it looked like a real board.

He turned to face us. "I think with the four of us together again, we can get through the interview, no matter what she asks. We got through a lot, the four of us."

"That's right, brother," Griff said, his voice thick.

Mag nodded. "And in an hour we'll have the money to fix up the Gull and clear our debts."

"My debts," Dyl said firmly.

I shook my head. "All of ours."

It was time.

FIELD JOURNAL

When she slipped away that night long ago, I watched. I saw their van.

I could have summoned our father and stopped her.
Stopped the two of them.
Father asked if I knew anything, and I lied.

He was so angry, as if he knew.
He slammed his office door, summoned help to chase them.
But I'd bought them time.

Now we're together. And we'll face this "interview" together, too.

And in an hour it'll be over, and everyone will go swimming,
or for a hike,
or we'll gather around that sweet ersatz fire.

And maybe her children will come to know me, and like me.
And understand why their Cap and I planned it this way.
How little time we had…he had.

How unhappy they were, under the world's rule.
And they seem to have found their happiness, in the world they
created as they drove toward it.

Two hopeful young sorcerers.

Their children, though…they were merely along for the ride. And I
fear… Oh, we'll talk about that soon enough, face-to-face.

I can't draw hands. Even Picasso had a hard time with them.
But if I could, I'd sketch my fingers, crossed.

2002
The island
Day 3, morning

"Well," Pauline said. "Here we are." She seemed dazed and uncertain, now that her big interview was underway.

The seven of us sat in the shade under the *Popoki Kai*'s gently flapping blue sunshade. It was a calm morning on the water, and the boat rocked only slightly, a soothing motion, the awning's shadow stretching and contracting.

Pauline was perched awkwardly on the molded bench on the starboard side, the twins flanking her. I sat opposite them, Dyl on my right and Mama on my left. In the stern, Charlie sat cross-legged on the deck. Every time I looked her way, she mouthed, *One hour.*

Only an hour, and this would be over for good.

Soon we'd be back on the island, watching the boat speed toward Santa Barbara with Pauline aboard, and we'd never have to see her again.

Griff tried to sound relaxed, as if he hadn't rehearsed our opening line: "We thought it might be helpful if one of us demonstrated a pop-up for you, to start."

"Thank you, Griffin. Maybe you can demonstrate for me later. I—" Pauline glanced around at each of us, ending with a long, confused look at Mama. "I know you didn't expect me. And I know this is a private time. But you've all been so kind."

Mama nodded encouragement.

"Your father," Pauline started, then halted again, darting another nervous glance at Mama. Why?

Mag coaxed, "Cap Merrick. He got his name from the hat he always wore. A Greek fishing captain's hat." Another gem lifted straight from our anodyne, talking-point script.

"Yes." Pauline held a notebook and pen, but hadn't written a word. I discreetly checked my watch—fifty-eight minutes left. At this rate, we had nothing to worry about.

"I wrote so many questions for you," Pauline said uncertainly. "Hundreds. On the plane. In the shed my first day. Nothing seemed right. And when I decided on 'Is this the truth?' I guess I was—I was being unfair. How could it be the truth? I knew it wasn't."

I tensed, but Pauline went on. "How could one souvenir picture capture the lives of six people, over so many years. Part of what I meant by it is, I guess, were you happy? As happy as the photo suggests?"

My brothers and I looked at each other, visibly relieved.

"I was," Mag said. "I can't imagine a happier upbringing. Look how miserable most people in this country are. Grinding away for money from big corporations their whole lives, indoors. Rushing around to stores, never pausing to take anything in. Never imagining anything better even exists. We had so much freedom. So much love."

Griff said, "Exactly. I'm immensely grateful to our parents for fighting convention so that we could have a more…pure existence. From when we were born, they instilled a deep sense of gratitude in us for the natural world. They—they lived softly on the land. They consumed so little. Made use of what we had. Consumer culture is absolutely sick."

Pauline nodded thoughtfully. "So you never had…worries?"

The four of us couldn't help quick glances at each other, but Griff quickly filled the silence. "We had everything we needed. I mean, sure, sometimes we stayed in a town a few extra days to…for Cap to earn money for gas or repairs."

"And you always felt confident that this was possible. He did garage work, right? On a day-hire basis?"

"He was a very skilled mechanic," Dyl said. "He could make pressure plates for a clutch when they weren't in stock, and they were better than the originals."

Pauline smiled kindly at this spiel. It had taken great effort for Dyl to participate at all, I knew. And maybe Pauline understood that, because she didn't follow up.

We braced ourselves for what might come next. Could she know about Cap's full employment history, somehow? Images flashed at me—white packets, Cap scrabbling under a Sapphire Resort golf cart for one *day-hire job* that was decidedly not mechanical.

"Mama traded her lotions and oils for us," Griff said. He looked at me for help but I was half-lost in the past, and could only muster a nod and a strange-sounding "yes."

"And she gathered windfall fruit." Mag looked at Mama with genuine appreciation. "We were all resourceful and frugal, and our parents made sure we never needed for anything. We ate healthy food. They provided well."

Pauline's voice was wobbly with distress, her eyes apologetic. "Oh. I know that. I didn't mean to suggest—" She glanced at Mama again. But this time Mama didn't nod encouragingly. She looked down at her hands. Hurt by the implication that she and Cap had been poor parents, I guessed, and felt a wave of protectiveness for her.

"We should get back to surfing," Mag suggested firmly. He showed Pauline his little balsa-wood board. And Pauline watched respectfully as he showed her Cap's style of cutback, how it was old-fashioned but coming back into favor. He talked about longboards and short boards. Our roof rack.

"Oh!" he said. "Cap earned money shaping boards. He was a true artist. Write that down."

Pauline complied.

Between Mag and Griff, the interview flowed on well from there. It could hardly be called an interview, really. It was my twin brothers talking excitedly about how our calisthenics made us champion paddlers, about alternative waxing methods, the most environmentally friendly wet suits and booties, the importance of protecting tide pools and reefs. At one point, they ranked their top-twenty surf breaks.

Dyl and I contributed little, and Mama still said nothing at all, but I watched in awe as my brothers warmed to their task. They paced, gestured, their voices rising, faces animated. Pauline seemed transfixed. She really was not a very good reporter.

Eleven minutes left. Soon it would be over.

But in the middle of an impassioned soliloquy from Griff on kelp bed and algae bloom management in Monterey Bay, Pauline raised both hands. "This is all very interesting," she said. "I'm grateful. I've let things go a little off track, though. You see—" She cleared her throat. "Your father and I… The museum exhibit led me to him, indirectly. An article in a newsletter, with your picture in it. I called around at the Brand and, well, a fundraising employee had heard someone rumored to be in the photo had recently collapsed and hinted at the name of his hospital… I'm not proud of that. But anyway I phoned him there, and then we wrote, once he was out. He had me mail letters to a bait shop… I can tell you more of the specifics later. I *want* to. But the important thing to know is our plans for my trip here were…rushed. Because…"

Mama was tense, not meeting anyone's eyes.

"Well, because of how quickly his illness took him. I tried to prepare, but clearly I didn't do a good job."

Pauline looked intently at me. "Ronan. You've been quiet. Were *you* happy?"

The boys looked confused, too surprised to rush in and help me, though I felt Dyl stiffen beside me.

"Pauline," Mama murmured.

She seemed so oddly casual, so *familiar* with Pauline. It didn't make sense.

"I'm sorry," Pauline said. "But it's. It's something I've wondered. Worried about for a long time."

"I was happy," I said. But it came out child-like and defensive.

Pauline nodded. "When I wrote 'Is this the truth?' I was especially interested in you. After all, you're the one who left."

I glanced at the boys, whose eyes were still wide with confusion, at Mama, who was now staring out to sea with a pained expression.

"I left when I was grown-up. Practically."

Pauline pressed on. "But when you were younger, did you ever wish for a regular home, or...? I understand you slept outdoors sometimes."

"Yes, we all did, and we loved it. Cap took care of us."

At my side, Mama looked down at her hands. *What was going on?*

"Is— Did Cap suggest I wasn't happy growing up? Me in particular?"

It's a logical assumption, I reminded myself. It didn't mean Cap had told her about the photo...

Pauline shook her head. "No, but I can understand it, why you left. Remember what I said earlier this morning. I just want to understand. To know if you'd ever wished someone had made a different life possible for you."

"I made a different life possible for myself."

"By running."

"I was an adult, ready for something different."

"Is seventeen an adult?"

"We matured early." I grasped for words. "I don't mean that negatively. It was a good thing. It was—" I cast around to my brothers for help.

"We were very comfortable, sleeping in hammocks when it was hot," Griff said, coming to my aid, but there was hurt in his eyes.

"Our father didn't believe in air-conditioning," Mag added.

"That's…admirable. But—" Pauline rummaged in the fuchsia tote bag at her feet. "This may help me organize my thoughts."

Nine minutes.

For a moment, before I saw what she was reaching for, I almost pitied her. She needed props to get through this, too. Then I feared she might pull out *Dreamers*, and braced myself. It was the reason we all sat here together for this bizarre gathering, eighty miles from the museum where it had been blown up and hung.

"I'm sorry. One minute…" Still, she scrambled.

Mag raised his eyebrows at me, but then made a funny face. A reassuring face, like *We're almost home.*

Eight minutes left.

Pauline went on, "The fact is, I haven't been entirely honest with you all, regarding how much I know about the family. I know that will feel unfair…hurtful, even. That wasn't my intention. Or your father's. Or your mother's."

What?

She turned to Mama, who remained impassive. "I insisted on a bit of time to get to know you all, to feel things out. Before explaining everything and… Here it is."

She pulled out a journal and set it on her lap.

A journal with dark green spiral binding at the top. The cover had a distinctive, ornate green botanical design of kelp twining around the edges, a cream background. Words identifying each part of the plant, elegant green arrows. "Mer" in loopy script in the center.

Mer for Merrick...because mer *means* sea *in French*, Mama had said, so long ago.

Dyl's field journal.

His only valued possession, protector of his innermost thoughts, his observations and recordings. Not just about the natural world, but his world. Our world. And Pauline was flipping through it as casually as if it was hers now.

Dyl had seen everything. Shadow and sun. Our struggles, our arguments. Our fractures. But through everything, we'd respected his privacy.

I stayed very still. We all did.

Inside I roiled. I had gone from fear to relief and back again so many times it physically hurt. Far more than my bruised shoulder. A quick look around at my brothers told me they felt the same. Dyl most of all. He was so shocked, so horribly *frozen*, staring at his journal in the invader's lap. After his bravery up on the hill just now, it broke my heart.

Mama sat and did nothing. Said nothing. Just like always.

When had Pauline taken the journal? I tried to remember the last time I'd seen Dyl writing in it, here on the island. We'd been so busy, so distracted...

"There's something in here I want to read to you," Pauline said. "Maybe it will help me explain. It's about running away, about fathers and daughters."

Pauline was going to twist something Dyl had written to say Cap had been a terrible father. Overbearing, neglectful. That I'd run away from him because I hated him. All of her digging suggested it. Her hints about fathers and daughters...she'd write it in her article, and that would be Cap's legacy.

I couldn't let her.

Only a few minutes left in this charade, but I couldn't bear it a second longer.

I rose calmly, crossed the boat to where Pauline sat. I took the green-and-cream journal from her, closed it, and returned it to Dyl. He clutched it gratefully, his eyes swimming.

I sat next to him again and held his hand, then looked straight at Pauline. "I didn't leave for the reasons you think."

"Ronan?" Pauline asked. "What are you—" She stared at Dyl's journal. "I've upset you."

"You didn't need to sneak around. Pretend to be our friend when you were stealing our stories behind our back."

Pauline was all innocent confusion. "What do you mean?"

We all talked over each other:

"This interview is over," Griff said. "You have enough, Ms. Cowley."

"No, Griff," Mama said.

"Charlie, will you take her back now?" Mag asked.

Charlie stood, the boat keys in her hand, looking from one to another of us, trying to figure out what she should do.

"The reason I left," I said, my voice rising above the others'. "It wasn't Cap's fault. It was the photo. I hate that photo. But it's out there forever."

Griff shook his head slightly. Mouthed, *What are you doing?* Mag made frantic chomping gestures on the little balsa-wood surfboard, reminding me to wade back into safe waters.

I looked at my family, each of them equally baffled, hanging on my words. The twins still sat across from me, and Mama and Dyl on either side of me. The larger half and the smaller half. We'd broken into those same groups, when Cap had said we were too conspicuous, the six of us by the Gull. "The photo split us up," I said. "And—"

Mag jumped in, hoping to get us back to our plan. "She means we separated for a little while because of the picture. It made it hard to have the privacy we all liked. You know, Cap would never willingly be part of advertising for the big surf outfitters. He didn't approve of their practices, their environmental stance. That was in 1986, right? Griff? It was just a month, and it wasn't so bad, actually—"

"No, Mag," I interrupted. "I know you're trying to help me. But that's not what I mean. I need to say this."

I thought of that separation. Though there'd been a throb of guilt, constantly, in my head—*we had to do this because of you, because of you, because of you*—it had not been enough to lessen my thrill at having time with Mama. On a ramble with her. Just her and me and Dyl. The smaller half. I didn't resent it that time; there had been no choice for Cap, who was desperately trying to keep us together by splitting us apart for a while.

And even the fact that my camera was the reason we had to separate—that guilt hadn't been enough to stop me from bringing it along. Imagining the pictures I could take during our ramble…

"What are you trying to say, Ronan?" Pauline seemed baffled, a little stunned.

I couldn't seem to finish what I'd begun.

Exhaustion, betrayal, guilt, regret, our constant swaying on the ocean—so familiar and so long forbidden—had worked on me and now I felt like someone tumbling through time.

Like wiping out, rolling and gulping underwater and not knowing, for a scary minute, which way was up and which was down.

You are thirty-two. You are here on Manzanita island with Mag and Griff and Dyl and Mama and Charlie. Cap is gone, in a blue urn. You have sons in Oregon, who are eight.

I wished I could be eight again.

Eight was a perfect age for the Gull. My world was just the right size to fit inside it. At eight I was old enough to see that my family lived apart from everyone else. But not so old that I wanted a life apart from them.

Mature enough to take care of Dyl on my own and to be proud of it, but not so old that I could see clearly what the responsibility was doing to me, costing me. The weight of it. I no longer believed everything Cap and Mama told me, but there was no bitterness blooming in me, no shame, no ache for anything different that would lead me away from them.

Not yet.

All of that was waiting, looming around a few more turns in the Gull's road.

"Ronan?" Pauline coaxed.

"The reason we split up that time— The souvenirs with us on them—" A timid start. I could still shift the conversation away and keep my secret.

"It's funny," I said instead. "One time someone vandalized Cap's board. They called him a *hypocrite*. It was like—like they'd reached into the darkest part of my heart and pulled out the word. Because I'd thought that of him, once in a while. How he wanted freedom, but kept me confined in his rules."

"Let's take a break." Griff stood.

"No, Griff. You all deserve to know this. It's more than time. That night someone painted *hypocrite* on Cap's board. It made me feel for him, understand him. It's so ironic. Because—"

Oh, let it go. We've earned the money for Dyl, now. End the interview and send Pauline on her merry way and don't ever look too closely at the past.

Are you all right? Charlie mouthed.

No. No, I wasn't.

And I wouldn't be if I kept on like I'd been all these years. My running hadn't stopped when I left the Gull. I'd run from the truth for far too long.

"I have a story for you, Pauline," I said quietly. "A story about who took *Dreamers*."

"What do you mean, who took *Dreamers*?" Griff asked, alarmed.

I couldn't look at him. Or any of them. But I forged on. "You can put this in your article for *SWELL*. And say how the person who took the picture, that picture of a perfect life, is a liar. And a coward."

It was harder than leaving the van fifteen years ago, because this was my second time, ripping myself apart from them. I knew how much it would hurt. And this time, there was no deluding myself that I would come back, or they would come for me.

I had begun crying, and the confession wasn't even out yet.

Finally I said it, my words broken, my voice so soft they almost got lost under the lap of waves. "It was me."

Silence.

I wiped my tears with the heels of my hands. But by the time I was done there were more, the dam broken, tears held back for so long I had no idea when the supply would run out. I hadn't cried since my twins were born. And those had been happy tears.

But there was sweet relief in them, too. I was so very tired of my secret.

"What are you saying, exactly?" Griff's voice had turned hard.

"I got that college boy's camera from the firepit, and it still worked. I took *Dreamers*. I gave it to the newspaper because I was mad at Cap one day. Or I—I thought that was why. Then. When really, it wasn't that at all. It was something I didn't even understand at the time. Maybe I still don't. But—I never—" I dared a glance at them.

Griff stared at me in shock. Dyl looked down at his field journal. And Mag gazed blankly off to sea.

Only Mama seemed unsurprised.

"So I wrecked everything. Not the boy from UC San Diego who'd photographed us that other time. And I even took a bunch more. I hid the film inside Rontu."

"Ronan," Charlie said gently from across the boat deck. But

if I looked at her, I'd never get the rest out. And I needed to say it now.

I breathed deep. "So *Dreamers* went onto the wires and was printed on souvenirs and beach towels and *Time* and got famous. I'm the *punk*. The sneak, the thief. What else did you call that college kid? Oh. Coward. Yes. Especially that, because when Cap found out, he wanted me to tell you. That's all he asked. But instead I ran away.

"*I'm* the reason for all of it. Everything falling apart. Not whoever first decided we looked good on a beach towel and bought one."

"Ronan," Mama said, dipping her head, shaking it slowly, so a long tendril of hair fell across her cheek. "Cap didn't want this."

"But he did. Because he knew. And maybe this is my punishment."

"No, Ronan," Mama said sadly.

"I'm sorry," I whispered. "When I took the picture, I was so happy. The last thing I wanted was to hurt you."

Pauline spoke in a soothing, low voice. "You put too much on yourself, Ronan. You were so young. So isolated."

"This is none of your business," Griff said sharply. "This is family business."

Mama: "Griffin. Don't speak to her like that, please?"

"It's all blown out." I stared down at my hands. "And it's my fault."

It's blown out—what you said when once-promising waves disappeared. *Gone to chop, turned to mush, fell apart*—it all meant the same thing.

Even when our life had begun breaking apart, I clung to the hope that it was all right. That if I was patient, it would go back to how it was.

How wrong I had been.

I looked at them. Each one in turn.

So I'd told them at last. I waited for accusations, for questions. Anything that would make it feel time was passing since they'd learned of my betrayal.

But they seemed too shocked to speak.

Even Charlie wasn't rushing to my defense. Even Dyl only looked down at his field journal, as if it might help him somehow. He had it open to a page near the back, and I could see a picture he'd pasted in—a copy of the *Triton* clipping, with Mama circled in yellow marker. I wondered when he'd done that.

Soon, when my confession sank in, he would scratch me out of that picture…

"I wanted to tell you about the photograph as soon as we saw it in the newspaper," I said, remembering my urge to come clean, at least to the boys. How shock and panic, then simple cowardice had settled in as the days went on. "And then when the souvenirs started. And the rest… I waited too long. I finally sent the postcard to the bait shop and I thought—if someone reaches out to me, I'll tell them how I took it, tell them everything. But no one did. And then the *Time* cover came out. And then I had my sons. And I knew Cap didn't want me back."

"Since we're no longer keeping secrets," Griff said angrily. "Want to know something about that postcard?"

"Don't, Griff," Mama murmured. "We're all…overwrought."

"No more secrets, right?" Griff turned to Mama. "Tell her about when he showed you that postcard."

Mama put her head in her hands.

Griff said, "He showed her as soon as it came, Ronan. Almost fifteen years ago. They *both* knew where you were all this time. And *he* wanted to reach out to you then, but *she* said no."

I expected to feel more shame when I told them. I expected their anger.

I did not expect this. Mama had known where I was all this time. She'd known, and not cared.

A burst of sound—my heart shattering? No. An aluminum chair toppling as I bumped it and ran away.

29

The smaller half

1986
Malibu, California
Sixteen years old

It's a ramble for the smaller half. Dyl and Mama and I will be on our own for a month.

The three of us pack very little. I bring *Island* and some clothes, Rontu-dog, a bit of Plumeria surf wax in an envelope. After much inner debate I bring my camera and film, secreted inside Rontu. I want to take pictures on this trip. And anyway, it must be safer than leaving them in the unattended Gull, which Cap plans to park behind the bait shop, hidden under a tarp. Our friends there agreed to shelter her until what Cap calls "the fuss" over the photograph dies down.

Mama slings her worn green canvas travel bag across her chest, Dyl straps on his dun-colored backpack, and we hug the others goodbye.

"One month," Cap says to us all. "Just until the fuss is over." Because he's certain it will not last long. Hugging Mama tight, he whispers something into her ear that the rest of us can't hear, and then we split into thirds.

The twins head southeast, toward the mountains and snowboards of Big Bear. Cap drives the Gull north to the bait shop in Monterey.

And Mama and Dyl and I will go northeast. She has a destination in mind, but wants to surprise us.

We hitch up, hopping onto an orange truck on I-5 north.

"Open fruit trucks are always the safest," Mama says, explaining that there's a whole community of pickers who use them, families with kids, grandmas, even, and the drivers can be trusted. She says never to hitch with only men. "Truckers and pickers, that's the way, will you remember that?" she asks.

For when? I think. Then I imagine I know why she's sharing her knowledge; she thinks that when I'm older, I'll want to go on rambles of my own, like she does. I've never craved them before. They sound lonely. But I like that she's passing this knowledge on to me before the twins.

Atop fragrant crates of oranges, we travel with two large families of pickers, farther inland than I ever remember going.

The first night we camp, stringing our hammocks in three almond trees, in the center of an orchard. "Blossoms not buds," Mama says, meaning the picking season for almonds is over, and we will be left in peace.

Mama and I speak in hushed voices while Dyl lingers on the soft ground below us next to his lantern, writing page after page in his field journal.

"What do you suppose he's noting in there with it so dark?" Mama whispers. "The sounds of the night animals and stars, or something he observed when it was light out?"

"Maybe neither," I whisper back. "He doesn't only write about nature. He writes about people, too."

"Sweet boy. Of course he does. Did he tell you?"

I explain how I glimpsed my name over his shoulder once and have resisted the temptation to peek at what he'd written about me, or anything else in Dyl world.

"You two have a special bond, don't you?"

I grab a branch above my head to swing my hammock back and forth. It's a cloudy night, and bands of stars vanish and reappear, so the sky changes every moment.

Dyl and I do have a special bond. Mama and I have one, too. The first seven years of my life, before Dyl was born, we spent so much more time together.

Now it's rarely just the two of us. She got busy with Dyl, and then I was, and she went on more rambles every year.

"Will you give me a hint about where we're going tomorrow?" I ask.

"Hmmmm. Water."

"A lake?"

"No. One more guess?"

"River."

"So it stays a surprise," she says, laughing. "Good night, Little Seal."

"Good night, Mama."

She rustles and shifts, and soon her breathing steadies into sleep.

Water, but I know it's not the ocean because we've gone east. I wonder if it will be a pond like the one she secretly taught me to swim in when I was three, a warm swimming hole, her Floating Forest, way up a hill hidden by thick trees. We always left early in the morning, before the twins rose to surf with Cap. I hadn't learned to surf yet.

She'd touch my cheek in the dark and I'd smell her, oranges and cloves. Open my eyes to see her there hovering over me, her finger to her lips. She'd help me down from my bunk, lead me past my sleeping brothers. Just the two of us holding hands on the cold sand, barefoot, in the shadows. On the way to her pond, she pointed out the best shells. *And this is called a liswe, and this is a tiger nassa…* She was my first and favorite teacher. She knew the names for everything.

"You have all the time in the world," she said, at the beginning of each lesson.

But only a few mornings later I swam on my own, paddling across the small swimming hole to where her red hair flashed in the sun.

"Aren't your little seal flippers amazing?" she had whispered. "How did that feel?" I remember being so happy I could only nod. A nod that meant *Good, easy. Thank you.*

I wish I had taken longer to learn. Cap might have let us park near the pond longer, if I hadn't. I shouldn't have let those early mornings with Mama end so soon. Just us, the boys in the van asleep, like we'd made an extra hour in the day that only we knew about.

I yawn now, listen to Dyl switching off his light below us, stowing his things, climbing up to his hammock. We have this month together now, and I love the smaller half. Only when I'm dropping off, half dreaming of running on the sand out to a beautiful morning swell, am I reminded again that I'm the reason the Merricks had to split up. A trip with Mama seems a small price to pay for what I've done. It's no price at all, in fact. It's a reward. Guilt jolts me fully awake, but only long enough to look for a few constellations. Orion, Ursa Major. I remember that forlorn college boy, and how he gazed up at the stars that night when I was fourteen. But despite everything, I can't be totally sorry for what his interest in us set in motion. His camera is deep in my backpack, hidden inside two socks and my knit hat. I will have so many opportunities to take pictures on this trip... That thought eclipses my guilt and I fall asleep.

The next day, Mama brings us to a creek, and we picnic near an open field. When a woman leads a white horse to drink from it, Mama admires the animal, asking its owner about her saddle, calls the animal "a beautiful roan, a blue roan, isn't he?" clearly impressing the owner as a fellow equestrian.

"When did you learn so much about horses, Mama?" Dyl beats me to the question, equally impressed.

"Oh. Long ago, as a girl."

"You rode one?" I ask.

"Hmmmm. I had lessons."

"Did you wear jeans, like that lady?" Dyl asks.

It sounds like a silly question, but I know Dyl, too, is trying to picture Mama on horseback, and we've never seen her in jeans. Only her swimsuits and fluttery skirts.

"We wore something called jodhpurs." For a moment her expression shows she's far away. Then she comes back to us. "Now let's explore those falls I told you about before it's too dark, does that sound nice?"

Mama rode horses. I'd write that in my field journal if I had one, and I'd bet anything Dyl will, later.

The trip yields other fragments of information. Mama has been to New York and France. Mama went to church and always sat in the same pew, which her family had bought. Mama had singing lessons every week. And dancing lessons, and a maid.

The fragments aren't enough, they could never be enough. But they form a picture, however hole-filled. They tell us one thing she never says directly: Mama grew up rich.

"We," she'd said. "*We* wore jodhpurs. *We* attended church." Where is this mysterious *we* now?

And why did they let her go?

The rhythm of our time inland has a different feel from Gull time. Partially because Mama eschews routine of any kind, unlike Cap. Partially because there are no waves to surf. The three of us wake at different hours, and after I get used to this, I fill my long stretches of time alone in the early morning with my stolen camera—hours when my body is usually in the ocean.

I take pictures of animals, and new east-west roads, and the families traveling on them.

One morning, I wander to a cul-de-sac. There's a broken sprinkler in front of one yellow house, a family visible past it through their open double door. When I kneel, the water gushing from the sprinkler looks like a bright morning swell. Like I'm surfing, viewing a citizen family from far out at sea. We're an ocean apart. As I stand, hastily hiding my camera, I can hear them laughing together. Not so far away, really.

A few nights later, a girl dumps her ESPRIT sweatshirt in a restroom trash can by Lake Elsinore, because she got red Sno-Cone stains on it. After she and her laughing friends leave, I emerge from the stall where I'd spied on them and, impulsively, rescue it. I pull it on, wandering the lakeshore alone. No Cap to disapprove. But I don't feel like myself, and an hour later, I stuff the sweatshirt down the same restroom trash bin.

I miss the Gull.

On our last night, swaying in our hammocks not far from where we'll meet the others tomorrow, the three of us discuss how we're so excited to reunite with them we probably won't be able to sleep. We can't wait to tell them of our adventures, but we've missed them.

I can't help asking Mama, "Do you miss that other family, Mama?"

She sounds genuinely confused, swinging next to me in the dark. "What other family?"

"The one you grew up in."

She shifts, rustles. I'm worried that I've upset her. She's given us a treasure of facts about her girlhood, and I was greedy to dig for more. I'm worried that I've even made her cry—something I've never seen, although she says she cried when each of us was born on the floor of the Gull.

At last she says, sounding composed and as if she's weighed her answer carefully, "I don't think of them as *another* family.

But it was another lifetime. And this lifetime is…" Petals rain down on me. "As sweet as almond blossoms. Good night, Little Seal. Good night, Dylly."

On our return hitch, we ride on a truck carrying lavender. The purple boughs are fragrant and velvety.

"*Lavare* means *to wash* in Latin," Mama says as the three of us inhale the sweet, clean smell of the purple buds.

We're reuniting; the trouble's over. I've been washed clean.

30

Disguises

1986
Monterey, California
Sixteen years old

After our separation, we meet the twins at a rest stop. Mama glows, enfolds them in her soft arms. Dyl takes my hand and we tell the twins everything we did while we were apart. It was thrilling to have Mama to ourselves, to get glimpses of her past, but I look forward to being back in the bunk tonight. Mag's restless turns, Griff's snores. Curling close to Dyl, poky elbows and all.

Mag is full of his own stories—chatty, even—about snowboarding. The rush, the etiquette that's not too different from surfing. He couldn't get enough of it.

But Griff is strangely silent and cool, like he has brought some of the mountain's ice back with him.

I piece it together from Mag's descriptions of "where I crashed" that the twins did not spend the last twenty days together. Griff went off alone after a week. He'd had enough of snowboarding and they separated.

"Where did you go?" I ask, shocked.

"Nowhere important." His forced smile is a mask I can't get behind.

We stop for a quick lunch in San Diamante, a sleepy, U-shaped cove above Santa Barbara. In the lacy shade of a scrub oak high above the dunes, we eat strips of dried choke-cherry paste. Mama peels off a wide piece of the jewel-like treat, pinches the center over her nose, and holds it to her eyes. "Rose-colored glasses, like the poem?"

Griff laughs at her little joke, and I feel comforted, knowing that Mama also has noticed he needs cheering up.

As we walk down the road to the shady lower-level blacktop where the Gull's supposed to meet us, I picture my beloved home, eager to get back to her. Feathery paint, little rusty awning-wings, her front lights like glossy white-and-gray eyes on a bird.

Except I don't see her. There's a converted station wagon, a beat-up Woody with two striped longboards on it...

Everyone else realizes before me.

Mama, who covers her mouth with her hand.

Mag, who stands still.

Griff, who drops his board and runs ahead.

Dyl, who clutches my elbow.

I don't know why they're upset just because it's not there yet. Cap is off working, or delayed by freeway traffic, and he will be here soon.

Dyl says, "She's in disguise."

And it hits me. Cap has painted the Gull black, and clipped her wings.

Outside, the Gull is foreign. Inside nothing has changed. We collapse onto our bunks, and Mama ducks her head from Cap's kiss.

"You should have warned us," Mama says.

Dyl moves close to me. Griff and I glance at each other in surprise—Mama, *should*ing Cap?

Cap, who doesn't swear, has an expression: "Don't *should* on anyone and don't let anyone *should* on you."

"I'm sorry," Cap says. He looks at each of us in turn, his expression remorseful. I've never seen him so pained, or so uncertain. "I didn't know how to get word to you in time."

"Tell them, too." Mama's barely audible.

"I'm sorry." There's a plaintive note in Cap's voice I've never heard before. "All of you. I didn't plan it, but I had to do it. There's more tourist junk with our picture on it. A beach towel. But the photo is cropped wider and in this one, most of her left side is showing."

Her white-and-pale-gray-and-putty-pink left side, with the clamped-down awning like a wing hugged close.

Cap unfurls a garish yellow towel with us on it; so I hadn't imagined that one, the day I'd picked salmon berries and mushrooms with Mama.

"I had to paint her," Cap repeats, pacing in the limited space of our home. "I got hassled by two cops just getting her to the bait shop. And both of them mentioned the picture. Our family's *fame*." He says it like it's a dirty word. And I know, to him, it is. "Tina thinks maybe a cop's envious because they're sure we're making money off that merchandise, or else it's not a cop but somebody else who's jealous and tipping them off."

"Who?" Mag asks.

"I don't know." Cap wads up the towel. "The same person who left the Kenny's advertisements with us in them at the Carve," he suggests, referring to one of the board shops where Cap occasionally earns cash, helping out. "They won't have anything to do with me now."

"What?" Griff asks. "When did that happen?"

Cap shakes his head. "That was a while back."

Who's doing this? Someone who would want Cap to look like a hypocrite. To lose work shaping boards, to get hassled for parking the Gull where he shouldn't. But who? Cap interacts with so few people. He's known from a distance only, among old-school vanners.

The man at the hotel? Angry that Cap stopped ferrying money for him? Of course we can't ask about that.

Cap goes on helplessly, "Tina offered me some old auto paint, no charge, and helped me paint her. No one has bothered me since. She's unrecognizable—it's the safest way."

"Where are her wings?" Dyl asks, near tears.

Cap comes over to our bunk and places his big hand over the crown of Dyl's head. "They're in storage at the bait shop. They're safe."

Dyl nods bravely.

"We'll paint her the way she was and put her wings on again when we're sure this fuss has died down," Cap says. "It won't be long. Someone is making mischief, that's all."

Dyl's tracing waves on the bunk, his finger movements barely perceptible.

Cap looks at me then, beseeching.

I dredge up my most encouraging, optimistic voice, the one I used on Dyl when he first learned to surf. "She's the same, Dyl. She's still our home. Actually, I think it's really clever, her camouflage. I didn't even see her, at first, in the shade, isn't that funny?"

Dyl doesn't find it funny.

But Cap casts me such a grateful look I have to glance down, pretend I'm smoothing Dyl's hair.

It's a silent reunion after that.

As I stroke Dyl's soft, long hair in our bunk, I think of how the lavender didn't wash me clean after all. I'll keep getting punished for what I've done.

But I get an idea, and tiptoe out.

Four hours later, when I come back inside the Gull—who

now looks more like a wingless raven—everyone stares at me, open-mouthed.

"It's so much cooler," I say, and let Dyl run his hands through my short locks.

I already miss my long, wild curls, which I stuffed in the rest stop ladies' room trash can, along with the stolen box of Raven Black hair dye.

Mag hops down from my bunk and examines my head roughly. "Who did that to you? Some chook on the beach?" He sounds ready to pound on whoever did it.

"Nobody. I did it. I like it."

Griff doesn't say anything, but he quietly goes over to Mama and Cap's bunk, murmurs something, and brings Mama to me.

Her eyes well up; she's the first to realize why I did it. "Because of the picture," she says.

"I've been thinking about it for months," I lie.

"Well," Mama says, wiping her cheeks. "Isn't that modern? It shows off your pretty eyes. You look like a...a little wood sprite."

Last of all, Cap, who comes down from the bunk to see why everyone sounds heated. Like Mama, he realizes right away that I've done it so I won't look like the girl in the picture. Pictures. Who knows how many towels are out there. The Hang Ten! notepad alone has our photo on every one of its fifty pages, Griff said.

I expect anger, for some reason, but Cap sinks to the rug across from me. "You didn't have to do that, Ronan."

"I wanted to change it. It's no big deal. Everyone stop freaking out, okay?"

Cap looks helplessly at the others. He is not one for hugs, but Mama drapes herself over him. And I swallow, holding back tears, then drape myself on her.

Griff says, "Maybe I'll cut mine, too."

"You match," Dyl says, meaning I now match the Gull. Cropped, dyed black.

"I guess it's not so hideous," says Mag. "You look punk."

31

Lost child

The next morning

Long before dawn the next day, after a fitful sleep, I wake with an overwhelming sense of pity for the Gull. It's only a feeling, intense but disconnected from reason, I'm so groggy and tired. It takes me a moment to remember *why* I feel sorry for her— then I recall her stolen wings, her brutal paint job.

My second thought is how unusually cold my neck is. Normally, when I wake, it's warm, with damp tendrils of hair stuck to it. Could it be true that I cut my hair yesterday, and dyed it dark to match my home? I reach up to my shorn head to confirm this, pull a piece down my forehead to check its color, and the ache for my long, wild white curls is so piercing I quickly rake my hair back. My whole body craves water. Water will make everything right again.

It's hours until cereal and exercises, but I tiptoe outside and drag my half suit from the drying rack. I tug it down quickly, hating the flat black paint on the Gull, her winglessness. I turn my back on her as soon as I can. *Water. Just get to the water.* There, it won't matter. I'll forget yesterday, and how I caused all of this.

Cap's already out here in the moonlight, his board hoisted overhead for the long walk down the beach. His eyes are on the horizon. Dark as it is, he's scouting waves. I will do the same, scanning the ocean for possibilities, imitating Cap's single-minded hunt.

I'm about to step into my wetsuit when I see it, not in the ocean but on the sand—a smooth, arched length of something shining. A mound of fish, opaline in the moonlight. But it's not the right time of year for grunion.

I race toward it, barefoot, wearing only the T-shirt I slept in. I know from the sound before I see its frantic flipper, its great, rolling eye. It can't be anything else, but still, there's a moment of denial. Not thousands of fish—one mammal. A whale. Just a baby, surely, no more than ten feet long. Only the distance of my own body, a little more than five feet, separates it from the waterline, but the tide is ebbing fast and the creature has panicked, letting out a broken moan that's pure ache, pure longing for home. It hurts to hear it, and I come close, push the wall of slippery flesh. I'll never be able to move it alone.

"Someone! MamaGriff! Help!" It comes in desperate pants as I scoop water onto the animal, flicks it probably doesn't even register as more than mist, but all I can think is it's drowning in our air. It's a windy night and they haven't risen yet and the Gull's far off—they won't hear.

Cap. He's barely a dot in the shallows, but I run, sloshing into the cold. "Cap!" I wave him down, and by a miracle he must glance back, maybe checking the wind in the trees to do some mysterious calculation, maybe giving one last thought to where his family sleeps. He sees me.

"Whale!" I yell, pointing. "Whale!"

I run back past the glistening hump of animal, up the steep trail to the Gull, and while minutes ago I couldn't bear to look at her exterior, now I'm thrilled when her ugly, sloppily painted side comes into view. I rush up and pound on her door, and Griff appears, bleary-eyed.

"Beached," I pant. "Blankets. Beached whale. Help us. Wake them up."

Awareness dawns on his tired face and Griff jolts into action. He stuffs his sheet and a blanket into my arms and I fly back down to the water to drench them, drape the sopping fabric on the whale's side.

Cap is next to the animal on his knees, digging furiously. A grave, no—a trough. He's trying to make a chute from its body to the ocean.

"Good," he says, helping me spread the wet blankets. "They're coming?"

"Yes."

Cap digs, I run back and forth to the water's edge, soaking the blanket.

Then Mama is there, digging, cooing to the poor lost child.

Dyl's here, too. Then the twins. Every piece of fabric we own is sopping. Every towel, blanket, sheet. Dig, soothe, soak, squeeze, drape. Over and over. Now the whale's inside two troughs, but they're not nearly deep enough to draw water and it seems impossible.

Cap—"We need more people. Mag, you go."

Mag is the fastest runner. He's gone forever while we five dig, soothe, soak, squeeze, drape.

People come. Our people. Mag has roused the couple who live in an alley lean-to behind the bait shop, and the wiry man with the braided gray beard who never talks to anyone but collects cans all day and sleeps under the pier. Five or six others. Then more. More panting, voices I know and most I don't, saying "poor thing" and "it's still alive," more strange hands digging desperately next to mine.

"Did you call them?" someone asks.

"Yes. Number on the pier."

"A juvenile. Sperm whale?"

"Yes. Female, almost two tons, I'd guess. Poor thing."

Dig, soak, squeeze, drape.

"There, there, baby," Mama coos.

"Close now," Cap says.

But mostly, we work in silence. The dozen of us roused from sleep, a small group of people who avoid people. Drench sheets, drape it, towels, the trenches beginning to fill, dig dig dig.

Just as I think I can't carry one more sodden blanket—my shoulders ache like my arms will fall off my body and surely, surely we cannot outrun the tide—a trickle of water touches the great creature's flank. Then it's a channel six feet wide.

"Faster!" I yell.

"Close now, baby," Mama murmurs.

Jubilation—it's moving.

Someone urges, "Give it a second."

"Don't stop now."

"Okay, give it space. All together on three. One, two, good. Leave it room."

We push with everything we have, helping it along as it flounders, a graceless and desperate shimmy of its torso. We heave, its fin hits water, then one whole side, then it's in, and as it submerges, we hold our breath, watching. One wrong flick of its exhausted, confused body and it will surge back onto land, farther than before, somewhere beyond our help. But it disappears into the waves just as the first light hits the water. A fragment of fin, a shared sigh as if every one of us on land can feel the great fish's relief.

By the time the ranger comes in his truck full of gear, the animal is at sea.

He nods. "Would've been too late." He seems like a kind man, but the others scatter, wary of his badge.

I watch our bedraggled group break up, a patchwork family I didn't know I had.

≈

The six of us stay close all day. We skip exercises—the only time except El Zafiro that has happened. We're limp and shivering after our rescue mission, but the water calls. Mama surfs with us, which she rarely does, and for hours, before the tourists come, we make our own private lineup. Nobody mentions the morning, and I think—I hope—it's because they feel like I do. They don't want to break the spell. In bright sun, it seems like something out of one of the bedtime stories I spin for Dyl, moonlight and magic and mythical creatures. There's a sunburned family sprawled out where the whale was, their red Igloo cooler and towels right where it got beached.

As I float next to Mama, she sees me looking over my shoulder at that spot and smiles in understanding but says only, "My watchful Little Seal."

Finally, exhausted, the six of us head to the Gull for a nap.

I hoist Dyl up to our bunk, climb after him and settle in close. It feels like nighttime, I'm so tired, but it's not even midmorning. Dyl curls on his side next to me, yawns once, and he's out, his warm body a small c inside my big C. Behind me come the familiar creaks and shivers of Mag and Griff climbing up to their own separate bunks, rustling into their covers. Cap and Mama crawl up the ladder into their room over the Gull's driver's seat.

Outside, there's the usual noise of beachgoers revving up for the afternoon. Distant radios, kids crying. Is it the weekend? It doesn't matter to us.

Mama and Cap murmur, laugh, go quiet.

I stare at the vanilla wall that hides my sleeping parents. Dyl's body is slack, he's deep in a dream, and Mag and Griff are already snoring, but I'm wide awake. I can't stop thinking of the creature we saved. Her cry of fear, and that huge, rolling eye. How scared she was to lose her bearings.

And how lucky we are, the six of us, together and safe in our home.

I haven't thought about my hair, or the Gull's disguise, all day.

The whale, so much bigger and more important than a little picture. Everything will be all right.

That night we string our hammocks up in the trees, close enough to hear each other if we call. It is warm, but not so hot that hammocks are necessary. Cap thinks it's smarter to sleep here at night for a while, just until we know the paint job has worked. We can keep an eye on the Gull and any trouble that might arise in the night.

"Just to be safe," he says.

As I'm getting Dyl settled, he whispers, "Ro."

"Yes?"

"We float. We float AND we glide."

It's such a happy thought that I whistle. I'm only whistling to Dyl, who's in the tree with Mama, next to me, so close that when one of them turns a puff of wind comes to me.

He returns my whistle, long and low, *who-whoooooo...hoooo.* The stress on the second syllable, a croon that was made up so long ago. It's pretty, musical, so I think Mama invented it.

Then someone else whistles. Mag or Griff. Mama—her whistle is as pretty as her voice. Then Cap.

Swaying in the cradle of my hammock, listening to his low whistle in the dark, I regret every time I've disobeyed his rules. I don't want a different father. I'll always choose Cap over some soul-dead citizen.

I won't use the camera again. It's hidden in the Gull, inside the wall behind our bunk, but as soon as I get the chance I'll paddle far out before dawn and throw it into the ocean. Mental pictures will be enough.

I start the whistles again. A little shy. But they all follow. Then someone else starts it.

We go on like this. Five, six times. Dyl dares, next, his excitement palpable in how he holds himself, rigid, waiting for the answers.

It's cool up here. The air is fresh and sweet, and tomorrow

stretches ahead, and I'm glad to be in a new place. When it's hot, go in the ocean. When it turns cold, get cozy in the Gull.

Grouchy? Hang up a hammock and trade whistles.

I feel sorry for any family who thinks they need more.

This is my cul-de-sac. I smile at the thought, picturing our circle glimpsed from above by a night bird. A ring of bodies. The navy blue rope hammocks wouldn't show up in the picture; probably, they'd melt into the dark night. This is my quiver, except it's a quiver of six, and it's all-year-round. We are each other's home.

Mama floats away, but she floats back right when you need her most.

We float, we glide, we need no one else.

32

Flight

1986
Half Moon Bay, California
One week before Ronan's seventeenth birthday

It's been a month since the morning we helped the whale, and no one has bothered us. We've all gotten used to our Gull's black-paint disguise and my matching hair, even joking about it once in a while.

"Maybe she will molt soon," Dyl said just this morning.

"Maybe Ro will," Mag said, laughing. Because the dye was cheap and my hair is brittle.

The swell has been perfect here, south of San Francisco. But it's turned cold, and tonight we will head south.

We're parked at a small rest stop and it's late, probably near midnight. We are all bedded down inside the Gull—all of us except Cap, who went to buy a windshield wiper from the late-night gas station half a mile off. We have made do with our worn wipers long enough, and he says we can't scrimp on safety.

There's a slight shudder, a little click from outside the front windshield, under his and Mama's bunk. Another click. He's hopped up on the bumper to snap the new blades in. In a minute, he will start our home's ignition and we'll soar down the highway.

The door opens and there's Cap's light step, a little whoosh of cold. A cozy feeling—all of us together for the long night on the road to where it's warm. We will whisper and tiptoe tomorrow morning, to let Cap sleep all afternoon after his overnight drive.

I stretch and curve around Dyl, and soon the delicious rocking of the Gull in flight will lull me to sleep like him and the twins and Mama—

"Ronan," Cap whispers. "Please come outside. I'll wait while you put some more clothes on—it's cold."

This has never happened. Perhaps he wants my help with something, sensing I'm awake?

I don't bundle up or put shoes on, and hurry out in my T-shirt and sweats. I shiver, my bare feet on scratchy, wet pine needles.

In the fog, Cap leads me over to the stump where Mama and I served our hasty dinner of nuts and windfall melons. Cap flicks on his portable lantern, careful not to bounce its light toward the Gull and the other four, who dream on, oblivious.

He lowers the light so I can see what he's spread across the stump.

I'm grateful that my face is in darkness. But I wish I could see his. His hat is tilted too far down, and the lantern casts strange shadows across his chin, all the way to the bleached-out neck of his rash guard shirt.

It is me. A poster of me. Cropped from the photo, blown up. Fuzzy and printed on cheap, curling paper, but unmistakably me, running toward the water with my board, in my green bikini top, my half suit like a skirt at my hips because I hadn't zipped it up my back yet. Me, the way I looked before I chopped my hair.

Perhaps he merely wants to warn me, a protective father. To

show me so we can burn it, so no one else can taunt me with it. To sympathize, to tell me first that I am on strangers' walls, that he and the other four have been cut out of this version, leaving me alone.

"They were selling these at the car wash." He reaches to the ground, lifting and unfurling a thick stack of duplicates, which he sets over the first poster on the stump.

"I'll pay you back" is all I can say. Though I wonder if he paid for them at all, or if he stole them, in his shock. "Thank you for showing me, I—"

"See here?" He crouches by the stump. "You might think it's just a smudge on the poster, or a shadow, or perhaps a flaw in the printing. But what does it look like?" He traces a small, jagged mark in the lower-right corner of the poster. The distinctive curves of a Parks Service trash can drainage slit…in the shape of a wave.

I wish I could be brave. Admit to it, right then. Say *Yes, I did it. I took it. Because I felt so much love for you all that day.*

I didn't do it to hurt us. Because he is admirably restrained. He is not shouting, or waving the poster around, like many fathers would. I know this somehow.

"I don't know," I lie. I pretend to examine the picture again. I feel so separate from the girl in it. That girl holding her board and looking north, her hair flying everywhere—she's not me.

He waits. He knows. It's in his voice, in how he's pointing to the wave shape on the poster.

But I don't say anything.

So he rises and leads me down the steep, railroad-tie trail, to the beach. It feels like it takes forever but I follow him, over the cold sand. He walks slowly, courteous with the lantern so that I don't stumble. But my instinctive shame tells me where he's taking me, and I know before we arrive what his lantern will illuminate next. A few yards from the end of the trail. A garbage can.

The kind I used for my timed photos. So clever of me, devising my crude system. Using the materials on hand, like Cap taught us all. Upturned garbage cans with drainage cutouts near the bottom, so I could position the camera lens for a clear view from inside.

This is the most common can in the parks system—there must be hundreds of them, scattered around our favorite beaches. It has a wave design, eight inches or so, repeated over and over around the bottom of the cylinder, and it's exactly the same as the mark on the photo. My photo.

"It wasn't that first boy at all." Cap settles patiently on the sand, careful to keep the wave in the lantern's glow. "Please sit, Ronan."

I kneel next to him.

"See, someone else took that picture by hiding a camera in one of these and setting a timer."

He waits for me to confess. He'll have a grudging respect for me, a sliver, if I do. But I can't. I'm seven years old again, and he's bored, teaching me to surf. He holds his approval just out of reach, knowing it will make me paddle until my arms ache.

At his side, I run my finger along the cutout in the rusted metal. Over and over, trying to comfort myself, when it is futile. Not so far away, a group of kids on the beach, maybe kids my age, laugh around a bonfire. I look past the garbage can, Cap with his lantern, at that far-away glow, and wish I was there. Part of their happy noise, a melody to the background music of unseen waves.

"It must have been hard to line the lens up with the cutout," he says. "Perhaps the camera was propped on something."

"A book." My confession.

He doesn't ask me why I took the picture. He asks, "How did you get the camera? Did you steal it?"

I nod.

"From a store?"

"From our fire."

He sighs sadly. "Of course. And it wasn't an accident that our picture appeared in the newspaper, was it?"

How does he know? I feel so seen through. So foolish. How had we gotten here, kneeling by a beach trash can in the middle of the night? Submitting the photo had seemed such an ingenious idea. Balancing out his crime with my own in a way that only I would ever care or know about.

I shake my head no.

"Did you take more?"

I nod. "Six rolls." I'd stolen fountain coins and resold the board wax Charlie mailed me to pay for them.

"And you still have them."

"Yes." I'm ashamed. But also, humiliation and anger begin to burn in my throat. I'm furious over my mistake, and at whoever blew up the picture, the picture I'd taken for my own private reasons, so much, zooming in on me… I'm furious that this is someone's idea of sexy, that you could make out the bandage on my left pinkie, the strip of pale skin beside my left bathing suit strap…and that distinctive wave pattern from the can's drain slit which gave me away.

Most of all, that he made me go through this, leading me to the garbage, making me confess, instead of saying right away *I know what you did, Ronan. Why'd you do it?* Caring enough to ask.

In the horrible silence, I grasp for words to explain myself, but this is all I come up with: "It's not as bad as what you did for the hotel man, passing bribes to cops for him."

I can tell he's shocked. I'm shocked. But it tastes good, the ugliness I spit out: "I could have given the newspaper a picture of that instead."

He pulls off his hat and rubs his dirty blond hair. It's not as satisfying as I thought it'd be, watching understanding dawn on his face. It's not like what I craved.

He's shrinking, right in front of me.

I want to say *We're even now! Let's both pretend we don't know. Let's go back to the way things were.*

But I can't get the words out.

I wait for him to hit back. He looks at me steadily, the green-eyed stare that's intimidated beachgoers from Imperial Beach to Port Washington, when they did something to deserve a peek under his hat.

But I don't flinch. I pull my shoulders back and stare straight back at him. I've studied Mama's features, her rounder eyes and softly curving brows that seem to rest in a permanent position of calm. But Cap is so rarely hatless on land, and I've never looked at my father closely, or long enough, to see his. I never noticed before how our eyes are exactly the same almond shape, under high eyebrows, like we're permanently surprised by the world.

I wish he would speak. Give me a sand grain of hope that we'll be able to move past this, with time. That he guesses how awful I must feel, as a sixteen-year-old girl, to see myself on a poster for strange men to buy in gas stations. Or that his hotel work was not the reason I needed to rebel. Not the only reason.

He doesn't—he only waits longer.

"Maybe I'll…" I flail. A car's red taillights float past, up on the road, and I say, "I'll hitch north."

He nods slowly. "If that's what you want. You're seventeen next week. And perhaps you've wanted to go for a long time, Ronan. I wonder, in fact, if that's not the reason you took your photographs. Though I know the others would miss you terribly."

But not you? Not you? You want me to go? His voice sounds sad and strained, but he's too proud to say it. And I'm too proud to ask him.

He didn't ask me why I submitted the picture. He supplied my answer.

"Are you going to tell them?"

He considers, then says, "You will, if you decide not to go."

As if it is a condition of me staying.

"And you will also…" Now he seems indecisive. His confused look before he threw the camera into the fire, like it pained him, what he was about to do, and he was fighting an internal battle, comes rushing back to me.

I wait for the rest of my penance. I will tell them. Wax all of our boards forever. Go to every gas station and souvenir place from here to San Diego and scour their shelves for posters or towels or notepads of any Merrick, burn them? Happily!

"You will dispose of the rest of your film," he finishes.

"All right."

"Good. It's settled, then." He rises. "You should go get warm. Your feet look so—" He stares off in the dark toward where the waves are. "Go inside and get warm."

Throwing out the film is such a small price to pay, considering what I've done to my family. A few curls of plastic, or whatever film is made of. It's nothing.

But I don't sleep that night, as the Gull shudders her way south. I imagine telling them. Their faces. Griff's expression will harden. Mag will say something mocking, his eyes flashing fire. Dyl will not look at me at all.

Mama…of any of them, Mama would be the only one to ask *Why?*

But I don't know how I'll answer.

No matter what I say, none of them will look at me the same.

The next dawn, in Santa Cruz, while everyone sleeps, I carry Rontu outside and shut the Gull's door as quietly as I can. I take her to a far-off picnic bench, open her Velcro belly and pull out clouds of white stuffing. In her paws, in her ears, she hides my pictures. I take out every film roll she's kept secret for me. One after the other, tightly rolled Army green dry-bags for soldiers' cigarettes. Six of them. I take them out of the bags, hide those back in Rontu, carefully replacing her stuffing, fluffing her gently as if she is a real puppy. I carry the film in my shorts pockets and Rontu in the crook of my right arm— she'll be my witness.

I walk away from the Gull on wet sand as the first light, purplish gray, breaks behind the hills at my left. I'll miss exercises, but Cap will know what I'm doing. I want him to.

I hunt for a long time, passing dumpsters, trash cans. Until I find a can like the one that told on me. A metal one with waves—it has to be that kind.

I reach into my pocket and hold a roll of film over it. The trash smells like sour beer and rotting fish. And I can't seem to let the film go.

I am late for exercises, but Cap offers me an understanding nod, trusting that I've done it. He hasn't given me a deadline for telling the others I took the picture. I'll do it today. Throw the film out tonight.

But the day passes. A regular day, not that different from the day I took the picture.

I don't make it to a garbage can that night.

Or the next morning.

Cap says nothing, but he doesn't speak to me except during meals.

Mag asks me, "What's up with you?"

Griff teases him for the way he's phrased this, and loses interest in how off I'm acting.

The next day, two nights after Cap confronted me, I try again. I find a trash can in a little strip of park abutting the beach. This one smells of cigarettes, and there are wasps stuck to a sticky soda cup. I wonder what could be on my undeveloped rolls, but tell myself I'm being silly and these aren't worth grieving over. They're images of rusty trash can, or blurry limbs, or fuzzy animals. Garbage belongs with garbage.

I can't do it.

≈

So I begin to think he's right. Maybe I do want to go. Maybe I have wanted to go for a long time. Otherwise I would not have taken such a risk with the camera.

That night, the night before I turn seventeen, I do something I've never done. When Dyl's sound asleep, and Cap's driving, I slip out of my bunk. I climb over Mag in his bunk, waking him. "What's going on?" he hisses.

"Shhhh." I'm already half out the window.

It's not as hard as I feared, climbing up onto the roof, positioning myself between the boards on the roof rack. It's a little narrow, and I can't use my usual surfing stance. But I'm doing it—sky surfing.

Griff joins me. Then, after a few minutes, Mag comes up.

"Why?" Mag asks, laughing.

I lie to him. "For my birthday."

The three of us ride the van like it's our board, like the road is the sea.

I close my eyes and tilt my face to the wind, trying to memorize the feeling.

The next morning, dawn

Cap and the big boys are in the water. Cap still hasn't spoken to me much since he found out. He's been cordial. No dirty looks, no impatience over when I'm going to tell the others.

But I know—if I tell them, this is what it'll be like from now on if I stay. Silence, distance, distrust…from all five of them. I won't belong anymore.

When he and the twins are far out, surfing, I ask Mama to take Dyl for a ramble without me because I don't feel so hot.

"Poor Little Seal," she says, and places a cool hand on my forehead. "But I think you *are* hot. Warm, at least."

"I just want to sleep," I say. Memorizing her sweet voice, her childish joke, the arch of her eyebrows, her scent—the one we share, at least for a little while longer—oranges and cloves.

"Ro," Dyl whispers when Mama's outside. "Read *Island*. It'll make you feel better."

"Thank you, Dyl, I will." I have a lump in my throat. I clear it, trying to pass it off as part of my sudden sickness.

I watch them leave through our bunk window. Mama's holding Dyl's hand, and they walk away, in no rush. Stopping to examine flowers, leaves, things I can't see. Mama's leaning down, her hair shining in the sun, and she's listening patiently to Dyl.

They leave me slowly. It's like they know I'm trying to imprint the picture of them in my mind forever.

I pack a few things. Not much, just what fits in my backpack. Then I take a last look around, trying to make the Gull look shabby and cramped, trying to see her the way strangers see her, to make it easier to go.

But she refuses to look ugly. She looks more beautiful than ever. Her shag-carpet remnant is bright red, and light's pouring in her tape-mended windows, and even Cap's vanilla wall of books looks like a work of art I got to live with.

Rontu-dog—Dyl will worry that I'm never coming back if I take her. And I *will* come back. I retrieve the big toy puppy from way down at the bottom of the quilt Dyl and I share. The plush is still warm from our feet, and this is what breaks me. Turns everything I look at wobbly and glassy. I have to go now or I won't be able to do it.

I scribble a short note for Dyl: "Take care of her until I come back, Love R." I stuff the message in Rontu-dog's collar and put her back under the blanket.

Then I remember the film in my backpack. I'd been carrying it with me for days, trying to destroy it. The film, which holds proof of our good and bad...of the six of us sunrise surfing at Trestles, and of so many other times. So many more good than bad.

I can't destroy it. I don't want to bring it with me, where it could only make me sad.

I'll leave it here. Part of the Gull. I'll get it when I visit, when things are different. I pull Rontu-dog back out from under our blanket and hide the film again, in the stuffing of her ears and legs. Dyl vowed he'd never look inside again, after the first time. He'd been so disappointed by the Highest CD Rates in Town! on her tiny plush heart, hated seeing her flayed open.

I tuck Rontu in and hurry outside.

One more look. One more glance at her clipped wings, the boards on her roof, the worn, rainbow-striped beach towel folded by the door for us to wipe the sand off our feet, softer than any cul-de-sac girl's welcome mat.

Then I go.

33

Children

I ran heedlessly along the beach, then to the interior of the island, stumbling along rocks.

The landscape changed, gray turning green, and I found myself on the east side. If I kept running, I wouldn't have to know they weren't following me.

At the place Mama had named Golden Cup, the sunny fishing hole ringed in yellow blossoms, my legs gave out.

I sat there, on the dock. Hidden from marine traffic.

I thought of how I'd run, that morning after my seventeenth birthday. Run so that I wouldn't lose courage. Run until I saw a lavender truck, purple blossoms. And it felt safe. Like a sign.

I'd hitched up to Oregon. Got work as a picker on the lavender farm. Bunked in the picker cabin. And Lou had been there, with his kindness. Not asking too many questions.

I couldn't regret running, not now that we had our boys. But Mama had known where I was, and not come. Cap had forgiven me, wanted me back. But not her.

He had told her about the picture, and she'd been angry? It wasn't fair. None of it was fair.

Now they despised me, and it was over. I'd return to my boys. Forget I came here, and the faint, foolish, ever-present hope that I could make things right with them. Like tearing up old photographs.

I pulled Rontu-dog from my pack, opened the seam in her soft belly, and dug into the white stuffing. In her right ear, my fingers met something soft but solid—a film canister in its miniature Army green dry-bag. Made for cigarettes, purchased in bulk from the army-navy surplus store to keep Mama's spices safe from damp.

I pulled out another, and another. Six in total. I tossed one in the water and watched it float, a puffy lily pad. One by one, I dropped the rest, until all six rode the surface of the sunny inlet.

They wouldn't leave quickly; the water was too calm.

But slowly, steadily, they'd be pulled from me. The tide would take them out to the open sea. I could watch, if I stayed long enough.

"You sure you want to do that?"

I turned: Mag. Dyl behind him. And far back, up on the trail he'd led me along the first day, Griff.

"You found me" was all I could manage.

"We followed you," Mag said. "Your tracks." He came up and sat near me, on my right side. Wordlessly, Dyl settled on my left.

They dangled their muddy bare feet in the water as the three of us watched my lily pads float. It was only thanks to the storm that there had even been mud for me to stamp footprints in.

"I fled the interview," I said wearily. "That's a line from some movie, isn't it?"

"We'll have to take your word for it." Mag held his palms up, *Beats me.* "Is that what you've been doing, up in Oregon?

Watching movies and picking lavender, and beating yourself up about a picture?"

"How are you not mad?" I asked, an ache in my chest.

"I am," Mag admitted. "I wish you'd trusted one of us with your secret, at least."

"I do, too," I said.

"Did that make you feel better?" Mag nodded at a film bag bobbing near his right ankle.

I watched it float for a moment. All I felt was profound loss. "No. But he asked me to throw the film away, right before I left. And I let him think I did."

Dyl swirled his toes in the water and asked, "Ro?"

"Yes?" I looked over at him.

"Why did you give that one picture to a newspaper?"

There. The question I'd waited fifteen years for someone to ask. I began to cry again, tears of relief, gratitude, regret for the time we'd missed.

Though maybe they wouldn't have understood back then, no matter what we wanted to believe. It was so easy, from a distance, to look at everything differently.

"We all have a right to bear witness to our own lives," Pauline had said. I'd desperately wanted that as a teen, without the words to articulate it or the confidence to believe I deserved it.

"I wanted to bear witness to my life, I guess," I told them. "I let him believe I submitted *Dreamers* because I thought he was a hypocrite, working for that creep at the hotel. I'll always be sad about that. Because I realized later, it was so much more. I sent that photo in because I didn't want him deciding which secrets I should keep. Which rules I should follow."

My brothers didn't answer at first. They seemed lost in memory, like me, as the three of us sat on the dock and watched my film surf away.

Throwing the film hadn't made me feel better. But telling

the truth had. I could forgive the girl who wanted to defy her father. Maybe I should've forgiven her a long time ago.

Dyl spoke very softly. "Mama said, just before we came after you, 'We were children who stole a van.'"

I'm not sure which part I welcomed more. The fact that Cap and Mama stole.

We don't steal.

Or the acknowledgment that they were children. Fallible, naive. That they'd made mistakes, and some of them had hurt us.

"Mama must have been about the age I was when I left, when they had you and Griff, Mag."

He nodded. "*Children.* She said they stole the Gull from a former boss of Cap's father. From the factory lot."

I marvel at this, try to picture it.

"I remember breaking a few rules myself," Mag said. "You weren't the only one. And let's not forget Bruce Balboa up on the trail." He turned to look over his shoulder at Griff. "He never admitted it, but he always dreamed of competing."

"But he's still furious at me, isn't he?" I, too, stared up at Griff, high on the trail.

Mag said, "Give him time."

"Ro? I used to crawl out our window, just to know I could. I wrote about it in my journal."

"Which Pauline stole," I said.

"No," Dyl said gravely. He hunted in his pack and pulled out his journal. Then a second one, exactly like the other. Green kelp, Mer on the cover. "She uses the same brand. French naval science booklets."

"Pauline?" I ask, astonished. The journal I'd snatched from her had been her own, not Dyl's?

"What?" Mag asked. "That's a freaky coincidence. Whoops. Guess we owe her an apology."

"*Pauline* shops at army-navy surplus stores?" I asked, trying

to make it align with her prim fuchsia pantsuits, her gentil-
ity… My head throbbed at this new fragment of information;
there was hardly room for it after all I'd discovered. A freaky
coincidence…or something not coincidental at all. Something
perfectly logical.

Pauline had said something. Alluded to an entry in her journal, about fathers and daughters. And those looks at Mama. Her
insistence that she always had a lot of respect for our family.
Always… Her admission that she and Cap had corresponded
long ago, and only revived the connection due to the photography exhibit.

If I tried, I could put it together; there was a vital truth in
there somewhere. Something important. But it was all too
much of a puzzle for me now. Two brothers sat beside me, and
one watched from above, like he wanted to keep us safe. I was
reeling from learning that things I'd been so certain of weren't
so certain after all.

The boys were here, but not Mama. Never Mama. *Mama
hadn't come for me when my postcard arrived, either. Mama. And
Cap had wanted to.*

Dyl stared at a bag of film, bobbing gently in a whirl of kelp
heading slowly but steadily out of Golden Cup. For a moment
it seemed that roll, the one that had traveled the farthest, might
float back to us. It crested a little wave, came nearer, then,
steadily, it picked up speed.

"What's on them?" Dyl asked.

"Pictures of our beaches. Of us. There's one of your elbow
on our bunk at night when you were ten, with the dark freeway behind you, out the window."

"You remember specific shots?" Mag asked, looking at me
steadily, surprised.

Every last one.

The film rolls were spreading out, receding from us more
quickly now. Soon they'd be lost for good.

A sudden movement next to me, a splash.

"Dyl!" I called. "It gets rough out there. What are you—What is he—"

"Come on, Dylly," Mag urged, next to me.

Soon I was rooting him on too. One stroke, two.

And then Dyl had a fingertip on the film. It inched away from him, but he was getting close. He tried another method—duck-diving under water, emerging with scientific precision under the little dry-bag. This time he got it, clasping it, turning, waving it at me in triumph.

"I'm not going to let him have all the fun." *Thud, splash*—Mag was in.

I jumped to my feet. "Mag! Griff warned me about riptides! Don't bother! I'm sure it's wrecked by now, anyway!"

Mag surfaced, had a hand on a second bag of film. "It seems fine!" he called. "It's in a nice little air bubble!"

Pounding on the dock behind me, a flash of earth-colored shorts, sandaled feet, a third splash.

"Don't, Griff! You're sweet, but come back!" I shouted after him.

He saved the third roll. Swam after a fourth.

I hurried to the end of the dock. And then I was in. One second on the sunny, warm wood, the next up to my forehead in cold salt water.

Mag created a wave for a roll halfway between us, shoving at the water with both hands to create a little swell, and the thing surfed toward me. "Got it!" I called.

There was one roll of film left, bobbing ten feet from me, on its way out of the cove. In a minute, we'd lose sight of it. I swam in my awkward sidestroke, courtesy of my shoulder, propelled by relief, by gratitude.

They understand.

"Get it?" Mag called. I hadn't realized how far out I'd drifted from him and the other two.

"Almost!" But the roll floated out of my grasp, teasing me.

You can't catch me! A child's game. My boys had gone through a phase where they loved it.

The current was more insistent, colder out here. A few more feet and I'd be out of the cove.

I turned, treating my bad arm gingerly, prepared to swim back. Five rolls saved. Three family members here with me… take the victory and cherish it.

But then I heard it: a steadily increasing buzz. A motorboat in the channel, probably a fishing charter headed out from Santa Barbara, and if they decided to veer this way to admire Manzanita Island on their way, I would be spotted.

I couldn't be the reason my family got busted.

I held my breath, submerged, waited until my lungs protested and forced me up.

When I resurfaced, the boat's motor was faint, but I couldn't see my brothers. And no matter how hard I kicked, the island wouldn't get bigger—my shoulder injury had stolen half of my paddling power. I tried again, determined, but this time pain shot across my right ankle. Flotsam? I'd had the bad luck to bang my ankle on a beer cooler or some other junk? But it bobbed next to me—a fat cross-section of invasive giant bamboo, like the hundreds scattered on the island.

I hugged the fat cylinder of wood and realized that my bad luck had really been good; the wood gave me enough buoyancy that I could gather myself, rest for a second, remind myself: *Be calm.*

And then I found grooves in my float. They were just like I remembered, the ones I carved into our old bunk for comfort. The pattern—up, down, swooping, sloping. If you were tracing it in the air, it would look like you were conducting a tiny symphony with one hand.

Just trace the waves, Ro.

I did. I traced my fingers on those beautiful, intricate carvings, carved from pure love, a gift from one child to another to make it through the night.

34

Little Seal

The water off of Manzanita Island

I don't know how long I've been treading water. Maybe an hour or more, because the sun is no longer directly overhead, but slightly behind me. I'm cold, and so, so tired. I've tried to swim with only my good shoulder and good leg, but the pain is piercing, unreal, and anyway no matter what I do, I can't get past the breakers. The current pulled me out, though I fought it.

So I float, grateful for my makeshift kickboard of bamboo. I remind myself that I am a good swimmer, that this water is my oldest friend.

I still have sight of the island, and I can't let it shrink anymore in my view. I'm so thirsty. These two worries have equal weight.

I keep thinking of cream soda. *Boylan's vanilla cream soda*, like we order at Statton's Drugstore in town. Poured over crushed ice in a curvy glass, and kind-eyed, craggy-faced Bill, the owner and soda jerk, always drops in five maraschino cherries for me without asking... If Bill could see me now, what would he say? *Quite a pickle you've got yourself into, Ava LeClair...*

This whole time, one command has pierced every passing image, precious and absurd: *Don't give up.* My thoughts drift. Images, scraps of memory, phrases, come and go. Memories of the past, of my first life in these waves. The life Cap and Mama chose for me. And memories of my second life. The one I chose.

The faces I love come often, making my heart contract and my cold, sea-wrinkled fingers tremble, and when this happens I recite the Latin names for lavender. In movies people concentrate on family to hang on, but picturing my sons hurts so much.

What wave washed me here? I'm Ronan and Ava, I'm seventeen and thirty-two, I'm the girl with a house on wheels and the woman with a farmhouse she'd do anything to get back to.

Jack, Bear…they could be swimming in this same ocean right now, after skate camp. Lou watching over them. Dear Lou, who saved me, took me in, gave me the kind of family I needed right then, *rooted, grounded, down-to-earth*, who let me be Ava LeClair. And Mama, my brothers, they'll feel so guilty if something happens to me, when it was my own foolishness that got me here. And Charlie, who I've only now rediscovered…

Lavandula pedunculata…

Lavandula stoechas…from the mint family.

The endless Pacific all around me is so blue, the exact shade of Royal Velvet lavender in full bloom. If I make it back, I'll tell my boys how the blue of the sea down here is pretty, but it can't compare with our lavender fields on a late afternoon in summer, the wind rippling the velvety stalks, the sun tipping the top buds in pure gold. I'll describe it until they see it clearly as a photograph. I'll tell them we've lived by an ocean all these years and didn't know it, and that our ocean is the most beautiful of all.

I'll tell them about the Gull. How it was hard, and we were different.

But how we had many perfect days, like the day I took the picture. The one I'd told Charlie about last night. I'll pick one at random and paint a picture of it.

I'll tell them everything. Like I should have all along.

I'm so tired. But I trace the waves in my wooden float. Up, down, swoop, slide. The soft wind is Dyl's sleepy breath and my sons', both at the same time.

There's a shape in the distance, it's Mama surfing. Cap's style was so natural, and I saw him surf so often, that I often forgot how good he was until someone else talked about him with admiration. But Mama. I didn't get to see her surf that much. She liked her secret spots. So when I did, it was a new realization each time, how gifted she was. Effortless on her board, unselfconscious, lost in her own world.

Lou, Jack, Bear, Dyl. Charlie, Magnus, Griffin. Cap, Lou, Bear. Strange pairs and trios floating to me, talking to me. Mama on her board. The hum of bees, the hive that Jack smashed with his whiffle bat when he was four, they've followed me here.

Mama on her board. I will let go soon. I know it, sure as anything. I am seeing things. Losing my grip on what's now and what's then, and soon I'll lose my grip on the wood.

The bees are close. But we destroyed that hive so long ago, I was sure of it…

I force my eyes open to face them. No bees. Only their sound. And then Mama, her hair bright as the sun on the water, holds out her hand. I blink, squint. She reaches down, quick and graceful, to pull me from the water onto her board.

"Little Seal, why don't we give those flippers a rest?"

The bees are an outboard motor on one of the DFW pontoons. Mama takes me to shore and they're all there, then they're not. I'm so tired it's hard to figure out.

Someone bundles me in blankets, chafes my hands and feet. Someone else holds a cup of water to my lips, thin slices of banana.

"You scared us, Ro." Charlie's voice, her hand squeezing my ankle. "I was running for the satellite phone on the boat when Mama scooped you out."

"Still impulsive," I say weakly, eyes half-closed, and she laughs.

Dyl's face above me, upside-down and kind; he's arranging a blanket under my head.

"The twins?" I ask him.

"They're right here. We've kept your film safe, too."

The twins are tending my banged-up ankle.

"...did quite a number on it."

"An eight-brace. We have what we need, just a bad sprain..."

We're under a shady canopy of some kind, but all I see clearly in my exhaustion is her.

In the photograph, Mama is nearly hidden in the glare of the sun. Beautiful, but unknowable.

But now I see her completely. A pained, intent expression I've never seen on her lovely face. But still, even in distress, she carries a peace with her that I've never felt from anyone else.

"You came for me," I say.

"Oh, sweetheart. Of course I did."

"You didn't then. Postcard."

"Didn't...? Didn't come for you on the farm when you first left? Is that what you mean? Drink."

I comply, nodding, trying to keep my eyes open.

"I thought it was what you wanted. You'd been restless for so long. But I checked up on you, on my rambles over the years. I've even seen your sons, your beautiful sons, Ronan."

"When?"

"Just rest now."

"Tell me."

"I visited you. And I thought I understood what you wanted. Because I ran, too. When I was seventeen. I ran from my family and never looked back. I missed you terribly—how can you not know that? And I'm so sorry, Ronan."

"Tell me about running. About your family," I muster.

"I can do better than that. I have pictures, right here on the island. A whole journal full of pictures and entries about me running away."

Pauline's blond hair, her evasion. How she happened to have the same brand of journal as Dyl—the green, seaweed-printed kind Mama had given him.

Corresponded with Cap.

I know about fathers.

About running away.

I have so much respect for your family...

Click. "Pauline. She's your family." Of course she is.

"Yes," Mama says. "My little sister, from Georgia. Eight years younger, only nine and a half when I left them." She looks behind her at someone: Pauline.

"Have her come here," I say, my voice hoarse.

Pauline's face looms close, eyes wide with worry.

"So you're not a reporter?" I ask.

"I've written exactly three pieces for a museum newsletter back home in Georgia," Pauline says with wry self-deprecation. "The Georgia Modern Art Museum's quarterly, and they only published those because I'm a donor. But *SWELL* had reached out to your father; that's the truth. He agreed I could come here as a journalist, in case I decided to back out of telling you...everything."

"Stalling," I say. I understand stalling.

Pauline jokes, relief in her voice, "But I *can* write a piece for *SWELL*, if you all like. I'll bet they'd run it. Are you sure you're all right?" She touches my arm. "I couldn't have borne it, losing my— Losing you."

"Say it." I'm exhausted, and the two syllables come with great effort.

"Losing my niece. Just when I've found you."

My eyes are heavy. I can't fight them much longer, but I have a thousand questions.

Pauline, Mama's little sister from Georgia.

"Ro?" Dyl says in awe. "Two months ago, an article about the exhibit led Pauline to us."

Mag added, "And Cap wanted to atone for what he'd done, Mama says. Mama and Pauline's father hired a private detective to find her when they first ran away together, but Cap threw them off the scent and didn't tell her."

"We were so young, and—" Mama says, then seems to think better of it. "Let's let her rest. I'll explain everything, when you've rested."

"*Dreamers*. You're not mad?" I say, sleep pulling me.

"I think it's time you forgave yourself for that picture, don't you?" Mama asked. "After all, it led Pauline to us. But maybe I should have told you not to feel guilty long ago. The day the newspaper came out."

"The day..."

"Yes. I knew it was you who took it."

"How?"

Mama smiles in wonderment. "It made a sound. A clicking like a baby bird. And that's one reason I thought you were getting ready to leave. And there is so much more I want to tell you. But later. Later. Now rest. You have all the time in the world to ask questions."

All the time in the world. I'm back in our floating-forest pond where she taught me to swim, safe and warm. She strokes my hair and she smells like oranges and cloves. I have a thousand questions.

But for now, knowing they're all here with me—that's enough.

FIELD JOURNAL—Pauline

We almost lost her. My niece.
A shift in the wind and she'd be gone.
Ella thinks this island wouldn't have let that happen.
I said we save ourselves.
She said, "I like having a sister to argue with, even if
she thinks I'm silly."

It will take some getting used to. Her strange way of thinking.
Sometimes I feel like I'm the big sister and she's the little one.

But that's all right. I've found her. Found all of them. I've
explained to all of them now that I wasn't sure, even when I
stepped onto the island, even when I saw them, if I would reveal
who I was. Our plans with their "Cap" to bring me here
had been so hasty, letters crossing in the mail,
our idea of SWELL as a pretext so rushed.
I didn't know what mental state he was in, or even if
it was fair, me accepting his invitation when he was so far gone.
And then he died before we'd made final decisions
on how, exactly, to reveal myself.
I thought they might not want to know what Cap had done,
concealing our father's first, early attempt to find their mother.
And I feared they'd be bitter I hadn't tried harder
to find them before the Dreamers *picture appeared*
in my museum newsletter, in my mailbox back in Georgia.
That I hadn't rescued them from the life he chose.
Not understanding that they didn't see it that way.

They didn't need saving.

Anyway, there was no hiding the truth from Ella,
who recognized me instantly.
And she said they would understand, that we had plenty of time,
and this island was the perfect place for me to tell them.
It seems she was right.
"See?" she said. "Magic."
I know it's the photograph that led me to them.
But I'll call that magic, if it makes them happy.

FIELD JOURNAL—Dyl

Ro is sleeping, and we're watching over her.
Across the lamp from me, my aunt is writing in your twin.
Twins really do run in our family.

I keep thinking how Ro's pictures were the reason she flew away
fifteen years ago, and, because she loves them more than
she'll admit, the reason she floated away today.
But they're also the reason Pauline found us.
When she wakes up, I'll tell her that. I think she'll understand
what I'm trying to say. How telling the truth can divide us,
and connect us, but the connecting part is stronger.
That doesn't sound quite right, but she'll know what I mean.
I can't paint stories like she can, but Ro and I
always understood each other.
Now Ro has lived both lives. Citizen life, Gull life. I haven't.
So I need to ask her something about that, too.

2002
The island
Day 3, evening

I sleep deeply, without dreams. And when I wake it's dark. We're at camp, in the clearing under the hammocks. Lamps circled around on the ground and in the trees, me in the center on a pile of everyone's sleeping bags.

"How did I get here?" I ask, laughing, mystified by all the people around me.

"We carried you," Charlie says. "On the twins' stretcher."

The surfboard.

I could sit up, but my head is in her lap, and in no hurry to leave it.

They all fuss over me, but Griff stays outside the circle, out of the lamplight. He helped save my film, but he's still hurt, I know.

I still have my thousand questions, but start with one.

"Mama, will you show us the pictures from when you were young?"

By lamplight and flashlight, we look at the pictures and mementos pasted into Pauline's journal. Everyone but Griff, who keeps his distance.

There are pictures of my mother, from before the Gull. I'm glad they exist.

The first thing Mama shows us is her name, in her own handwriting, on the inside cover. Her old name: Celine Cowley.

"I had a series of these," Mama explains, meaning the journals with the seaweed design and Mer decorating the outside. The one Pauline took out on the boat, the one she's written in faithfully, was an empty one that Mama had left behind.

Mama had bought the green notebooks in packs from an army-navy PO supply store in Valdosta, Georgia.

"Along with a hat," she says playfully, smoothing my hair.

Dyl, Mag, and I chime at once: "Cap's."

"Yes." And Mama goes on. "The journal Pauline uses is one I left behind."

"Why?" Dyl asks.

"Because I'd written my old name in it." And she invented a new name—Ella, because her mother liked Ella Fitzgerald. Merrick, because she and Cap thought it sounded right for the life they planned in the water, since *mer* means *sea*.

She fills in what's not captured in the photographs her sister saved in the journal. Her wealthy family. Her father, an officer. Mama meeting Cap at the boardwalk on Tybee Island one vacation, during his brief stint in the army as a tank engineer, a private. Him teaching her to surf there, on a river wave.

Cap's worldview shaped by the fate of his father, who'd worked himself to the bone and died young in a glove factory.

Cap, lowly, rebellious, only a half term's college to his name, rejected by her family. And then AWOL.

Secret visits to her second-story room in a big, cream-colored house with black shutters. How she'd run away twice before eloping with him for good. Cap had been named Jim Winter. The irony, the *smallness* of such a name shakes me, and I know why he left Jim Winter far behind and didn't look back…until fifty-two, near death. When Pauline found him thanks to a museum bulletin about the Brand exhibit, and a picture of him. And her sister.

"It haunted me, that I saw them run away that last night," Pauline explains. "I could have stopped them, told our father. But he was an...unforgiving man. Brutal, some would say."

Pauline and Mama touched hands and were silent for a moment, lost across the country and thirty-four years in the past, and then they returned to the island, the present.

"We should have told you more," Mama says. "But we wanted a fresh start. And we were worried about our status, our lack of paperwork, how we took the van. We thought it best if you knew nothing about where we'd come from. And we'd created this new world. We were so young, we didn't think things through."

I was young and impulsive, too, when I'd sent in the picture. About Mama's age. My first step in running away.

"I'm sorry I destroyed that world you two made," I tell Mama. "I didn't mean to."

Mama stated, "But you didn't! Boys?"

"No," Mag said. "Nobody could come close to destroying it. It's not like we've been vanless or miserable all these years."

"You're all just trying to make me feel better because of today," I say.

"That might be true," Charlie says lightly. "But Ella, explain what you told us while she was sleeping. This was something you said before you came *near* the island."

"Mama?" I ask.

"He picked this location for the paddle-out because of *you*, sweetheart." Mama tells me how Cap read *Island*, years after I'd left, and understood why I liked it. A story that took place on San Nicolas Island four hundred years ago, not far from where we sat right now.

Mama tells us he regretted his old-fashioned thinking. That's what she calls it. She doesn't use the word *chauvinism* or anything approaching it. But he'd seen the contradictions in himself, after I left.

"'Freedom for me but not for thee,' he said. He wished things had been different."

"And he wanted to come find me on the farm," I say, still not quite believing it. So he'd regretted that terrible night when he showed me the poster. I ache for the impossible—a chance to tell him *it's all right*. I did all right after I flew north…

"Yes. I'm sorry, Ronan. I truly didn't think it was what you wanted. That is everything to do with my father, how I ran away. Pauline has helped me see that."

She explains how on her rambles, and only on her rambles, she would allow herself to look at a photograph of her childhood home in Georgia, and her little sister, Pauline. The only picture she'd brought when she fled home—which had not been happy since their own *Mama*, a lover of flowers and rambles and stories, had died.

A photo she hid from all of us at the bottom of her clove jar.

"I should've known your heart would be torn, too," she says.

And for once I'm glad she hasn't called me Little Seal, but addressed me as an adult woman.

"I understand," I say.

"Truly?" Mama asks.

"Yes." And I mean it. To my surprise, I do understand. It is a great relief to let go of that burden I'd held inside without realizing it—my anger over being abandoned, lost under my guilt.

"There's something else you need to know. Near the end, he wasn't speaking much. But he told me, 'I finally have a saying for Ronan.'"

Mama leans close and whispers, sharing it only with me. And for a moment I'm heartbroken all over again.

"That's Dyl's," I say, fighting disappointment. "He must have forgotten." *Ronan is wise beyond her years?*

"No. Listen." She leans close again and whispers a little louder, "Ronan has eyes beyond her years."

35

Anthills

2002
The island
Day 3, evening

"I want to see the lookout at night," I tell my brothers.

It's our last night on the island. We'll throw the ashes tomorrow, and then we'll have to say goodbye.

Everyone says I should just rest, but I wear them down, finally winning them over when I agree that they can carry me up to the center of the 8 on a board like they toted Pauline yesterday. Dyl in front, so that I can see by my dancing flashlight when a leaf adheres to his honey-colored hair. Griff in back. I heard Mag insisting on that; he wants to make up for Griff's continued silence.

His breathing, behind me, is labored.

"Griff? I know you haven't forgiven me like the others," I say. He doesn't answer.

"It's all right. I can't be greedy."

"It's not a matter of forgiving." We follow three bends in the trail before he speaks again. "I entered my name in that contest, remember? What if I had gone through with it?"

"You didn't."

"I came close. And what if someone had taken a photo of me that day, and it happened to catch everyone's fancy. And chased us. And there's something else I was thinking about when you were caught in the riptide."

"What?"

Griff stops, asks Dyl to lower the board, and they rest me on the ground. "Stewart Tippetts," Griff says over my shoulder.

"Who?" I ask, baffled.

Griff gestures with his right forefinger in front of me. Tracing something invisible.

"A wave?" I ask, still confused.

He traces the invisible outline again. A sharp swoop, down and up. "A fake bite cut into a board," he says. "Stewart Tippetts is the real name of that Jaws guy. Remember him?"

"How could I forget?"

Griff signals to Dyl to lift me again and they resume climbing, carrying me.

"Cap told me something after he got sick," Griff says after a minute. "He figured out Jaws was the one who vandalized his board and had the cops hassle us, taunt us about being on souvenirs. Cap and Jaws... Stewart Tippetts...met before any of us were born, butted heads with each other over other stuff. The photo was only...an accessory."

I shake my head in disbelief. "So that's why he and his friends picked a fight with Mag at the party, and broke your board? Over some chip on his shoulder because, what? Cap was a better surfer?"

"They met, both working under the table at a garage in Central California, Cap told me. Before any of us were born. Cap and Mama had just run away from Georgia. '67, '68. And they needed cash. He told me something that must have been really hard for him. He said..." Griff hesitates. "At that very first garage gig, Jaws helped him swap a VIN-number placard, inside the driver's door."

"Years later, Cap tried to stop his boss at the hotel from hiring Jaws as another money runner. He was trying to protect him. He told Jaws, 'Don't get tangled up with them...' That he hated himself for it, that it was one of his biggest regrets and he was getting out."

I picture black hair, a dorsal-finned VW. Chapped lips forming the word *Duchess*.

"Cap tried to help Jaws, but Jaws didn't take the gesture kindly," I say.

"No," Mag says. "It really burned him. He didn't think it was a selfless act—"

Griff continued, "He couldn't imagine that kind of decency. He thought Cap was being petty. But of course he couldn't out Cap for the VIN, or his secret...gigs for the Sapphire..."

I finish, "So he hurt him in other ways instead."

I close my eyes, marveling at all of it. So Cap's "celebrity" hadn't caught the attention of cops by dark magic to taunt me. "What a small, hateful man."

"That's what we said to Cap, more or less," Mag says, from behind Griff. "I wanted to confront him. But he said, 'We can only pity him. He's chasing all the wrong waves.'"

Cap was a large, loving man. Despite his flaws. He'd gotten out of that hotel work, tried to protect others from it. I'll never get a chance to tell him I understand.

"And is the hotel still fronting for dealers as a side business, paying off cops?" I ask.

Mag shakes his head. "They stopped needing that *line of work* a few million ago."

We're almost at the top. Dyl, at the nose of the board, looks off at the dark sea coming into view. I touch his shoulder. "But it's all right now. Pauline has piles of money—she wants to help."

We're there. At the summit of the island, in the center of the 8.

"Here, let me down."

They try to stop me because of my ankle, but I insist on disembarking from my board.

Griff looks off at the winking lights. "Ronan. I know logically that you're not to blame. But."

But his heart hasn't caught up.

"I know," I say. "We have time." Not all the time in the world. But enough to let forgiveness come without forcing it.

I'm not sure I've quite forgiven Mama yet, after all. For not coming for me. But I'm patient, and hopeful.

That can come first.

The view from here is spectacular—lights of yachts berthed in the Catalina harbor, bobbing just enough to make them seem like they are shimmering, and the amber of hotel windows strung up and down the hills.

"Anthills," Mag says. "Cap took me up to the top of a hill in Santa Gabriel a few nights after I turned fifteen and showed me the lights in high-rise offices. He called it anthills."

"He brought me there, too," Griff says softly. "He said it was a secret. He told me he'd worked in an office when he was fifteen as a runner, and he never wanted to forget how stale the air was."

Mag added, "And his boss smelled like—"

"Rum and despair." I smile. "And then he had you do this." Slowly, I turn so that my back is to the winking lights of the hotels and boats in civilization, and instead I face open ocean.

"No way," Mag says. "You, too? Dyl?"

Dyl turns as I had done.

Then the four of us sit, looking out at the dark water.

"You could develop that film after nearly drowning for it," Mag says. "Aren't you curious how the pictures came out?"

The pictures span about two years of our lives, from when I'd obtained the camera to a few months before I fled the Gull. Twenty-four on each roll, times seven, meant I held 168 photographs on my lap. Some taken with the timer, others in moments when I'd stolen off alone. I began to look over them in my mind. Pictures of me, my family, our strange life. Pictures taken everywhere from the Mexican border to the Canadian.

"I'm sure they're ruined," I say. "They've been in a hot van for fifteen years, and just went for a swim."

None of the boys argue. But maybe this is an excuse, and I am merely afraid of what I'll see in the film if I allow it to uncoil itself and come out of the dark.

Even to print them for my eyes only would be hard. I'd have to look so clearly at what I'd given up. But it was pointless to think about... Even if the film wasn't ruined, it probably held only blurs. A sweep of rusty metal and sand, or leaves. *Dreamers* had been pure luck.

"What do you think would have happened if Cap hadn't sent the detective off our tail, that time Mama's father found him? Or if Pauline or someone had found us when we were little, and decided Cap and Mama were unfit?" Griff asks softly.

"If we'd been yanked from the life, you mean?" I ask.

We are silent, trying to imagine this, but it's only seconds before I shake my head—*No.*

And Mag says, "It's too awful to imagine."

Dyl says, "There's something I wanted to ask you. All of you. I wrote it down so I wouldn't forget how to say it." He goes to his pack and returns with his journal. He flips through it and I catch glimpses of his handwriting, of faded petals and bright, intricate diagrams, until he comes to what he wants and holds it out for the three of us to read over his shoulder:

Could we have had both?

"The van and the regular world?" I ask.

"Yes," Dyl says.

We're silent for a little while, thinking this over.

"Charlie had both, I guess," Griff says.

I shake my head. "Charlie's van time came when she was practically grown-up—it's not the same. But if we could've had both..." I think about it for a long time. "It would have been nice, having a young aunt outside the Gull," I allow. "As I got older."

My brothers nod, and if they can't fully grasp what it was like, being the only girl in the Gull, at least they're trying now.

"Maybe I would've been allowed to compete once in a while," Griff says.

"College," Dyl says quietly.

And Mag sums up his alternate life this way: "Marriage. Maybe kids."

"It's not too late, Mag," I say.

We all consider this idea. Could there have been a halfway life? One foot on citizen-land, one in surf? Straddling the two worlds? It doesn't seem possible.

"It was all-or-nothing with him," Mag says. "Cap committed. Like seeing the shoulder of a wave and developing it into what you want by throwing yourself at it. We couldn't have both."

We all agree on this. Imperfect as it was, the world we had was better.

Cap and Mama gave me beautiful places, and the time to know them well. Maybe my children ride the school bus to town every morning. But we spend long days outdoors, and our bodies are tuned to the rhythm of nature. It's because of my parents that we live that way. They gave me that.

They took from me... No. No lists of the taking.

They gave me much more than they took.

36

Closing the circle

The next morning, dawn

It's a calm morning at slack tide, the waves steady and easy to manage, as if even the wind has paused to pay deference to Cap. They are all out there waiting for me. I see the ring of bright boards and swimsuits, but they look away. Pretending they all suddenly had an urge to gaze off toward the pink horizon. They know I haven't been on a board in fifteen years.

I'm clumsy as I heave myself onto my borrowed board and begin to paddle. "Like riding a bicycle," Charlie said to me when we woke.

Hardly. I am older, heavier, in a life vest, with a bandaged ankle and injured shoulder. And this board is made of some substance that hadn't been invented the last time I surfed.

I try to paddle past the little breakers but I overcorrect, spill over, gulp salt water. They'll be watching me, even if they pretend not to. They don't want me floating out of reach again.

I untangle my leash, heave myself back on and try again. Cap chose this place because of me. Maybe the waves don't want me out there, but he does.

I stop thinking and let my body take over, and it starts to come back. Maybe, just maybe when Cap was teaching me to surf, and I overheard him saying "she is okay just floating out there in one place forever, it's the damndest thing," he wasn't being condescending. Maybe there was a grudging admiration in it, an admission that he wished he could stay in one place sometimes, too.

My infuriating, stubborn, flawed, beautiful father.

I could float here forever.

But they're waiting for me.

I paddle to the opening they've left for me, between Mama and Dyl. We all straddle our boards, and the sun is high enough that the ripples we surround are gold. From here, facing the island, I can see the flowery outline of Mama's tribute to the Gull. She and Dyl rose in the dark to fix it up with fresh boughs; it had been damaged in the storm.

Mama begins, paddling to the center, saying something I can't make out, and maybe we're not meant to hear it. Maybe she's singing a private song for him. She throws a winged seedpod, and I imagine the green arrow bobbing cheerfully, never sinking. It will make land, possibly on some island Cap never visited. After a long time, she shakes out the blue urn and tips it, and we watch the cupfuls of gray sand that were once Cap surf small waves.

The sun is in my eyes so I can't see her face when she returns to my side, but her movements are calm, comforting.

The rest of us take turns paddling to the center.

Charlie whispers her limerick from Bassett. When she paddles back to her place, she looks at me and her cheeks shine with tears. She will visit the farm soon, we've decided. And she has invited me and the boys to stay with her during their next school break. There's a killer skate camp in Laguna, she has told me.

Mag is next. I've seen his tribute already—from his pocket he pulls a picture from Pauline's journal. One of my favorites, of Cap surfing Tybee, in Georgia, when he was sixteen and courting Mama. Mama took it, and Cap's straddling his board, beaming at her. He didn't have his hat yet, and his pale hair is buzzed short. But his smile is the same as Mag's. Mag says his words, then repockets the picture.

Griff offers a dried hosta leaf with something written on it. Maybe it's a letter, or a poem, or a sketch. Griff, so easygoing and caring, so quick to forgive, has been slow to forgive me for *Dreamers*, and all it wrought. I know he's still trying.

I won't give up on him.

Dyl's next. He leaves a crown he's woven of manzanita branches to resemble Cap's fisherman hat. There was much discussion about the real hat, Cap's cap. We considered giving it a water burial along with its wearer. But in the end, everyone agreed it should stay on the dashboard of the Gull, which Mag and Griff are anxious to retrieve and tune up.

Dyl's replica hat bobs where Mama threw the glistening ashes. It tilts and, ever so slowly, drops out of sight.

Then it's my turn. I paddle to the center.

I've brought my token, tucked behind my suit zipper. I thought for a long time about what to throw. I decided on lavender, because it is purple, the royal color, and Cap is surf royalty. Because lavender washes things clean, and because I think Cap would have liked to walk the fields with me.

Tucked behind my wet suit's right sleeve, I have the locks of hair from my sons. They gave them to me so I wouldn't miss them, but now I pull them out and set them in the middle of the purple blossoms, the flecks of floating ashes that are my dad.

If Cap had known his grandsons, he'd have teased them for skateboarding, but he'd have seen their joy and their fearlessness. They have some of Cap's best qualities.

So do I.

I close my eyes and think of my favorite line from Cap's morning promises. I'd resented that ritual as a teenager, but now I find it beautiful.

I close my eyes 'til it all drops away.

I close my eyes 'til it all drops away. What's left is what I want.

For me, what's left is an image of rolling blue. Not the sea—our lavender, back home.

I watch the locks sink down under the flotilla of petals. I watch as it all glistens, floats, as sprigs and petals break away.

It's still not enough. It'll never be enough. I wipe my cheek and—quickly, casually, because I don't want anyone else to realize what I'm doing—I dip my fingers in the water by a lavender sprig. So my tears are in there, too.

Whatever mistakes he made, whatever pain he might have caused us in pursuit of his dreams, we still worship him for trying. He wanted something different for all of us.

Mama says, "Goodbye, love."

Then she looks up from the ashes at me, a look I'll try to decipher for years. Contrition, gratitude? I'll never know. Maybe she just wants to be sure I'm really here.

I whisper to the waves, where Cap lives, "Thank you."

Then I paddle back to where I'd been, closing the circle.

The Brand Museum, Los Angeles
CALIFORNIA DREAMERS:
West Coast Beach Photography of the '70s and '80s
Spring 2002 Program
Addendum
Ronan Avery Merrick

35 mm film photographs mounted on Bristol board, 1985–1986
Ronan Avery Merrick was recently identified as the photographer of
The California Dreamers, 12-by-18-foot print mounted on
California cedar, featured in the South Hall exhibit.
From birth until seventeen, Merrick, her parents, and her three
brothers lived a nomadic life, roaming West Coast beaches in their
1968 Grumman Olson step van, which they nicknamed the Gull.
The family followed their parents' ideals of treading lightly on the
land, rejecting traditional schooling and consumerism
in favor of an untethered, outdoor existence.
Merrick's recently discovered photographs are a remarkable
window into her life on the road and in the water with her family.
Without their knowledge, Merrick rigged a crude method for taking
pictures with an APDOO self-timer attached to a secondhand
Leica DRP camera, often hiding it inside upturned beach garbage
cans and positioning the lens behind drainage slits.
Photos courtesy of the Merrick family. Installation support for this
late addition to the exhibit courtesy of the Surfrider Foundation.

1. Road at Night, 1985, Huntington Beach, Calif.
2. Dyl's Lonely Otter Friend, 1985, San Francisco, Calif.
3. Gull Tangled in Six-pack Ring, 1985, La Jolla, Calif.
4. Our Secret Sea, 1986, El Zafiro, Calif.

5. Cul-de-sac Girl from My Far-off Wave,
1986, Santa Barbara, Calif.
6. Dinner Rations, Four Walnuts and Apple, Rest Stop,
1986, Pismo Beach, Calif.
7. Cap and Mama by Their Boards,
1986, Trestles Beach, Calif.
8. Vanilla Library, *1986, Monterey, Calif.*
9. Twins on Dawn Patrol, *1986, Gold Beach, Ore.*
10. We Glide, *1986, Undisclosed location*

★ ★ ★ ★ ★

BEHIND THE BOOK

Every hardcore surfer knows the Paskowitzes, "the First Family of Surfing." For twenty-five years beginning in the '60s, Dorian, or "Doc" Paskowitz, his wife, Juliette, and their nine children lived off the grid in a camper van. Surfing, traveling. Soaking up sun and waves and freedom. Rejecting school, wealth, and convention.

Doc hadn't started out as a rebel. A Texas boy, he surfed the Gulf of Mexico and Hawai'i, but regarded it strictly as a hobby. He was driven, a lauded physician—until, approaching forty, he turned his back on it all. The world valued his achievements, but they made him miserable.

"My spirit shrank until there was nothing left," he said. So he set out in an RV to find it again, bringing his fast-growing family along for the ride.

This was not the #vanlife of today, with its 600-thread-count linens, three-wick Diptyque candles, and Lark-filtered scenic photographs. But in the waves and their Spartan rolling home, the family found bliss. At least, so Doc claimed in his book, *Surfing and Health*.

In my twenties, with a 401(k) and a career at a New York business magazine, my own spirit had shrunk. In a park one cold fall lunch hour, I read an article about the Paskowitz Surf School in California, run by Doc's sons. I'd first heard about the family while at Stanford, where Doc's book was included in a famous alum display. But the surf school felt especially exotic and appealing in that moment when I felt so stuck, unsure how I'd come to spend my days reporting on the "400 Richest Americans" from a desk near a collection of Fabergé eggs.

Haven't we all dreamed of quitting our jobs for an endless summer?

Dreamed, and then stayed put—that's what most of us do.

When I saw the 2007 documentary about the family, *Surf-wise*, I became even more fascinated by Doc's idealism, and how gutsy he was to chart a different course. But the film captured the full range of the Paskowitz kids' feelings about their nomadic upbringing, and they weren't all positive. As a new mom of a girl, I asked more questions now. Would I resent my parents later if they forbade school? If I were the only daughter among nine siblings, would I struggle? Suffer under the lack of privacy, the rules about food (no sugar! no body fat!)?

The Merricks in *The California Dreamers* are not the Paskowitzes. They're my own creation; to use a surf term, the story found its own break. It celebrates surfing, and nonconformism, and the unique, casual beauty of California in the '80s, but also tries to answer the question that haunted me after devouring stories of off-the-grid families: who gets to define freedom for us?

In the novel, I've explored how difficult it is for outsiders to fully understand another life, and how even those who lived it can struggle to see it clearly enough. As the siblings gather to paddle out in honor of their father, it takes all their courage to swim inward, too—to look squarely at the past.

As a girl, my protagonist, Ronan, insists, "I don't want a different father. I'll always choose Cap over some soul-dead citizen." But as she grows up, she realizes life's not so simple. Full of beauty, a dream to those who gaze at her family's picture, but never simple.

ACKNOWLEDGMENTS

These things usually begin, "This book wouldn't exist without…"

This time *I* wouldn't exist without the brilliant cancer team at Providence Portland Medical Center, including Doctors Amanda Hayman, Kirsten Kinsman, Donald Lum, my primary physician Megan Smith, and every nurse, tech, facilities crew member, and volunteer. Thank you.

Get every screening, folks. Colonoscopies, mammograms, skin, prostate, and whatever other fantastic new scan will exist by the time you read this.

My agent, Stefanie Lieberman, has had my back through nearly a decade of health, career, creative, and personal ups and downs—and with this one, there were a lot of downs. But I'm so proud of all four of my books. Our books.

Melanie Fried loved this story way back in 2017 when she first considered publishing *The Summer List* and asked during our phone call what else I was working on. I had seven words: "the only girl in a surf-van family." But she immediately got me, and after three other books together, my ace editor gave Ro and her family the fierce and focused attention they deserved. Thanks also to the entire team at Graydon House, including Susan Swinwood, Justine Sha, Ciara Loader, cover designer Amy Wetton, Greg Stephenson, Susan Dyrkton, and Marina Green.

Kelsey and Wesley Mason sparked our family's love of photography, and *The California Dreamers* is as much about photography as surfing. I couldn't have dreamed up better in-laws or a dearer found family than my Toronto Masons: Tiff, Dave, Natalie, and Luke.

Love and thanks to my Mike, who understands me as well as the lure of the Pacific, who graduated from Queen's University in Canada and drove straight to Venice Beach, where he bought a surfboard within days, and who makes life in often-gray PDX an endless summer. I love you so much.

Miranda, you're a gifted photographer and California girl forever, even if we brought you up to Portland nine months after you were born in Newport. Thanks for saying this premise sounded "cool" years ago. Thanks for our beach trips, past and future. Lusm.

Mom, Carrie, and Erin, love you and let's all go to Asilomar soon?

Huge thanks to my writing family for encouragement, early reads, and blurbs: the Rose City Book Pub JustWriteIt,Fool! Critique Group, Julie Clark, Jessica Anya Blau, Allison Larkin, Tracey Lange, Rene Denfeld, Lynn Paul, and Emily Strelow.

Jillian Henderson, lavender expert and good friend, helped me understand Ro's farm life.

Thanks Molly Steinblatt, Adam Hobbins, Aaron Rich, and everyone at Janklow & Nesbit, as well as dear Penny Lewis, Leeann Lewis, Zuzana Sakova, Gabi Fiore, Sarah Shine, Kirsten and Mark Pennington, Stacy Thomas, Josh and Megan Channel, Christine Rains, Harvey Simmons, David and Susan Hanson, and Karen Lerner.

Endless shakas to Broadway Books, Beach Books, Parnassus Books, Rakestraw Books, Lido Village Books, Zibby Owens and Zibby's Bookshop, Vroman's, Powell's, and every indie bookseller. Every day, Shandra Battern and the entire Hollywood Library staff in Portland create a welcoming space for readers and writers, including this one.

Solidarity in the struggle and wishes for no wasps to the PDX Writers' picnic crew—especially Gigi Little, Steve Arndt, Carmel Breathnach, Parag Shah, and Kate Ristau.

Love and respect to the off-grid surfers whose stories and pictures inspired me: the Paskowitz family, Myra Roche, George Freeth Jr., Asher Pacey, Warren Miller, photographer Loomis Dean, and everyone in his August 28, 1950, *Life* article on San Onofre "beach bums."

Finally, enormous gratitude to Eli's surf school in Laguna Beach. *Toes on the nose.*